LONG GROWS THE DARK

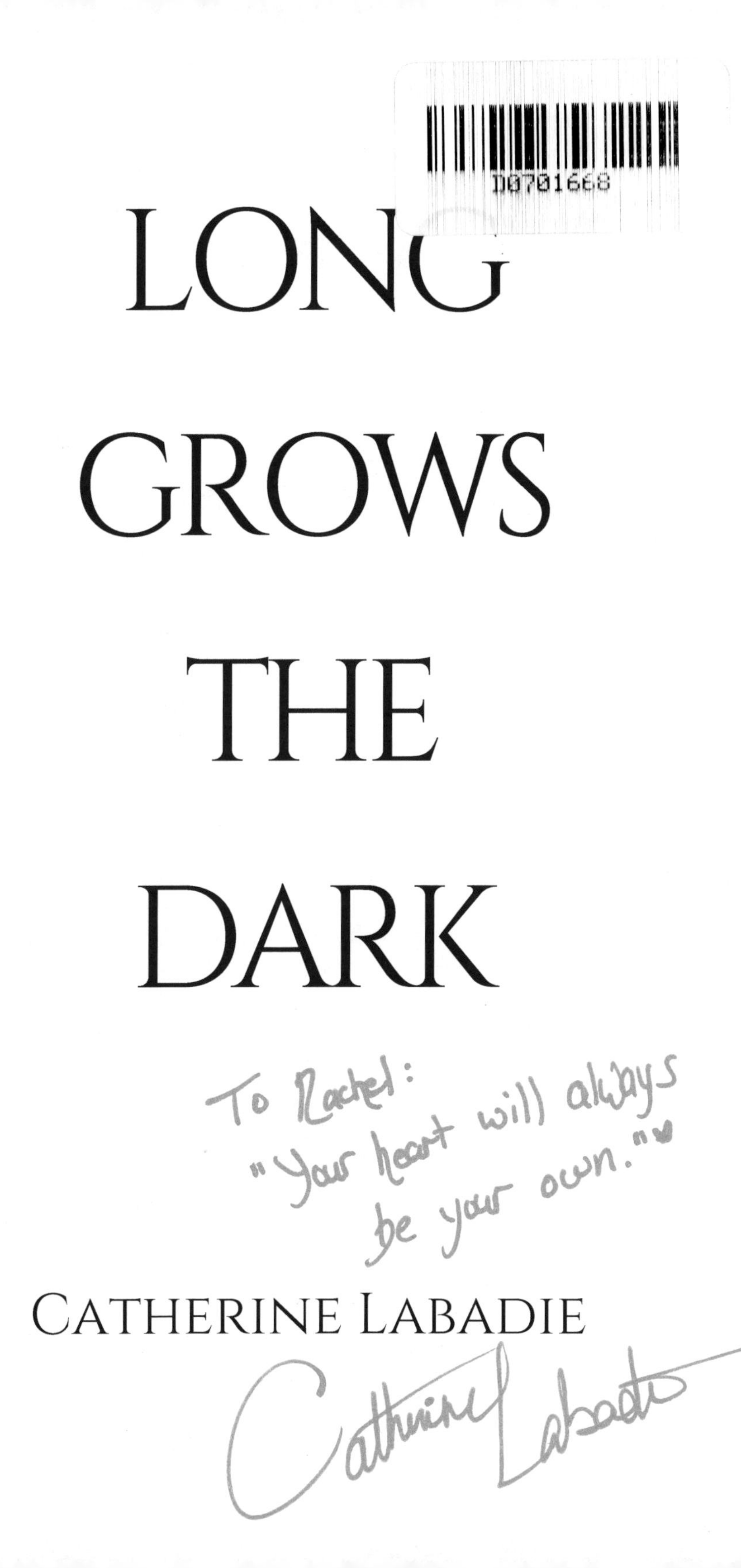

CATHERINE LABADIE

Cover design by Daniel Labadie
Interior design by Catherine Labadie

ISBN-10: 0692172475
ISBN-13: 978-0692172476

Printed in the United States of America.
First Printing 2018.

http://authorcatlabadie.wixsite.com/catherinelabadie

To Daniel, for believing.
To Kerrie, for listening.
To Mum, with love.

PROLOGUE

Before

Glenna felt a howl of frustration building up inside her, threatening to tear from her throat at any moment. The anticipation of battle clogged the air nearly as much as the humidity of the midsummer evening. A bead of sweat trickled down her back, tracing the length of her spine under her peasant blouse as it left a clammy trail on her skin. Her hands trembled as she helped Leland pull on a gauntlet. To her dismay, she observed a tremor in his hands as well.

As she picked up his sword belt from the chair beside her so she could strap it over his chest, Leland gently took it from her quivering fingers.

"I can do that," he said, his rich voice soft and comforting.

"Nonsense," Glenna snorted, pushing a tendril of damp hair away from her forehead as she reclaimed the belt from him; she had braided the black strands into submission earlier, but the locks insisted on slipping free. "Who better than me to equip the champion of Oloetha for this fateful challenge?" Her bravado was weak, a mask to conceal her terror over the possibility that he would lose this fight.

Leland fell silent as she finished strapping his armor onto his rigorously maintained body. She took the opportunity to concentrate, murmuring every spell she knew to strengthen his armor and empower his sword in the melodious tone she used for enchantments. Killing magic sounded ugly, guttural, but protection spells resonated like melodies sung by a choir. She could confidently say she was an expert with either method.

Finally, only the helm remained, the bronze teeth of the hellish creature it depicted gleaming. It rested on a simple wooden table beside a small bottle of wine and a jug of water, both half empty; Glenna had drunk the tart wine and had a mind to finish the rest, but the water had been for the trial's combatant.

She stalled, walking slowly to retrieve the helm. She could see the moon rising as she looked out of the window to observe the gate outside; it was almost time for the match. When she turned back to the helm, she saw Leland checking to make sure his golden long sword was clear from its scabbard. A huge shudder ran from her neck to her toes as she observed him, but she bit her tongue and picked up the helmet. Every protest she could call to mind crowded behind her lips as she touched it and felt the magic it contained zing through her veins. Her words vied for escape so the world would know exactly how she felt about this method of combat: madness, foolishness, hopeless. If it would work, Glenna would say anything to free Leland from this fate.

Anything at all.

Looking down at the ground, she held out the helm for him to put on. She felt his gloved hand brush her fingers as he took it.

"Listen, Glenna," he began, attempting to assuage her concerns; she held herself completely still as he took her hand. "We have been through fire, and we have been through war. We have slain our brothers among our enemies, and we have come too far to falter now. I will win. You, Niles, and even Abelard have taught me...have taught me so much." His voice threatened to break as he squeezed her hand, but he held fast. Glenna looked up at him, unable to hide the fury in her iron gray eyes.

"No war we've fought has been like this," Glenna murmured. "No duel you've fought can match the difficulty of this one. In this case, magic will prove worthier than steel." She failed to keep the anger out of her words, though her fury couldn't ever be directed at him.

"Regardless, I will prevail," Leland retorted, taken aback by her anger. She struggled for the type of waspish reply that would have ordinarily come the moment she bid it, but it evaded her.

"Damn it," she swore at last, "You're like a child wandering into the pit of the beast, and there's nothing I can do to protect you!" She threw back his hand with disgust. If tears were coming, she wanted to make sure he'd never see them. "Someone dies by match's end, as the land has decreed."

"Then Averill will die, and I will take his place. I have strength enough to accomplish that," he replied. His voice sounded muffled, and she faced him once more to see he had donned the helm. The demonic helm had frightened her as a child when Leland's predecessor had been its bearer, as it was meant to, but now it drew her in. The only thing she noticed now was the gleam of resolve in his bright-steel eyes.

Do you know what happens once you take up his mantle? Will you remain the same, my dearest Leland? Her thoughts pressed to be spoken, but she held them in silence. Frustrated and confused, she looked down at the ground, toying with the simple necklace decorating her white throat.

"Oh, Leland," Glenna began after the uncomfortable pause. "I can't believe I live in a world where someone could take everything we love away so easily."

"So you think I shouldn't fight?" Leland questioned, approaching her slowly. A laugh escaped her, as vibrant as it was bitter.

"You don't have a choice anymore." As she spoke, a firm knock at the door startled them both.

"That will be Jael," Leland said, watching her.

Their eyes met once more, her blunt iron irises meeting his steel ones, and the wordless connection they shared, perhaps had always shared, flowed through them like it too was magic. Perhaps it was: as if sensing her need, Leland stepped forward, pulling Glenna into such a tight embrace that she thought she'd break.

If only, her thoughts echoed, *if only I could change everything that happened. If only I was the one.*

Nearly overcome, Glenna choked back her anguish and fled the room.

1

Gwendoline snapped her casting book shut and sank even further into her chair. She didn't usually give up so easily, but scanning a few paragraphs into her spell book had convinced her to discontinue her research.

"Well? Anything?" The boy seated across from her asked, his forehead furrowed anxiously. His name continued to evade her, and her forgetfulness itched like a mental mosquito bite.

"No, and this is the best resource I have," Gwendoline explained, wincing as she looked up at the sharp hedgehog quills protruding from her café companion's goatee and eyebrows. "Honestly, this is a really clever curse. She managed to hex only your facial hair so it would turn into quills—"

"It's not just my face," he stifled a groan as he shifted in his seat, cringing. She bit the inside of her cheek to contain a giggle.

"I'm afraid you'll have to go to the district clinic instead of the campus one. They can usually help cure revenge hexes," she said once she'd regained her composure.

"That's all the way across town!" He protested, losing his temper. "I asked you out because I heard you were smart, and this is the best you can do?" It took her a moment to realize he was trying to insult her.

"Seriously?" Gwendoline shouted so loudly that every head in the coffee shop turned towards their corner table to stare. Her date—Ryan! She suddenly recalled his name—gazed up at her blankly, shocked by her outburst. She considered punching him, but managed to refrain mostly because the quills on his face would scratch her fist. "You asked me out before your girlfriend found out you cheated on her. She cast a sleeper hex on you so the next girl you tried to flirt with would see you suddenly sprout spikes. Of course, *of course* that next girl you made suggestive comments to would be me, so I had the pleasure of watching this hex unfold in real time. Maybe next time you'll think before you cheat on one of the best hex witches on campus!"

"Hey—" he began, unchastened. His face flushed unbecomingly.

"If I'd known you were a cheating bastard, I wouldn't have gone out with you in the first place. Anyone with a quarter of the talent your ex has would be able to fix this by themselves, so think about that. I have the talent, of course, but I don't have time for lazy horndogs like you," she declared firmly.

"But—"

"Away with you," she murmured. A throatier tone echoed her words, and a light gleamed in her amaranthine eyes. Frost crept over the prickles protruding from Ryan's incredulous face, forming a translucent web. He winced as the ice bit into his skin.

"You can do that, but you can't undo this stupid hex?" he grumbled.

"If you're not out of this café in thirty seconds that frost will spread downwards," she explained, smiling serenely.

Probably for the best, Gwendoline thought as her failed date sprinted out of the coffee shop. Dismissing his presence, she reopened her book and carelessly sifted through the pages.

No longer absorbed in the dramatic but somehow underwhelming confrontation with Ryan, Gwendoline took a few moments to look around the room. Grateful for once not to recognize anyone she knew, she settled further into her chair and glared down at the book resting on the smudged glass of the table. As if responding to her gaze, the russet leather cover of the book rippled.

"Don't give me that," she hissed at it, drumming her fingertips against the cover. "I know you had the cure in there somewhere. But you knew he was bad news when he walked in, didn't you?" In response, the pages seemed to shift as if the slightest of breezes had stirred them. Gwendoline sighed and flipped the book open again. Sensing her mood, a few extra pages flicked over on their own, leading to a story that materialized in fine, calligraphic ink that undulated over the page before settling. She read a sentence, curious, then smiled and ran her fingertip gently over the inner spine of the book. Somehow, the pages always knew what she was in the mood to read.

Like the vast city of Starford, which was full of magic prone citizens, Gwendoline's book was an antique rarity. Enchantments and spells were common in this world, but she lived in a part of the globe where particularly magical folk gathered. Even so, this book was something few people had ever seen. Everyone, from the lowest hedge witch whose only magic involved enchanting her robe to stay warm hours after her bath, to the talented sorceress who had hexed her cheating boyfriend with hedgehog quills, had a familiar, an object or creature used to channel enchantments.

In a great city chock full of the peculiarities of magic, Gwendoline and her stepmother had been known for their eccentricities. Her stepmother had been a high profile player in one of Starford city's cooperations...until she'd been caught embezzling and tampering with people's memories, that is. Gwendoline supposed the rumors had peaked when her stepmother had abandoned her teenaged daughter with signed emancipation papers and a hefty guilt inheritance earned through dubious methods to avoid the law. But this wasn't the case, since now and then she still got weird looks from people who noticed her carrying around a huge dusty book while carrying on a conversation with its limitless pages.

Always more of a solo act after her parents' deaths when she was a kid, she tried not to mind them. Besides, she'd always accepted her book as rare and special: from the moment she'd laid eyes on it, cast aside at some fancy flea market, she'd known it was meant to be with her. After all these years of owning the journal, the only thing she knew about the book was that it was centuries old and that it was distinctly hers.

"Gwendoline, it's been ages!" someone addressed her with mock solemnity as they threw themselves into the slightly rickety chair Ryan had previously occupied. Recognizing the voice, Gwendoline held up a finger to silence her new companion. She didn't respond until she'd finished skimming her current paragraph.

"Everleigh," she spoke warily, looking up and into a pair of bewitching jade eyes.

"Hallewell," Everleigh quipped Gwendoline's last name with a serious tone, matching the staring contest. Each of them held the stare for at least ten seconds, but Everleigh broke the contest by flicking her focus downward to glance at the book on the table. As usual, she spoke first.

"You haven't cast it yet, for one thing," she began accusingly, "and for another, where's your date? I timed my drop-in to this rotten dump precisely so I could spy on you together. Honestly, what type of guy brings a date to the campus café?" A waitress walked by and threw her a dirty look as Everleigh said the words "rotten dump," but she barely noticed. Gwendoline reluctantly shut her book again and sighed at Everleigh; with her exhale, a shimmering cloud slipped from between her lips like cigarette smoke.

"No, I haven't tried any spells yet because I was waiting until after my so-called date to experiment with something so...time-consuming." *And by time-consuming, I mean pointless and potentially dangerous,* she thought. "Also, I had a class in the Alumni building and I had to rush to get here on time."

Everleigh shook her head at her, clasping her elfin hands together over her black pleated mini skirt. "You're stalling because you're worried that your creepy book will be damaged from the scrying you told me you were determined to try a week ago. Wouldn't be a loss, if you ask me...you need a regular familiar or channeling tool. What about a wicked sharp crystal, or perhaps a cuddly pet?"

"You're not at all sorry that my date didn't go well?" Gwendoline asked, widening her eyes in an unspoken plea for sympathy.

"All right, I'm sorry your date turned out to be yet another prick," Everleigh conceded. "In fact, I'm so sorry for you that I'll give you five minutes without nagging you about delving into your stupid book."

Gwendoline snorted. Everleigh was an avid listener and the sort of chipper friend most people enjoyed having around, but once started, a conversation with her became hard to drop. Unless of course

Gwendoline had what Everleigh would consider a better topic, which was gossip, but she wanted to save the crotch quills story for when she really needed a break.

"Speaking of which, where is your familiar?" Gwendoline asked, making a show of searching under and around the table for the creature. "I mean Smaug, not your boyfriend."

Everleigh sighed and picked up a wrinkled straw wrapper from the table, drawing it between her fingers to smooth out the crinkles. "I won't let you see him until you tell me when exactly you plan to snoop around your book," she said, a delighted tone of mischief in her voice; she tossed her rippling brunette curls over her shoulder, a look of triumph in her serpentine eyes. Gwendoline groaned, leaning forward until her forehead rested on the cool edge of the table. A second later, something tapped the back of her head, almost snagging on several of the midnight dark strands. Looking up, she saw Everleigh had transformed the straw wrapper into a cheap plastic fairy wand.

"That's right, no cuteness therapy for you until you get your homework done," Everleigh cooed, smacking her again with her wand to emphasize her point. "Don't rest your head there, dear, it'll leave a mark."

Ignoring the last comment, Gwendoline sat up.

"Homework? As if. The homework I have involves practicing my mastery of defensive shields before the practical test next Monday, not trying to peer into the soul of a book that may or may not appreciate the intrusion."

"Books don't have souls, Gwendoline," Everleigh frowned at her. Gwendoline feigned a gasp and scooped up her book, clutching it to her chest with melodramatic horror.

"She didn't mean it, Niles," she crooned at the book she cradled in her arms like a baby. "You are full of history and stories and countless spells recorded in your pages!"

"Wow. Codependent, much?" Everleigh frowned deeper. "I'll amend my previous statement: books aren't *supposed* to have souls. Or names...what kind of name is Niles, anyway?" She spoke ominously, but her solemn words were ruined by the appearance of a golden snake slithering out from beneath her buoyant hair and coiling itself around her neck like a choker. It released an audible hissss that would have sent other girls screaming, its black tongue flickering in and out of its mouth. Distracted, Everleigh took hold of her familiar and eased it from off her neck.

"My book can't be a little eccentric without you harassing me about it, but you can be the only person in the city to have a poisonous serpent for a familiar?" Gwendoline grumbled.

Everleigh coaxed the snake from her hands to the table, guiding it towards Gwendoline with a few gentle words that no one else would be able to understand; her green eyes gleamed with luminescence as she spoke, but the color soon faded. The small creature drifted towards Gwendoline right up until it reached her outstretched fingers, but at the last moment it reversed direction and returned to Everleigh's hands. Forming a circle around the enchantress's slender wrist, it hissed again: a strange sheen glimmered over each shining scale of its thin body, and then it went still.

"Even Smaug knows you're full of shit," Everleigh declared matter of factly. Gwendoline nodded in agreement.

"True. Look at me, I can't even get a proper date," she said. Her companion narrowed her eyes.

"No more sympathy," Everleigh said; looking up as the café door opened, she waved someone over. "Look, here's Colt! He'll encourage you to submit to my will." A smile slanted her pretty pink lips, lips that the boy who walked in no doubt planned on kissing.

Gwendoline turned to watch a red-headed boy who was the living equivalent of a mountain of muscle enter the coffee shop and head towards their table. Sure enough, when he reached them, he bent down and pressed his mouth onto Everleigh's with a quiet passion that would have made Gwendoline blush had she not seen all of this many times before. Another thing that had given her pause when she'd met him was the antique sword he had slung over his shoulder as casually as if medieval times were current, but she knew already that the sword was Colt's casting tool; one of his ancestors had inherited it after a great war, he claimed, and it had bonded to him when he'd discovered it in his grandfather's attic. Inconvenient as it seemed, as fairytale like as his story sounded, he always carried the historic blade with him. As casting tools went, his wasn't as much of an oddity as hers, or as Everleigh's.

"Never mind all that," she said, addressing Colt. "I just had a terrible date, and now Everleigh won't stop bothering me about prying into my book." Colt didn't answer until he'd waved hello to the waitress and pulled up a chair to seat himself beside Everleigh, who looked between the two of them expectantly.

"Well?" she asked. Colt gazed steadily at Gwendoline, his sea colored eyes clear as he considered her.

"Did you address the problem?" He asked her seriously, his deep voice resonant within his large frame.

"No, I didn't. I don't...I haven't had time yet," she answered, a frown creasing her brow.

"Did you tell Everleigh what you told me last week?"He asked the follow-up question as he slipped his arm around Everleigh's slender shoulders. Her snake, waking up, slithered ponderously from her wrist up her shoulder and onto Colt's arm, hissing again, this time with contentment.

Gwendoline's frown deepened. "Yeah, I told her."

"Well then," Colt spoke like the case was closed. "I guess you'd better do it then. She always stops harassing you once you obey." Everleigh laughed, reaching over to squeeze his bicep, and Colt smiled indulgently at her in return. Infuriated, Gwendoline picked up her book again and clutched it tightly to her.

"Listen, I—"she began. Colt interrupted, but kindly.

"This is serious, Gwendoline. Really. If what you told me is true, the book might ask you to do something dangerous, like sacrifice a virgin on an altar made of neighborhood cats. Books, even magical ones, aren't supposed to make requests." Colt had always had a way about him, a manner of seeming to care about the problems of every person he spoke to, like a politician but with honor and scruples. When he directed his concern towards her, any anger she felt often evaporated on contact.

"I shouldn't have told you what Niles said," she admitted glumly, both she and her companions knowing that she was about to concede.

"You didn't, actually," Everleigh nitpicked. "You gave us the gist, you didn't show us the actual page where it...it talked to you."

"And I'm not going to," Gwendoline said firmly. "You both may have convinced me to handle this, but I don't let anyone spy on Niles but me. I—"

Before she could continue, a disturbance in the café startled them all. The door slammed violently open, knocking the retro bell clean off; Colt hummed a spell under his breath and summoned the bell to his hand so no one would trip over it on the floor. The excitable looking teen who could have been a freshman at Starford university took no notice of the courtesy, since she appeared to be out of breath from running. Hair frizzed into a sweaty mess, the newcomer made a beeline for her friend as she burst out with her gossip loud enough for the whole café to hear.

"Madam Kinsley is dead! The cops are investigating, and they don't think it was from natural causes—"

Every eye in the room turned to focus on the unintentional herald. The girl's dark skin flushed with embarrassment when she realized she'd shouted her news instead of communicating just with her friend behind the counter. For a few seconds, silence reigned as everyone took in the news.

Governor Kinsley is really dead? Gwendoline marveled; the coffee she'd imbibed felt like a stone in her stomach as she ruffled the pages of her casting book nervously. The old lady was a fixture in this town, even if she hadn't done any real governing in a while, and news of her possible murder was welcomed by no one.

Then, as if she hadn't announced the most momentous news the city had heard in over fifty years, the student dashed back out to spread the news.

2

Before

Glenna marched down the hall, her silken slippers whispering against the marble floors. She winced as they pinched her feet, but kept walking because *Fate help her* she was so late. Jael might just have her head, and Leland...well, he'd be as happy to see her as always, never mind that she was almost an hour tardy to make sure he was prepared for his betrothal ceremony.

Leland...she paused, lost in thought. As usual, thinking about the official betrothal ceremony and following castle-wide party made her feel listless and forlorn. She could see his face in her mind, with his red hair and long nose and those perceptive gray eyes. She could mentally see the pure love in his gaze when he gazed upon the princess, the woman he'd dreamed of ever since he and Glenna were only youths adventuring in the gardens and training to be knight and sorceress.

That's what hurt, that she could see it so well now. Before, when he was technically unbetrothed, she could imagine he was gazing at her that way. Before, she could dream of him in the daylight, and occasionally pretend he was hers. Last night, when she came to the reality of the grand event taking place the next day, her dreams had darkened and her mind turned to sleeplessness.

Now...*he's Jael's. Officially.*

Realizing she had come to a dazed halt in the middle of the hall when a servant brushed past her in a bustle of hurry with some last minute linens, she shook herself and resumed her determined walk.

He's Jael's, she repeated to herself harshly. The two words she forced herself to admit tasted of poison, like they were polluting her bloodstream further whenever she considered them.

She approached Jael's quarters with some apprehension, tugging her bodice and her skirts into place so no one could accuse her of being untidy. No one being Jael, who had been a terror throughout the whole process of planning the ceremony and the ball that was to follow. Taking a deep breath, she knocked on the door and waited to be admitted to the room.

"Is that Glenna? Is it her?" She heard Jael's voice chirp. A lady in waiting, a young pink-cheeked girl who probably only had enough magic to mend tears in the fabric of Jael's many dresses, opened the door and ushered Glenna in. Glenna stared, not because of the maid, but because of the maid's smile. None of Jael's ladies had smiled for weeks, let alone welcomed anyone in who dared to disrupt whatever fragile peace they had coaxed into place.

"Did he send you? Is everything all right?" Jael asked anxiously, stepping off her fitting stool to rush to Glenna. The sight of her, this slip of a girl who had become a vision of sunshine curls and flowing golden skirts topped off with a topaz studded diadem, brought to the forefront all of the mixed feelings Glenna had about this day. Before today, she could occasionally pretend that Jael was hideous, and search for flaws to squirrel away for later when she could still imagine Leland entering the room to choose her instead of the princess. Faced now with the sight of the radiant betrothal dress and the shy but excited grin Jael bestowed upon her, Glenna felt a familiar knot form in her stomach.

"He didn't send me," she managed to say, wishing the words would chafe her throat like sand so she would have an excuse not to talk any longer. "You asked me to manage all the details to make sure your day goes smoothly, so here I am to see if you need help." From anyone else, this request would have been met with her highest level of scorn: she was a sorceress, a warrior and an occasional bodyguard, not an event planner. But Jael knew how skilled she was at arranging events, and since they were friends Glenna hadn't had the option to refuse.

"Oh, now I recall!" Jael exclaimed, clutching her hands together. "I don't need anything just yet, but you certainly do!"

Careless, she took both of Glenna's hands, clad though they were in fine silk gloves that chafed against the rough palms they hid, and led her to the trio of mirrors where she had been standing on the fitting stool. The servants and ladies orbiting the princess fluttered like birds, fanning outwards to clear her path. In their opinion, the princess might be friendly from experiencing a betrothal glow now, but recent weeks had taught them to steer clear whenever tiny but rage filled little Jael went on a rampage.

Glenna found herself compelled to sit at the vanity beside the tall mirrors, and at a cue from Jael the ladies suddenly swarmed around her with various items they were somehow able to identify from the chaos strewn across the vanity.

"Hang on—" she protested as the women began to tug at her unruly hair with fine combs and brushes, and to smear beauty potions on her skin without asking her permission. Jael, amused, released a slightly manic laugh and stood apart from the fray, her green eyes dancing. A fox with curiously gold fur and a pale pink ribbon adorning its neck dashed out from under the vanity and bounded into the princess's arms; she stroked it smugly.

"You've done so much for Leland and me, Glenna, so it's only fair I find something to do for you in return. It's not much, but a little pampering should do you some good," Jael explained, and then snapped at one of the ladies. "No, no, not like that! I want sleeker, more elegant! Oh, and turn her away from the mirror so she can't see the results until the end!" The ladies whisked Glenna around so her back faced the vanity, resuming their beautifying process without missing a beat.

Ordinarily she would have thought the whole procedure would be a waste of time: most days she dressed in muted shades of black and gray, often donning trousers and a loose shirt so she could practice her weaponry or ride her horse without hindrance. But after so many long days and nights craving to be touched even casually, the gentle but firm hands of the ladies as they styled her disorderly, pin-straight hair and smoothed cool lotions onto her wind-chapped skin, she felt strange and powerless to fight back.

"You have your speech written for the ceremony?" Glenna asked, at least attempting to do what had been asked of her. Jael nodded, cooing at her fox familiar and toying with the ribbon around its neck.

"I wrote that ages ago...I hope Leland is moved by what I say. It's so poignant when the groom-to-be tears up for the bride...even if this is just the betrothal ceremony," she said.

"I'm sure he'll be stirred by anything you say," Glenna felt a bitter smile begin to stretch her lips, but she quelled it as one of the ladies dotted expensive scarlet color there. Jael smiled at her, suddenly a timid bride-to-be.

"How completely sweet you've been to us...to me, Glenna. I know you and Leland have always been best friends, so it's truly grand that you've accepted me as you have. I can't imagine that was easy for you, especially because of how spoiled I was when you met me," Jael said, admitting her flaws with the ease of one who had learned to work around them. "But then, war changes us all, I suppose, and a war amongst kindred even more so."

Glenna closed her eyes to look back into the past. *Leland and Glenna, noble children in training together to be a knight of the realm and a sorceress for the princess we'd never met...Leland and Glenna, growing up together and becoming inseparable...Glenna falling in love with Leland...imagining a future together...*

She forced herself to remember the rest, clenching her hands into tight fists where they rested in her lap. *Leland, meeting the young orphaned Princess Jael and falling in love with her...Glenna urging him to remember he was only a knight out of jealousy...Leland setting forth to become one of the three land-blooded knights, just to become worthy of Jael...Leland and Jael, falling in love...Leland and Jael, braving quest and combat to lead her to her rightful throne...then the secluded proposal in the woods...*

"You're done! My, you were quiet as a barn mouse!" Jael exclaimed, unceremoniously dumping her fox from her arms to approach Glenna. Glenna started to ask her how would she know how quiet a barn mouse was, since Jael was not the type of person to frequent barns and stables, but the ladies swiveled her around a final time so she could look into the mirror and see the results of their work.

She had to admit, they had done a superb job. Glenna's brows rose, as she hardly recognized the woman in the mirror. Her sleek black hair, shot through with silver that had revealed itself once she'd shown a preference for winter magic, had been brushed into submission and twisted into a style so elegant she felt that one wrong turn of her head would send the masterpiece tumbling down. Her skin, pale and bloodless on occasion, had been coaxed into an enticing flush, her dark tinted lips a place the eye was instantly drawn to. Her eyes...well, nothing could be done about permanent touch of melancholy in the slate irises, but they had been outlined and enhanced to give her a mysterious yet inviting look. The lavender dress completed the look that Glenna could not have accomplished herself had she tried her hardest.

"What do you think?" Jael interrupted her astonishment. "I could tell my ladies had a time concealing the sleepless circles under your eyes—really, dear, you must learn to relax on occasion—but things have turned out for the best, haven't they?"

"Your ladies are artists, Jael," Glenna said, standing so quickly she almost tumbled the vanity over. She hated herself for thinking it, but she couldn't help wondering how Leland would react if he saw her like this, at what had to be her most beautiful. It took great willpower not to run to where she knew Leland would be to beg him not to marry Jael.

Meanwhile, Jael beamed and clasped Glenna's hands in her own again. "I'm glad you like it. Wait until Niles sees you!"

"Niles?" Glenna questioned, caught off guard by the mention of Leland's fellow knight of the land.

Jael winked mischievously. "Surely you know...Glenna, how can you not have noticed how he looks at you?" Looking down, she adjusted the fit of her friend's dress as she spoke. Nonplussed, Glenna summoned her thoughts on Niles into her mind: they'd trained together with magic after Leland had focused more on physical combat, they'd schemed together during the war, and she trusted him as a true friend. But...Niles looked at her? That way? She couldn't believe it.

"You know, he returns from negotiating with the barons today. Maybe you've never thought about it, but perhaps it's worth seeing what would come about if you offered him some encouragement?"

Glenna monitored Jael's expression, searching for any sign of cunning or artifice in her words. *Maybe she's discovered somehow that I have feelings for her betrothed? Is this an attempt to distract me?*

But the princess's eyes were as wide and innocent as always. She could be ruthless when crossed, but strategic manipulation among friends was not Jael's way.

"I haven't noticed, I must admit..." she began, picturing the slender but strong knight in her mind's eye.

"Really? You haven't seen how he watches you, how he orbits your sphere like an albatross drawn to the sea?" Jael asked incredulously. Finished with grooming Glenna, she turned back to her own toilette and pinched her cheeks while peering into a mirror.

"Not at all," she replied. *Also, my heart belongs to another.*

"Well, if you ask me, I think this is something you should pursue," Jael hesitated before she continued, the concern of a friend outweighing her wish not to offend. "Surely you must get lonely on occasion, and at the very least Niles seems like he'd be good company and perhaps warm you in the dark."

"Jael!" Glenna exclaimed.

"What? It's not like either of us has no experience with that sort of companionship..." Jael turned, a saucy grin decorating her pert bow lips; a few of her ladies frowned at her brazen words, causing her to scowl. "Enough with the false virtue, you old hens. I know you've spied on me and the future prince together, and Penelope, *you're* the one who smuggled him into my boudoir last week."

"I think it's time for me to go, my lady," Glenna said formally, trying and failing to conceal how unsettled she was. Jael wasn't wrong about the fact that neither of them were virgins, but she didn't appreciate the interference in her love life. She hadn't approached Leland with her feelings all that time ago because she hadn't wanted to risk their friendship, a decision she regretted but not completely. In Niles's case, she wouldn't risk a perfectly healthy friendship against a handful of sweaty but satisfying nights.

Jael's smile curved down into a guilty expression, and she shuffled her feet sheepishly. "I suppose you do have to go, but please understand that I just want you to be as happy as I am. Perhaps I meddle in the wrong ways sometimes, but I...I really do think you should give it a chance with Niles. Maybe it wouldn't be the worst thing if you encouraged him."

"Perhaps," Glenna admitted, not even entertaining the possibility in her head. "I'm not angry with you. But I really must go check on—"

"As you wish," Jael conceded, waving her out of the room. "Go, and let the rest of my realm be astounded at your beauty!" Her fox jumped back into her arms as Jael sat back down at the vanity to primp some more. Glenna exited the room full of women, trying not to seem like she was fleeing.

She still had a great deal to do to make sure all the little details were in order, but she found her feet taking her to the armory, where she knew Leland would be. She felt like she could breathe fully and deeply now that she had left Jael and her shoes no longer seemed to pinch her as much as she rushed through the halls and down the stairs to her destination. When she reached the sturdy wooden door, she paused to let her breath catch up with her and to cool her flaming cheeks. Hesitating, she placed her hand on the door to push it open and entered.

The armory had no other occupants at the moment: all were busy with preparations for the day, so for once the vigilant training program Leland, Niles, and their protégée Abelard had enforced as ruling knights of the land rested on standby. Leland, dashing with his strong arms, red hair, and the fancy clothes Jael had personally selected for him to wear to the ceremony, sat casually on one of the many benches, polishing his sword. If she hadn't known better, Glenna could have pretended it was any other day. The two of them could have been about to trade off spells in a mock battle in the training arena, his corporeal sword clashing against her enchanted basket handle blade in a shower of indigo sparks. He looked up when he saw her, his gray eyes kind and filled with happiness so potent it forced her to smile.

"Glenna! You're all dressed up!" He exclaimed, clearly delighted. "I swear I haven't seen you in a dress in at least two years."

"Well, I've been busy protecting a princess and setting up a kingdom...what's your excuse for looking slovenly?" she replied. Her smile drooped slightly, but she held it in place and approached Leland to sit beside him on the plain wooden bench. "Are you ready?"

"I've been ready since I met her, honestly. Fate's blood, she made me work hard, but I can't tell you how glad I am to finally be able to claim her," he disclosed his feelings in the same quiet tone he always used, but his expression and voice were so jubilant she had no doubt as to the depth of his emotion.

"I'm happy for you both," she lied, but then spoke some truth to soothe her conscience. "You both deserve the absolute best, and so does Oloetha. You're going to be one of the greatest things that will happen to this land." She allowed herself one moment to touch him, simply placing a hand on his brawny shoulder to connect. He smiled at her, placing his hand over hers in return.

Unlike Jael, they could communicate so well together that many words were rarely necessary between them. Unlike Jael, they had labored through battles together, fought for the queendom with their lives on the line. But perhaps that was unfair: Jael had shown bravery as well, and as a princess without an heir she couldn't have been expected to be on the front lines of a bloody conflict.

Suddenly, Leland set his sword aside and scooped her up into an impromptu waltz about the room, laughing as he did so. Glenna, swept off her feet, felt his infectious laughter fill her as she danced with him.

"I thought your first dance was supposed to be with the princess?" she teased, allowing herself to be caught up in the moment.

"Technically yes...but how could I neglect the friend that helped me win her in the first place?" he said; then he stopped dancing. "Glenna, I can't even tell you how much is means to me that you've helped me get to this point. I've never been happier, and a lot of that is due to you. I could ask for no better swordsister."

"My pleasure, future prince." She couldn't, she just couldn't stop drinking in his face, which his sincere eyes and that noble, slightly crooked nose and those lips she'd wanted to kiss for forever. Was she imagining his glance towards her own lips? Was it only a fantasy that his hand tightened around her waist?

"I thought to find the newly betrothed couple in here, but perhaps I've intruded on the wrong scene?" A voice startled them both, and they stepped apart. In the doorway, a man stood casually leaning against the entryway. His eyes, as changeable as autumn leaves and sharing their colors, scanned them both. His focus had always been sharp, but his gaze seemed keen to cut Glenna open just to see what he'd find beneath the surface.

"Just two old friends celebrating my betrothal, Niles," Leland released Glenna and stepped forward to greet him, shaking his hand warmly. "So you've returned from your expedition in time for the ceremony...did you have any luck with the negotiations?"

"Some. Enough to—" Niles began, drawing his eyes away from Glenna to address his friend and fellow blooded knight.

"Never mind, we can talk business another day," Leland brushed aside his reply. "You still have to prepare for the ceremony, and I'm sure Glenna has other tasks to occupy her."

"What, my travel stained clothes and the smell of horses isn't suitable for your betrothal ceremony?" Niles quipped, a wry smile twisting his mouth. "Remind me to tell the princess it's rude to discriminate against her honored guests."

"Remember, Niles, Jael has no sense of humor when it comes to ceremonies and event planning," Glenna said.

Recollecting Jael's declaration that Niles was interested in her, she observed him as undetectably as she could. Where she and Leland had fought as comrades in arms, Niles had moved in the shadows, manipulating key players on both sides and slitting throats in the dark when certain players dared venture outside their allotted role. True, his eyes kept returning and returning to her, but perhaps that was because she rarely dressed up as much as other castle dwellers did. Leland hadn't been wrong: it had been several months since she'd bothered with a dress, let alone something as delicate as this gown.

He's probably surprised to see me looking like a girl and not a stable boy, she mused, self-consciously smoothing the multilayered folds of her skirts. Their eyes met, and held. Niles came to her and took her hand, grasping it in formal greeting as if Leland wasn't in the room. Even through the gloves, Glenna felt a spark that was either magic he'd channeled or a coincidence, and quickly pulled her hand away.

"You should go prepare, Niles," she said hurriedly, turning back to Leland, who had re-seated himself to finish polishing his sword to the brightest sheen it could muster. "I'll follow you out." She wished Niles would stop looking at her, not just because she was aware of what it might mean now, but because he seemed to sense that she wanted another moment alone with Leland.

"As you wish," Niles said, moving to leave the room. "I'd like to have a word with you before the ceremony, Glenna, if I may."

Heart sinking, she nodded. Once he was gone, she allowed herself a final moment to pretend Leland was excited and preparing for her. She watched him as he worked, and he looked up at her again, smiling.

"What is it? You seem sad," he asked, his dreamy smile fading into a look of concern. Reaching out to him, she brushed her fingertips against his face, wishing it was her skin and not her glove touching him.

"Nostalgia, I suppose," she lied again.

Then she forced herself to leave, each step away from him more difficult. Right before she exited, she noticed one of Leland's crimson handkerchiefs, the ones he would occasionally use to polish his weapon or his armor, laying abandoned by the door. Quickly glancing back to see if Leland would notice, she summoned the rag to her fingertips with a hushed spell and clutched it tightly in her fist as she departed.

3

"Today our prestigious Madam Governor passed away in what can only be called a mysterious set of circumstances. Found in her home shortly after eight a.m. this morning, Madam Kinsley suffered a fatal injury to the throat that caused her to bleed out. The authorities are doing everything they can to find whoever was involved with the murder."

"Along with the investigation of the murder of Madam Kinsley, there have been protests and riots all over Starford and other surrounding towns all the way to the border regarding the right of succession. The current heir of the Kinsley line has been abroad for much of his life, and some feel the time might be right to hold a democratic election to choose the best leader for our city and state. The search for the killer of Madam Kinsley as well as the heir of her bloodline will continue over the coming days—"

"Give me a break," Gwendoline, fed up with flipping through the various Starford news channels, snapped at the television as she turned it off with a wave of her hand.

"I know," Colt, sitting beside her on the sofa, tossed back a handful of the cheap popcorn they'd made in honor of the evening news. "But stop being a drama queen and turning the TV off because you don't like what they're saying."

"It's not that I don't like it, but I'm already tired of the speculation." she grumbled, allowing Colt to turn the news back on. "Madam Kinsley wasn't well liked, but she's barely cold and they're already tearing all the regions apart with rumors."

"Well yeah, Gwendoline, I'm moderately sorry she's gone before her time, but the unrest the Governor's death will cause might actually change things around here," Colt said. They'd propped up their feet on the scratched surface of her coffee table, and he nudged one of her sock covered feet with his own. She bumped him back, leaning over to steal a handful of his popcorn since she'd already devoured hers.

Could things really change? Starford had a status quo to uphold, or so most people who lived there thought. Unlike a town filled with equal parts mortals and magical folk, each state was ruled more like a kingdom, and the line of casters and sorcerers who presided over the land had remained unbroken for time uncounted. Starford in particular was crucial to the health of the nation, since it was so central to the land and the core of magical commerce. Talk of an election taking place rang with an air of absurdity, because the land was still ruled by laws set by the old gods who demanded ancient blood ties to the earth. Even if most actively denied true belief in the old gods, deep down everyone accepted the reality of a higher power who might come calling if certain unbreakable rules were abandoned.

Regardless, Gwendoline wasn't concerned with all of that. All she'd wanted to do at the end of the day was take a hot bath and get some of her homework done in front of the television with the biggest glass of wine she could find. She'd had her bath—her wet hair dripped occasionally on the pages of her Practical Casting textbook—and she had her mug of sparkling wine, but the TV had been nothing but unhelpful.

Colt had decided to get his homework done at her house tonight. Everleigh had a mandatory parental dinner on Tuesday nights, and even her boyfriend of several years wasn't welcome at this one family function. Gwendoline had heard her bemoan this weekly commitment more than once, as any college student with a busy social schedule might, but she knew Everleigh secretly loved how involved her parents were with her life.

"How are things with your parents?" Gwendoline asked Colt; finally giving up on studying, she slipped her textbook to the ground with a thump and picked up her wine mug instead. "Is your Dad still trying to get you to drop out?"

"Of course," Colt sighed, tossing his own battered textbook aside and raising his arms in a long stretch. "He knows I'm talented, and he knows I could make a difference with my gifts once I decide what I actually want to do. Hell, even without magic I could make a career from any of the sports that I play."

"Yes, we know you're a god," Gwendoline teased. He cast a glare her way before he stole her mug and finished its contents. Courteously, he sat up long enough to refill the cup from the condensation covered bottle on the coffee table before he reclined again.

"Anyway...my old man's latest tactic is the tried and true passive aggressive guilting strategy. Lately he keeps reminiscing about my mother and talking about how he doesn't have any other family to share the business with," Colt told her.

"That's so unfair!" Gwendoline tried to empathize. "You shouldn't have to give up your life because he wants you to run his shop when he retires."

"Agreed. But I can't help thinking..." Colt's expression became pensive as he tilted his head back to stare at the ceiling thoughtfully. "Maybe I owe him, you know? He's been so great about everything else, especially since Mom passed."

Gwendoline remembered the dark days that she and Everleigh had helped Colt through together when his mother had gotten sick and then eventually died. The Hallewell family hadn't been together for very long, since her mother had died when she was an infant, and shortly after her father had remarried when she was five. Then he'd passed away, and when Gwendoline was fourteen her dubious relationship with her stepmother had come to an end as well. She' basically been raising herself for most of that time, so the independence and empty house wasn't a novelty...nevertheless, in her own way Gwendoline had lost enough parents for a lifetime, and she had been able to relate to Colt's circumstances. For now, she simply laid a hand on his arm and let him sit in silence for a moment or two.

"Want to just spend the night? I have more booze, more popcorn, and plenty of our favorite sitcom episodes at the ready," Gwendoline eventually asked, attempting to cheer him up. "We can either talk more, or get blind drunk on a school night. Which would you prefer?"

"I'll spend the night if you want, but we won't be watching sitcoms," Colt whispered, his brooding session over as he leaned in close with a teasing smile of his own. On anyone else his charm would have been a temptation, but she'd known him long enough to see through to the mischief underneath. Groaning, she slumped down in her seat.

"I don't want to dig through my book tonight. I don't want to ever do that, actually," she complained. "No further messages have appeared since the first one, and maybe they won't at all. Maybe it was a magical fluke."

"Is that what you really think?" Colt voiced his skepticism.

She held her ground for the space of a second before she gave in. "No. But I still don't want to, and I don't think it's a good idea."

"You promised Everleigh you would. You promised me too, actually," Colt reminded her smugly. "Real friends don't break promises. Isn't that something you always say?"

"Shut up," Gwendoline struggled to conceal a laugh. "I only say that when I want to get my way."

"Well, now it's a two way street," Colt poked her side, nudging one of her ticklish spots with the expertise of a long-time friend. "I can stick around either to support you or make sure you actually go through with the snooping."

Dodging his nudge, she shook her head. "All right, I'll do it, but I'd rather be alone. Niles isn't partial to anyone else, as you know."

"Of course. Remember that time you tried to show me some of your notes and it burned me?" Colt rose to his feet, stretching with his arms towards the ceiling as he winced. "I'm surprised my palms aren't still scarred from that."

"I refuse to allow you to hold me responsible for that, I told you he was ornery that day!" Gwendoline laughed, since Colt had barely yelped from the shock of magic the book had inflicted on him.

After a few minutes more of careless banter, Colt packed up his textbooks and left her house so she could be alone. Alone with Niles, alone so she could possibly irritate whatever ancient power made her book so mysterious. Even now, the book sat glaring at her from the chair where she'd set it. Books couldn't glare, she knew that, but the pages sent her a troubling vibe all the same.

"I know we've been together for almost seven years," Gwendoline began explaining aloud, coaxing the book to float to her with a hummed spell. "I mean, think about it: I find you at a flea market, my magic suddenly spikes, and now after all this time being predictable, you write to me personally. Can't you understand my concern?" The book came to her hands, strangely warm to the touch in a way that made her spine tingle.

"With all the unrest that's about to happen in Starford, old friends like us should stick together, that's for sure. It's been you and me for so long now...so please don't take this as a sign of disloyalty," she continued, hesitantly opening the book to the page she knew would still be there. Normally the book erased everything she had already read until she asked for or needed it again, but the words on this page had refused to fade with any spell, even when she'd pitched the heavy tome across the room in a temper. She regarded that lapse as a low point for both of them.

"But...I mean, books aren't supposed to talk back," she whispered, tracing her finger over the words on a slightly torn page near the end of the book.

Gwendoline Hallewell, I need you. Will you help me?

There were the words, and there was the bloodstain in the corner where Gwendoline had cut her finger while searching for a spell to cure one of Everleigh's infrequent zits. (That too had refused to disappear, not until Everleigh discovered a special cleanser from the very unglamorous grocery store.)

Reading the words again, she knew Colt and Everleigh had been right about looking into the book. What kind of book asks for help?

But she hardly knew where to start. She had always gone to her book to look for spells, so any spell about scrying into a casting object would have had to come from the book. Sighing, she gulped down the last of her wine and set the glass down on the coffee table. Staring at the book in her lap, an idea came to her. It was so simple; she almost laughed aloud thinking she'd nearly missed it. Summoning a pen to her, she uncapped it and held her hand poised to write.

Suppose it's a nasty demon or something of that nature...suppose it lies to you. What will you do then? Her thoughts intruded, unwelcoming and grim. *You were too scared to write back the first time you saw the page. What's changed?*

What *had* changed? The fact that now she was tipsy enough to disregard the risk?

Whatever. It's worth a shot. Gwendoline grit her teeth and began to write.

What do you want?

Almost instantly, fresh words appeared on the page.

Good, I almost thought you'd never write back. If I could talk to you like a person and not in this form, I would have convinced you by now.

You sound normal enough, for an insentient object that isn't supposed to hold conversations with its readers.

She wrote back. A pause took place, then more words.

I'm sorry if I scared you. This age being what it is there's no possible way for me to explain what's going on in a way that you'd believe me. Especially as a book…and, well, especially because it's you.

Especially because of me? What's ***that*** *supposed to mean?*

I hint to you that I'm more than a book and the thing you focus on is that I may or may not have insulted you. That might be why.

Gwendoline paused this time, allowing a moment to concede to his point. Then she felt foolish, so stupid as to lose the point of why she was doing this at all. Her curiosity took over, and she hurriedly wrote back in handwriting so messy she wondered if he'd be able to understand it.

If you've been here all along, why start talking to me now? What's changed?

I woke up once certain conditions of the spell were met, Gwendoline. I'm going to have to talk to you in person to properly explain all of this.

How are you going to do that?

That's what I need help with. There's one final condition, and there's a very strong chance you're going to hate it.

Gwendoline bit her lip, conflicted. Chills patterned her skin, ominous and yet thrilling, somehow.

Why don't you tell me what it is and I'll decide if I'll help you or not? Also, let there be no confusion: I'm not pledging my soul to you or sacrificing any virgins. There has to be a line drawn somewhere.

If I was that kind of book, the only virgin I'd want would be you, and I'm fairly certain that ship has sailed…

Hey!

Apologies. Are you ready?

As I'll ever be.

A long pause followed her last statement, as if he was rushing to write to her too. Finally, the fateful words appeared. Gwendoline felt her heart thumping incredibly fast as she read them.

The spell that sealed me in this book is threefold. It needed a spirit, heart, and soul connection, and it needs those again to reverse the cast. Unknowingly, you provided two, the right number to wake my soul up so I could convince you to complete the final link. One, you named me, and named me correctly, which represented the spirit connection. Two...well, that paper cut wasn't a total accident. I was awake enough to will the other links to start breaking. Regardless, your blood finished the heart connection.

That's morbid.

I know...but necessary. More than the threefold ties, timing is important. Finally...and this is where you come in...I need the soul connection. There's a reason this book came to you specifically, that it waited through years of strangers' writings to come to you.

Just come out with it. What do you need me for?

I need you to kiss me.

Gwendoline's mouth dropped open, and if she'd been holding her mug of wine she would have dropped it. *Kiss* him? Kiss *Niles*? Giving her casting book a name had seemed like a joke at the beginning, even though the name also seemed perfect for the task. It surprised her, but now after a few moments writing back and forth, she had almost stopped thinking of him as a book.

For some reason, she believed him, and she felt incredibly stupid for doing so. Was she crazy to consider pressing her lips to a stupid spell book, let alone hold a serious conversation with one?

A strained giggle escaped her. *This has to be the wine. I must have drunk way more than I thought.*

Believe it or not, I can hear you laughing. Technically, I can hear when you talk, too, but it seemed more sensational to go about this conversation writing to each other.

She'd dropped her pen and got an ink stain on her red pajama pants. Annoyed, Gwendoline reclaimed the pen and wrote back.

Kiss you? You want me to <u>kiss</u> you? You're a book! Books shouldn't talk, or ask for kisses, or be smart asses with aesthetic goals.

I think we can both agree by now that I'm not just a book. And I think you're going to kiss me... and who knows, maybe you'll like it.

That was a little creepy.

Yes, I realize it's hard to flirt while trapped in book form. If only someone would save me from my parchment prison...

Enough.

Another pause ruled. Gwendoline felt breath-less.

It's almost like I really am about to kiss someone, she thought; uncomfortable, she dismissed the idea.

So you'll do it?

I'm thinking.

Think faster, these pages are getting scratchy.

Seriously?

This appears to be another situation where humor doesn't translate well through this method of communication.

Gwendoline thought of one more question.

Wait, so if you need me to free you from the book...are you human? What do you look like? Am I going to be shocked into a heart-attack because some alien or goblin crawls out of my casting book grousing for some human meat?

Instead of writing back, a page turned in the book and a rapid sketch began to draw itself on the fresh surface. A slender face appeared beneath a well-tousled mop of dark hair swept back from a regal forehead. The waves were black, but not thoroughly dark like hers: in the sun, light would reflect upon it in a way that reminded her of a comforting bonfire on winter nights, or perhaps fresh ink dotting a white page. A strong, stubble covered jaw, the stern brow, the lips quirked in the faintest of smiles...Gwendoline realized that he must be trying to show her his appearance.

All at once, the simple sketch bloomed with color and detail, so she could see the rugged skin and the deep-set, curiously amber eyes. For some reason she couldn't quite pinpoint, the face felt familiar to her, and she traced her fingertip down the bridge of the picture's dignified nose, against the shadows around the eyes. On the page beside the picture, more words appeared.

So...I wouldn't precisely be kissing a book...I'd be kissing you to turn you human again?

Sounds like a fairytale, doesn't it?

I'm not so sure, Gwendoline thought, but didn't write. Unable to tear her eyes away from the portrait of the young man, she gazed into the solemn eyes of the picture to will more answers forward. An impression of the pleasant scrape of his stubble against her cheek startled her, the intimacy of the feeling ringing with a distinct sense of familiarity. Equally so did this face seem known to her, and it made perfect sense that Niles would look like this if he was actually telling her the truth. And yet...

This is insane. She felt like she was standing on the edge of a diving board, balancing on the end just to see how far she could sway forward until she lost her balance. Fear and exhilaration may have been good friends in a situation like this, but all at once all she could feel was the alarm. But was she afraid that he would break free of her casting book if she did as he asked, or that he wouldn't?

I don't think I can do this.

Of course you can. At least...think about it, Gwendoline. Please.

He seemed so natural, so real, and she'd never met him. She'd never known she could meet him, had never known there might be a real reason her book was such an oddity. She was scared of how easy it would be to give in, and how quickly he had almost convinced her to help him.

I promise you I'll consider it.

Gwendoline wrote her last message in a tolerably legible scrawl before slamming her book shut. She felt drained, though she hadn't cast a single spell. Part of her wanted to call either Colt or Everleigh, but when she found her phone she realized that she'd rather keep this to herself after all. Besides, would they even believe her?

4

Before

Evening, sultry and seductive, had crept over the land at last, indicating that the betrothal ceremony was due to start at any moment. Per Jael's request, everlasting candles had been lit all over the main hall and ballroom; each dancing flame bestowed upon the room a festive yet beguiling aura. The wedding between the princess and Leland would be a brighter, morningtide occasion, but betrothal ceremonies were meant to convey a sense of romance and rising anticipation. Where a wedding was a public, political celebration of love, the betrothal ceremony was a binding contract of two souls being bound together. In its own way, a betrothal held far more significance.

Since it was nearly midsummer, Jael had arbitrarily decided that all of her ladies should wear ivory roses in their hair, so Glenna had removed her formal gloves and ventured into the garden to slip some of the freshest roses she could find into her coiffed locks before anyone else laid claim to the better blooms. She already knew Leland wouldn't notice the enhancement to her beauty, so she didn't know why she cared about which flowers she got. Maybe the heady scent would help soothe her through the ceremony so she could keep her emotions in check.

"I didn't expect to find you here," Niles spoke, appearing behind her as silently as if he'd been conjured. Glenna, who had been lost in contemplation as she'd fingered the soft petals of a shy rosebud, coaxing them into bloom with her magic, hadn't expected him either, but she managed not to startle too obviously. "I thought you'd be with Jael."

"She wanted a few moments alone before the procession to the great hall," she told him.

When she faced him, she couldn't help but take in how good he looked, partially because of what Jael had intimated about his feelings for her. Niles would be performing the ceremony, so it was fitting that he should be so well-dressed, but the distinguished line of his jaw and his clever features conveyed a dignity all their own. He was not as tall as Leland, who towered over all the men Glenna had ever known, but he surpassed the height of average men, and had broad enough shoulders to showcase his strength. His body, lithe as a dancer's and suntanned from weeks on horseback, moved with its usual subtle grace towards her. Staring at him as she was, she hardly noticed the fancy but minimal charcoal suit, aside from the fact that it framed his figure so well.

How odd, she mused. *We've been friends for ages, and I've really never* noticed *him like this before?* She had to remind herself that Jael's words might not be true, since neither one of them had had any tangible proof.

"How are you?" Niles asked, stepping forward; they began an impromptu walk down the lane. "Jael has been a terror, I've heard, and you've had your hands full with planning the event."

"It's been all right, I suppose. I'll be glad when the whole thing's over." Glenna shrugged, demurring.

"That's understandable. It will be nice when Leland isn't so damned nauseating about how in love he is," Niles replied.

"You surprise me, Niles. I didn't expect you to be the unsentimental type."

"Why is that?" he queried. Noticing another fully blooming rose, she paused to pluck it; twirling the thorny stem in her hands, she resumed her meandering down the path as her lilac gown gently swished about her legs. Dresses could feel freeing, after all, if no one was forcing her to wear them, and as long as she wasn't intending to engage in any physical activity.

"You've always been an advocate of the legendary romance of the princess and her knight," she explained, teasing a little. "You almost sounded like a meddling matchmaker woman, back when the whole castle was pushing them together. If Jael hadn't been intimidated by you at the time, you would've made her laugh."

"I expect that is the case," Niles chuckled, clasping his hands behind his back as they strolled. "But don't misunderstand me: it's not that I'm unsentimental. It's more the fact that someone who is alone can't appreciate every love struck glance or supposedly secret public kiss."

"Oh, I understand that." *More than you know,* Glenna added silently. "The affection can be...wearying, at times."

"For you more than anyone else," Niles said, his shadowed eyes piercing her. Her feet stopped walking briefly as her heart stuttered in alarm.

"How do you mean?" She asked at last, twisting the stem of the rose she'd plucked in her hands.

"You're in love with Leland, and he's about to marry someone else, someone you consider a good friend," he said, speaking the facts that tore at her in the night so casually she wanted to strike him. "Between the sorrow of lost love and the guilt of coveting a man that belongs to your friend and your princess, I can't imagine that dilemma would be easy for you to handle."

She ogled him, mortified that anyone else had been able to see through her carefully constructed façade of platonic friendship. It didn't occur to her to try to deny the truth; Niles was too smart to believe any protest she could think of now that he knew the truth, and he wouldn't have spoken unless he was positive.

She opened and closed her mouth twice before words, breathy and broken, escaped her. "How did you know?"

"Oh, I know quite a lot," Niles said. His mouth quirked into a smile and he gestured for them to continue walking. Hesitating briefly, she did so.

"If you're so sure of how I feel about Leland, you're acting rather heartless about the whole situation," she accused him. "In fact, if you've knows about this for a while, why say anything to me about it at all? There's no reason to speak unless you were seeking to hurt me. Is that what you wanted?" *He doesn't even have the grace to look abashed,* she thought, furious.

"On the contrary, the last thing I want to do is hurt you. I've just returned from a journey involving a lot of exceedingly dull negotiations, so I've had a lot of time to think about this." He rambled, momentarily lost in thought. He looked up at the sky, where the sun gracefully dipped into the line of the horizon.

"Niles?" she spoke to summon him back to the present.

Unexpectedly, he took hold of her slender arm, whirling her into him. She glimpsed his brows drawn down seriously over his intense eyes before his lips landed on hers, tender and firm simultaneously. It was not her first kiss, but Glenna felt a similar rush of surprise and exhilaration that always made her feel tipsy. She didn't have time to feel anything else but a startling rush of pleasure in being kissed that left her breathless; he withdrew, not just from the kiss but from her, stepping back with only his hand on her elbow to keep her steady.

"Glenna..." he began to speak, but the huskiness in his voice made him clear his throat. "I wanted to give you something else to think about tonight. Someone else. Me."

Her heart felt like it was shredding into pieces, a razor-sharp sensation that made her eyes water. But that wasn't the only thing that hurt her; during the kiss, she had squeezed the stem of the rose so tightly a thorn had pierced her skin, and deeply. Oddly detached, she lifted her hand to inspect the puncture wound, observing the thin stream of blood that marred her white skin and continued on to stain a silken rose petal as well.

"Oh, I—" Glenna tried to speak, scrambling for something to say, anything to say to improve the silence. Niles hushed her, taking her injured hand in his own and looking at the cut. Wordless, he curled her fingers open and brought the hand to his lips. She thought he was about to kiss that as well, but he simply *blew* on the wound. An electrifying quality buzzed in the air around them both briefly, before disappearing along with her cut. Glenna lowered her hand after he released it, staring up at him dumbly with no words worthy of the moment. He too seemed nervous, suddenly shy.

"You don't need to tell me anything now. But if you felt like you didn't have anyone...now you do," Niles said, sincerity crystallizing his voice in her memory.

Speak, say something, *fool!* Glenna urged herself, but no words and no answers came. Niles bowed slightly before her, then headed back to the castle on the same path they'd been strolling on minutes before. She lingered, rooted to the spot where she'd been kissed by someone she had previously considered only a friend.

When she did muster the will to think past her problems and focus on Jael's and Leland's ceremony, she noticed she still had the rose she had plucked clasped in her newly healed hand. The petals, formerly stained with just a drop or two of her blood, had blushed into the deepest of reds and bloomed to fullness. She blushed too, her cheeks turning as red as the rose. Whose magic had accomplished this, hers or Niles's?

Never mind, she thought. Shaking herself, she cast the rose down and turned on her heel to walk back to the castle.

When she stood beside Leland and Abelard—the newest and youngest knight of the trio tied to the goddess Fate—at the start of the ceremony an hour later, she still had no answers. Indeed, she was full of Leland, staring up into his face with her heart in her throat. How could she even think of anything else when her true love stood beside her, awaiting the arrival of his betrothed?

She couldn't bear it. She'd thought she could, but the urge to rush back down the ivory carpeted aisle was filling her to the brim, and it took all of her self-control to stay. When Leland looked down at her, his expression full of eagerness to see Jael appear in her ceremonial finery, it took all of her strength to smile back.

At least he will be happy with her, she told herself. *And he can be yours for the moment. In the candlelight, no one will see your heart's desire.*

Jael materialized at last, as dramatically as anyone who knew her could have predicted. The doors to the hall, eased open by a pair of footmen, revealed her standing in the entrance. She had the grace to blush, as if she wasn't drinking in the attention from the other royals and nobility that had gathered, but then she saw Leland. The two beamed at each other, the gloriously noble soon-to-be Prince and the resplendent bride-to-be, and Jael glided down the aisle as poised as a winged angel. Indeed, the candlelight reflected off her golden hair, and the bright topaz gems in her tiara, lending her a perfect halo.

As awed by them both as everyone else in the hall, Glenna couldn't take her eyes off of Leland. *How could he think of me when* Jael *is in the room? He couldn't possibly.*

A sense of being observed distracted her, though, and guessing what it was, she looked over to where Niles stood at the top of the aisle, waiting to officiate for the couple in love. Instead of focusing on Jael, the most beautiful woman in the queendom, he seemed mesmerized by Glenna. An odd look crossed his face when he noticed her eyes on him, then he inclined his head to her to acknowledge her attention.

The two lovers met in front of Niles, clasping their hands together and slowly kneeling as was proper. Bowing their heads as if praying, they spoke in unison loudly enough for the hall to hear.

"We two wish our hearts to be tied together this night. We two wish our spirits to be pledged together this night. We two wish our souls to be sealed as one this night. We believe Fate has willed this."

"I see," said Niles, formally speaking the words of the betrothal pledge; he placed a hand on each of their heads, subtly taking care not to muss Jael's curls for fear of her later wrath. "And what have you two spirits, hearts, and souls to offer to one another and to Fate tonight?"

"Naught but love, and with marriage my worldly goods," Leland said, his deep voice resonating through the hall. Already, he sounded like the king he would be after he and Jael produced an heir.

"Naught but love, and with marriage my name and my worldly goods," Jael echoed, altering her statement from Leland's to fit her superior social status. She was a princess who ruled in her own right, who would become queen once her children followed in her steps and became their own princes or princesses.

"I see," Niles repeated solemnly. "But how do we gathered here know you are sincere? What proof have you that such a grim pledge will be upheld?" Sensing the light sarcasm in his voice, Glenna had to muscle down a particularly stubborn giggle. In this situation where her emotions were in such turmoil, the urge to laugh irritated her.

"I pledge my sword. Should I break my oath, may it be broken in pieces beside my honor," Leland said; it took a moment, but the sword slung over his back began to glow with faint silver light.

"I pledge my familiar," Jael spoke after him; beside her, her golden fox familiar appeared as if from nowhere, softly luminescent as it crouched beside the princess. "Should I break my oath, may she be lost with my good name and my honor."

"As you have spoken, so may it be," Niles began the conclusion for the first, most formal part of the ceremony. "I equip your two souls with—"

THUD.

The hall doors burst open, followed by a blast of wind so cold that webs of frost raced in from the entryway to spread over the polished marble floors. Glenna stepped forward in front of Leland and Jael, instantly ready for magical combat as she had been trained, and Niles took his place beside her as they watched the door. A shape had begun to form in the doorway of the hall, brought in by the frigid air that made her feel exposed and naked even though she wore the flowing summer dress.

The shape formed at last, coalescing into the figure of a tall, broad-shouldered, giant of a man who surpassed even Leland in height. Evidently dressed for the occasion in a deep crimson ensemble, the lines of his long body and aristocratic features conveyed contempt in its purest form. He exuded such an aura of power that the lengthy strides he took towards the betrothed couple and the majesty in his bearing were unnecessary to convey the authority of his person. Before he spoke, Glenna knew his voice would ring in the hall for a long time after.

"What a magnificent ceremony. What a stunning couple. Indeed, what a well-spoken ceremony." The man drew his gloved hands together, clasping them together in a single mockery of applause. "It's almost a shame that all of it is for naught."

"Naught?" Glenna questioned, the first to speak. "Your boorish arrival will not stop this event." She fought the instinct to shrink back as a killer's focus directed his attention her way. Interest flickered across the brutal features of the intruder, but thankfully he dismissed her challenge.

"I have come to put an end to this façade. Jael will not bind herself to this knight," he spoke with the air of someone who is always obeyed, and quickly.

"And what gives you the right to speak?" Leland said, rising from his kneeling position to stand tall. Knowing him as well as she did, Glenna knew his hand would be itching to grip the hilt of his sword. Anxious herself, she began to twirl her right hand slightly, summoning a white outlined flame to her palm.

The man looked upon Leland with a measure of distaste curling his aristocratic lips. "I have the only right. The princess will tell you that herself."

Everyone collectively turned to Jael, questioning in silence. Now that Glenna's focus had returned to her, she could see that the princess was still kneeling. She rose to her feet slowly, as feeble as an old woman though she waved away Leland's offered hand. Her chin tilted up in a defiant pose.

"Lord Averill. We did not expect you here tonight, if at all until the next succession," she said.

"Not only did you not expect me, but you failed to invite me, Princess. Some would consider that a gross breach of etiquette," the man named Averill retorted, his unusual eyes focusing exclusively on petite Jael. The way he looked at her made Glenna's skin crawl, and she sensed Leland tensing. Guessing no one would notice, she began to hum softly under her breath to empower the flames she conjured in both hands. *Hurt either of them and I'll incinerate you to ash, she thought.*

"We had not thought such lowly proceedings as a betrothal ceremony would concern someone as...influential as you, my Lord," Jael spoke demurely, almost how a maid would speak to a king. "You are of course welcome to observe and bless the proceedings of this evening's ceremony."

"And if we are discussing etiquette, barging in here and stealing attention from the couple being celebrated is hardly well-mannered."

Niles jibed, cocking his head to stare curiously at the newcomer. Averill observed him in return, as if fascinated by a talking dog.

"If by 'influential' you meant 'blooded sovereign of the land ordained by Fate,' Jael, we understand each other. I know you know why I'm here, so why don't you explain to your guests why your false betrothal ceremony has been cut short?" Averill seemed to only have eyes for Jael, and he widened his haughty lips into the grin of a ravenous jackal. To Glenna's disgust, she noticed that the nobility of his bearing was marred by the sharply pointed teeth in his smile.

"You are not welcome here no matter what your reason for bursting through the doors," Leland spoke at last. He was no coward, but the power Averill exuded took strength to overcome.

"Leland," Jael spoke to him with a tone of sharp desperation in her voice. "He has a right to be here. And..." She paused, clutching the skirts of her dress so tightly in her fist the gossamer fabric suffered the danger of tearing. Around her ankles, her fox familiar growled, hackles raised at the intruder to the hall. Jael was unmistakably terrified, frozen in place and hypnotized by Averill's blue-white eyes.

"Tell him," he said. "It's time you told all of them who really rules the land."

So commanded, Jael spoke. "When each ruler is crowned, young or old, presiding prince or princess becoming reigning king or queen, Fate use the Lords to link them to the land so wild magic won't wreak havoc on the people. Lord Averill visits each royal heir old enough to learn of the burden placed upon them and each new ruler the night before their coronation and...blesses them with the blood of the land so Fate will not curse their rule. That is why he has the right to come and go as he pleases." She looked down at her hands, twisting them somehow further into her skirts; Leland noticed her trembling and touched her arm, concerned, as beside her the fox whined piteously.

"What do you mean 'bless them with the blood?'" Niles asked. Glenna felt a light touch on her arm, and the flames spinning in her hands flared, then quieted to embers.

He's lending me power, but hiding the flames, she realized. *So Averill doesn't notice.*

"It is an honor to be blessed with blood linked from the source of magic in the land. My Lord himself exchanges the blood, giving and receiving in turn by a...bite to the neck," Jael explained, her mouth curling in revulsion. Leland abandoned all of his weak pretenses at being civil, drawing his sword and standing in front of her.

"He...he bit you?" Glenna asked, trying to be secretive about moving protectively in front of Jael beside Leland. She hadn't known Jael as a child, really, since they hadn't run in the same circles, but she'd been there for the coronation. Belatedly, she remembered the princess's wan, shaky appearance the morning of the coronation. She'd assumed it was only nerves, or simply exhaustion, but now the weakness made sense.

The princess nodded. "My blood went to the source so the earth would recognize my sovereignty... and I received the blood in return."

"Enough of these overdue lessons. I am not interested in further educating fools who have forgotten the past that led them to the present," Averill interjected, staring between everyone directly at Jael. "Tell them the rest."

"I..." Jael began, but she choked, frightened tears coursing down her face. She brushed them away angrily, and Leland took an aggressive step forward towards Averill. Niles and a silent Abelard seized him, holding him back with their hands on his shoulders to keep him from making a rash decision.

"My parents told me it would be a simple thing, done and over in the span of a few minutes," Jael started again. "However...Lord Averill took a special interest in me. He said he would return when it was time for me to wed. He...he said it was time blood ruled the land in truth once more."

Several of the guests, sensing the danger this being had brought into Jael's palace, had been making their way towards the exits as surreptitiously as possible. Glenna had willed all of them to get away, both for their own sakes and so that there would be no audience to this ruined ceremony.

So far Averill hadn't noticed, or if he'd observed the emptying hall he hadn't cared. But after he spoke, he lifted his arm and slowly closed his fingers into a fist. Three of the small group of guests let out terrible screams, shrieks that were cut off as they froze into solid ice before shattering into thousands of pieces. Mere seconds had passed, the deaths had been so instantaneous.

Glenna choked back her revulsion as lumps of ice skittered across the marble floor.

"That's right," Averill spoke in a silken voice, as if he hadn't just murdered three people with one nonchalant gesture. "I've come to collect on that promise."

5

Music filled the small practice room Gwendoline had reserved for her own use, beautiful notes that danced in a playful melody from the violin she played with practiced skill.

Well, ordinarily she played proficiently. This afternoon she'd missed more notes and key changes than she had in years. Part of that might have been due to the fact that the music she usually played had come from her casting book, and she had refused to open it for two days now.

Determined to continue, to make this new piece she'd composed over the past few months work, she channeled magic into the music her violin made by humming a harmony to the melody as she played. The practice room was plainly decorated aside from the soundproofing on the walls, but under her influence ornate vines of silver coated greenery twined down over the walls and floor. Springtime flowers bloomed at each rise of the music she played, filling the room with the delicious scent of honeysuckle. Gwendoline smiled, caught up in the moment as she transformed the drab room into a small portal into paradise as her music conjured her vision into reality.

Until she flubbed yet another string of notes, slipping so badly she couldn't stumble her way back to the main melody. Giant thorns sprouted on the vines, spearing each flower with a killing blow before the whole vision faded into nothing.

"*Shit!*" Gwendoline shouted at no one as she lowered her violin. She was tempted to hurl the infernal thing against the wall, but breaking her primary instrument wouldn't solve her problems.

Besides, she had somewhere to be. Practicing her musical hobby could wait for another time.

Still irritated, Gwendoline spared a glance into her book bag as she lifted it to her shoulder so she could glare at her casting book. Just because she didn't dare open it didn't mean she would leave it at her house, even if at times the temptation to write to Niles again made her itch with impatience. At least she'd refrained from telling Everleigh and Colt what had taken place: she'd only told them the book hadn't sent any more messages in spite of her scrying.

What's wrong with me? She wondered. Resolved to think about something else, as if she could will her troubles away with pure determination, she tugged her phone free from the back pocket of her jeans and opened up her messages. She'd set up a date with a random guy from her preferred relationship seeking app, and she'd rather show up early to that than stay here messing up the music she normally played to relax.

Gwendoline forced all other thoughts out of her head as she left the practice room and made her way out towards her car. It was easy to allow her usual semi-hopeful anticipation of a date to occupy her as she freshened her makeup, curled her hair with a quick spell, and changed from her casual shirt to a more revealing black top. She didn't intend to take anything too far on this date until she made sure the guy wasn't a creep, but predicting the outcomes of matches on this app wasn't easy.

Once she was satisfied with her looks, she drove to the chain restaurant whose most important feature was a well stocked bar and went inside. A server who seemed engrossed with staring at with what the black top put on display led her to the end of the bar. She asked for a Singapore Sling without a second thought as she took her seat. The music in the restaurant was loud and classless, but easy enough to ignore after a sip or two of her drink.

Then the waiting game began. Gwendoline checked her phone several times as she finished her first drink, hoping for a message explaining her date's tardiness. By the time she'd finished her second drink, she was unhappily flipping through the photos of guys on the dating app, searching for a last ditch effort at not going home alone tonight.

After her fifth drink, when the bartender and wait staff kept giving her sympathetic looks, she decided that she was done with men for good. Well, done with boys at least. The sort of man she wished she could catch would never dream of making plans with someone just to stand them up later without a single explanation.

Gwendoline knew she was too intoxicated to drive home, but drunk enough to risk an illegal spell that would drive her car home for her while she lounged carelessly in the driver's seat. As she let the magic guide her home, she finally quit resisting and pulled her heavy casting book into her lap. She wasn't quite bold enough to open it yet, though she was hoping she would be by the time she got home. Her fingertips tapped the beat of one of her songs on the cover as she tried to force her inebriated mind into reasonable activity. The expectant energy thrumming through her body felt all-consuming.

All things considered, she felt as nervous and excited as if she was bringing her date home with her after all.

As soon as her car pulled into the driveway, she rushed inside with her casting book clutched tight against her chest. After kicking her shoes off, she grabbed a pen and settled herself on the edge of her sofa, flipping open the pages before she could reason herself out of her recklessness.

She saw a new message when she opened the page, right under all the other lines of text she and Niles had wrote two nights ago. They hadn't disappeared, after all. She read through them again with fresh eyes without realizing that she was smiling by the end.

You play beautifully. I've never heard music like yours. Don't worry, I haven't been spying on you at all. But your music was almost impossible to ignore.

She had to admit she was drawn to him, enticed in a way she couldn't explain. She wanted to be wary of manipulation, or of strange magic befuddling her, but the only difference she could feel in herself was curiosity and the odd and comforting sense of familiarity when she looked at what was apparently Niles's true face.

I just got stood up on a date, and for some reason you were the first person I wanted to tell about it. Can you explain that?

She hadn't meant to tell him about her sorrow of the night. Wasn't it humiliating, after all, to be stood up?

I could explain it better if you freed me, I think.

She should have expected an answer like that. Gwendoline twirled the pen in her hand, allowing it to drop when her gin-dulled reflexes failed to catch it. That reckless feeling was growing stronger, teaming up with her lack of inhibitions to help her actually consider Niles's request. Needing only one more push, she flipped the pages over to study the portrait he'd painted for her. He looked...she couldn't describe it. She had to meet him.

No buts. Just do it. She told herself firmly, and without giving herself further time to think, without writing anything else, she brought the book to her face and touched her lips to the lips in the picture.

It wasn't that she instantly felt a spark or anything dazzling at all. She felt nothing except the cool paper against her skin...and then there was something, warm skin and lips on hers, and then he materialized out of the book to kiss her back.

Objectively, she had believed him. Experiencing the reality stunned her so thoroughly her mind struggled to catch up.

The antique book thumped to the floor beside the couch where she was sitting, and a man stood before her, stooping to continue their kiss. Niles—that was his name, she had named him long ago, and it simply fit—held her face in his hands, his fingers tangled in her hair, kissing her so soundly that they might have been lifelong lovers. But the thing that frightened her, against all odds, was the fact that she was kissing him back, tasting him and exploring him as if she'd never done this with anyone before. Other boys had come and gone, each one as unremarkable as the last...but she'd never been kissed like this.

It took all her effort, but she lifted her hands and placed them on his unyielding chest to push him away. He lingered for another moment, the tip of his tongue tracing her bottom lip before withdrawing.

Gwendoline finally opened her eyes, looking into the face of the man she had summoned from the book. That nagging sense of familiarity struck her again, but not because she had just seen the exact same face in the sketch Niles had painted for her. She felt like she knew him, had always known him, like they were connected on a level she couldn't understand.

"How drunk *are* you, Gwendoline?" Niles asked, lifting his hand to touch his fingertips to his lips thoughtfully. "I'm not complaining, but the alcohol taste was quite strong." He was teasing her, almost like it was a defense mechanism, but after that kiss she couldn't summon a single coherent thing to say.

"You really do look just like her," Niles said, filling her silence as he brushed a few tendrils of hair back from her face before stepping back. "I mean, in a sense I could see you, but to actually see you now...it really is you." He seemed amazed and out of breath, as if he'd been running hard for miles.

Gwendoline wasn't in such great shape herself: her face felt like it was on fire, her heart beat against her ribs threatening to burst, and her hands didn't seem to remember how to stay still. She didn't know how to feel, and her emotions knew it; crowding together, they seemed intent on mashing every button of her mental control panel all at once.

"And...it's you," she said at last, once she caught her breath.

"How...How does it feel to be in the outside world again?"

Niles looked around the room before answering. "Not as strange as you might think. That book is old, older than anyone realizes, but I wasn't aware of too much since I was sent into it until recently. I'm not an omniscient ancient creature."

"Judging by your flirting, I'd say it's been a while since you were in the game," Gwendoline jibed, her wits kicking in at last. Niles cracked a smile at her, causing her heart to pick up its figurative sprinting shoes once again.

Damn, he's sort of beautiful, Gwendoline thought, *like a suave European pilot on a mission to save the world.* They smiled at each other, tentative and unsure how to continue. Niles hesitated before sinking into the seat beside her with surprising grace for someone who had been confined to the form of an inanimate book for so long.

"I expect you have a lot of questions...like how I got into the book, why I keep talking about recognizing you, and why I'm here now," he said. "I promise you'll understand it all once I give your memories back."

And there it is, Gwendoline thought, a thread of fear and sinking disappointment snaking through her body again as she drew back from him. *What did you expect, a free boyfriend provided by your casting book? Like there wouldn't be buckets of crazy attached?*

"My memories? I remember everything anyone else would at my age."

"Yes, you as Gwendoline do," he conceded in a gracious tone; she couldn't help but notice his eyes dwelled on her face, almost like he'd been starving for a glimpse. "But since you are an incomplete soul, you need Glenna's memories as well to be completely whole."

"Incomplete?" She asked. His words rang in her ears, absurd.

"Yes. Look, no matter how I say this, you're going to want to run once I tell you why I'm here. Furthermore, that spell has weakened me...it will take some time to return to how I was before." This had to be true: Gwendoline noted his pallor, and how he winced when he shifted his weight in her chair, and even the trembling of his hands due to apparent exhaustion. In this moment she pitied him, and despite the strangeness of her entire evening she reached out to take his hand in hers.

"Gwendoline, you are a reincarnation of a powerful sorceress from long ago who split her soul as a sacrifice for the people she loved most. She's the one who convinced me to bind myself to the book and wait for her to return," Niles's enlightening words washed over her; she felt frozen in place, a doe in headlights. "She salvaged her memories and the parts of herself that were relevant, and I need to give them to you."

It was too much, far too much; she couldn't ask enough questions if the day was twice as long. Looking at the man before her, a cold sweat broke out over her skin, and bile rose in her throat. His expression of concern didn't help matters, and with a head rush she knew she was going to be sick.

"Bullshit," she croaked, before she smacked her hands over her mouth and rushed for the bathroom.

Like a sleepwalker, Gwendoline poured a heap of granola into her bowl and splashed way too much milk over it. She had a full day of classes ahead of her, and the dreams she'd had the night before had been wild beyond even her usual norms.

That'll teach me to drink a gallon of gin before trying to sleep, she thought, irrationally angry with the headache that hammered at her temples. On autopilot, she lifted her hand palm up to summon her channeling book to her, and it flew effortlessly to her from where it had been in the living room. *Time to cure this hangover before it screws me over for the rest of the day...*

When she opened her book, Gwendoline knew instantly that something was off. For the most part, it behaved the same as it had the day before. If she had asked it to, it would have summoned her a remedy for headaches faster than she could blink. However, she could sense that the essence that had made her book her book had disappeared. And then...

It wasn't a dream.

It all came screaming back to her, from the uncomfortable hours at that bar, to the kiss, to the eventual embarrassment of throwing up and barricading herself in her room to avoid the stranger she had set free from her spell book. After a few futile attempts, he had stopped knocking and pleading with her to talk to him and fallen silent.

I wonder where he went? I didn't exactly ask him to leave, but...

Curious regarding her visitor, Gwendoline padded out to the living room in her flat slippers, wincing as she almost knocked over her pot of bleeding heart flowers. She managed to right the vase, but only because another pair of hands grabbed the side of the pot and steadied it. She stared at the hands, miserably wishing that she was hallucinating.

"You're still here," she said, staring resolutely at the blushing petals of the flowers in the pot.

"Good morning to you too, Gwendoline," Niles said; unsurprisingly, he sounded as grumpy as she felt. "I understood you needed some time alone to digest the strangeness of someone falling out of your casting book, but I think you forgot that the man in question didn't have anywhere else to go." Abashed, Gwendoline sensed her cheeks blush as pink as the flowers.

"I suppose that's true," she said after a moment, looking up at him. "But you had my couch, didn't you? I always leave blankets out here."

"Yes, all things considered I was very comfortable on my own, left to re-learn what it means to have a real body again," Niles snapped sarcastically. His disheveled dark hair stuck up in various directions, and his face was puffy from sleep, but his dusky eyes were alert as they watched her for a reaction. Gwendoline's guilt increased.

"Well, like you said it's a lot to deal with, so I'll let you stay here for a bit until you—"

Until what? she thought. *Until he gets a job and saves enough money to move out and become a functioning adult?* She didn't expect someone who had been cursed to live in a book for who knows how many years would understand how to operate on their own in modern society. Besides, it's not like she worked for a living either: she'd inherited enough money to keep her comfortable until she graduated and could get a proper job.

For the first time, she noticed what clothes he was wearing. Instead of fussy old robes or 18th century menswear as she'd half expected, Niles wore simple dark jeans and a white t-shirt, clothing so nondescript and yet so simply attractive on his lean body that Gwendoline had to stare. Had he been wearing the same thing last night? She couldn't remember. All she could recall about him were his insistent pleas for her to "reclaim her memories."

More importantly, she recalled that overwhelming kiss. The memory of it made pinpricks sizzle over her skin.

"Have you been wearing that this whole time?" She queried, looking him up and down. Niles's lips quirked into a half cocked grin; he crossed his muscular arms over his chest.

"I knew you'd notice," he said. "I transmuted the new clothes from my old ones. This is the first time I've worn modern clothes, but I didn't think the garb of yesteryear would suit me if I wanted to accompany you to class today."

"Class?" Gwendoline questioned, the nausea from the night before swimming through her again. She pictured the tall stranger following her around, claiming to be her visitor, distracting her as she tried to work, and (oh shit) meeting her friends. She'd have to explain him to Colt and Everleigh, or lie and risk them catching her in her deceit...and what a conversation that would turn out to be.

"Yes," Niles confirmed. "I can't persuade you to listen to me unless you trust me. We don't have all the time in the world for you to gain confidence in me, but this would be a start. You need to remember, and I...I need to be human again." An ancient, timeless look came into his eyes, which glowed amber around the edge of the irises, just for a second or two. It was mesmerizing, in a sense, the way he stared off into the distance as if lost in profound thought.

"It's Saturday," Gwendoline interrupted his musings, sputtering the lie. "I don't have classes today, so you can just—"

"Just what? I'm a man without a history in this age," Niles returned to the present to smirk at her. "Besides, it's *not* Saturday, it's the last Wednesday in September, and you have a full class load today if I'm remembering correctly."

Gwendoline gaped at him. "How would you know that? You were a book less than twelve hours ago." As always when she was in a sassy mood, her hands crept to her hips and rested on them defiantly. He laughed at her, striding past her into the kitchen.

"I was never just a book, even if I was asleep for centuries, or even if you didn't know about me," he said, pausing in front of the fridge and staring at it curiously. "Besides, even if I was only a book, you relied on me far too much. I don't know if it's natural to record so many plans and daily to-do lists in a spell book, but at least it helped me learn your schedule and habits." Confident as he sounded about her schedule, the big black box standing in her kitchen seemed to befuddle him, and he tugged on the handle tentatively. When it opened with a whoosh of cold air to reveal her meager food supply, he laughed with delighted astonishment.

Gwendoline loitered in the doorway to her small, bright kitchen, her heart softening. She still couldn't shake the feeling that she knew him, this man who kept pulling her condiments out of the fridge to sniff and taste them, like he was an old friend she had once trusted and relied on. Magic often manifested strange things in even stranger ways, and it was better to be wary than dead...but hadn't she trusted her mysterious book enough to freaking kiss the pages when it—he—had asked? If he wanted to spend the day with her...what was the harm?

So he kept talking about "reclaiming her other half" and "destiny" and all of that...maybe she could listen, and it didn't mean she had to do a single thing about it.

"Don't eat that," she surrendered with a sigh, going to him and forcibly prying a bottle of sriracha from his hand. "Let's get you a proper breakfast."

Curse those pancakes, Gwendoline thought later in the afternoon in the middle of her defensive theory class. Her day hadn't quite been a disaster, but traipsing around Starford University with Niles had been both more of a chore and more of a laugh than she'd expected. Her schedule had been packed for a Wednesday, and Niles hadn't helped do anything but distract her throughout the day.

During breakfast, she had made him promise not to discuss their conversation from the night before until after classes; she'd guessed he was the type who couldn't leave the topic alone indefinitely, and as a pushy person herself, she wouldn't demand perfection in that area. Gwendoline, red-faced and embarrassed, had stammered her way through a request that the kiss be kept secret as well. Niles, though he'd given her a slow, impudent smile, had acquiesced and kept his mouth shut. She had no idea if he'd blab if they eventually did see Colt and Everleigh.

During her first class—the history of magic through literature—Niles had sat beside her stoically, rigid as a general in his plastic seat as the lack of magical reference in Jane Austen's works and timeline had been discussed. Gwendoline had been quite proud of him, smiling as she took notes in her familiar channeling book.

When the bell was almost about to ring class's end, Niles had leaned over to her and whispered conversationally: "You know, my departure from the book sort of damaged its memory, and much of your non-casting content may have been erased. The book won't really work for anything but spell related notes now unless you cast specific separate spells on it."

"You wait until now to tell me this? I have a test next week!" She'd shrieked at him, bashing his arm with her leather and canvas book bag.

Two classes later, Niles wasted a lot of time by asking several obscure channeling questions that the teacher couldn't answer and sparking some animated debate. Gwendoline had glared daggers at him for a half-hour before she gave up and let the remaining twenty minutes of class pass in a mortified slump. The class after that, her favorite set of lessons involving her academic focus on elemental magic, Niles melted every single painstaking, elaborate ice sculpture she managed to design, carve, and realistically color without any movement or any obvious casting. She'd become so frustrated with him that she snapped and tried to cast the crotch quill spell her date from the previous day had suffered from, but either it hadn't worked properly, or he'd cured it without any effort. She was more willing to bet on the latter, since previous instructors had told her that her magic style was rare and potent, and she knew next to nothing about Niles and the strength of power he might possess.

But Gwendoline had to admit she hadn't enjoyed a day quite so much in a long time. Even while disrupting her classes and distracting her, Niles had managed to delight and amuse her several times. He'd whispered creative answers to her during a written test, amplifying his voice from where he waited outside the room and altering it so no one else could hear. This of course was strictly against the rules; she didn't know how he bypassed the anti-cheating wards.

He also empowered her magic just by looking at her with his amber eyes during a practical assessment. Her most relaxing class, a free cast session meant to help students learn from each other and expel stress from the day, had been filled with inventive channeling and him teaching her magical tidbits that astounded even someone with her considerable expertise.

Once, only once, when their hands had brushed together while they were frivolously enchanting a fountain to spew fire, the fountain of harmless amethyst flames had transformed into a cascade of glowing butterflies that looked suspiciously like tiny fairies. Gwendoline had laughed, awed by their temporary creation of life, and when their eyes met again she was stunned again by that baffling sense of recognition.

Finally, classes had drawn to an end and Gwendoline had driven her and Niles to a local park where they could talk with reasonable privacy. Besides, if anyone she knew saw her, they might assume she was on another disastrous date and keep their distance. Everyone but Everleigh, and by extension, Colt. It would so much easier if she could keep this strange secret and the even stranger man she'd conjured from her book to herself, but she knew her friends.

She'd grabbed dinner for them both from a little deli near the school; he'd been so enchanted with the whole store that he'd lingered there for fifteen minutes, scanning the shelves and chatting up the employees. When she'd finally tugged him out the door, Gwendoline took Niles to that park and into a gazebo to pelt him with questions between bites. He barely had time to tear into his sandwich before she began.

"You don't use a familiar. Why?"

Niles shrugged. "Some people gain power over time and don't necessarily need a familiar to channel. Glenna didn't need one either, though she liked to have her book around her to make keeping track of her spells easier."

"Really?" Gwendoline had never heard of such a thing. Niles tried to speak around a mouthful of food, but, seeming to think better of his lack of manners, waited until he swallowed to explain further.

"It was more common in my day to channel magic through personal will alone. More and more people learning and using other means to harness their own magic means a larger variety of magically talented people," he divulged. "Aside from that, Glenna was gifted and powerful. As you are and will continue to be as you age." Gwendoline felt uneasy whenever he spoke of this Glenna, and the sense of remembrance soured instead of comforted.

"She must have been talented, since she trapped you inside of a book for centuries," she said sarcastically, putting no stock into her own words. "And, what was the other thing you kept shouting last night, she split her *soul*? I've never heard of such a thing, and even if I had I wouldn't think I would be the one to inherit such a legacy."

"She didn't trap me, as I've told you. Also, it makes sense that you would doubt her power and determination in the face of catastrophe. Glenna was always doubting herself," he replied, studying her as he took another bite. An irrational surge of anger sparked through her, but she focused her ire on the extra bread of her own sandwich. To her chagrin, she accidentally froze half of the bread solid with a touch; disgusted, she set her sandwich aside and munched on her side of chips instead.

"I resent you treating me like I'm not my own person. You may not know me well yet, but even if what you say is true, which I highly doubt, I'll always be Gwendoline," she snapped.

"Of course. I meant no offense." Leaning over his food with a tiny bit of mayonnaise clinging to his chin, he still looked noble as he nodded her way. "Anyway, we need to get on with making things right and returning your soul fragments. I hadn't realized how many lesser magical people lived openly in this time. Averill will eat them alive."

Gwendoline half expected a shiver to rattle her bones at the name, but she felt nothing but a vague sense of unease. "Who?"

"Let me see your book," Niles ordered suddenly, setting his food aside and wiping his face off with a flimsy napkin. Tempted to say no, she placed a hand on the tome protectively—thanks to habit, she'd set it on the table beside her—and curled her fingertips over the spine. Instead of making a grab for it like she'd anticipated, he folded his hands in front of him and gazed at her steadily. She felt like they were in a battle of wills she wasn't sure she needed to win.

"Gwendoline. There's some part of you that believes what I'm telling you, and there's a reason you've been looking at me askance, wondering who I remind you of," he said, leaning forward earnestly. "I saw last night that it wasn't practical to push you into knowledge you weren't ready for. But I need to try to normalize this for you, to prepare you for what's coming."

"What's coming?" she asked, her grip still tight on her book. Niles opened his mouth to speak again, then hesitated.

"Let's get the first part of the story straight before I tell the second," he finally said. "Will you please let me see the book?"

"I..."

You're being stupid. He literally materialized from the pages last night, and suddenly you're worried about him looking through the book again? Gwendoline thought, conflicted. It was about more than that, she knew, more about her final decision on trusting him and believing his story. Would she do it, or wouldn't she?

"Gwendoline!" She didn't have to decide. Everleigh's ear-splitting

greeting from all the way across the park shattered the moment. Peering around Niles, she saw Everleigh waving; Colt walked tall beside her, carrying Everleigh's school bag with an amused expression.

This was the last thing Gwendoline needed. She had her reasons for not telling her friends one of the craziest things to ever happen to her, and those became more and more apparent the closer her friends came to their table. By the time Everleigh took in Niles's appearance, her fiendish grin spoke volumes.

Here we go, Gwendoline groaned internally.

6

Before

The shards of ice that had once been courtiers and friends had begun to melt on the ground, pink tinged and bizarre. The message was clear: no one was to leave the great hall, and all were to bear witness to this scene.

Glenna's shock numbed her against reacting to the violence in her own home. In her hands, the deadly fire magic that had swirled there sputtered into nothing, and she struggled for half a second to reclaim her power and leash her wrath. Nearby, Abelard had drawn his sword. Jael couldn't conceal the horror she felt at this bald-faced murder, and Leland only had eyes for her. Niles alone masked his reaction with stillness.

Averill captivated the attention of the whole room, rulers and hostage audience both. But his focus rested entirely on Jael, who returned his predatory gaze with the hypnotized concentration of prey.

"You remember, princess? You remember my promise?" Averill spoke to her, hunger in every line of his angular face; he was not a hideous man, though his size and brutish figure belied the nobility of his features. His milk white hair complimented his severe countenance with the picturesque quality of a brutish masterpiece.

Jael nodded, pausing to steady her voice before she replied. "I recall. You said one of the founders of magic should rule the land, and should stamp out all interference from ungifted people. You said you'd come back for me to take what was yours."

Averill's grin widened, making Glenna shudder at his resemblance to a wolf. "Here I am. Are you prepared to accept?"

Leland, who had been straining against Niles's grip on his arm, burst forward protectively, his sword out and the tip poised against the intruding Lord's throat in an instant. Abelard took his place in front of Jael, ready to kill any and all threats to his princess. Any other man would have cowered or flinched, but Averill merely blinked at the best knight in the realm as if studying a moth.

"You have offended us long enough with your presence, sir," Leland growled, his deep voice resolute. "From what I understand, you as the Lord of the land are necessary to maintain the balance of magic. We've all heard tales...but no matter. I don't care who you are, frankly, so I advise you to take care."

"Take care?" Averill questioned, one immaculate eyebrow arching incredulously. "You would do well to take your own advice, boy."

Glenna saw the attack coming before it happened, but she couldn't do anything about it: Averill ignored the sword all but pricking his throat and held his hand up at Leland's shoulder level. Leland grit his teeth together as an invisible hand forced him to bend, then kneel onto the ground before Averill. A cruel smile flickered across the Lord's face as he continued to force him down until, in spite of Leland's efforts to fight the force grinding him into the floor, he lay belly down on the ground.

"Know your place, knight," Averill said, stepping over Leland to approach Jael. Niles advanced in front of her and Abelard, nondescript with his lack of obvious magic, but dangerous nonetheless. Nodding to Glenna, he indicated that she should go to Leland to make sure he was all right. Needing no further prompting, she extinguished the battle flames in her palms and rushed to the prostrate body trapped on the ground.

"Are you—" Glenna began, but Leland ignored her, using his strength to force his head up to glare at Averill.

"Don't you touch her!"

"He won't," Niles assured Leland as he stared down the man hunting Jael. "You may not have the manners to avoid a celebration you were not invited to, Lord Averill, but that what you're seeking must be given by consent of the princess."

How would he know that? Is he bluffing? Glenna wondered, helplessly looking between each member of their group. Her eyes met Niles's, and she saw from the hidden panic in his eyes that he was indeed bluffing, taking a gamble that Averill did need or at least want Jael's permission to take power. The rest of the world, all the petrified, silent courtiers and onlookers, even strong Abelard, had faded to irrelevance.

"Step aside. This is none of your affair," Averill insisted, sizing up Niles in a way he had not with Leland.

"No," Jael spoke, her comment as sudden as her voice was quiet. A whisper would have deafened her, but still, she had captured the focus of everyone present.

"No?" Averill questioned.

"No," Jael insisted, louder. "No. I am not prepared to accept you as my prince or future king. I don't believe a union with you would benefit Oloetha or myself. I don't believe this is what Fate has in store for me, or for my people. We have been ruled by tyrants before, my Lord, tyrants with appetites less unwholesome than yours. To speak plainly...the land will have to weep blood from every root and every grain of soil before I *ever* join myself or my people to you!"

By the end of her speech her tone had gained strength, though her fear was perceptible. Abelard had to steady her, taking her arm in his. Leland, sensing her need, slowly rose to his knees. His breath came in harsh pants, he could barely lift his head, but he fought the hex placed on him with all his strength.

"Lady," Averill answered, a dark smile revealing the points of his ivory teeth. "*I* am the land. *I* am the blood."

Glenna, pausing her task of empowering Leland to rise to his feet, felt dread needle her pores as magic darker and older than any she had ever experienced before filled the main hall. No stranger to darkness and the forbidden, Glenna did not fear ghosts and shadows...but this. This was blood magic, land magic, wielded by a Lord who lived as a god in the land. Frost slicked the floors and walls of the vast room, and a personal chill burrowed into her heart and settled within it. Dark thoughts, sibilant whispers she only murmured to herself in the night at the blackest hour before dawn, crowded her consciousness and demanded to be heard.

Who is she to deserve Leland, the man you loved long before she ever thought of him? How could he ignore you, Glenna, how could he prefer her selfish spirit, her tiny body, to your dark radiance? Your supple flesh, your strength compared to her utter weakness?

He was meant to be yours...Jael is just in the way...

Woozy, Glenna swayed where she stood and blinked rapidly. When she could focus again, when she was able to tamp down the terrible thoughts that had escaped the prison she kept them in, she saw the brightness of the hall and the absence of the frost and darkness that had transformed her breath into vapor.

Averill had departed, but not for good, and not without a warning. Jael lay in a swoon upon the ground, her skirts giving her the appearance of a golden cloud. Her neck, smeared and stained with blood, was marred with two precise, deep puncture marks. Glenna rushed to her side, shame filling her breast at the thought of what she had been contemplating. Niles steadied her as she stumbled over the steps, pulling her against his chest so she didn't collapse of dizziness, and Leland reached the princess first.

"Jael?" He shook her gently, his voice breaking with concern. To everyone's relief, she stirred with a moan as her eyes fluttered open.

Then she screamed, a terrified shriek of horror as she clawed at her neck. Glenna intervened, seizing Jael's scrabbling fingers before she could do further harm to herself.

"I can't! I won't! Not for anything!" Jael moaned between cries of pure fright. She turned, burying her head in Leland's chest as she sobbed, shuddering with revulsion.

"He'll be back," she whispered at last, "and next time he won't leave."

Glenna winced as she limped down the hall leading to her quarters. The stupid shoes Jael had begged her to wear had finally worn a blister or two onto her feet, almost causing her to shuffle the rest of the way to her room. Unprepared for such a frantic day, her body ached from her head to her soles; healing the blisters was barely worth the effort.

Lord Averill, sadistic and manipulative as he was, had reappeared from misty legend to grab for power he could easily seize by force. They had just been through a war, a conflict against their own so Jael could take her rightful place on the throne, and now an even greater enemy arose to challenge them. The future—formerly so hopeful with the two young, brave leaders—had been fouled by a threat both powerful and dangerous.

Along with the hazards on the horizon, another fact tormented Glenna. The pain in her heart had finally blossomed into such sorrow that it was all she could do to hold the tears back from her tired eyes.

In defiance of Averill's threats, Leland and a calm, single-minded Jael had gone through with the betrothal ceremony in the privacy of their own rooms under Niles's guidance. Glenna had dutifully stood watch, and fled as soon as the time was appropriate. She had walked, then run, then slowed down to a walk again as far as she could from the scene of her heartbreak. It had burned before when the possibility of their betrothal and eventual marriage was only a storm cloud looming ever closer. Now that they were joined to their souls, the embers of her past pain cowered in the face of the agony scorching her heart now.

Just think, Glenna thought bitterly as she lingered outside her own bedroom door, pressing her forehead against the cool, sturdy wood. *When they do marry in a year's time, the wedding might kill you off at last. If*

Averill doesn't destroy us all first, that is.

Guilt over thinking only of herself, shame over worrying about anything but the upcoming feud with Lord Averill filled her with such a sense of inadequacy and defeat that she could hardly push open her door without expending maximum effort.

"Glenna?" Niles's voice barely made her look up and to her right, where he strode down the hall towards her. Belatedly, she recalled that she had asked him to come to her after the subdued ceremony to discuss defenses for the princess and Leland. The betrothed couple.

"Good, you're here," she managed to say, exhaustion infusing her voice. "We have much to discuss."

"I should think so," Niles said, caution written in the tight lines around his eyes. Glenna beckoned him inside, ignoring the impropriety of inviting him into her boudoir. If the other inhabitants of the castle were smart, they'd be safely tucked into their beds by now. Whatever celebration had been planned after the original ceremony, Averill's arrival had cancelled that as well. Jael would have been livid at that, had she been in her usual perfectionist state of mind.

Once the two of them were inside, Glenna closed and locked the door behind them. Just to be safe, she enclosed the doorknob in her gloved hand and channeled a spell into it, effectively sealing the door with magic. Sensing her intention, Niles walked about the perimeter of her spacious room, laying a hand on each wall to arrange the wards that would prevent anyone overhearing their conversation. Once finished, the two of them seated themselves at the breakfast table near her windows; the open curtains allowed enough light in from the moon that neither one of them felt the need to light a candle. The air in the room felt close, muggy in a way that had the tiniest trickle of sweat inching its way down her neck.

"Well?" Niles invited her to begin.

"Out of everyone who was shocked when Lord Averill showed up today, you seemed the least surprised. Why?" Glenna asked bluntly, crossing her arms over the thin fabric of her lilac dress.

"I read a great deal of books," Niles tried to quip, then thought better of it. "That's not entirely untrue...let's just say that unlike Leland and Abelard, I took interest in my history lessons. We have plenty of books in the library, and while most of them were vague, I knew about the old gods who are tied to the land. I never expected to actually meet one, however."

"Did your books say anything about a Lord demanding to marry into the royal family to rule the people as well as the land magic?" Glenna asked, more interested in tactics than a lesson on times past. "Did they mention any loopholes, any weaknesses we could exploit?"

"Not to the best of my recollection. Many of the authors seemed to be more focused on the 'right of the land to demand blood' and all of that. I'd have to look again to be sure—"

"Then do it. We need to get ahead of him before a catastrophe happens," she snapped, her fraught nerves getting the better of her. Regretting her sharpness, she shook her head to clear it, placing her fingertips against her temples to cool her skin with a touch of magic.

Niles observed her, his hard, wary eyes softening from black to ocher. "You will do no one any good unless you rest, Glenna. There will be enough sleepless nights in the future, I'm sure."

"I'm afraid my wakeful midnights are starting early," Glenna laughed, the cynical sound ringing harsh: she hadn't slept well for weeks already, thanks to the royal betrothal. "I wish I could turn back time and start over."

Start over...if only she could. If only she could go back several years to prevent Leland from meeting Jael, somehow, or speak her feelings before he was drawn to the princess like a priest to an angel.

"Aside from the possible calamity about to descend on us all, would you say you're all right? I don't want to leave you like this..." Niles reached across the table to take her hand. Glenna allowed it, studying him as he turned over her hand and uncurled her fingers.

"Your gloves are singed," he remarked with a dry laugh, indicating the scorch marks that had nearly burned through the ivory silk.

"In the heat of the moment I didn't thinking about protecting my finery from my fire," Glenna replied.

"In the *heat* of the moment?" Niles chuckled again, appreciating her accidental play on words. A not reluctant smile lighted upon Glenna's lips, and she couldn't hold back a laugh of her own. For a few moments, all they could do was laugh at such a silly, inconsequential detail as singed gloves.

When the laughter faded, Glenna found her heart beating faster within her as she stared at Niles. He gazed steadily back at her, his hands still holding hers across the breakfast table. The moonlight shining on his face showed each handsome, familiar feature, and she allowed her mind to wonder what it would be like to be with him.

"Stay?" she murmured the request.

Niles didn't reply. He rose from his chair, only to approach her and turn her chair towards him as he knelt in front of her. His irises softened to black, rich and expressive, and she couldn't look away as he focused on her hands, removing her gloves with mesmerizing slowness. The charred fabric slipped easily off her slender fingers, and he cast them to the floor. Still looking up at her, he pressed his warm lips to the center of her palm, sending a thrill of heat over her skin. He kissed her other palm, then each wrist. An ivory rose petal fell on his face, brushing against his cheek and jaw before it fell to the floor. Glenna was amazed, until she remembered the roses she'd slipped into her hair what seemed like eons ago when they'd encountered each other in the garden. Deprived of water, the petals would naturally begin to fall.

Niles half-smiled, unable to shake the intensity of the moment even for a second. Still silent, he retrieved the petal from where it had fallen beside him and cupped it in his hands. Drawing it close to his face, he murmured a spell to the fragment of nature; instead of sailing out of his hands and back to the rich, scarlet carpet lining her floors, several more identical petals began to drift down from the ceiling like rain. Glenna looked up, an unexpected sense of delight filling her as the soft petals fell on her face and hair.

When her focus returned to Niles, she glimpsed, just for a second, the true force of his feelings for her. The wonder of the moment swept her away, chasing other thoughts completely out of her head.

When a petal fell from her ceiling onto Niles's hair and upturned face, she leaned down to take his face in her now bare hands and touch her lips to his. He kissed her back, showing her tenderness she had not experienced for a long time, if ever. Since she had initiated the kiss and therefore expected it this time, she was able to fully appreciate how Niles simply tasted like *Niles,* all bourbon and spice, a phenomenon that made their kiss as unique as it was lovely.

By some unspoken agreement, they both rose to their feet. Glenna stepped into him, encircling her arms about his neck to hold him as closely as he held her. They explored each other with kisses, somehow preserving the tenderness of the moment while surrendering to the urgency of desire. Niles dipped her supple body back in his arms, one hand tangled in her soft hair while his other rested on her back to balance her. She thought she'd fall, and her dizziness increased as he kissed a trail from her neck down to the dip of her dress where fabric covered her breasts. His mouth brushed against her collarbone and she shivered, though not from any chill.

"Niles…" She spoke without realizing, seeking to tell him something without knowing what it was. He hushed her, kissing his way back up to her lips, where their mouths met again with a craving that had somehow increased. This time when they held each other close, no space remained between them, and his hands swept all over her body, lingering near her hips as he held her to him. She felt his arousal press against her thigh, which jolted her into reality as she couldn't doubt what was about to happen any longer.

This is Niles. Oh, she could hurt him with this frenzied memory, and hurt him too deeply to recover from. Instead, she arched her body against his, kissing him more deeply and encouraging him to go further.

They stumbled to the bed, Niles shedding his jacket, cravat, and shirt between kisses. Before she could begin to stammer out a request to help her get out of her own clothes, Niles whirled her around and quite practically tore the innumerable buttons of her outer dress to get to the corset beneath. Glenna slipped out of the dress as he worked at the ties, and after discarding her other various undergarments, she was free and exposed. Goosebumps spread over her skin along with a flush of embarrassment that made her want to cover herself with her hands.

Niles pushed her down onto the bed—now covered with petals, even though his spell had run its course—and studied her, no discomfiture in his expression. Silent except for short, panting breaths that revealed the depth of his desire, he shed the rest of his clothing and joined her on her bed, trapping her wrists in each hand as he stretched his lean body over hers. They began to move in love's familiar rhythm, tentatively at first before at last he entered her and their energy built to a tumult.

Glenna had no idea how long they stayed joined, kissing and gasping for breath; she only knew that she took real pleasure in the true closeness of another human being, especially someone like Niles. When they reached the highest point, first her and then him, she was blinded by sensation.

Then they slept, tangled in her bed with the petals and sheets rumpled around them.

She woke only once that night, gripped by the misery of a broken heart in spite of Niles's presence. A few tears of guilt and longing escaped her in spite of her will to keep them at bay. Then, Glenna felt her fist clenched tight around something. When she uncurled her fingers, she saw a red cloth, still vibrant in spite of its wrinkled state.

*Leland...*she thought, choosing to hold the simple polishing cloth tighter as she eventually fell back into a sound sleep.

7

"So close..." Niles sighed. Frustration showed on his face as Colt and Everleigh approached, but he altered his expression to one of neutral friendliness in the blink of an eye. An odd sense of regret washed over her as Gwendoline wondered what he might have said if they didn't have company.

"There might be an election instead of a succession of rule this year. Did you hear the news?" Colt said once he and Everleigh were in a more normal hearing range. Tempted to blurt out her story, Gwendoline limited herself to shaking her head.

"You know how Starford has pretty much been in the power of one family for the longest time? The other family lines died out? That might not be true, and in a big way!" Everleigh cackled; Smaug, her snake familiar, was curled around her chestnut hair as a headband.

"How exciting," Niles interjected sardonically. Everleigh feigned a startle, as if she hadn't noticed his presence at all.

"Gwendoline! Did we interrupt your *date*?"

"Considering I don't know how you tracked me down, I wouldn't say 'interrupted' so much as 'stalked with the intent to eavesdrop and interfere,'" Gwendoline grumbled; Niles caught her eye and smiled.

"Well, you've developed this habit of spending time alone at the park to chill out after your classes..." Colt said, hunching apologetically as he pulled out a chair at the table for Everleigh and then seated himself between the two girls.

"Does *everybody* know my schedule?" Gwendoline protested; anxious as she was, a sheen of frost began to spread over the rusty metal table.

"You're a predictable person," Everleigh said; humming a tune under her breath, steam suddenly rose from the opening of the travel mug she cupped in her delicate hands, and she took a dainty sip. "Better we keep tabs on each other in this big, big city than get screwed over by some creep. Or let you continue messing about with that damn book without some sort of monitoring."

*About that...*Gwendoline thought, dreading the eventual explanation she'd have to get through. *They'll think I'm insane, and they might be absolutely right.*

"Niles, this is—"

"Colt and Everleigh. Yeah, I...heard a lot about you." Niles's gaze lingered on Everleigh a second too long, leading her to stare at him so hard Gwendoline could just hear the gears turning in her mind.

Colt reached across the table to shake Niles's hand, polite as a courtier. Gwendoline, watching anxiously, saw the latter flinch as if a static shock had burned him. Looking between her and Colt, Niles's face appeared filled with equal parts astonishment, triumph, and...regret. The regret lingered the longest, and when he laughed it echoed with bitterness.

"It fucking worked..." he said, under his breath. Only Gwendoline heard him.

"Niles? *Niles?*" Everleigh finally spoke up, beginning to put the pieces together. She glared at Gwendoline, suspicious. Colt, concerned with Niles's stricken face, leaned forward. He had his hand on the hilt of his sword, worn on a belt around his waist for once, and he slowly stretched his other hand out to Niles.

"He's fine, Colt," Everleigh snapped, seizing her boyfriend's hand and forcing him to withdraw. "Keep your healing to yourself."

"You heal?" Niles asked, breaking out of his daze. Wary, Colt nodded.

"Did you need—"

"No. But it's helpful to know you retained...just about everything," Niles said; his gaze shifted to Gwendoline long enough to reveal more of that bitterness she was beginning to question. "*Almost* everything." Another hollow laugh escaped him.

Tempted to smack him, tempted to hit anything that put her into this frustrating, confusing, overwhelming situation where she knew absolutely nothing, Gwendoline grabbed her book with both hands, willing strength back into her mind and body.

What do you want to do? Trust, or don't? She asked herself.

"What is going *on*, Gwendoline?" Everleigh demanded, her voice slowly rising to a shriek. "I know this sounds insane, but when you called this guy Niles, did you actually mean *Niles*? As in, the pet name you use for your magic book?"

The only thing Gwendoline could decide to do was to pretend ignorance. "What are you implying?"

"I don't even know," Everleigh growled; irritated by the tension in the air, Smaug unwound himself from his mistress's hair and slithered down her arm to form a bracelet around her wrist. "I'm hoping you happened to meet someone named Niles between now and when I saw you yesterday, not that you found a stranger you convinced to go under the name Niles so...well, so he could get under you—"

"Everleigh Northwood!" Gwendoline felt the sting of outrage from her friend's implication, but laughter bubbled up to the surface in spite of that. The idea that she would make such a wild request of a date was only just crazier than some of the things she'd done to either get a date or progress a date into the bedroom.

Colt laughed with her, a booming reverberation in his chest that never failed to cheer any one of his many friends. "I love you, 'Leigh, but that's fucking ridiculous."

"Not that getting under Gwendoline would be a disaster, but I can honestly tell you that your idea isn't the case," Niles said; he seemed to have returned to his normal, impish self without a trace left of the regret she'd seen before. His comment even made Colt laugh louder.

"Someone had better explain what 'the case' is then," Everleigh, not amused with being the butt of the hilarity, sat up regally in her seat and frowned at them all. "Something is up, and I want to know what it is."

"Yes, mother," Gwendoline grumbled, a kick of annoyance pursing her lips. She had little room for Everleigh's habitual meddling right now.

Everleigh for once had the sense to look contrite when Gwendoline glared at her, and opened her mouth to speak. "Gwendoline, really, I'm just asking. What's going on?"

Instead of explaining, Gwendoline closed her eyes, mentally compiling an acceptable version of the events that had led her to free Niles from her book—minus her sad episode at that bar, and minus how she'd reacted to Niles kissing her back. Then, knocking graciously at the mental doors to her friends' minds, she projected her story to them in a swirl of colors and memories tinted by her own subconscious. She had communicated with them this way once or twice before, but under normal circumstances it wasn't efficient and it made her nauseous. Still, since they could see the true story from her mind, they'd be more likely to believe her.

No one at their table had the chance to form a coherent response. All of them stiffened as an abrupt wave of power flooded the park, malevolent and dark. Gwendoline peeked out from under the roof of the gazebo at the sky, wondering if clouds had blocked the sun. However, she found that she couldn't move, couldn't breathe as what felt like an invisible magic hand frisked what could only be called her power signature. The feel of whatever this being was felt revolting and cold, like sandpaper on an open wound.

So, pawn, you returned to the land? A malevolent force cruelly shoved its way into the cracked doors of her mind, seizing hold of her mental self and holding her trembling psyche in its tight grip. *How foolish. And how foolish of you to forget that the channels you broadcast on are not always private.*

Frantic to free herself from whatever spell held her in place, Gwendoline strained to move even an inch from where she was sitting. If she could have used her magic, she would have, but she didn't have any idea in which direction to send her power. Equally disturbed, her friends struggled in their seats without much success. Somehow the invader tampering with her mind had been able to grab hold of her friends through the connection she had initiated.

Niles alone seemed relatively unscathed by the toxic magic resonating through the forced mental connection. He wasn't totally impervious to harm, however: the color rising in his sharply defined cheeks belied his outward calm, and an eerie shadow outlined his form in response to the onslaught.

"What is this?" Gwendoline finally managed to ask aloud, straining towards her book from her seat. A spear of pain halted her movement, jabbing behind her eyes.

I wasn't even looking for you. I had heard my right to rule in Starford would be challenged by a young enchantress, so I was searching for her. The circle truly does come around, doesn't it?

Reaching across the table, as apparently only he could in this situation, Niles took Gwendoline's white knuckled hand in his own. Understanding his intention, she gritted her teeth and let her own magic wash over her, humming a cleansing incantation under her breath.

As suddenly as it came, the repulsive invading force evaporated and freed them all. But not without one last assault.

Run away then...Gwendoline, is it? It will be no trouble to find you all again. In the meantime, I'll leave you a reminder of what it means to oppose me.

Gwendoline cried out, clutching at her abdomen with both hands. Niles came to her as she groaned with agony, kneeling before her to shove her scrabbling hands aside to inspect her for any injury. The pain abruptly stopped when he touched her, but she saw Niles's face turn completely white as he stared at her stomach.

"What is it? What's the matter?" she asked him once she regained her breath, looking down. In spite of the pain, the awful voice hadn't inflicted any lasting damage. But from Niles's face, she had thought she might be dying.

"Is she all right?" Colt, aside from her, had been the most afflicted:

sweat beaded his strong brow, and he gasped for air as if he'd been strangled.

Niles hesitated before he nodded; he stared at her stomach a moment longer, still deathly pale, but when he looked up at her face some blood returned to his skin. "I had thought...but she's fine. It was just a dream, of sorts."

"A nightmare, you mean," Everleigh. "What the hell was that? How did it break into our minds?"

"That," Niles said after a moment, returning in his chair and sinking into it as if he was a thousand years old, "would be Averill."

"Did it say anything to any of you?" Gwendoline asked, dreading an affirmative. Everleigh and Colt shook their heads, but Niles added his experience to their knowledge.

"He didn't speak to me, exactly. But that last message was for me, since right now I'm the only person in this circle who remembers how things ended last time." Glancing again at Gwendoline, fury swirling together with sadness in fire colored eyes that threatened to consume anything they observed, he shuddered.

A minute or two passed in total silence while they all recovered from the sick feeling the invasion of that presence had given them. Then Niles began to explain, clearly recapping a shorter version of events to save time and energy.

"You saw what Gwendoline showed you, which is true. I'm from the distant past, and I preserved myself and Glenna's soul memories so we could return and defeat the evil we failed to eradicate before. Gwendoline is the reincarnation of Glenna, which is why she was the one who had to free me from the casting book. The three ties to Fate need to be in place to vanquish Averill, which is where you come in."

The story sounded fantastic, unbelievable to the extreme even for a magic based world. Worse, Gwendoline realized that she believed him almost wholeheartedly and without too many questions. *How can this be?*

"So what you're saying is that Gwendoline is a reincarnated sorceress sent to destroy Averill, as in Averill Kinsley? Starford's heir and our future lord and master?" Everleigh's voice was calm as she cut in, but her body language was so tense that Gwendoline could almost hear her grinding her teeth. "And you were trapped in that book to make it all happen?"

"I wasn't trapped," Niles sighed, clearly wishing that someone would remember this simple detail. "I went in willingly."

"You let yourself, your soul, as you say, be trapped in a book for hundreds of years just for kicks, then?" Everleigh queried belligerently, crossing her arms even tighter over her chest. Niles flushed.

"It was my whole being, actually: spirit, heart and soul," he quibbled.

"But why though? How did you even know Gwendoline would even find the spell book at all, let alone at the right time?" Everleigh insisted.

"Fate has a way of working things to her advantage, sometimes," he hedged any explanation. Gwendoline tapped the cover of her book anxiously, wondered why he was suddenly so reticent. His personality had seemed open enough before, when it was just the two of them sharing a meal in the gazebo.

"And if the threat of Averill is real, which I'm not saying it isn't...I felt that...that thing too," Colt interjected, sounding apologetic for arguing. "If he's as strong as you say and apparently immortal, what stopped him from nuking us in our seats when he had us by the balls just now? And since he's lived here all this time and known about us, why didn't he act sooner?" He slouched in his chair, long, meaty legs stretched out in a way that made him resemble a lion at rest.

"Nuking?" Niles questioned, unfamiliar with the word. He looked to Gwendoline for explanation.

"The modern equivalent to a huge fiery comet from the sky streaking down from the sun to destroy us all," she answered, almost smiling when his eyes went a little wide.

"Oh. It is...inefficient to kill through a mental connection such as the one we experienced, even for someone so powerful. Often, you're more likely to break the victim's mind before you stop their heart, and once the mind is broken so is the link you've used to kill them. I had hoped to keep our presence concealed until we confronted him...but it's too late for that now."

"I think I know why he didn't just end us," Everleigh said; apart from the aggressive tension that knotted her pretty brows and stiffened her spine, she seemed satisfied that she finally knew something Gwendoline and Niles didn't. "Averill is Madam Kinsley's only heir, supposedly, but now almost completely by accident Starford's council has discovered a very old bloodline that has one heir viable for leadership. There might be an actual election this year, instead of the usual automatic succession. He probably wants to win by popular vote, so no one will oppose him once he's in power. If he were to come here and start killing college students in gazebos, people might talk."

"An election? Really? I thought that was just talk," Gwendoline voiced her surprise; a stray breeze blew a few strands of hair into her mouth, but she spat them out so she could ask more questions. "I can't believe it."

"You and Niles just told us that he magically appeared out of the casting book you've had for years last night, and that you're the reincarnation of an ancient witch who fought Averill before. But you find the possibility of a democratic election hard to believe?" Colt pointed out.

"A new bloodline might cause too much unrest and make magic in general misbehave. Who is the heir they found?" Gwendoline asked instead of acknowledging Colt's statement. She may not have been able to shake the feeling of DANGER that had screamed in her mind since Niles showed up with his lips fixed on hers the night before, but somehow a trust was beginning to form between them that she had no control over.

"That's the funny part, which we were going to tell you until we got distracted," Everleigh said. Gradually relaxing, her limbs loosened enough for her to slouch, but then she abruptly tensed again.

"Yeah?" Gwendoline encouraged her friend to talk; practicing what she'd learned earlier that day in class, she clenched her left hand into a fist and concentrated, summoning moisture from the air into her hand and willing it to form a shape. When she opened her hand, a tiny ice sculpture of a fox rested there, unmelting and pristine. She passed the little creature over by magic, floating it over to Everleigh.

Niles's expression caught her notice: he seemed taken aback, squinting at the fox to study it. "Why a fox?"

"I've always been partial to foxes," Everleigh said, cooing at the ice creature, which suddenly animated and leapt about the table. Niles stared at it warily, a wistful look in his eyes.

"So..." Gwendoline interrupted, watching him carefully. "What's the funny part, Everleigh?"

"Oh, the police contacted me last night..."

"I was over at her house, and they came in all official, like they were about to make an arrest," Colt elaborated; taking a moment aside, he and Everleigh observed the tiny ice fox that gamboled over the table and onto Gwendoline's spell book, chasing its tail. "I thought maybe they suspected her of having something to do with the governor's murder."

"As if," Everleigh scoffed. "But the humorous part came when they told me that I was a contender for leadership."

"Seriously?" Gwendoline questioned. "What the hell?"

"I know! But they said they searched through a bunch of 'vaulted documents' and my family name kept coming up in the records. I'll have to go through a few magical tests to confirm their theories that I'm the heir apparent...but I don't think I will." Everleigh seemed unconcerned with the matter, but she was the only one.

"Seriously?" Gwendoline exclaimed again, smacking her hand down on the dancing fox atop her book to quell the distraction; Everleigh pouted as a tiny puddle of water spread from beneath her fingers. "Why not?"

"I don't think it's necessary. They're probably wrong, and even if they're right, can you imagine me running this huge city and the outlying towns? Starford is the capital of the magical world! It would be a catastrophe...or worse, it would bore me," Everleigh retorted casually. Uncurling Smaug from her wrist, she wound him between her fingers carefully, watching him hiss loudly at her.

"I told her she should take the test," Colt said. "It wouldn't hurt to find out for sure if she was the true heir. With everything going to hell since Madam Kinsley quit actively governing, it might be a good thing to have fresh management."

"It won't be the safest thing she could do, but Everleigh passing the test to become heir would settle a lot of questions," Niles finally spoke again. "And it can't be a coincidence that they found you now, since this sounds like one of those things Fate might arrange on so events turn out to her liking."

"Who asked you? You've been here less than five minutes and you think you get a vote?" Everleigh snapped, turning her snake in his direction so Smaug could glare at him too; then his words sunk in.

"I think Averill's presence gives him the right to an opinion," Gwendoline said, quieter than she normally would have spoken. The name thrilled through her, triggering a gut response of panic and fear now that she'd felt his presence for herself. She couldn't recall details, but the knowledge of having been through a similar situation before gave her a dizzying amount of déjà vu. The four at the table fell silent, lost in thought.

"I can't imagine a popular vote would be enough reason for Averill not to simply end us." Colt spoke again, falling into the habit of holding on to his sword hilt as if ready for combat at any moment.

"Since it's a new day and age where he can't rule a smaller population by force, he's making the effort to win the people over so they want him to be in charge," Niles mused aloud, leaning forward on his elbows and steepling the tips of his fingers together. "If all the pieces are in place—and just about all of them are—then even he couldn't destroy us without a fight. My power has grown over time, and I might be strong enough to match him in magical strength...but never mind. He'd have to go public to remove all of us from the situation, and that wouldn't suit his plan of encouraging the people to want him to rule. Aside from that...well, if I'm guessing correctly there is one brunette reason he wouldn't slaughter us all in our sleep."

"What do Colt and I have to do with all of this? I'm not saying we won't help you if that's what it comes down to...but I don't see how we're directly involved," Everleigh said. "Averill couldn't know that I have a very, very doubtful connection to the 'throne,' and even if he did know, I'm only a 20-something enchantress who poses little to no threat."

"He mentioned you," Gwendoline said reluctantly. "When he was in my head, he told me he was looking for the enchantress who would challenge his legitimacy." Everleigh paled at her words.

"Have you all decided to believe me?" Niles asked abruptly, changing tactics. An air of authority came over him, lending strength to his words that Gwendoline had not heard before. It suited him, like he was born to lead.

"This is all pure speculation. You could be a freaking lunatic and none of us would know yet, having just met you," Everleigh chattered.

That's not true...I've known him for years, Gwendoline thought, surprising herself with her defensiveness. *Did* she know him? She felt like she did. Twenty-four hours and she was hooked beyond belief...what did that say about her naivety? But even Everleigh, having experienced Gwendoline's image of events and Averill's toxic presence in the same hour, appeared to be fighting off the same conviction of the truth.

"I'll withhold judgment until we hear the rest of what you have to say," Colt said, fair as usual. Niles nodded, as if he had expected their answers. Then he faced Gwendoline, angling his body towards hers.

"Gwendoline?" he asked, speaking to her as if she was the only person around for miles; his tawny eyes, amber shot through with gold, utterly captivated her. Dizzyingly, she felt a tingle against her hair that brought an inexplicable mental image of falling rose petals to the forefront of her mind. She felt like she was suffocating. How ridiculous that she was part of this odd legend, this strange world where books carried handsome men of nobility and a person could live more than once.

"I believe you," she exhaled, caught in his gaze. "Damn."

Everleigh threw her hands up in the air, huffing with exasperation.

Apparently decided on something, Niles nodded firmly and addressed the group. "The pieces I referred to were brought together by Fate. Believe in Fate or not, as you will, but typically whoever has the ruling power maintains a spirit, heart, and soul connection to the ancient, mysterious land magic. In the old days, we had knights who represented each thread: Leland was our spirit knight, Abelard our heart, and I was the soul connection. Obviously things have changed, but not as much as you'd think. I doubt Madam Kinsley set up knights or council members in line with the old laws, which is part of the reason Starford has been suffering. But now the required pieces are in place for another confrontation with the Lord of the land, as Fate has willed." A sinking dread set over Gwendoline as he spoke despite the trust she had chosen to place in him.

"I, obviously, am still the soul tie to Fate, which means that my magic focuses on what could be called an introspective aspect. But heart and spirit...Colt, there's no easy way to tell you this, but you are the reincarnation of Leland the same way that Gwendoline is the almost exact replica of Glenna. You are the spirit tie, which is why you have the rare two-sided gift of healing or breaking with magic: the spirit is the intermediate tie between the more physical aspect of the heart, and the more mysterious aspect of the soul."

Colt, who had somehow stretched out further in his chair and had the appearance of being half-asleep, made no move to indicate that he was listening. Nevertheless, the invisible aura around him felt sharp edged, revealing his doubt.

"I'm less willing to believe you now," he said, opening his eyes fully to give Niles a warning look. Due to his size and the sonorous quality of his voice, his words became a threat.

Unimpressed, Niles narrowed his eyes right back. "How long have you had that sword, Colt? Family heirloom, isn't it?"

"Does it matter?" Colt asked, bristling at the mocking tone. "Lots of people have magical heirlooms, and lots of people aren't reincarnations or heirs to destiny." Niles rolled his eyes.

"The beautiful thing about this is that it doesn't matter if you agree or not. You're alive and present regardless, which is apparently enough for Fate. Besides, I have no fragments or memories to give you. Your belief is not required." He brushed off Colt's skepticism like it was dust on his shoes.

Sensing an unwanted return to the topic of memories, Gwendoline intercepted further questions from the others. "You said there are three ties: you've only mentioned two. Am I the heart tie?"

"I'm afraid not. Glenna would have laughed at that," Niles chuckled. "You're sort of the bonus piece, a chosen nearly exact reincarnation of Glenna. I think she was sort of the binding, the glue that holds all of the pieces together. As you are in this time."

"So who's the last piece?" Everleigh asked. In spite of her doubts, she seemed hopeful with her wide jade eyes, wishing to be included even if she didn't want to believe what she heard. As if sensing this, Niles's stern expression softened.

"It's you, of course. You're not a reincarnation, a split soul, in the same sense Colt and Gwendoline are. But you're a descendant of Abelard and of the old ruler of his time, and that makes you a part of this fight. Also...the resemblance you bear to someone I used to know, someone Averill was captivated by, is quite uncanny. That could be the reason he's kept his distance until now."

"Enough talk," Colt barked; Gwendoline stared at him, taken aback by his uncharacteristic display of aggression. "What are we supposed to do with this information? Storm the Kinsley estate demanding trial by combat?"

"If necessary, but we'll probably need to play our cards with more care," Niles said bluntly. "I can't find the words to tell you how dire the situation is. If Averill gains control, especially with the people's blessing that someone as powerful as him doesn't really need, this world will turn incredibly dark."

"This world? He'd only have jurisdiction of the city and its territories, definitely just the state," Everleigh contradicted.

"That wouldn't last long. Averill has always hated lesser magical people, and would cleanse the lands of them if he could. Trust me...I know."

"That's the issue, isn't it?" Gwendoline observed, sitting up in her chair and stretching; the air was turning cool with the evening, and a shiver stopped her mid-stretch. "Trust...whether we do or don't."

"I think you believe me, against your so-called better judgment. No one would sit here and listen to this story as long as you three have if they didn't," Niles said. He caught Gwendoline's gaze and held it. Without realizing it, they leaned towards each other, challenging for dominance.

"For another thing," Niles said, still looking at Gwendoline in a way that made it impossible for her to break eye contact, "I have another sign for you. Everleigh, your familiar is a golden serpent. That's a rather rare breed of snake, wouldn't you say? Especially for this area?"

Everleigh stopped Smaug from winding endlessly through her fingers, clutching him to her defensively like a living noodle. "He came to me out of the woods when I was about to start high school. What's so wrong with that? Most people find their familiars in similar ways."

"Nothing at all. It's just coincidence, I suppose, that the house symbol for Princess Jael Northwood's family was a serpent, which signals favor from Fate and good fortune for the bloodline. You're no reincarnation, but being a descendant of both a ruler and a knight possessing the heart tie is no small matter," Niles spoke casually, but his eyes were fixed on Gwendoline like he couldn't find it in him to look away, and she doubted his further commitment to the conversation.

What is *this?* Gwendoline wondered, not for the first time as she leaned forward with her elbows on the table towards him. She'd never felt a connection to someone like this, a lure so compelling it raised goosebumps on her skin.

"It's not that unusual," Colt intervened in the moment that had snared the two of them, placing his meaty hand on Gwendoline's shoulder to draw her back. "Everleigh's snake, I mean. There have been stranger familiars."

"I hope this gutless behavior isn't typical for you. Leland was known for his bravery, not his lack of a backbone." Niles snapped waspishly, placing his hands behind his head and leaning back as if nothing in the world mattered to him.

"Are you kidding me? You—" Everleigh stopped Colt from rising out of his seat to advance on Niles. Exchanging concerned looks with Gwendoline, she tugged at her boyfriend to lead him away. He'd never made a point of engaging in fights before, though he'd been provoked into enough to teach him how to win, but this combative side of Colt emerging under Niles's goading troubled them greatly.

"I think it's time you take your boy toy home, Gwendoline. I promise we'll think about...everything," she said, wincing as Colt wrapped a too-tight arm around her waist protectively.

"So you believe us?"

Us? Gwendoline doubted herself, briefly wondering if the whole past two days were a gin induced black out. *Since when is it us? Yesterday you were a girl trapped in a disastrous dating cycle, culminating in a douchebag with quills instead of hair...today, you're emotionally tied to a man who crawled out of your spell book and told you you're a reincarnation of someone else? Really smart, Gwendoline.*

Niles hadn't missed her slip up: out of the corner of her eye, she saw a grin upturn his lips.

"We'll see," Everleigh finally said when Colt neglected to answer. "I'll...I'll get that test done and we'll see if I'm even eligible to oppose Averill. After that...I don't know."

"You're the heir," Niles assured her, not a shred of doubt in his demeanor. His entire bearing exuded confidence in his declaration.

Everleigh shrugged, her eyes round with an approaching fear she didn't want to succumb to. Colt, perceiving her distress, nodded a belligerent farewell to Niles and Gwendoline and guided his girlfriend down the steps leading out of the little gazebo.

"I'm sorry they weren't as receptive as I was, I guess. I did spend the night barricaded in my room, but..." Gwendoline babbled, speaking to fill the black hole of silence that followed the departure of her friends. "I don't know why he lost his temper, Colt isn't normally so aggressive."

"Don't apologize. I did goad him further than I intended, which was my mistake," Niles insisted, watching them walk through the park back to wherever they'd parked Colt's car. "This meeting went how I'd expected it to. Well...mostly. I didn't expect Leland to actually be here."

"Why not? You said you're here because I'm here, so if your story is true, why wouldn't he be here?" Another question occurred to Gwendoline. "And if you have memories to give me, why wouldn't you have memories to give Leland? Colt." This whole fractured soul thing was only increasing her confusion: even she had started referring to Colt by his supposed previous name.

Instead of answering, Niles rose to his feet with feline grace and offered her his hand to help her up. "I'll tell you another time. Maybe we should head back, since the sun's going down."

"Another time? I thought you were in a rush to slay off Averill." Instead of taking his offered hand, Gwendoline pulled her school bag off the back of her chair and handed it to him, carrying only her casting book out of the gazebo.

"I am. But I want to do things right this time, and that requires patience...as long as we can afford it," Niles said. They began walking, leaving the gazebo to go back to where Gwendoline had parked her ancient but serviceable black BMW.

"Do things right? How?" she asked Niles. He didn't answer at first as they trudged through the grass.

"You'll just have to see, won't you?" he said at last. For the whole drive back to her stepmother's house, he remained cryptically silent.

8

Before

Something soft brushed against Glenna's face, first over her cheekbones, then her lips, then her eyelids. It took effort to rise up out of her dreamless sleep, but she found the strength to wake when she recalled who the person touching her face had to be.

"Niles?" she asked, opening her eyes.

There he was, cradling her in his arms as they lay in her tussled bed, somehow looking fresh so early in the morning. True, his dark hair stuck up in odd places, and his stubble looked more advanced than she normally saw it, but his eyes were such a bright autumnal color that she found it hard to look away. She didn't think she wanted to, except to perhaps observe the muscles in his chest and arms. She hadn't seen Niles without a shirt in years, let alone completely nude; she could feel his body against her, pleasantly warm, and the effect swept across her sweetly, reflecting the coziness she normally experienced only on the coldest of nights in front of a warm fire with a cup of herbal tea.

Casting secretively, she cleansed her mouth of morning breath and tamed her skin so it didn't look too puffy from her slumber. It had to be barely dawn: the sun had scarcely risen in the sky yet, but it gleamed dimly around Glenna's curtains as if determined to peek in on last night's lovers.

"Hello," Niles replied; it wasn't quite he who had been kissing her awake, as she'd thought. He'd taken one of the slightly flattened rose petals from the bed and used it to trace the planes of her face with its silken texture. "I hate to wake you, but the servants could knock at any moment. I wasn't sure if you would approve of them finding me in your bed." His tone lowered slightly and he held her close. "I, for one, would be open to staying right here."

"After the wild encounters they've had walking in on Jael and Leland, I don't think the sight of a man in my bed would perturb them at all," Glenna smiled, snuggling into his arms. He grinned back at her, diving in for a deep kiss that recalled memories of the night before. When his hands found her hair and wound themselves into the tangles, she reached up to hold him to her, seeking to lose herself in the moment as her nerves sang with desire.

The cloth clutched in her hand, Leland's red handkerchief, brushed against Niles's back and this time everything from the night before washed over her mind: Averill, the danger ahead to the people she cared about, the finality of the betrothal ceremony. She couldn't help it: as the emotions pierced her, she stiffened, turning her face away from Niles's eager kisses.

"Glenna?" Niles paused, poised over her in a position so arousing it ordinarily would have wound her up. Instead, the only feeling that shoved its way past every other confusing impression was guilt, and she stared up at him helplessly. Her hand had fallen back against the pillows as she'd gone limp, and Niles finally noticed the scrappy cloth gripped tight in her fingers.

This time, he was the one who tensed.

Glenna wished she could read him better, that she'd paid more attention to him all these years. Maybe then she'd be able to see past the anger in his eyes, or be able to cajole him out of the self-loathing curl of his lips. Without a word, Niles removed himself from proximity to her in one smooth movement, vacating her bed to gather his clothes from where he'd cast them on the floor.

"Niles..." she began, without the slightest clue on how follow up her address. He turned his back to her as he slipped into his trousers and laced them, then faced her again.

"My apologies. How boorish of me to linger all night when you obviously wished to be...well, not alone, but not with me," he said, his voice as crisp as the morning frost on a windowpane.

"Niles!" Glenna called his name more urgently, sitting up in bed. He paused his search for his shirt and jacket, his eyes lingering on her swaying breasts. He hesitated, arousal parting his lips, but then he withdrew in a way that conveyed his disgust for his lack of self-control. Wounded, she pulled up the bed sheets over her chest.

"If a gentleman is not welcome, perhaps it would be better to let him know before he...before I..." Niles himself didn't seem to be able to find the right words to say either; locating his boots, he perched on a chair to shove his stocking feet into them before he stood again.

"No!" Glenna leapt out of bed with more swiftness than she thought she'd be capable of in such a moment. Wrapping the thin sheet around her curves—and shedding a few squashed petals from her hair and back as she walked—she pursued Niles as he gathered his things and proceeded to her door to leave.

"I..." *I what?* "I asked you to stay," she murmured, looking up at him as the knot in her throat somehow made her eyes water dangerously. Niles, half in and half out of the room, looked down at her with contempt in his eyes. His dark gaze softened, becoming almost tender when he saw that she was close to tears.

"Yes, you did. Everyone needs a warm body sometimes," he said; his cheeks flushed, signaling his embarrassment over being so ungallant. "I knew, Glenna. I knew that I wasn't what you wanted. Who you wanted. I...I'd hoped to make you forget about anything else but me."

"You did," she protested earnestly; she wanted to reach out to him, to pull him back into her room, but she resisted the act that would reveal her inexplicable desperation. "You did make me forget."

How could she tell him that their one night, each kiss and caress they had shared with such zeal, had been the only thing that could have chased another man out of her mind last night? He was not her first evening visitor, but she had never experienced anything similar to their togetherness before now. How could she tell him that only he could have accomplished that sweet oblivion with her?

"I did?" Niles smiled bitterly, though his black eyes were warm and filled with longing. She nodded solemnly, attempting to persuade him with her eyes to come back in. He stepped forward, enticed...but then he saw the red kerchief still clutched in her hand as she was propping open the door.

"Not for long," he said. Bowing to her mockingly, every inch of him taut with hurt pride, he took his leave and disappeared down the hall.

Frustrated with her bad decisions, Glenna slammed the door as hard as she could behind him, tears streaming down her cheeks. Her anger increasing because she couldn't force herself into composure, she turned back to her bedroom, looking for something, anything to destroy. Her glare fell on the remaining petals that lay in scattered piles about the room, and with a choked scream she cast her hand out as if striking an enemy. A crackling sound echoed through the space, and all of the petals froze to solid ice. With another wave of her hand, she gathered each icy part into a whole; another gesture sent the whirl of petals crashing to the ground, shattering the fragile ice into thousands of glistening shards.

The destruction didn't satisfy her, but after a moment she was able to calm her tears and clear her mind somewhat. *There are more important things at hand, Glenna. Time enough to fret over wounded loversand losing friends if we survive the coming storm.*

It took a great amount of resolve to prepare herself for the day ahead when all Glenna wanted to do was crawl back into her bed and sleep for a fortnight. A servant popped in to bring her a simple breakfast of fresh eggs and toast, which she found she wasn't hungry enough to eat. Another came to help her dress. This was a formality Jael had insisted upon when she'd asked Glenna to live in the royalty wing of the castle as a member of the family instead of with the other mages, and the servant ordinarily went right back out the door without accomplishing her task. Most of the time, Glenna figured she could dress herself and style her own hair, but today she found herself beckoning the maid in to brush out her tangled hair.

"Is my lady well?" the maid, blonde and apple-cheeked in a way all the kitchen and stable boys surely found pleasing, dared to ask as Glenna sat staring stony-faced into her vanity mirror.

"Your lady can't seem to do anything right these days," Glenna sighed. "I don't suppose you have any advice when it comes to having relations with one man when you're in love with another?" *Stupid! Haven't you forgotten how maids gossip?*

Taken aback, the maid shook her head with her blue eyes wide. "The only thing I know is that you should speak your feelings as you have the chance. If you wait, you might be sorrier than you'll have thought possible."

Touched by her words, Glenna had to soften. "Oh? Did you have a sweetheart you lost?"

"Not quite," the maid suddenly beamed with the brightness of a sunflower. "We caught each other in time. We'll be married after the princess's nuptials."

Another happy couple. Am I to be surrounded by them forever? Not totally displeased that this maid had found joy, Glenna forced a smile onto her face, which she maintained as the maid chattered about her partner—he was a soldier, and he was partial to rhubarb pie—until the girl paused over her hair.

"You know, my lady, I think I have just the thing to coax some proper curls into your locks. May I go and fetch it?"

Glenna allowed the maid to go. Alone at last, she found she had no idea what to do with her day. Aggravated by her sluggishness, she threw herself into the chair by the breakfast table, looking out the window. Seeing nothing outside to interest her, she decided to do some research on old gods of the land and hummed softly to summon her casting book to her. She did not have a familiar like Jael or Leland or any other soldier who often had a weapon for a casting tool, but if she'd had one, it would have been her spell book. It simplified her magic, helping her focus her spells with artistic details that pleased her.

The book flew to her from her large bookshelf across the room, sliding into place on the table in front of her with the pages already fluttering open.

"Right," Glenna said. "If you would, could you find me lore on the old blood of the land?" It never hurt to be polite to whatever spirit or strange magic controlled the aged volume: in response, the book flipped through several blank pages until it paused to allow spidery black text to fill the surface.

Fate divided the world according to Her will. She appointed a Lord to each Land to hold the wild Magic in check. Because of Her generosity, little sacrifice was required from the Children of the Land: each ruler upon succession must bond to the Lord and the Land with a portion of Blood. Should a ruler abuse their power, the Blood taken by the Lord of the Land would bind the ruler further to the Land and end their life if necessary. Should a Lord abuse his power, a ruler alone could challenge the blooded Lord with Heart, Spirit, and Soul to initiate a change in the Land. The victor of their grievous combat, frowned upon by Fate Herself, must swiftly bind either a new ruler to the Lord or a new Lord to the Land lest the wild Magic run free once more. Wild magic, contained by Fate and Her Lords—

The script continued in a similar long-winded fashion for several more paragraphs, but the left page kept turning over her current one with an annoying level of insistence. Glenna flattened her hand over the left page, holding down the struggling paper until it wriggled enough to gift her with a deep paper cut.

"See here, I'm already in a rough mood," she scolded it around the bloody slice in her skin she had paused to suck the sting out of. "Is that why you're acting up? Don't want me touching you after what I did last night?" In place of answering—as if a book could retort—the page turned over with a distinct air of smug victory. Almost amused, Glenna scanned the words that began to write themselves on the worn paper with a measure of curiosity, but her blood chilled as red ink outlined the words of the page in a different, more chaotic hand than before.

When sacrifice is required at the moment of lost hope,
one must be ready to answer the call of Fate.
One must summon the strength to break thy Heart, bind thy Spirit, and rend thy Soul to preserve hope for the future. To Split ones' Soul is no simple feat, nor a painless one. To suffer defeat, to face annihilation, is worse.
What Fate Herself has writ must be obeyed. Even if the three ties and thy very Soul be at stake.

Why this talk of souls? Glenna marveled at the increasing chills creeping up and down her arms. She tried to close the book, first casually, then attempting to force the covers together with both hands. Neither of them budged or gave the remotest indication that they would close, and the words seemed to be etched onto her mind's eye long after she'd stopped focusing on them. To her horror, the book flipped to the opening page of its own free will and began repeating the message, over and over and over again in increasingly bright ink.

Red is the color of Fate, and Scarlet the color of the Blood, Glenna thought, the words not entirely her own. *Crimson be the tide that will sweep over the land should hope fade to dark.*

The room grew warm, then hot, as if bonfires were burning in the vicinity. Yet her chills remained, wracking her body with shivers she could not explain. When the book flipped to the last page with a t-t-t-t- noise as the parchment fluttered against itself, she felt the cold settle into her bones.

Prepare Yourself.

Glenna's mind filled with fog, the blankness affixing her in place as she stared at the words. There was not a shadow of doubt in her mind that Fate herself had been the one to initiate this interaction. Bound to silence by an invisible force, she couldn't voice or even properly think of any questions to ask the Presence in her bedroom before it departed with a sigh that warmed her cheeks even as it filled her eyelashes with frost.

An image smoldered in the remains of her vision, an impression of an elegant female, hands as pale as the moon, recording the words from the vision with a feathered quill that was the rich red of blood.

She thought she'd have a moment to process what had happened to her, but Glenna sensed a presence in the room besides herself. This was not a supernatural presence, but a human one; turning, she saw that her maid had returned, a beatific smile on her sweet face.

"Did you find what you needed?" Glenna asked, trying to smile back with her heart still pounding from her contact with something as simply other as Fate. The maid nodded, holding up a potion with her fetching smile in place, and came forward to resume brushing

Glenna's hair.

As the brush swept through her locks once more, Glenna studied the now blank pages of her book as if they might give her more answers at any second. Her heart almost stopped as red dripped onto the page, bright blood dissolving into the pages too swiftly to analyze. She felt the wetness on her hair, the blood soaking through the strands.

Looking up into her mirror, she stifled a scream at what she saw.

The maid was shaking her head as if repeatedly saying no, still brushing Glenna's dark hair like nothing had changed, but her eyes were the sightless orbs of the dead, and a wide, seeping gash opened and closed as her head bobbed up and down. Blood dripped from the wound, coating the already decaying body and the brush that swept through her hair.

All the while, as the maid started to gurgle an eerie death rattle, an elated smile remained on her face.

Glenna leapt out of her chair with a shriek, backing away from the animated corpse. Her attacker groaned, the sound a whining, choking abomination that burbled wetly. The jagged slit stretched from ear to ear, open for good as an impossible amount of shockingly garnet blood flowed from the mortal wound. Unperturbed by her own physical distress, she studied Glenna with eyes as blank as a stone.

"A MESSAGE...FOR JAEL..." Somehow words tore from the young girl's lips before she lunged, sending the vanity flying. Acting by instinct, Glenna cupped her hands into an archaic shape for casting a particular spell. Sizzling energy zapped the atmosphere of the room as a dagger sized lightning bolt materialized in her hand. The maid's poor, deformed corpse didn't stand a chance: the lightning hit her straight in the gut, singeing her bloody uniform and scorching the skin underneath. She fell to the ground, still pouring out an improbably quantity of blood from her throat.

Then, gargling again, she began to crawl towards Glenna.

9

Days passed between further talk about Gwendoline's and Colt's supposed reincarnations, along with the other fantastical tales Niles had told them all. Everleigh decided to be tested by the town elders to find out if her bloodline was the right one to make her the official heir, but no one had heard anything of the results yet. Everleigh herself had been quiet lately and, according to Colt, keeping even him at a distance. Gwendoline worried about her friend, anxious for the burden Everleigh might have to carry if the town council actually found her to be the heir. Judging by Niles's grim certainty, the results would confirm his expectations.

Gwendoline herself was eager to ask Niles more questions, to hear more about his story if nothing else, but each time she tried, her new roommate told her not yet and distracted her with whatever he had on hand.

And oh, did he have a lot on hand. Gwendoline had supposed that after being virtually trapped in a book for an undefined number of decades, Niles would be eager to learn the ways of a world that would be totally foreign to the whole of his experience. In spite of her assumption, he managed to impress and frustrate her simultaneously as he attempted to integrate what knowledge he had into his new daily life. One morning she could wake up to the sound of him trying to learn to rollerblade in the house, and another to a sweet scene of him cooking them a gourmet breakfast of biscuits from scratch and homemade jam.

"How did you learn how to cook so quickly?" Gwendoline asked him one Sunday morning, her mouth half full of cinnamon rolls so stuffed with the warm spice they nearly burned her tongue. "I can't even bake this good!"

"Memories have been coming back, of my time in the book," Niles answered, brushing his flour covered hands on the stained, lemon tree printed apron tied around his waist. "Not memories, per-say...more like images of the things people who used to own the book wrote. When it was just Glenna's casting book, she used to leave it in the royal library with a charm on it to absorb the information from the surrounding books. Maybe I learned that way, since over the years that book went a lot of places and absorbed a great deal of information." Heedless of her waving him away, he served another frosting smothered roll onto her messy plate.

"But recipes for baked goods? And what about that music you've been playing on my piano? Or the gardening?" Gwendoline raised her eyebrows as she took another bite of her sweet roll. Niles served a roll for himself and took a seat beside her at her kitchen bar.

"You make it sound so tame, like an elderly lady had my book the whole time. I also know a vast amount of unique spells relating to all subjects, things that could strip the skin from your bones or simply make you grow straw instead of hair. I could turn the world upside down with my knowledge, if I wanted," he protested; the mischievous sparkle in his eyes let her know he wasn't fully serious.

"What else do you know?" She asked, curious.

"The powerful hexes and curses at my disposal don't interest you? Very well. I have journal entries from at least seven teenagers who misguidedly used the casting book as their diary. Which era are you interested in? I know more about being an adolescent in the past than I ever cared to." Gwendoline felt her face flush as she recalled one or two diary entries she herself had recorded in the book several years ago, and prayed he didn't remember any of those. If he did, he had enough tact to not bring them up.

"Aside from that, I also know certain techniques regarding... physical magic we could try out later, if you're willing," Niles said suggestively. A lazy smiled played about his lips, luxurious as a cat stretching out to bat at a new toy. She only frowned at him.

"Techniques you learned from what people wrote in the book?"

"I knew a lot of things before I disappeared into the book," he laughed, taking a seat beside her at the kitchen bar. Their eyes met, and a strange image of her body being dipped back in his arms fluttered across her mind's eye. The thing that scared her was the fact that the image was most definitely a memory, not a picture she had conjured up in the present.

"Did you do that?" she demanded.

"Do what?" He tried to play innocent, but she glared at him until he came clean. "Yes, I did, but not on purpose. I seem to be having trouble...containing myself and my power as I did before. It must be the adjustment to being human again."

"You say you have the soul connection to Fate," Gwendoline began. "Does that mean you can see souls, or interact with them? If you can project images like that?"

"In a sense, yes, I can. I'm better than most at perusing memories and ideas and filtering through the impressions that make each mind—each soul—unique. It takes a lot of work and the headache afterwards is nigh unbearable, but if I wanted I could convince someone susceptible to persuasion to do my bidding, or simply alter their thoughts," Niles explained. Abruptly, his eyes shifted from amber to black, and he looked away from her, placing his hands flat on the cool granite countertop and taking a steadying breath. "In particular, now that I have Glenna's memories to look after, it's hard to balance reality and memory and keep my sanity."

"So...a memory. That was a memory, you accidentally showed me," Gwendoline asked, indulging in another bite of her breakfast so she'd have something to do instead of awkwardly watch him control his magic. "You and...Glenna?"

"Yeah," he said simply. He didn't seem to want to elaborate, since he turned away, and she didn't want to push him, but the girl in the memory looked too much like Gwendoline for her to ignore.

"Your memory, or hers, specifically?"

"Hers, I think. I was there too, so in that case it's hard to tell, but it's safe to say that the part of the soul that is Glenna's is reaching out to you, longing to be whole," he replied. Looking up at the ceiling, he took another deep breath before he returned his focus to Gwendoline, a tired expression tightening his face. "I know you don't want to hear about the memories, I know...but they're there, and eventually we'll need to address them."

Instead of responding to his probe to see where she stood on taking her memories back, Gwendoline tried to bring the conversation back to a lighter note. "You and Glenna were an item?"

"No, we weren't," Niles said, frowning at her. "Don't change the subject. I made you these rolls because cinnamon is your favorite and I wanted to talk."

"Did you know cinnamon was my favorite because it was actually Glenna's favorite?" she asked, teasing.

"Maybe. I don't know, if it was her favorite, I must only know it now subconsciously," Niles thoughtfully leaned forward, his forearms resting on the edge of the bar. "She was my friend, but she liked to keep to herself and getting to know the little things like that wouldn't have been easy even if I'd had more of a chance to be with her."

"So, judging from that memory, you were the sort of friends who frequently dallied in bed together?"

For someone who's supposed to be a reincarnation of the person Niles would have been dallying with, you're taking an awfully calloused approach to this conversation, she thought, a little guilty. Her abashed feelings increased when she observed the look on Niles's face and the way his dark brow creased in indignation.

"*You* might be like that, but she wasn't. We weren't like that," he said, rising from his chair and heading over to the sink to begin washing the pile of dishes precariously perched on the ceramic edge. His insult stung—intentional or not—but she didn't have time to retort before more memories assaulted her mind. This time she was sure they were his, and that he didn't have control over what his mind shared with hers.

Her face the same, an exact replica of Glenna from her strong cheekbones to the full lips he'd kissed and wanted to kiss again and again. Her eyes, but starry violet, not the iron gray he'd known. Her hair, but full sable with no snow white strands to be seen, and curled by nature instead of sleek and straight. Her beauty, the silvered glow of early dawn instead of the cool, sensual darkness that made him remember...oh, what he remembered...the last he'd seen her...

A spark of pain in her gut, the same place Averill had hurt her in the gazebo, cast her out, violently pushing her away so that her physical body nearly collapsed to the floor off the bar stool. Dazed, she blinked several times, gripping the edge of the counter for dear life. Around her, her magic formed a swirling cocoon of transparent mist that dissipated within seconds as the pain faded. Niles was by her side in an instant, tilting her chin up to look into her eyes to make sure she was all right.

"I'm so sorry, I didn't mean to do that. That memory was...well, that's not one I'm willing to share," he said. His hard gaze softened into concern as she continued to blink away the rush of confusing images she'd glimpsed, panic causing her heart to thump far too quickly.

"I think I understand you a little better now," she said at last, looking up at the tall man tipping her chin up to face him so he'd know for certain that she was fine. Once he was sure, he steadied her in her seat; she waited for him to withdraw, but he didn't.

"Oh? You learned something from that jumble even I can't sort out?" An ironic smile played about his mouth, but it faded when she answered.

"You really loved her, didn't you? Nothing short of that would have persuaded you to seal yourself in that book for all those long years," Gwendoline realized, her voice breathy and almost girlishly high. Almost out of her control just as Niles couldn't seem to keep his memories and his mind under wraps, her magic reached for him, a static charged spell that guided his body closer to hers.

Why are you doing this? She asked herself, even as she leaned into him. She didn't have an answer.

"Yes. I loved her. I can even say I loved her more than my vocabulary could express," Niles said, speaking so softly that she had to strain to hear him. "But we were not well suited. We both knew that, in the end."

"In the end?"

"In the end," he repeated shortly, avoiding the obligation to answer her. "You'll know what that means soon enough once you take these memories back."

"I—" Gwendoline began, but he quieted her with the lightest kiss on her lips. It barely felt like anything, just the merest touch that her mind didn't even have time to register, but the cooling and then heating effect on her body made her hair stand on end. Her trademark mist, visible only when her emotions were slipping from her control, swirled around them both, tinted the same unique shade of her eyes.

Unexpected relief coursed through her before the guilt returned to make her palms clammy.

"This can't wait forever, Gwendoline," he met her gaze, his tone soothing even if his words were firm. "We can only put this off for so long, and once Everleigh finds out she's eligible to rule, the hour grows late if we want to save Oloetha...or Starford. Regardless, even more is at stake than just these lands."

"Morbid," she quipped, the word a joke between them from when they'd been writing to each other in her casting book.

Just days ago I was only a college student...now I'm having conversations about "saving the land" and questioning everything I know about my childhood friends and myself, she mused, unintentionally pursing her lips together to try to hold onto the feeling of his lips on hers. *Not to mention kissing a guy—a scary, damaged guy—I don't know and have no business kissing.*

When she came back to the present, she found that her lips refused to obey her command not to smile at Niles, who smiled back and cupped her face in his hands, thrilling her with another breathlessly light kiss. She noticed for the first time the interesting calluses on his hands, and wondered what weapon he'd practiced with to earn them.

"Sorry if I'm invading your personal space and shaking up everything you know about your world," he said at last, beginning to step away. "And, technically I suppose I should apologize for kissing you without express permission, but after all this time I find you as irresistible as..." he trailed off, the light in his warm eyes darkening a little.

As irresistible as she was. The thought sent a stab of absurd jealousy into her heart, but his expression troubled her more. She liked this one, with his quips and love of baking and his confidence. This man shouldn't have to be sad often, at least not on her account, Gwendoline decided.

"Chalk it up to disorientation from being human again?" she asked, smiling to reassure him. He cocked his head, confused as what "chalk it up" meant. Completely charmed, Gwendoline laughed and turned away from him, returning her focus to her cinnamon roll. An idea occurred to her, and she asked him about it as he returned to scrubbing the sticky dishes in the full sink.

"Why don't you have any memories to give Colt, if he's been reincarnated like I have? Also, how did the reincarnation come about? Who brought us back?" she asked, kicking her feet cheerfully as she perched in her chair. Of course, Niles answered her questions from last to first.

"Fate brought you back. Fate—I guess you would consider her a sort of goddess, in this time—tamed the wild magic in the land so her adopted children could use it. Fate set up a system with Lords and blood in the lands to keep hold on the magic so it won't turn on us and make the land wild again. She's not all-knowing, necessarily, but she knows and can accurately predict a hell of a lot of outcomes, and she has the power to pull strings to bring things...into her alignment, shall we say," Niles explained patiently, splashing suds and water all over the blue paisley apron he wore as a bundt pan slipped from his hands and banged against the sink.

"Lords...like Averill," Gwendoline deduced.

"Yes. For all of this world there are only four or five Lords, but Averill possesses one of the larger portions. Being the greedy bastard we know him to be, I don't understand how he won favor with Fate to be chosen for that kind of role, but I'm assuming it's because he helped her tame the magic at the dawn of mankind's age. So, he's here to vex us all, and Fate simply brought us all back to resolve this conflict," Niles continued. Gwendoline watched the movement of muscles in his forearms as he scrubbed, physically fascinated.

"So she's on our side? She wants us to..." *To what? Fight her battles for her, win? Punish a Lord who's out of control, or reward him for taking initiative?* Gwendoline had never been the religious sort, and felt less inclined to be so now.

"I wouldn't say she's on our side, but her bringing us all back to fight him just as he's reemerged from whatever hole he's been hiding in all these years might be a good sign she's willing to help us," he filled in her silence. They paused a moment, briefly steeped in their own thoughts, before Gwendoline recalled her original question.

"Why doesn't Colt have memories, Niles? And why do you hate him?" she asked softly, longing to push for an answer despite her desire to nurture this fragile peace between them. He stopped moving, freezing into a fine featured sculpture of a man covered in dishwater and one or two errant dustings of flour.

"I don't hate him. Leland and I were friends, brothers in arms, and there were few things about me that he didn't know. He died before I could be sure Glenna captured the part of him that made him himself, and I didn't sense any remnants of him with me in the book. So, I mourned the loss of my friend all this time, only to be confronted with his reincarnation who apparently has nothing of his courage and honor," he spoke at last in a rippling murmur. "Besides...it was hard enough not to blame Leland for having what I wanted without realizing it."

"Died? Leland *died*?" Gwendoline, distracted from defending Colt, couldn't believe it. She supposed it was stupid to be surprised at news of a historical person's death, since one had to die to be reincarnated, but some part of her, deep down in a place she never liked to look—introspection was not her favorite—recoiled at the idea of Colt...of Leland being gone. Even though he would have been buried under the earth long before she was born.

As if sensing her unexpected surge of anguish, sorrow she felt deeply to the core, Niles finally turned to look at her. "I'm sorry."

She knew he meant it, somehow.

They both startled as Gwendoline's rusty doorbell emitted what sounded like a dying gasp of a chime. Shaken out of the spell her and Niles both seemed to be under, she leapt from her seat and rushed down the hall to the front door. At this point anyone would be welcome if they could provide a distraction from the tense bubble of remembrances, real and imagined, that had filtered through her house alongside the delicious scent of cinnamon rolls.

"Everleigh?" Gwendoline tentatively greeted her friend as she pried open the stubbornly heavy wood door. Everleigh shoved past her, her nose in the air as she caught scent of the rolls.

"Food first, talk later," she said, letting her nose lead her way down the hallway leading to both the living room and kitchen. Nonplussed, Gwendoline followed, catching Everleigh's fashionable leather purse as she tossed it to her. In seconds, she'd made herself at home and began consuming the biggest cinnamon roll from the pan with record speed.

"I haven't seen you eat like that since we were in middle school, when Isaiah Brown said he liked curvy girls," Gwendoline said, staring with a fair measure of disgust as a glob of frosting slid down Everleigh's fingers and wrist back onto the plate. Instead of laughing like she normally would, Everleigh frowned at Gwendoline and nodded to the green purse.

"There's a letter in there. Read it," she commanded around a mouthful of frosting. "I told Colt I'd meet him here, and I want to get two shocked responses out of the way before I have to deal with his drama."

Curious, Gwendoline did as she was told and pulled the folded sheet of creamy, official looking paper from the handbag. Niles dried his hands on a towel and approached to read over her shoulder. His presence, the nearness of him which made her think distracting thoughts about how his mouth would feel on her neck, diverted her, but she made the effort to focus and skimmed the letter.

"They want to get on 'training' me right away. I ask you, why couldn't they have done this shit earlier? Surely they knew the old bat was going to keel over sometime, and they never thought to look for an heir until now?" Everleigh babbled once she was sure they were finished. Niles looked up from the letter to watch her, hearing the obvious panic in her voice.

"You'll be fine," he told her, using a similar soothing voice to the one he had used for Gwendoline earlier. "It's in your blood to succeed at this, and you'll have lots of people to help you."

"Sure, sure," Everleigh whispered, her sarcasm falling short as she stared down at her now empty plate.

"So. You're the heir to the oldest leading family of Starford, older than the Kinsley line," Gwendoline stated, trying to wrap her mind around the fact that one of her old friends would possibly be leading thousands of people all too soon. "Should I curtsy? Should I prostrate myself before you?"

"Who's prostrating themselves?" Colt's booming voice echoed in the hallway, drawing notice even before he entered the room where they all stood. "If anyone's bowing, it should be Everleigh because she—"

Gwendoline stared at him as he entered, shrugging off his faded jacket and revealing the freckled, mostly tan, and expertly sculpted biceps exposed where his t-shirt did not cover. He'd always looked good to her—she'd even had a small crush on him, years ago when she was an angry punk girl with bright blue hair and black fingernail polish that never chipped—but she'd never truly noticed him as anything but Everleigh's boyfriend. Her feelings, or lack thereof, had not changed, but she had the strangest sensation that someone had handed her a pair of glasses to try on, and looking through them she could begin to see things she hadn't before. Colt was *hot,* and he was a good guy, which she had never been able to find elsewhere. The sudden unwelcome thoughts that filled her head made her cheeks flush, and she guiltily dismissed them as best she could.

"Everleigh?" Colt's focus was not on her, but on his girlfriend, who made herself busy scraping sugary goo off her lips and chin with a napkin. In spite of his diverted focus, he stepped closer to Gwendoline and leaned against the counter beside her. Embarrassed by her disobedient mind, Gwendoline hastily moved away once she handed Colt the letter Everleigh had requested they read.

He took his time, reading slow to take in every word so he could speak intelligently about the information. Gwendoline wished she could say she knew how he'd react, but all she could do was wait with the others to see what he'd say.

"So?"

"So...? Everleigh asked, nonplussed as to the tranquility of his answer.

"So what? Just because you're the first heir to the Northwood bloodline that they've found doesn't mean you'll be the last," Colt said, tossing the letter in his hands onto the countertop disdainfully. "It's your choice if you want to take part in this, not your obligation. And for the record, my vote is for you to stay out of this."

"Oh? That's your professional opinion, is it?" Everleigh lifted the letter up with two delicate fingers, pinching the paper between them like it could explode at any time. Her eyes narrowed as she studied her boyfriend. Niles cleared his throat and spoke up.

"It's unlikely they'll find someone else. Historically, the Northwood bloodline Everleigh comes from only has one heir alive at a time. They've always been fertile enough to produce a child, but no more than the one," he explained, untying the strings around his neck and waist to remove the dishwater damp apron. "Besides, why would she not claim her birthright? It's an honor to lead, and she would have help."

"Who's help? Yours?" Colt demanded, his tone indicating that Niles offering his help would be unsatisfactory. Taken aback by the bristly attitude, Niles held his hands palm up in surrender.

"If she wants it she has my loyalty, and I think she'll need it, but I'm not who I meant. Gwendoline will help her, of course, and there's a whole council willing to guide her and train her to lead and use the land magic she'll gain access to."

"Land magic?" Gwendoline asked, curious. Niles waved his hand impatiently, and she wondered how often he got annoyed with answering her questions when it would be easier to simply give her Glenna's memories.

"It's what binds magic together. It's subtle, powerful, and most people don't have more than a spoonful of access to it," he explained; the bemused looks the other three people in the room spurred him on to further elaboration. "Land magic...it's like roots. No, like veins in the body. There's a reason it's tied to blood, which makes it tied to magic bearing people and tied to the land. As I said, it's tricky to access for most people, but the current ruler of the land would be able to tap into it with minimal exertion."

"What would I need it for?" Everleigh asked, perking up at the mention of such power. Gwendoline noticed how she referred to herself instead of abstractly mentioning whoever would end up presiding over Starford like a queen.

Niles shrugged. "It was my understanding that it was only used to augment the user's own magic so they could ensure fertility of the land and people and keep enemies away. I'm sure it had innumerable other uses, but unlike other magic using land magic too much has a price, so Jael and her predecessors called on it only in times of need."

"Oh," Everleigh deflated, disappointment curling her smudged lips. Niles studied her, then slid his dark, calculating eyes in Colt's direction.

"Leland would have inherited the same access once he and Jael married, enhancing his own magic and binding him to her more than just legally," he told him, leaning forward on the counter as if he hadn't dropped a conversational bomb. Everleigh gasped, duly startled, but Colt met Niles's hard gaze with a steady expression. Gwendoline marveled at his comparative lack of surprise, cutting her eyes to Everleigh to see a gentle smile softening her features. She held her slender hand out to Colt with the expectation that he'd take it. Ignoring her for perhaps the first time in his life, he kept his focus on Niles with the same uncharacteristic frown still marring his strong face.

"If we're going to believe in this story of reincarnation, believe Niles is telling the truth and isn't some insane stalker in Gwendoline's long line of dubious past boyfriends—"

"Hey, none of those were my fault!" Gwendoline protested; Everleigh arched her eyebrows at her friend from where she sat on her bar stool, invoking at least a dozen memories of frantic phone calls pleading for an excuse to escape a bad date and tearful break-ups. Colt continued again, uninterrupted.

"I haven't decided to believe all of this yet, but I do remember him saying that you weren't Jael. Since you aren't, there's no reason to risk getting hurt or caught up in a war no one really wants," he finished at last. "And you, Gwendoline. What makes you so ready to trust him?" Somehow she knew Niles was silently seething without looking at him, and she puzzled once again over the baffling emotional tie they'd shared since he'd emerged from her book. No...since long before he'd climbed from those pages. How could she explain that to someone so ready to doubt?

Gwendoline shook her head, her dark hair swishing about her face; as if helpless, she raised her hands, palms up in defeat. "He was a familiar I named when I was a younger, then the person in my book, then the man who materialized from it. I don't know how, but I...know him, in a sense, like I remember him from before." *Glenna's memories...my memories...are returning whether I'm ready for them or not,* she declined voicing that thought.

"And you trust that sense? You trust him?" Everleigh spoke before Colt could cut in with his atypical negativity again, her wide eyes pleading with Gwendoline. Smaug had emerged from her pocket amid all the discussion; he perched distractingly on Everleigh's shoulder with his gleaming eyes fixed on Gwendoline. She knew that what she was really asking, what her friend of many years was truly wanting to know: did Gwendoline think it was worth the risk for Everleigh to pursue her right to rule?

Niles, asking a different sort of question without saying a word, observed her with the cool darkness of his eyes. *Why do you keep testing me?* Gwendoline wanted to shout at him. *You of all people should remember the moment I put my faith in you.*

"I do," she said at last, tilting her chin up to show her confidence. Everleigh's tight, tense shoulders relaxed and she straightened, imbued with Gwendoline's confidence. Almost unwillingly, her gaze turned to Colt as if she was concerned about his approval.

"But it worth the risk?" He questioned, challenging her as he took an unwitting step in her direction. That strange feeling jumped in

Gwendoline again, and to her surprise she noticed that Colt's throat bobbed nervously as well.

"I think it is," she spoke finally, rushing her words to keep Niles and Everleigh from clueing in on whatever had snapped taut between her and Colt. "We all felt that...that strange darkness pass over us when Averill sought us out. I don't think it would turn out well if we let him bully his way to the top with empty promises and take over." She half expected him to argue that they'd never actually met Averill to pass judgment on him, but even this new, belligerent version of Colt could not contest the ominous nature of the shadow that had passed over the four of them as they'd talked in the gazebo.

“"You wanted me to take the test, Colt. Everything seems to fit with what Niles is saying. Starford's council found me through the campus blood drive. Now you want me to back out and let Averill take over?" Everleigh demanded. "How well do you think that will go, him ruling over us and abusing or killing anyone who doesn't have enough magic based on his standards?"

Setting his jaw with a stubborn grind of his teeth, Colt shook his head and crossed his large arms over his broad chest. "Let's not make it our problem until it has to be. It might not end up being an issue if we keep to ourselves, anyway," he said. He looked at Everleigh and his tone softened, and he reached out to place his hands on her shoulders as she turned away from him to regard Niles.

"I think I want to try to make this right. I don't know what happened before, and I know I'm not a new version of Jael, but I am an undisputed descendant of Abelard's bloodline, and he must have inherited the throne or whatever after she was gone," she spoke quietly, arresting the room's attention in that special way that had gained her A's on every speech she'd ever given throughout her academic career. “I know that I felt...Averill is evil, even if I don’t know exactly how evil yet, and I want to put a stop to that.”

Gwendoline was caught off guard by the contrast of Everleigh's brilliant courage and Colt’s spinelessness. A haunted look had chilled Niles’s eyes into further blackness, if possible, and she wondered how it might have been to know Leland back in the day. He sounded like one of the finest royal knights in the queendom, set to marry the princess of the land: what would he think of his new self in Colt, whose best answer was to stay out of the fight and hope no one threw a punch their way?

Since Gwendoline’s coping mechanism had always been silence and observation, she caught the tension emanating from Colt as he focused entirely on massaging Everleigh’s slender shoulders. Her scrutiny drew his notice, and for the briefest instant when their eyes met, Gwendoline had a sense that maybe he had been having a memory flashback or two as well.

But that’s impossible, she reminded herself. There weren’t any memories to save.

For a moment, both of their expressions hummed with unexplainable guilt. A tie snapped taut between them again, blurring everything and everyone else in Gwendoline’s small kitchen into insignificance. Her hands trembled slightly, the fingertips icy while her palms burned, and she approached him with the stuttered gait of a sleepwalker.

Then she realized she really *was* cold. In fact, her whole house felt like it was freezing, frosty enough to transform her breath into a fine mist. Her movements had slowed to almost nothing, as if she was a patch of film an editor had paused to study. She saw Colt’s mouth moving, like he was speaking, but his attention had returned to

Everleigh.

Gwendoline couldn't turn her head too far, so she could see Niles, but she heard him shout words whose meaning eluded her comprehension. Or was he shouting? All she caught was a whisper, a sigh that sounded so close to her ear that she would have startled had she been able to move. Flicking her eyes around rapidly, she felt helpless as she saw the red-tinged frost as delicate as a spider's web feathering out over her windows and walls. The phenomenon should have been transparent, but instead the sheet of ice somehow blocked any daylight coming through her kitchen window.

Colt, Everleigh, and Niles suffered from the same confusion, trapped standing or sitting where they were as the ice crept towards them and threatened to engulf them all. Their nearly opaque breath fogged from their lips in pale clouds, and the silence that echoed in the room felt as complete as the peace that falls onto a forest during a heavy snow. Gwendoline had always been fond of snowy evenings, and of the cold, but this bitter chill frightened her.

Then he was there, among them, striding through Gwendoline's front door and down the hall with the firm sounds of his arrival breaking the thin sheet of quiet. Averill marched into her kitchen and tossed his fine dark coat carelessly on the back of her stuffy cream sofa, acting like he was just another of her brunch guests and not the villain they expected him to be. He faced them at last, leaning a shoulder carelessly against one of the ice covered walls with an amused curl of his lips decorating his face.

Gwendoline couldn't do much, could scarcely move a muscle, but the one thing she found she could do was speak.

"What the fuck, Averill?" The irreverent words shot from her lips, tasting of boldness she didn't quite feel, and Averill's baleful attention focused on her.

His smile grew to show all of his teeth.

10

Before

The blood filling her mouth tasted more of salt than anything else, and the iron tang didn't bother her as much as she remembered. Nevertheless disgusted, Glenna spat the gobbet out onto her once immaculate carpet and clambered to her feet, muscles feebly protesting. In her hand, she clutched the charred remains of what had once been the poor maid's heart, the fibers crumbling to ash in her fingers.

Who knew the only thing that would make her stop would be blasting her heart into oblivion?

Below her, the smoking corpse of the girl smoldered in silence, finally at peace. At least, Glenna hoped she was at peace. How someone so plain and human at the core could be changed into such a mindless, violent beast was beyond her, but at least her soul probably hadn't been damaged.

A strange, shrill sound ricocheted through her bedroom, and a flash of annoyance heated her through, even though her extremities refused any warmth. She at last concluded with a detached clarity that the unbearable screeching echoing in her ears was coming from her only when her chamber doors flew open to admit a bustle of people. As if ashamed by the arrival of guests, her throat closed to choke off the incessant outcry.

Glenna, who had had her back to the door, turned to face the group, composed mainly of servants and a few guards. Deep in her frozen chest, a twinge of surprise stirred at the sight of Niles heading the assembly, a rash of wildness in his pitch black eyes. They'd all raced to the source of the screaming, and it showed by their ruddy cheeks and puffing breath.

"Glenna?" Niles asked in a voice so quiet she could barely hear her name on his lips. His hands had been raised, ready to cast a spell that would incapacitate or kill an attacker, but he lowered them to a placating stance as he took a single step towards her. His face held no trace of the disgust he'd displayed earlier when he'd left her bedroom, only concern that would have wounded her had she not been made of stone in this moment.

Cocking her head to the side, she imagined how she looked to him now, coated head to toe specks of someone else's blood and gore. He had seen her bloody before, weary and stained from battle, but nothing to this extent.

I have killed and killed again for Oloetha...yet here I stand, shrieking like a ninny, her thoughts mocked her. Absurdly self-conscious, Glenna dropped the ashen heart on top of the maid and smoothed her hand down her dress. Instead of coming away clean, she smeared ash over the sticky patches on her dress, and her palm came away messier than before.

"It wasn't her fault," Glenna spoke to Niles at last; her voice sounded unfamiliar, like it belonged to someone else. "*He* sent her as a message to Jael." She took care to look at him, look only at his dark eyes and scruffy jaw and the clear-cut line of his nose, but her words felt strangled from her, and her body shook like a fallen leaf blasted by a gale.

"Averill did this," Niles spoke as a confirmation, not a question; he stepped forward again, seeking to calm her. "All right, we're going to take care of this. Are you hurt?" He advanced another stride, all while searching her crimson stained face to gauge any reaction that might be there. She expected more of a response from herself as well, but the only thing she felt was a twitch in her left eye. Nonplussed, she opened her mouth to answer, to say anything that would wipe that painfully concerned look off his face.

Instead of words, silence filled the space, an awful quiet that emphasized the ragged breaths Glenna couldn't contain. She found she could control her body enough to still her shudders, but there were no words to describe the horror of what she'd experienced.

That poor girl...

And Niles kept coming closer, reaching towards her to perhaps take her arms or embrace her. The idea of him touching her when she was like this, bloody and somehow unclean, made her shrink back, wincing again at the tension in her muscles. The trembling threatened to begin again, but she quelled it. A veil fell over Niles's eyes, and he paused in front of her.

"Go tell Leland what happened. I'll tell Jael as soon...as soon as I freshen up," Glenna said, unaware of how bizarre her hoarsely-spoken, duly polite speech sounded.

To add to the absurdity, she collapsed to the floor beside the maid's corpse as her legs refused to support her weight any longer.

The bandage wrapped around her forearm felt too tight against Glenna's tender skin, as she'd known it would. Leland, usually so talented with healing wounds of all shapes and sizes, had found that this particular slice in her flesh refused to fully heal in spite of his magic.

"Let's hope this is just a slow healing injury, and not one that won't heal at all," Leland broke the pattern of the gentle hum he'd been coaxing deep from his own throat to voice his thoughts. "There are other spells and methods I can try, but those are a little more time-consuming, so it'll have to wait."

"Of course," Glenna demurred, her teeth gritting together as his wide hands smoothed the gauzy dressing over the wound once more. Already, the material had absorbed the thinnest line of scarlet, proof that her blood would seep through the enchanted stitches until who knows when.

Perfect, she growled internally. Days had passed since the maid had been cursed and died so terribly in her room—a room which she had yet to return to even once—and more "messages" had been sent crawling and groaning into the castle in search of Jael and her closest allies. So far no one but those stricken by the curse had died, and as far as they knew the blight had not spread farther than the nearest few towns. But the numbers sent to the palace had steadily increased as time passed. The servants, and eventually the royalty, had taken to calling the cursed ones the Rotten due to the reek of decaying flesh that forewarned their approach.

Unable to contain her irritation, Glenna shook away Leland's ministrations and rose from the ornate chair Jael had insisted on shoving into Leland's chambers. His room had few windows, especially compared to the wide expanse of glass Glenna had designed for her own quarters, but they let enough light in for her to see what lay about the room. Various garments cast onto the floor in any direction, dust covered boots discarded haphazardly in front of the doorway, and a bed with sheets so wrinkled it made her wonder if it was ever made up at all. Compared to Jael's rigorous dedication to neatness, this careless disarray suited her much better.

"You must be exhausted," Glenna spoke at last, her own voice hoarse with weariness. "It's not like you to do things halfway."

Leland passed his hand over his face, briefly pressing his knuckles to his eyes to gather his thoughts. "Working with the healers' guild hasn't ever been a task I relish, and given the current crisis, they're less cooperative than normal." He blinked rapidly as moisture flooded his stormy gray eyes after a wide yawn. "I've had to take charge and cast most of the rituals on my own—or teach them the finer points—so my own magic wears thinner by the day. I've had to store power in my sword whenever I have any to spare in case of emergency."

Conversation had never been a skill that came easily to someone as stalwart as Leland or as reclusive as Glenna, and the words faded into silence almost as quickly as they were spoken. Still, the casual rapport they'd built over the years lent itself to companionable quietude, even in the worst of times, and he clearly felt comfortable enough in her presence to let the stillness reign. For once, however, she had more to say.

"Did you ever expect your betrothal season to be this eventful?" Glenna asked, placing her cold fingertips against the even chillier glass. Even the weather, unseasonably fair for midsummer, had turned as if cursed with a similar affliction as the Rotten. Behind her, she heard the distinct sound of Leland beginning to channel magic into his sword with low, gentle murmurs of words no other would be able to decipher. She wondered if he'd heard her, or perhaps chosen not to reply, but eventually he paused his channeling to speak.

"I expected life as a royal consort to be a challenge. Jael is not without enemies, but those are battles I can fight and win for her easily. I've fought for her before; I killed the usurper along with anyone else against our cause. We were to look to the future together, win wars together, have a family together. This particular fight against a being who is nothing like anything I've encountered before was not something I ever expected...especially because she concealed Averill's existence from me," Leland said.

Glenna wasn't observing him, but somehow she sensed the frustration causing him to tighten his grip on his gently glowing sword. This frustrated feeling she shared. True, Jael had had no way of knowing for sure if Averill would show up in her life again to demand she kneel before him, but she'd known of him and of a promise—a threat—he'd made. If the memory was too painful to share with her closest friends, Leland at least should have been told. If Averill had come to her at her coronation, she should have communicated his intentions, ready as she was to dismiss it all as a bad dream.

We could have been preparing for a tangible danger all this time, researching and readying ourselves to protect Jael and the queendom, Glenna mused with no small glut of bitterness. *How selfish of her to hold her silence this long.*

When it came to Jael, Glenna was aware of how ungenerous she could be when it came to inspecting her flaws, but she felt justified in this case.

"I understand why she didn't, or couldn't tell me, and it's not information I would have pressed her for unless I needed to know," Leland continued, oblivious to Glenna's toxic thoughts. "All that to say, as far as what's supposed to be a charmed time in my life turning out to be fraught with more difficulty than either of us could have anticipated? Well...we're hopeful. We're together, betrothed regardless of Averill, and this doesn't have to be the end."

She turned her head to the side, away from the window so she could casually gauge his expression. He'd looked up from his sword, which no longer gleamed from the magical energy he'd siphoned into it, and in spite of the fatigue darkening his laugh lines and the corners of his eyes, she felt rather than saw the depth of the hope he believed in for his and Jael's future.

In the light of something so genuine, bright enough to make her think a halo of sunlight should be bursting through the small window to make the gold in Leland's red hair glow, she felt that old pain pluck her heartstrings again. When had she stopped trying to be the better person by distracting herself from her undying love for another woman's betrothed? Glenna didn't know.

I almost died, and died alone. The recollection of charring that poor maid's corpse into ash made her shudder, and at the same time inexplicably want to press her lips to Leland's. What would he do if she finally gave in to that impulse?

Hesitant, yet exhilarated with the possibility, she left her position at the window and approached Leland. He gazed up at her with that steady, resolute quality she'd always admired about him. She didn't only want to kiss his lips, she wanted to taste the line of his jaw and nip at his skin, and more than she dared allow herself to think. If she let him see her heart, would he embrace it? Might he feel this link as well?

No, she told herself; staring directly into his unguarded eyes revealed only his trust in her as his friend, nothing more. *No, he doesn't. And it's time to go back to pretending you don't either.*

Then, as if to punish herself for wanting Leland to the point of betraying Jael and all her friends, she reached out and laid her hand on his sword. It took her only a few seconds to siphon every spare vestige of magic within herself into his sword.

"Glenna—" Leland began.

She didn't want to hear it, his insistence that she should take care of herself and not worry about him, or his gratitude for sharing this piece of herself with him. She wanted to feel the weariness that came with her magic being almost completely spent, at least for the next couple of hours. So, she shook her head wearily and held her index finger over his lips, hovering without making contact. When she took her hand away from his sword, a few golden sparks jumped from the metal and landed harmlessly on her skin, heating it briefly.

"Leland, here you are. I've been—" Niles entered the room, striding in briskly as he adjusted the fit of the worn leather gloves on his hands. He'd spoken with the casual bearing of someone who held no formalities with the space of his best friend, but all his relaxation seeped from his features the moment he saw Glenna. More specifically, saw her standing so close to Leland that they were all but touching. His expression had been serious before, but somehow without shifting a hair his whole form went on guard.

"Glenna, its good you're here. Jael has summoned us to the assembly chambers to discuss the Rotten, and I think she'll want you there as well. You two being such close friends and all." He tossed the words at her carelessly, like they wouldn't sting once they hit their mark. She wished she had a snappy retort, or something that would assuage his anger at her, but even if she'd had the words, she would have kept them to herself.

He has every right to feel ill used. And, knowing what he does, he has every right to want me away from Leland. So she pursed her lips and said nothing.

"Niles! Were you in a brawl?" Leland, oblivious as always to the tension in the room, stood and sheathed his now fully charged sword. Belatedly, Glenna noticed the dark, sludge-like blood that clung to Niles's boots, waistcoat, and gloves.

"A large group of the accursed ventured a little too close to the castle, so Abelard and I cleaned them out," Niles explained.

"You didn't send for me? I could have helped...not that there's much sport in executing a mindless horde of undead," Leland seemed indignant, but relatively unperturbed compared to how anxious he had seemed when in Glenna's company alone. His bravado struck her as odd, but again she held her tongue.

Niles, too, seemed to share her empathy for Leland; it must have been the exhaustion visibly lining his features. "Exterminations of this nature aren't difficult for me, Leland. The healers may not be able to function without you, but the other knights and I do fairly well."

"Still, warn me next time you plan to go out," Leland insisted, standing and rolling his neck over his shoulders to loosen his muscles.

"It helps that the speed of this strange blight is slowed by how long it takes the creatures to crawl to our doors."

"Slow or not, they keep coming, and Jael has finally come to her senses about confronting this head on," Niles snapped, uncharacteristically irritable. "Sorry, Leland, but she's taken her sweet time waiting for this to resolve itself instead of dealing with it as a sovereign should."

"She's scared, and rightly so," Glenna surprised herself by speaking up on Jael's behalf; woman to woman, she understood the princess's fear. "Averill doesn't only want her crown."

"She will have to challenge him nonetheless, before all this has a chance of ending. I'm looking forward to dancing at your wedding, after all," Niles softened his harsh assessment of the situation at the end, smiling slightly as he referenced an event sure to cheer Leland. No one dared voice the thought that, when all was said and done, there might not be a wedding, let alone anything worth celebrating.

"Well, we shouldn't keep Jael waiting," Leland broke the brooding atmosphere with an awkward interjection. "You should clean up first, Niles. She won't want to see anything resembling gore."

"Right," Niles agreed; with a shrug of his shoulders, a barely perceptible wave of magic shone around him until he looked freshly washed without a trace of blood on him. Leland nodded a bland approval before clapping his friend on the shoulder and making his way out of the room.

Glenna watched him depart, dreading the vacuum of stillness he'd leave behind. Seeking escape, or anything to avoid the awkwardness between her and Niles, she held her head high and moved to follow Leland.

*Please don't stop me...*she thought. I *can bear much besides your* *judgment right now.*

She almost made it to the door without hearing his footsteps following her, but then she felt his firm grip on her arm. For a second she imagined he would pull her close to him, back into the safety of his chest, but when he didn't she held her breath and faced him with her expression as blank as she could manage.

"I know you've been through quite a few trials, but you need to stop and think before you keep on this path," Niles began, his tone earnest. "As...overwhelming as the tide of your feelings must be, the time has passed for you to move in on Leland."

"I'm aware," Glenna held her stance as still as she would be if she were standing by Jael's side in a court ritual.

"He's with Jael. He's *betrothed* to Jael," Niles said. She steeled herself against the dull throb of pain that thumped near her heart.

"You don't need to remind me, Niles," she said, trying to slip her arm out of his grasp. It tightened, not enough to hurt her but enough so that she couldn't get away.

"Don't I? Sometimes it seems like you've forgotten." He didn't have to specify how she might have forgotten, since she felt shamed nonetheless.

"I don't see how this would be any business of yours, since you and I apparently have no relationship to speak of," Glenna stepped back; it was a small step, but the movement persuaded Niles to release her, albeit slowly.

"Have we not?" he asked. She dared direct her gaze into his instead of his lips—lips that looked chapped but soft, lips that had claimed hers so very long ago— and couldn't feel surprise over what she saw there. Open, magnetic Niles hadn't had the practice in hiding his true heart that she had, and his feelings for her shone forth transparently. But instead of comforting her, looking through the unguarded windows of his soul made her wish to collapse in an ungainly heap of shame.

Wouldn't it be easier to let this happen? Wouldn't it be easier to just be loved? Her thoughts scrambled for a resolution that wouldn't slam the door shut on Niles's heart.

Glenna hadn't answered, and her failure to reply communicated more than she'd intended. Niles withdrew at last, coldness filling his bearing similar to how he'd left her the morning after the night of passion she still couldn't forget.

"Regardless," he began again. "I have a relationship with Leland and Jael as my friends, and I greatly wish for their happiness. I...you know, maybe it isn't my place, feeling as I do, but I don't see a way down this road you want to take that would end happily for anyone." There it was, the damnable pity echoing in the background of his words. Glenna clutched the folds of her dress in her hands, heat emanating from her palms like a blush on her cheeks.

"There is no road. There is no other path anyone is taking," Glenna said, clipping her words like she was pruning thorns from a rose. "Leland and Jael are betrothed. That is the end."

Somehow she hurt physically, like actual thorns had pierced her skin. Damn Niles for interfering. Damn him for making her speak the one fact that made every other terrible thing in the world almost unbearable. Her eyes threatened to fill, traitorous tears betraying her unrest, but she quelled them with a simple cast of her magic. She hated using this spell because it dried her eyes out too much for several minutes, but rather that than let him see her tears again. Ever again.

Niles opened his mouth to speak, then slowly closed it, at a loss for words. Glenna wondered how long it had been since they had found tranquility in each others' company. How long since he'd developed feelings for her? Months? Years? Maybe she'd never know.

"Glenna, for your sake I almost wish things were different—"

"Do you?" She scoffed at him, her façade of ice threatening to crack. "That wouldn't serve your purposes very well if Leland miraculously realized how I felt and left Jael."

Niles studied her. "My purposes? What 'purposes' do you think I have?" Glenna shook her head, backing away from him.

"I'd like you much better if you kept out of my business and tried to go back to being my friend instead of my keeper."

"That's what you think I'm doing? Following you around and harassing you for fun?" Niles's anger began to show as he paced to the side, his voice rising. "Do you think I find pleasure in your misery? That I've enjoyed watching you want him for as long as I have?"

"How should I know?" Glenna snapped. "And you've been gone for months, so it can't have been too much of a trial for you."

"I left because of *you,*" Niles said, speaking like she'd torn this confession out of him by force. "Why do you think I signed up to leave for months on end of isolated travel trying to reason with stubborn diplomats? I couldn't stand it anymore."

"Stand what? The pressure of having to make sure I keep my mouth shut about how I feel?" She felt it almost physically, the tension in the air making her skin feel tight and prickly.

"Why am I the villain in your story? Why do you assume the worst of me?" He ceased pacing, pausing in front of her as he spoke. "If you must know, the pressure was on *me* to keep my mouth shut regarding my feelings for you. I doubted you'd welcome any confession from me...perhaps especially from me."

"You never actually confessed anything to me. You just told me you wanted to be an option."

Now you're playing stupid on purpose, Glenna chided herself for how low she'd sunk, but her flustered mind refused to acknowledge her pettiness.

"And you don't know what that means? Still?" Niles shook his head incredulously, turning away from her as he ran a hand through his hair; after a moment, he released a pent up breath and continued. "Is it fair to make me say it when you and I both know you won't say it back?"

"Can't," Glenna corrected him, her words falling softly. "Not won't. It would be...well, it would be better for everyone if I could, I know that."

Why can't you? She demanded of herself, dissatisfaction rising within her yet again. *He is honorable, charismatic, and strong...you can't deny the attraction you feel, so what else is needed? What else is there?* But she knew, down to the aching heart lying in patched together tatters, seams threatening to burst, that the "what else" she was looking for couldn't be satisfied by the man before her.

Niles turned back to her, perhaps waiting for her to say more. When the silence stretched on, a dry laugh burst from his lips. "See, this is all incredibly funny...I mean, I knew this is where things would go the minute I realized you loved Leland. But still, when I came back because I had to for the ceremony and saw you hurting, saw you in that dress with the roses in your hair...I don't know. I don't know what I thought."

"You are a hopeful person, Niles," Glenna sought to comfort him. "I have always admired your optimism." She caught her mistake when he turned on her, though his smile savored of bitterness more than anger.

"Your admiration is the greatest solace I could've asked for." Taken aback, Glenna crossed her arms over her chest defensively.

"Admiration for your character is all I can give you right now, which I believe I have made clear before this. I'm deeply sorry if I've hurt you by...allowing you to be intimate with me, but are you truly arrogant enough to assume one night with me entitles you to my heart and that I therefore *owe* you my love?" How easy it was, to make him the target of the dark feelings swirling within her.

"You owe no one your love, least of all me if that is your choice," Niles gathered his dignity about him simply by rising to his full height and studying her with those hot, dark eyes. "But why throw your heart away on someone who is so wholly dedicated to another? Wouldn't you agree that life is too short to waste on pining for a lost dream?"

Approaching her again, he paused before her and took both of her cold hands in his, holding them lightly. Her chill, magically enhanced by her sadness, lessened as a faint warmth licked over her skin and made her hair stand on end. Unexpectedly, the wound she had received from the Rotten tingled, almost like it was healing at last.

Choose me. I think we could be worth the risk. The brush of Niles's thoughts meeting her own, knocking at her mind seeking entry made her lean into him. Not only were they the only two people in the room, but for a moment Glenna felt like the universe contained just their two souls, shining bright as they briefly connected. A hint of wonder flickered in his eyes as well, the bright fire colors burning so intensely she wondered if he could feel the heat physically.

Then she recoiled, not so much from his touch or the ensuing sensations, but more from seeing an opening to wound his spirit deeply enough to push him away from her for good. If she spoke, that would be the end. His pride would not allow him to return to her again.

Say it, she told herself firmly, blinking to dispel tears she had already enchanted away. *He deserves someone who can care for him wholeheartedly. Not you.*

"I'm *your* lost dream, Niles. I am who I am, and I can't make my heart obey my will. If I can't have Leland, that will have to be my reality...but it can't be you. It'll just be me. As far as I know, that's all there ever will be," she said.

Her words struck true. He drew back into himself, mental walls of stone slamming down around his thoughts to keep her out. The loss of contact, however feather-light it had been, made goosebumps rise all along her skin as if someone had let in a draft of winter air.

"As you wish," he said, releasing her hands with such casual ease a stranger might never have known what had transpired between them. The heat in his eyes had died as she'd dashed his hopes well and truly to pieces, but even he could not control the gentle focus that rooted her in place from its strength.

True to form, he acted the ideal gentleman as he inclined his upper body in a slight bow to her. "I will not trouble you with this matter again." Glenna wanted to say something else, whatever words would have the power to remove the pain or even undo what harm she had just caused him, but he took his leave of her before she could come up with anything worthwhile to say.

"Thank you," she whispered to no one as she stood alone in the gloom.

"I thought this council was supposed to be just the four of us," Leland grumbled to Glenna, his expression stoic and stern in case any of the generals or captains bothered to look in their direction. "War is supposed to be exciting and terrifying, not a group of old men and royals shut up in a room for hours listening to statistical drivel."

"This is where most of wars take place, actually: rooms full of the nobility planning and bickering with their leaders. You should know that by now, Leland," Glenna sighed, equally bored. True, she reveled in the boredom because numbing her mind helped her avoid actively thinking about her problems, but listening to the bare bones like casualty statistics and pointless strategy arguments for hours would bore even her to tears.

"Jael will officially be queen, and you her king, once you marry and bear children. It is to be expected she behave like one on occasion, especially dire circumstances like this where the realm might actually perish," she explained, tapping her fingers on the cover of the book on her lap in a random pattern.

Bored and at the same time restless, Glenna flipped through the empty pages of her temperamental spell book. She had tried to recall more of the information Fate had shown her in red ink before the cursed maid had attacked her, but to no avail. Indeed, the pages had remained resolutely blank for days now, abandoning her to her own pitiable lack of knowledge.

I know you know something, she directed her thoughts to the book as she placed her hand palm down on the cover. *I know something we need to bring Jael and Oloetha through this intact is in there. Tell me!*

She had almost expected her fervent entreaty to the silent object to pay off, but the pages remained stubbornly blank as she flipped through her book. If she could, she would have snarled in frustration, but she doubted anyone else in the council would appreciate her outburst. As it was, she grunted angrily and cursed under her breath, suggesting the tome in her hands do something to itself it couldn't possibly accomplish.

"What exactly are you up to?" Leland inclined his head subtly in her direction, peering down curiously at the book as a lock of hair flopped onto his forehead. Glenna stared at him for a moment, struggling to make her reply sound more coherent than she actually felt. *Should I tell him about what the book showed me before? Should I lie?*

"I've left my book in the royal library for weeks at a time to help it absorb information from the environment. I was hoping it could tell me something about our predicament, something that might help us remove Averill, or at least end this blight of the Rotten," she ended up saying.

Leland sat up in his chair, proving his restless lounging wasn't a pose he regularly took. "It can do that?"

Glenna nodded. "I'm hoping so. Actually...I know it can. If I can persuade it to share its secrets again, I might be able to piece together a solution before—"

Perhaps something had been listening within the pages, or something had been triggered by Leland reaching out to touch the smooth leather cover, but the magical zing that raced through the volume was unmistakable. Muttering her thanks under her breath, she eagerly dove into the book, flipping through the pages in search of that same archaic script she had seen before. Thankfully, the same passage detailing how Fate had arranged the world long ago and the relationship between a Lord and a current ruler appeared, and an extra paragraph or two showed up beneath the original text.

Wild magic flows through the Land still, contained by Fate's will and the power of her Lords. To end the existence of a Lord is to fight against Destiny, but should a Lord abandon his throne in name or deed, a ruler or a champion may challenge that Lord to single combat.
If Fate supports the contest, if the Heart, Spirit, and Soul are true, a champion may defeat a Lord.
Mark you well: if the ties to Fate are not in place, a Lord will not bow to the will of a lesser ruler standing alone.

Single combat? To the death? Glenna's grip on either side of the book tightened as she stared unseeingly at the fine, elegant letters decorating the pages. She imagined Leland, massive, broad-shouldered, the unceasingly brave and undisputed champion of the realm, stepping into a square to fight against a being like Averill.

No, she thought, imagining those coldest of blue eyes boring through her to the bone. *He will not do this. I must find another way.* Her gaze refocused onto the words once more, seeking to remind her of the fact that there was no other way, but she slammed the book closed in rebellion.

The slam echoed in the drafty council hall, and several aged heads with serious faces turned in her direction. Well used to disapproval from a court who thought a steward's only child had no place taking the position of court sorceress from other noble daughters, Glenna met their stares with a studiously haughty expression. Beside her, she sensed Leland stiffen into a soldier's posture under their scrutiny.

Abruptly, he stood, towering over the rest of the members of the council even more so than when he had been seated. Jael, who had been instructing the minister of agriculture to begin storing as much food as he could for refugees of overtaken villages, stopped speaking and arched her brow at her betrothed in surprise.

"Everyone out, except for Princess Jael, Lord Niles, and Lady Glenna," he commanded in a tone that would brook no arguments; when a few of the older ministers at the long table looked like they wanted to grumble, one look from the tall knight silenced them. After a moment, the room was empty except for the four of them.

"Where is Abelard? He should hear this," Leland asked, somehow more at ease now that only his close friends were present.

"Leland, there's nothing to hear—" Glenna tried to stop him, her heart still pumping furiously at the idea of the combat he would undoubtedly bring to Jael's and Niles's attention. Niles, who had previously avoided noticing her at all, studied her with a sharp attention that made her feel exposed.

"I asked him to supervise the security of our walls while we were all enclosed here," Jael explained; behind her, her familiar curled up in the plush chair her mistress had just stood from. "Leland, I don't appreciate you dismissing my council while we're working to bring this terrible situation to heel."

"You'll appreciate it much more when I tell you what Glenna just discovered," he replied. "I've always known her book helped her know things other people didn't—or couldn't—but it just handed us a possible key to victory." Jael's face lit up with hope, though from her ensuing frown Glenna deduced that she didn't want to risk hoping for a positive outcome.

"Glenna?" Jael turned to her where she had remained seated in her simple chair. She wished she had the power to deny she'd discovered anything useful, but there wouldn't be a point: Leland had read over her shoulder and seen the same words already.

"If...If Averill is as you have said, there is only one way to defeat him without unleashing the wild magic on our land again," she spoke haltingly, looking down at the spiraling grains in the wood of the table so wisps of her braided hair fell over her face. "Single combat to the death of you yourself or a champion you appoint. If the cause is just, the Lord of the land can be defeated."

"Aren't there other factors? Is it that simple?" Niles asked her. His questions and his bearing hadn't altered, nor had he moved an eyelash, but the tension in his words didn't surprise Glenna at all.

"The ties of Fate are mentioned, so I'm pretty sure it has to be one of the knights or Jael herself. If I can defeat him—" Leland's eyes shone with a feverish light, fairly glowing with the building enthusiasm of a warrior born for combat.

"You? Why should it have to be you?" Jael interrupted, scoffing at his zeal as she crossed her arms over her ample chest. "It might as well be me, since I am the one he has come to challenge."

"You?" It was Leland's turn to scoff. "You are princess. You will not fight."

Glenna stared between the two of them, her customary silence weighing on her more than it normally did. Their devotion to each other was evident in their stubbornness that neither of them should enter the yawning maw of danger. It was of no comfort to her that she didn't wish for either Jael or Leland to fight.

Who should sacrifice themselves, my sometimes best friend or the love of my life?

"I am the only one who can fight him, Jael. My knights represent our ties to her, and I am the head of our knights, since I was the first to show my gift from Fate," Leland said. His tone was gentle, and he approached Jael so he could tenderly take her hands in his own. "I will save us, Jael."

"No," she insisted again, still stubborn even as her voice cracked. She tried to pull her hands away, but he clutched them tighter.

"Who should I send in my place, my love? Niles? He is an assassin, a knife in the dark and a diplomat, not your standard warrior. Or perhaps our youngest knight, Abelard? Shall I take advantage of his hero worship and send him to a contest he will definitely fail? At least I have good odds to win," he tried to reason with her, his tone that of a companion even as he spoke of death and ruin. Jael wilted slightly under his tender reproof.

"May I see the book?" Niles interjected himself into their moment, his words business-like; Leland's assessment of his skills didn't appear to offend him. He motioned for Glenna to pass him her casting book, barely glancing her way as he did so. Clutching the volume in her arms defensively, she considered withholding it just to be petty. Instead, she set the book on the table and slid it across the smooth surface to reach him.

Silence hovered uncomfortably in the room as Niles flipped through the blank, worn pages until he came across the passage in question. Jael moved to peer over his shoulder, looking to read the archaic script for herself, and Leland stood in ponderous determination that all but declared his determination to fight Averill himself. Glenna remained where she was, stock still as she analyzed Niles's reaction. Instead of surprise or concern, she saw his face harden as his jaw clenched.

"Did you know this?" she asked him softly, wondering at his silence as he contemplated the text. He didn't lift his eyes from the page as he replied.

"Not for sure, no. I came across a passage alluding to this in a few of the histories recently, but it wasn't as clear as this," he said, then snorted. "Of course, the writers made it their business to be as vague as possible when recording anything that might actually be useful in the future, so that's not saying much."

"Why didn't you say anything?" Glenna asked, though she suspected his answer. *Look at me, please,* her thoughts begged Niles, but of course he couldn't hear her.

"We have no certainty that Averill will even consent to the fight," he finally said after a long pause. "I was hoping to come across another solution, or at least a hint of one, by now. I planned to keep this to myself until I was sure there was no other way." Their eyes met, just for a moment, and in those amber depths Glenna saw—or rather felt—an echo of her own guilt. Leland may be his rival for my heart, but he's also the best friend Niles has ever known.

Jael huffed, her frustration evident as she shook Leland off and began to pace back and forth. "It doesn't matter who read what text where! Leland will not take this fight...in fact, no one will if I have anything to say about it. Single combat is ridiculous, and dangerous, and—" she paused, running out of breath. Leland took the opportunity to interrupt.

"All this discussion is pointless! This is the only way. I can no longer sit back and watch your people—our people, Jael—suffer under this curse." Losing patience with Jael's protective behavior, Leland's voice rose. Uncomfortable with the confrontation, Glenna wished to intervene—though she found herself more inclined to Jael's point of view—but she felt a strange sensation dulling his words into silence.

Red pulsed dully at the edges of her vision, in time with her heartbeat, and an odd, tuneless strain of music weaved in and out of her perception. Was it just her, or was a curtain of fog sweeping through the room, teasing the white-streaked tendrils of her hair like she was underwater? Dazed, Glenna flinched as something warm dripped onto her face.

Without knowing how she knew it, she knew the liquid was fresh blood.

Dread filled her as she slowly lifted her eyes to the vaulted ceiling of the council room, expecting to see the worst. Dimly, she sensed Leland, Jael, and Niles watching her as this eerie phenomenon took place, but she couldn't speak either to ask for help or reassure them of her safety. Then the fog descended, obscuring her vision so she couldn't find the source of the blood, and she began speaking words that were not her own.

"When sacrifice is required at the moment of lost hope, one must answer the call of Fate. Summon the strength to break thy Heart, bind thy Spirit, and rend thine Soul to preserve hope for the future." Glenna gasped, choking as her breath rasped in and out of her too quickly; these were not her words, Fate was here, somehow speaking through her, and the invasion pained her to the point of agony. *"To split one's Soul is no simple feat, nor a painless one. But to suffer defeat, to face annihilation, is worse. What is writ must be obeyed...even if the ties and thy Soul be at stake."*

She choked again, a croaky scream tearing from her as the foggy presence began to lift. All she could see was the fog, and the red, the inexplicable blood raining down on her pale face...and behind it all, a flash of gold that could have reflected from either twisting scales or inhuman irises.

She felt someone catch her as she crumpled to the ground. Was it Niles or Leland? It did not feel like a man: the arms were too delicate and the hands too small and soft aside from the light archer's calluses. She caught a whiff of geranium and felt silk somewhere near her face...Jael, then. Almost giddy, she laughed weakly.

"How are you holding me up? You can barely carry your fox up the stairs if she's wriggling," Glenna remarked, not realizing she was trembling from head to toe; it took much of her remaining strength to open her eyes and look around. Concern crumpled the symmetrical lines of Jael's face, but her emerald eyes brightened as Glenna laughed.

"I'm not holding you up, silly, I just kept you from cracking your head against the floor," she said, smoothing the hair away from Glenna's face completely heedless of the blood making it stick to her skin. A few tears, salty yet pure, fell onto the strands from Jael's eyes. They didn't make a difference to the crimson mess, but Glenna's heart softened painfully with affection for her sweet friend.

"Is she all right?" Leland's voice broke into her awareness, too loud in the echoing silence of the room; Niles had knelt beside Jael, who lifted her head to stare at her betrothed reproachfully.

Then, something near the doorway of the big room distracted her; her royal mask of indifference fell into place with record speed. Irrationally annoyed she'd been forgotten, Glenna struggled to sit up to see what she was looking at, but Niles's hands came from nowhere and eased her back onto the cushion of Jael's lap.

"Princess! Are you all right?" Glenna recognized the voice of one of the castle messengers, though she couldn't see his face. She did see Jael nod, then lift one of her perfect eyebrows at him as in indication for him to state his business. The breathless lad took a moment to compose himself before he spoke again, words that sent goosebumps racing down Glenna's skin.

"A procession marches on the castle, my lady! Our scouts say there's at least ten score of the Rotten out there...

11

"You are looking so much better than the last time I saw you," Averill intimated casually, as if he and Gwendoline had run into each other after a class they shared.

"Really? I can't remember seeing you, so you must be a pretty forgettable guy," Gwendoline struggled against the invisible atmospheric soup that kept her frozen in place, but to no avail.

She'd also lied through her teeth: this Averill looked anything but forgettable. Taller than most, hulking and bigger than Colt while somehow maintaining a savage, rapier-like grace that would have had most women swooning, this man would capture full attention in any room he entered. Coupled with the crisp, silvered hair cut and styled to perfection and the animalistic blue eyes, his presence struck her like a physical blow.

"Glenna was a frigid bitch, but you? You seem to be more human," he studied her as he stepped forward. Treating her as he would a slave he was inspecting before purchasing, he gripped her jaw in his hand and turned her face from side to side. His hands felt surprisingly normal, but the sting of power she couldn't identify or comprehend fully made her grit her teeth.

"Remarkable. But then, reincarnations have always been interesting to me," he spoke conversationally, his gaze boring into her like he would strip the skin from her body and leave her innards exposed to the elements.

Then, just as fast, he lost interest in her and moved forward to her friends. Gwendoline dreaded the moment he would focus on Niles, specifically because she could see how hard he was fighting this in his face. True, Niles kept his expression tightly reined into indifference, but his eyes burned hot, fire mixing with the black of the abyss, the hatred reflected there somehow thrilling her to the core.

But Averill didn't pay any heed to the struggling Niles; once his focus locked onto Everleigh, even Gwendoline knew that he would not be distracted.

"Ah. I expected you to be similar, Everleigh...but I never expected you to be so beautiful," he began, taking one of her delicate hands in his and bringing it to his lips for a kiss. Gwendoline would have laughed at such a cheesy display, but nothing about this moment, about the hunger in those captivating eyes, merited amusement. Everleigh herself furrowed her brow and bit her lip to hold her silence as he touched her.

"Similar? To who?" Gwendoline asked, her words slow, spoken as they were through a thick veil of enchantment. Averill dashed her hopes by not turning to her.

"Jael herself was a beauty, as are you, though she resembled a golden sunrise rather than the serene beauty of autumn. But how you could have grown into this goddess, this woman truly worthy of being a queen, astounds me," he continued speaking to Everleigh as he rose to his full and considerable height. Before him, Everleigh appeared unmoving, as if she was only a wax figure.

"From what I understand, beautiful or not, Jael hadn't wanted anything to do with you, and I know for a fact Everleigh would rather you fuck right off...so why bother sticking around? Desperate men aren't attractive." Sounding braver than she felt, Gwendoline covered her fear with the bravado that usually saved her from dates gone bad and other dangers.

"Y-Yeah," Everleigh struggled to speak, the single word escaping her with a following gasp of air. "F-Fuck off, you creepy—"

"Save your ire for those undeserving of magic. Such profane words are unbecoming from the mouth of royalty," Averill touched his fingertips to Everleigh's full lips, casting further magic that choked off whatever else she might have said to him. "Besides, you don't really feel antagonistic towards me, not yet. I sense your fear, yes, but why should you hate me? You're not the same person Jael was, and her misguided grievances are not yours."

Gwendoline felt stirrings of revulsion in her gut as he noticed a smudge of frosting from Everleigh's lips on his finger and, without breaking eye contact with her, brought that same finger to his mouth and licked away the stain. Everleigh whimpered, almost too quietly to hear, her eyes wide and white like those of a preyed upon rabbit.

"Back. Off." Colt's voice rang out clear in spite of his magical imprisonment, and somehow he'd managed to take a step towards Averill and Everleigh. Gwendoline had never seen him this angry, since she'd only known Colt as a gentle giant who she was lucky enough to be friends with, and the murderous intent in his tense posture filled her with fear.

This is real. Somehow, this is real. Her mind swam with the dizzying realization.

Averill, imperious and unmoved, didn't seem to be bothered by Colt's microscopic advancement. His aristocratic lips, almost unnaturally perfect, quirked up in the type of smile that forewarned sardonic laughter.

"The almost prince? Well, what you can't remember won't hurt you. Life would be so much less difficult for us all if you would accept what's to come. Accept the hand that was dealt before any of you were born...the first time, that is." He looked pointedly between Colt and Gwendoline, a derisive laugh marking his words; she didn't know what he was implying, but when she looked at Colt she sensed a depth to his bewilderment that she couldn't match.

Barely distracted from Everleigh, Averill turned back to her after speaking and cupped her fairy-like face in his hand. Colt groaned, a sound of profound frustration, and Gwendoline glimpsed Niles in her peripheral mouthing words she couldn't make out. *Is he trying to cast something? Will it help?*

"Aren't you supposed to be an immortal, super powerful being? Why do you feel the need to stoop low enough to consort with mortals?" Gwendoline tried to goad him, anything to pull his attention away from her friends.

"Immortality can be a trial, and it is common for my kind, what few of us there may be, to take a companion," Averill turned the most feral eyes she'd ever seen on her, his words conversational even if his dark tone threatened violence. "And what better match for me than the queen of the lands I've watched over for millennia? Who better than a strong ruler like Everleigh, the closest thing to what Jael once was?"

"The thing about finding a companion," Gwendoline began furiously, clenching her trembling hands into fists; it struck her as odd that out of the four of them, she was the only one allowed to speak without a struggle, "is that to find happiness both parties need to consent to the relationship."

He did laugh this time, releasing his tender, possessive hold on a petrified Everleigh as he approached Gwendoline.

"That remains to be seen. Regardless, she will consent, in the end, and we all know why. I'm not sure if you all will be around to bear witness, but I will taste her again and we will rule as we are meant to: side by side, with only those worthy of magic's gifts underneath our rule," he said. Another snake of fear slithered over her skin as she heard the conviction in his voice, calm but certain.

"But you, Gwendoline. How would you taste? I could taste Glenna's misery in the air the few times our paths crossed...her blood would have been bitter, acrid to the point of disgust. But you? You have been happier in this life...less regret, less restraint. Would that make you taste sweeter, I wonder?"

Terror pricked at Gwendoline's skin as he leaned in close to her, or more specifically, to her neck. She sensed rather than saw Niles forcefully push against the magical boundary keeping him and the others in place. Was it in her imagination that the room grew colder as more ice crept along the walls, floors, and now her furniture? Though it was irrelevant, she saw a layer of frost spreading over her kitchen countertop into the tray of once warm cinnamon rolls.

Keep casting, Gwendoline's mentally pleaded with Niles to somehow find a way to force this evil out of her home. Averill, delighting in her discomfort, simply inhaled her scent as he pushed back the soft, dark waves away from her pale neck. She shuddered.

"You played a particularly vital role in delaying the inevitable," he murmured against her skin, his tone the volume of a lover's even if his speech was nothing but menacing. "I shall enjoy taking everything from you, make no mistake."

Within the few seconds it took him to speak, Gwendoline felt frozen anew, stripped of whatever resistance she'd had to the magic taking over her friends and her home. She would have been shivering, had she been allowed to. If she could have, she would have admitted to not having a clue what Averill was talking about.

Somehow, her silence informed him of her lack of knowledge. Averill laughed heartily, his regular volume startling her at such close proximity. His mirth diminished to a dry chuckle as he withdrew from breathing in her scent and stood before them as a victor before the conquered. "How intriguing. Am I the only one who recalls the details of our last encounter?"

Gwendoline risked a glance at Niles, thought it hurt her eyes to move too much. His lips had formed a hard line, and she hoped that meant he was concentrating on his magic instead of responding to the obvious provocation. Since Averill had entered her kitchen, she'd known that her power, strong as she was, was no match for someone like him. His presence instilled a sense of insignificance that nothing could shake. Niles, however...

Gwendoline tried to refrain from questioning her faith in him yet again, but Averill sensed her flickering uncertainty. "It's no wonder you would believe him so quickly, even without proof. Your souls, numerous as some of you may have, cry out to one another. But, Niles, you didn't immediately tell them all that transpired so long ago? Now, that is unexpected."

It was Niles's turn in the hot seat, apparently, since Averill turned to mock him. All at once, a breeze flavoring of heat and the desert filled Gwendoline's house, melting the ice into rivulets of water and thawing the spell holding everyone in place enough for the four friends to collectively breathe freely again. The biting wind whipped through Niles's hair as he squared off with the intruder, all energy spent on shoving Averill's presence elsewhere.

Gwendoline half expected Averill to laugh, pushing back with a display of his own power, but he merely blinked, seeming to wait out the burst of magic Niles had thrown at him. Had he, too, caught a glimpse of the deep darkness twisting impossibly in the blackness of Niles's eyes?

"You could not do that before," he said at last, reluctant curiosity in his voice. "I crawled out of the abyss some time ago, taking my time to prepare for my rise in this time...but I did not sense you in the deep at all. Where have you come by that power?"

Niles did not reply, choosing instead to stare at Averill with an inscrutable expression. Gwendoline could sense that something was terribly, awfully wrong with him, something unrelated to Averill at all. The shadows that always drifted around Niles, just out of reach for her mind's eye, coalesced into a dark entity that appeared to be working of its own accord. She got the feeling that he was not as in control of the situation as he looked.

"So we beat you before? How wonderful." Gwendoline intervened hastily, barely aware of her words in her clumsy attempt to distract Averill. "It didn't really do much to squash that ego of yours, huh?"

She hadn't expected it to, but it worked: Averill finally looked away from Niles and turned his predatory focus on her. Out of the corner of her eye, she saw Everleigh frantically shaking her head, silently pleading for Gwendoline to keep her mouth shut.

"I have returned, since you failed the first time. In fact, I am in line to take the throne already, and taking Everleigh will solidify my claim once word of her bloodline gets out." he spoke softly. "Still, it is interesting that as yet you have no memories of that encounter. Which leads me to wonder about the nature of the fancy little spell regarding your souls. Will your new soul remain yet unscarred until your memories return? Shall I test what it means to have more than one soul?"

Gwendoline felt a spike of fear as Averill reached out to her. For a moment, when it looked like he would take hold of one of her breasts, she flinched at the perversion...but then he kept reaching, and his hand passed *through* her, into her chest.

"Shall we see what would happen if I were to pull one soul out for the world to see?"

"No! Leave her be!" Colt shouted, his voice inordinately loud compared to the whispers of before. Niles had freed him enough to advance towards Averill, though each step he took made him wince, and his hand trembled as he reached for his sword. Gwendoline found she couldn't breathe as her eyes darted between Colt and Niles, who had one hand raised palm up with a growing fireball bathed in the shadows of the void in the center.

"Make me, little boy," Averill laughed at them all, content in his own strength now he had a grip on something within Gwendoline that made her feel horribly in danger and exposed to the world.

"Stop!" Everleigh spoke at last, causing everyone to turn to her in surprise. Briefly, she wilted under the attention, her hazel eyes wide and her skin pale. Smaug, still curled around her hair as a headband, lifted his head and hissed at Averill; this encouraged her enough to straighten her spine and make her stand tall. "I think it'd be a good idea if you just made your demands and gave me time to consider them. Apparently, some of us are far too old to practice these theatrics any longer." In spite of the invasion currently happening to her body, Gwendoline felt the faintest twinge of pride over how regal her best friend sounded.

Averill, too, looked impressed; he stepped back from Gwendoline, pulling his hand away with a gentle tug that nonetheless brought her gasping to her knees with the agony.

"Quite so, I suppose. I will give you the same options I gave Jael." He paused, watching passively as Niles rushed to Gwendoline's side and helped her to her feet.

*Please don't let me puke, oh please...*Gwendoline fought the nausea washing over her, irrationally concerned with the embarrassing outcome.

"Bow to me and accept me as your ruler and companion, privately as well as publicly, and I will spare your friends and your land. Refuse, and I will unleash the magic of the land as I did before and the horrors will resume until you are alone and friendless." Somehow whiter than before, Everleigh pursed her lips and gazed steadily at her opponent.

"I will need time to consider," Everleigh said at last, her fists clenched at her sides. "At least enough time to prepare for the future if I were to accept." Colt moved to go to her, inevitably to protest, but Averill held up a hand, chuckling as he brought him to his knees with a wordless spell.

"You mean you need time to plot your escape," he laughed, the sound warm in spite of his personal chill. "You may have the time, because you and I both know there is no way out for you this time, no delay that will change your destiny. The loophole that worked for you before will not succeed a second time."

At his words, Everleigh's façade of detached courtesy cracked long enough for Gwendoline to see the terror stirring just beneath the surface. Everleigh had no memories, and therefore lacked the inexplicable, ancient sense of dread Gwendoline herself had recently become aware of. But prey knew when a predator stalked them, and there was no mistaking the possessive glint in Averill's eyes.

"You've spoken your threats, now shouldn't you leave?" Niles spoke, twirling the fireball in his hand into a swirling pillar of death. "You are no more interesting now than you were back then." Gwendoline wished he hadn't drawn Averill's attention back on himself, but Niles seemed to be fully in control of his magic.

Averill had gone back to ignoring all else but Everleigh, his gaze fixed on her with the unexpectedly fervent zeal of a religious man; when he spoke, his tone mesmerized them all. "Please consider, Everleigh, what it would mean to be with me. I have been with this world almost since its dawn, and the things I have seen...humans are weak, and the magic resents being bound to this day. We will dispose of those who are unworthy, and rule over the rest as it should have been from the beginning. If the lands were to be ruled by a denizen of the stars, one of Fate's own kind, as well as the offspring of this earth...oh, the things we could do! The power we would wield...and you, you would not be corrupted, I have seen it—"

"Stop," Everleigh whispered, the freckles standing out on her skin as she paled further; her feet had carried her backwards, until she leaned against a chair for support. "Stop, *stop talking*!"

Surprisingly, Averill did; for a long, dragging moment, he scrutinized her in neutral silence. Colt struggled to rise to his feet, his cheeks ruddy from the effort as he fought the magic holding him down.

"But you are weak still, and tied to flawed beings. That would not be the case once you ascended, Princess," he murmured, to himself as much as to her. Then he came back to himself and the familiar push of power reentered the room in force. Gwendoline and the others were suddenly able to rise to their feet and move without the hindrance of binding magic, but no one cast a spell against the Lord of the land.

"I will return for you in one month's time. That should give you enough days to ponder your decision," Averill said, rising to his considerable height as he frowned down at them. "It should also be sufficient time to call off your friends from their predictable scheming. It would be best to prepare them for your absence in the future, as I will be laying the foundation for our joined rulership during the coming weeks."

Gwendoline expected more fanfare or more arguments from Colt and Niles before the threat would leave, but Averill simply turned and walked out. With him all the cold building in the room and the deep sea pressure vanished. The only evidence he'd even been there were the frozen tray of cinnamon rolls and the unease the four of them felt.

They looked around at each other before Colt, who seemed to have borne the brunt of the magical pressure, stumbled over to Everleigh to take her face in his hands, kissing her and murmuring reassurances. She answered, but her wide eyes and flat expression revealed her lingering fear.

Gwendoline, used to comforting her own self, was startled when Niles approached her and put his hands on her shoulders. She looked up at him, shivering in the thin Sunday morning pajamas she'd forgotten she'd been wearing, and was struck by the intensity in his expression. His lips pressed together in a harsh line, and he looked very much like he wanted to be as affectionate with her as Colt was acting with Everleigh, but for some reason he thought it needful to restrain himself.

Instead, he turned Gwendoline's head to the side slightly and scrutinized her neck. "I wondered if he...if he bit you," he said, his voice measured.

"What would happen if he did?" she asked. She wanted to ask him what all that shadow magic had been about, but his tone and the circumstance didn't invite that sort of question right then.

"I'm not sure, but I don't think it would be pleasant," Niles frowned. He withdrew from her with an air of great reluctance. Looking around, Gwendoline saw Colt and Everleigh had emerged from their private cocoon and were watching her and Niles. Something had changed between all of them, perhaps because no one doubted Niles's story any longer. Colt even nodded at the other guy, acknowledging the truth.

His fear for Everleigh must have made all of this very, very real, Gwendoline surmised internally.

Fear was a powerful motivator, she had to admit. Glancing at Niles, then around at everyone who had decided she was the person to look to next, she realized they were waiting for her to speak.

"All right," she exhaled at last, feigning exasperation in spite of how nervous she was. "So we have about a month to put that bastard in the dirt."

12

Before

It took over an hour for the grim procession to circle the castle. Many of the blank, gray-faced individuals came, all unique in their own way: young and old, rich and poor, with a few local nobility mixed in beside the lowest of peasants. The only feature they shared was their ashen skin, curiously vacant eyes, and the jagged red line nearly separating their heads from their necks. The Rotten of previous days had taught Glenna to fear this steady blankness, though she still had done her part in warding them off from the castle. This, however...she knew these folk were not the same, and it took much of her will to remain seated impassively on her horse.

Glenna glanced at the wound the Rotten had left on her body. Except there was nothing but smooth skin on her forearm: the wound that had stubbornly refused to heal or fade had disappeared without a trace after her encounter with Fate in the council room.

The messenger informing them of the macabre march on the castle had arrived at a fortuitous time: no decision had been made regarding whether or not Leland would challenge Averill to the duel. Glenna had hastily cleaned the blood from her skin with a spell and prepared to ride out with Niles and the future sovereigns.

In their quartet, each person had always had a role that suited them like a favorite pair of boots: Jael was the undisputed leader, and Leland could always be counted on for either a sympathetic confidant or a brave defender. Niles was a more complex character, but when it came to their small circle of friendship, Glenna sensed his influence ran much deeper.

And Glenna herself? In this rain, in this crisis threatening the queendom, she felt she was only a shadow. Anything she could do or had done hurt more than it helped, and now she was fading, washing out with the tide. She felt as gray as the people surrounding the castle, growing fainter by the hour. Would it be so bad if she faded for good?

Not yet, Glenna thought, shaking her head side to side in her indigo hood to dispel the ugly, unwanted thoughts. *Not just yet.*

"Are you all right?" A male voice to her left caught her attention, and she glanced over to nod at Abelard. It took effort, but she managed to grant him a smile.

"I'm fine," she told him; he blushed and ducked his head. On another man as big as he was, this bashfulness would have come across as affected, but Abelard had always been shy around women.

"I was asked to keep an eye on you after your...ordeal," he admitted after a few seconds, looking down at her with his cocoa eyes from atop his horse, which was so massive it made Glenna feel like the gray stallion she rode was no taller than Jael's childhood pony.

Who asked? She wondered, trying not to loathe herself for hoping it was Leland. Instead, she nodded at Abelard and turned to look forward again, down the stony path that led up to the castle.

"What the hell is taking so long?" Leland turned his equally massive war horse to face Glenna where she, Abelard, and somewhere behind them Jael waited for Averill to make his inevitable appearance. "We've been out here for almost an hour watching these poor devils surround our home, and the evil bastard hasn't bothered to show up?" In anyone else, this show of impatience would have been bravado to hide a sizeable dose of fear, but Leland usually couldn't wait to get into a fight if he knew it was inevitable.

"Leland, we were never sure he was going to come at all," Glenna reminded him gently, tugging on the reins of her own beast as the creature danced impatiently beneath her. "This could merely be the prelude to an attack, which we're here to quell before they overwhelm the wards."

"He'll be here," Niles's voice carried back to her on the damp breeze; sitting atop his steed beside Leland, he still faced forward, focused on the path ahead. Glenna could only see the back of his upright form, but another twinge of regret troubled her at the sight of his broad shoulders resolutely braced for whatever came next. When was the last time she'd seen him smile, or laugh?

"There!" One of the numerous cavalry men raised himself up in the stirrups and pointed, not down the obvious path, but deep into the forest that stretched over the grounds for miles. A cold wind blowing in from the direction of the forest made all Glenna's hair stand on end.

The group turned, facing the direction their comrade had indicated. At first, Glenna only saw the fog and the dense line of trees, things she'd seen for most of her life. But then a large, white shape appeared behind the tree line, striding imperially towards the castle.

At first it was too far away to see clearly, but as it approached she realized what it was.

The biggest wolf she'd ever seen, larger than any war horse and taller to boot, progressed their way with its crystal blue eyes scanning the assembly as if looking for someone: undoubtedly, the creature was intelligent. The layers of fur were white, white without the blemish of any other color, and the bright contrast made the horizon around the creature drearier somehow. Upon closer inspection, while the horses danced nervously under their riders as the wolf advanced, she glimpsed a jagged pink scar curling the right side of the black lips into a compelling grimace.

"That beast is enormous!" Leland exclaimed partially under his breath, the remark more of an inconvenienced grumble rather than a sign of trepidation.

Once the wolf had stalked only a stone's throw away, Niles addressed the creature. "What brings you here, Averill?"

Impossibly, the wolf paused its pacing and opened a red, red mouth to speak in a voice that was both guttural and refined. "I will not speak with servants. Return here with your mistress or not at all." Glenna resisted the urge to look behind her, since that would betray Jael's location with her attention.

"We are the only ones who will speak with you. You may as well state your business," Leland spoke firmly, resplendent on his battle-trained stallion as the beast stamped his hooves impatiently. The wolf form that Averill had taken laughed, its blanched hackles rising.

"Lady, do you fear me? Come forth, or others will suffer the consequences of your cowardice." Backing up his warning, he growled, the deep resonance louder because of his size. Glenna felt her own hackles rising.

"Is your only skill threatening my people, my Lord?" Jael's voice rang clear from behind the front line of their party as Glenna heard the hoof beats of the golden mare dancing her princess forward. "That seems in poor taste for the man who would be king."

Leland reached for the reigns of Jael's steed as she maneuvered to stand beside and then pass him, but she gave him a look and he let her go. Glenna had the bizarre idea of how brilliantly this scene might translate into a painting: the princess in a white and gold lined cloak, facing off with the beast against the green landscape submerged in the dreary miasma of impending rain.

"And how do you find your land, my Lady? Pleasant, of late?" Averill gazed at her earnestly, hunger in his bright eyes; he pawed the ground, looking like he wanted to pounce.

"My land is still *my* land, Lord Averill, and I intend to keep it," Jael pushed her hood back, the flaxen color of her untamed curls lending the scene even more of a dramatic quality.

"You declared that the land will have to weep blood from every pore before you joined yourself to me, Jael, and I have delivered," Averill said. "The entertainment has only begun, and you will see all that I can do if you continue to refuse me." Gesturing with a nod, he drew their attention to the crowd of mysteriously unaggressive Rotten lined up around the castle, ignoring all else as they stared up at the fortress.

Jael stood silent for a long time, so silent Glenna wondered if Averill had overpowered her defenses with a spell. When she spoke again, her voice wavered.

"There is nothing else you would accept as payment to leave my queendom for good?" Glenna winced, helpless as she saw the direction the conversation was going. Averill's wolfish grin widened.

Abruptly, a presence knocked at her mind, familiar and not unwelcome.

We cannot let him take Jael, Niles told her. Not only for her sake, but for the queendom. *Fate knows what he would do once he has her...he might kill Leland, or everyone nearby just for pleasure.*

Agreed, Glenna sent back. She paused before she intervened again, blinking back a stubborn tear that threatened to fall any second. Then, she dove into Leland's mind and pressed at his consciousness, pleading for entrance, which he gave as soon as he realized it was her.

Challenge him, she encouraged, *challenge him before she surrenders herself.*

Leland needed no further urging.

"You will not have her, beast, and you will not take our queendom with your greed," he said, his strong voice reverberating through the air; here, in the prelude of battle, he was most beautiful in Glenna's eyes.

"Leland, no!" Jael turned back to her friends, her wide eyes pleading for them to stay silent.

"Oh? Shall I not?" Averill, amused by Leland's outburst, paced forward, eye level with the tall knight on his horse. Anyone else would have retreated in fear, especially the horse, which barely stood steady under his master.

"Fate herself has decreed that a ruler may challenge a Lord who has besmirched his title and duty. You are one such Lord, and as the princess's champion, I challenge you to single combat to right the balance of the land." Leland's challenge, while worded formally, disguised neither his wrath, nor his obvious willingness to battle right on the spot.

Averill, though his wolf guise did not allow his expressions to come across as they might have for a man, appeared shocked. That didn't last long: the astonishment that pricked up his ears transfigured to harsh delight in a matter of seconds. His dark lips curled back to expose the points of exquisitely sharp teeth made whiter by the scarlet of his mouth; if his mouth had been shaped for laughing, he would have roared with mirth.

Glenna shuddered as his gaze swept the assembled cavalry, fighting to show no unease as the wolf noticed her. But Averill's cobalt eyes lingered on her; he'd been looking for her amongst the cluster of men and horses. The blue appeared so bright it almost burned, dazzling her into blindness.

Come, child, a voice, seductive and dangerous, summoned, luring her forward with dark thoughts. *Poor fool, tainted by Fate's will...what will she do, I wonder, if I corrupt such a vessel? It would not be the first time I've taken what was hers.*

All she could see was blue, slicing through her mental wards like they were made of shapeless sand.

Dimly, she was aware of her body dismounting her horse and striding forward as slow as one of the Rotten; her stallion, perhaps recognizing the malignant scent in the air, whinnied behind her, but she did not stop. Someone, several people in fact, shouted her name, but Glenna didn't care: she had to keep walking, forward to follow the blue light straight towards the jaws of the immense wolf ahead.

Then, the mists over her befuddled mind lifted abruptly. She stood with Averill right at her back as she faced her friends, holding her own dagger to her throat with the blade already drawing forth droplets of her blood. She would have screamed, or at least cried out, but air hissed past her teeth without a sound.

Niles, Leland, and Jael had dismounted their own horses, and they stood a few feet away from Glenna, terror for her sake paling their faces. Jael clutched at her hair, desperation in her beautiful face. Leland was shouting at her still, perhaps attempting to wake her from the stupor that had already lifted; he had drawn his sword, and now he held it ready to wield in combat or use to channel his healing magic should the knife sink deeper into her flesh. Niles stood unarmed, the farthest ahead of the group and therefore the closest to her, dark fire consuming his deep eyes; perhaps he knew Leland's magic would not work in this case.

"This is not a debate, Jael, and there are no alternatives for you or for Oloetha. Fate has decreed that I accept any such challenge given to me, but she did not bind me to any particular safeguards beforehand or afterwards." Averill said, gazing past the two knights at the princess; his long tongue darted out to lick his lips. "There are consequences for disrespect, as you know. Something precious might be lost to you as punishment. In this case, I believe this woman is beloved by all of you. Some of you more than others."

"J-Jael—" The name clawed its way free of the vice holding her silent, but she choked as the knife pressed harder against her windpipe. Warm blood dripped down her skin, and fruitlessly she struggled to pull the weapon away from her vulnerable neck. Jael covered her mouth with both hands, silently screaming as she watched the painfully slow execution.

"If you must accept the challenge, why not make things more interesting?" Niles had taken another step forward; unlike the others, very little emotion showed on his face. The most Glenna could tell was that he was calculating something, determining how risky the venture would be.

"I doubt you could come up with anything to interest me," their adversary sighed, boredom apparent even on his animal features. Glenna winced as the blade cut deeper.

"Are you not immortal? I should think you'd be intrigued by a wager," Niles goaded, though his tone lacked the usual sting of mockery. Was that desperation she heard, a crack in the iron fisted control he usually endeavored to maintain?

Averill shuffled a paw against the ground, pawing the dirt impatiently. "Your efforts to sway me are as transparent as they are pathetic. Jael did her people a disservice if she appointed you to be her ambassador."

"I believe this arrangement will appeal to you nonetheless," Niles didn't glance away from the wolf for a moment, but Glenna, terrified and bound in her suicidal position as she was, detected the hesitation before he continued. "If you release Glenna to us alive, I offer you my soul as forfeit if you defeat Leland in single combat."

The knife in Glenna's hand ceased its advance as Averill finally took interest. Her heart paused and her breath caught in her throat. *No. Oh, Niles...*

"Niles, no!" Jael called, voicing the protest Glenna could not. Her pitch nearly rose into a shriek that was "unbecoming for a royal," and a few rebellious tears escaped from her eyes. Leland was forever waxing eloquent on the charms of her eyes, and here the wet green of them stood out strikingly against the backdrop of the summer landscape.

"What have I to do with souls?" Averill remarked disdainfully. But his unearthly eyes gleamed to betray his interest, and for the moment his attention rested solely on the black haired mage standing before him with a defiantly straight spine.

"Let us not play games, my Lord. You and I both know the power a soul can contain. If you were to kill me, the soul is lost to you. Power hungry as you are, doesn't the prospect of *owning* a soul fascinate you?" Niles said.

"Very few beings have the power to harvest a soul from a body. Only Fate herself could do it without causing some...trauma to the essence. However, you do intrigue me." The wolf stepped forward, passing Glenna so closely she felt his coarse fur brush against the fabric of her cloak; more than ever, she longed to break this spell holding her captive and her life in the balance, even if the reprieve was only long enough to sink her knife up to the hilt into Averill's heart.

Niles stood his ground, unflinching as the beast approached him. Another man might have fled, but he didn't shift a hair. He didn't turn when Leland moved to stand beside him, murder in his normally kind eyes. Light glowed around the edges of his sword, blurring the outline, futile power that was glorious nevertheless. Glenna stood alone, watching the exchange.

"How bitter it is, to crave what Fate has given to another," Averill murmured, the nobility in his voice merging with what could only be called pity, a paradox coming from someone so ruthless. "You would offer your soul for something that would never be yours?"

"You'll get nothing," Leland interjected, ready violence barely hidden in his words as he glared. "The bargain was for his soul if I lost the fight, and I don't intend to suffer defeat." The wolf swung his large head his way, grinning again.

"If only you could just kill me, right? If only my unlawful death wouldn't cause a chain reaction that would destroy the world...that would simplify things for someone like you who sees the world in black and white," he said. "But you know nothing of the world. You are not fit to rule by her side. You are not fit to rule at all."

Almost hypnotized, Leland stared into the face of the creature as his angry eyes glazed over with something unrecognizable. Glenna, recognizing the alluring timbre that helped Averill entrance his victims, wondered what secret thoughts troubled Leland.

"Do you accept the wager or not?" Niles interrupted, breaking the spell. For some reason, the seductive tone had no effect on him, and he merely gazed up at the wolf with clear-eyed concentration. He hadn't looked at Glenna during the whole exchange.

The wolf turned back to her, grinning as he licked his lips and showed rows of sharp, flesh-rending tooth.

"Run along, pawn," Averill taunted her. "Your freedom has been bought...for a time."

Suddenly, she was in control of her body again, which slumped from exhaustion caused by fighting for dominance over her own limbs. The adrenaline and fear that had been the only thing holding her upright diminished at the sight of his satisfied animal's smile. Seeing red again, that curious detachment that didn't belong to her filled her up and made her rise to her full height and she marched back to her princess, head held high.

"I will return at twilight, in three days time. Prepare yourselves for the inevitable," the wolf said, turning to walk away. "Oh, and Jael...you will only be able to save one of them, at contest's end. I hope you choose wisely."

"Leave us," Jael ordered: by the lift of her chin, Glenna could tell she wished to sound stronger, to be the powerful authoritative ruler her people needed her to be, but all that was visible was her fear and anguish. Averill, perhaps noticing the same thing, the brokenness of spirit, sardonically dipped his muzzle in a bow and took his leave of them by walking back the way he came.

No one moved a muscle until they saw him disappear back into the trees, and then chaos ruled. The men watching, prevented by Averill's magic from acting in any way, made much noise shifting in their saddles and muttering amongst themselves, holding drawn weapons like they were unsure how to use them after all.

Glenna reached her friends, and they stood around her in brief silence. Leland hummed, reaching out to the wound on her neck, healing it with a complicated cast. The connection between healer and wounded always bore a hint of the divine in its weaving, but this time she could feel his fear for her through the barrier.

Then he rounded on Niles, brows drawn down into a dark scowl.

"You bloody fool!" he swore, holding the mage's arm fast in an unbreakable grip; his red face betrayed his fury, but his voice cracked with emotion. Jael swatted his gloved hand away before pulling Niles into a tight embrace.

"Thank you for saving her," she murmured, closing her eyes as a few tears slipped free to catch in her eyelashes.

Somehow, through all the conflict and the war they'd been through to put Jael on the throne, Glenna hadn't realized until this moment that the princess loved her. *Really* loved her, as sisters cared for one another. It wasn't quite enough, but for the first time since she could remember, she didn't feel completely isolated.

Glenna watched them all as if from a great distance; realizing she was still holding the knife, she let her fingers go limp so it fell to the ground with a dull thump. Then Leland was holding her, hugging her stiff body to him as if to reassure himself of her reality. He was too strong, and she felt her crushed ribs groan in protest.

"We are going to get through this, all of us," he told her, releasing her after she failed to respond to his embrace; she winced at the compassion in his eyes as he withdrew and cupped her face in his hands. For an instant, the merest of seconds, it felt like this touch was something more, for him as well instead of just her. If she could stop being numb for a moment, Glenna would have been surprised, but the caress ended almost as soon as it began.

Leland turned back to Jael as she let go of Niles, their voices fading into a low hum of noise as they conferred together, looking around at the men they'd gathered and at the circle of silent Rotten that still surrounded their fortress home. Uncomfortable, Glenna turned to Niles. How were you supposed to address someone who had offered their soul to save your life? She opened her mouth to speak, but she found her throat was bone dry, and no words came to mind regardless of her speechlessness.

"Don't say anything," Niles said to her, his words commanding even if his tone was moderate. "It is my honor to do this for...for my friends. My family." They stood facing each other, arms loose at their sides as they studied each other's faces for insight.

"But...your soul...for what?" How bright his eyes were, the ocher blending with a curious onyx; would she burn up if he looked at her too long? Glenna was nothing in the face of this warmth: she was dry bones and gray nothing, she was only a shadow. Bright stars like Jael and Leland gave her life and light, and Niles warmed the eternal cold that filled her to the brim yet left her forever empty.

Warm...would she ever feel warm again? It was summer, but she couldn't recall that last time she had felt anything but cold.

Glenna heard Niles's breath catch, heard his heart thump louder as she reached out with her mind to touch his. The soft touch was fleeting, a feathery, secret stroke of her consciousness against his. She hadn't noticed, but she and Niles had come close physically as they reached out to each other with their spirits: she stood in front of him with her hands on his chest, resting her forehead against the place where his heart lay beating beneath his tunic. He had placed his hands on her shoulders, holding them and her as if she were fragile as a dove. This was not the painful draw, ever-present and ever-agonizing, that she experienced for Leland almost every moment.

This she didn't have a name for.

The world broke in again, separating them without consideration of their feelings. Their eyes met again, and she saw the sheen of emotion making his bright.

Niles...

"Isn't there anything we can do to help them? We can't just let them wander off to die!" Jael asked, tears filling her eyes as the procession of gray people, of unspoken accord, followed the path Averill had taken to dissolve into the trees.

"They're already gone, love," Leland said, reaching a hand out to grip her shoulder.

If we're not careful, all of us will be gone, she thought, clutching her slender neck with her cold hands defensively. *Only darkness will remain.*

13

"Sorry!" Gwendoline half called, half whispered in the direction of her neighbor's smoking garbage cans. She'd set her alarm just late enough to make sure most of her neighbors would have headed off to work by this time, but the cranky lady directly to the left of her house kept peeking through the blinds to glare across the fence.

"This is stupid," Gwendoline grumbled under her breath as she lowered her hands to rest limply at her sides. She studied the charred lines in the grass of her backyard's lawn, noting with frustration their inaccurate trails towards the makeshift targets she'd set up. She'd been out here for over two hours, right after she'd set a soundproof enchantment on Niles's ears so he wouldn't hear her practicing what little defensive magic she knew.

But in the time that had passed, the only thing she'd improved was her piss poor aim. Summoning fire magic big enough and hot enough to kill someone on contact led to difficulty sending the lethal blast to the correct target. At least she'd remembered to lay a protective blanket charm over anything she might hit. Her grass and Mrs. Willick's garbage cans would get the worst of it, smoking and collapsing together instead of melting instantaneously.

It's going to work this time, Gwendoline told herself, told her magic as she brought her palms together to coax another fireball to life between them. *And after this, we fuck up Averill!*

She believed in her own bluster long enough for the fireball to shriek down towards the indestructible targets she'd conjured from stray branches, ricochet off the edge, and fly over the fence to smash through the abused garbage cans yet again.

"SHIT!" Gwendoline shouted, loud enough to rustle any birds from the trees if any had stayed to brave her practice session. Mrs. Willick cracked the blinds open wider, pointing her finger at Gwendoline and then the singed cans as she shook her head.

"Screw you, grouchy bitch," Gwendoline muttered, tempted to sling a hex towards her neighbor on purpose just for being nosy.

"Good morning to you too, lovely!" Niles's voice scared her completely, so much so that she yelped in alarm as she whirled around. "Thanks for that hex, by the way. Waking up deaf and struggling through a series of cleansing charms is a great way to start the day, wouldn't you agree?"

"Oh, I'm sorry," she snapped, too grumpy to resist the jab. "I didn't want my desperate struggle learning to fight Averill to interrupt your beauty sleep."

She expected him to say something like *"You know what will help with fighting Averill? Getting Glenna's memories!"* Instead, he casually vaulted over Mrs. Willick's chain link fence and righted the tumbled garbage cans. The old lady smiled flirtatiously at him through the window as her blinds shot up, but he ignored her as he jumped back to Gwendoline's side.

"What exactly are you trying to get right?" Niles asked, cocking his head to the side. He seemed to be fighting off a smile as he observed the jagged wounds in her yard and the off kilter targets.

"Why do you want to know? So you can mock my failure?" Gwendoline grunted as she shook her hair free from its useless hair tie and finger combed out the mess before putting it up again. "It's not like I've ever had to practice this kind of stuff before. Deadly enemies aren't really a norm in Starford."

"So defensive!" Niles chided her as he hid another smile and shed the leather jacket he'd been wearing as he approached her. "Glenna hated not being perfect at something right away as well. It's what made her such a...how would you put it...badass."

Gwendoline watched him he rolled up his sleeves. "I didn't know where to start. I studied basic self-defense, both physical and magical, but I don't know how much good what will do here. So, I practiced the only thing I was sure would kill most people the quickest: a fat fireball directly to the face. Or, in Averill's case, maybe lower."

"That's good," Niles nodded thoughtfully, raising his hands as he summoned his magic. "But isn't your affinity with ice, rather than fire?"

"Yes, but I thought ice might be a little too slow in this case, so I went with fire," she replied. The shadows coalescing in his hands spun indistinctly before settling into the form of two large circular blades made from the darkest metal she'd ever seen.

"You're not using your imagination, then. In most cases, things like freezing a man's heart in his chest or trapping him in a vortex of razor sharp ice shards would do the trick. But what about a weapon made from and enhanced by your own power?" Niles challenged her to think as he adjusted his grip on the twin glaives he'd fashioned. The blades, black steel with a glittering texture that reminded her of polished obsidian, really did suit him.

Gwendoline hesitated, already picturing what kind of weapon she'd summon. The mental image had popped into her head too quick to be purely from her own inspiration. She recognized the feeling, guessed who this idea had come from...but for the first time, this surprise recollection didn't make her afraid.

Biting her lip, she lifted her right hand towards the sky and let her cold magic do its work to build the sword she desired. When she was finished, she gripped the crystalline hilt and rested the slender blade gently on the palm of her other hand. Pale blue steel, a basket woven handle that appeared too delicate for battle, and a single star sapphire set into the base where all the strands met.

Hello, old friend. The thought wasn't hers alone, but Gwendoline found that she welcomed it.

Niles stared at her sword as if he'd been struck. "What...what made you conjure that?"

"I'm not sure," Gwendoline admitted honestly. "But I think that we both recognize this sword. Glenna's, right?"

"Yes," Niles confirmed; his throat bobbed as he swallowed. "It's hers. But...did you have a memory, or was this instinct?"

"A little of both. I could see it in my head, strangely distinct, but it feels...it feels right, somehow," she told him. "I think something about freeing you from my book set off a chain of events...some stuff has been coming back, things I didn't notice at first, but this is the clearest event I've experienced." Gwendoline explained haltingly, the sword that had felt like a rightful extension of her arm suddenly heavy.

Heavier still weighed the knowledge that her memories, her previous self as Glenna, was returning whether she was ready for it or not.

Niles, saying nothing, seemed at a loss for words. She waited for him to speak, to once again encourage her to take Glenna's soul fragments, but he remained silent as he stared at her sword.

"Niles?" she tried to stir him from his reverie, and after a moment he looked up at her. All traces of his unease faded as he refocused on her face, forcing himself to smile as he returned to the present

"Do you think her skill at fencing has come back to you yet?" he asked in his usual teasing manner. "I know the perfect way to find out."

Guessing his intention, Gwendoline gulped; her sword dropped limply to her side. For Niles, his past as one of the best warriors in the land was not so distant.

"What's your affinity?" she asked, shamelessly stalling; she would have guessed fire, or a mix of flame and enchantment similar to what Everleigh practiced, but the black stillness outlined in white confused her conjecture.

"Anything my opponent isn't good at," Niles grinned as he readied himself.

Instead of replying, Gwendoline took her chance and charged Niles, lunging towards him with the point of her blade angled towards his heart. Part of her knew that this was a poor opportunity, but she wanted to see what Niles had to throw at her. But he only blocked her attack by lifting one of his glaives to parry.

"Lazy," he remarked. "With that sort of weapon, you need to be more discreet. You're not a bruiser with a battle axe hacking your way through the battlefield. Speed is essential: you should be moving continuously, and no one should be able to predict your next strike."

Taking his words to heart, Gwendoline launched towards him almost before he finished speaking. He blocked her attack more seriously this time, flowing from that into an undercut with his own blades that put her on the defensive. She had worried that he would take it easy on her, something she abhorred: she preferred learning with no holds barred rather than coddling from any teacher she'd ever had. Instead he challenged her, not enough to overwhelm her limited skill set, but enough to help her learn.

And then, as the minutes passed in a clash of enchanted battle, Gwendoline found that he was teaching her less and less, and she was fighting him as if she'd been a warrior her whole life. It wasn't just blade on blade either: ice sparkled on the edge of the spinning glaives, and though he used no magic on her, she felt the sting of his power every time their weapons connected. The sparks of his magic interacting with hers struck a chord within her, and she realized as she fought that Glenna was more a part of her already than she had wanted to admit before.

Gwendoline pressed her attack, her arm trembling from exhaustion after an hour of sparring as she sought to break Niles's defense. She wasn't used to this sort of practice, but standing out here in the morning sun clashing blades with Niles exhilarated her so the weariness became pleasant. Seeing an opportunity, she feinted an upward thrust and caught one of his glaives on her sword. By the time she took the strike she'd planned, ice had spread down the length of her blade and trapped the two weapons together. Choosing to fight dirty, she knocked him down with a blast of winter air from her other hand. She was flushed already with the triumph of disarming him.

But she hadn't expected him to react so quickly to her attack. As he fell, the glaive dissolved into mist in one of his hands as he used it to grab her unguarded wrist and pull her down with him. They landed hard on the prickly grass, but Niles was underneath her so she didn't really feel the fall.

What she did feel was tension, a sizzling in the air not caused by magic. Their weapons, called forth from nothing, disappeared as Gwendoline lifted herself off him slightly by covering his wrists. He'd pulled her down with him, so she didn't want to chance losing completely because she was distracted.

*Distracted...*she mused, her mouth dry. *More like totally taken in by pieces of a past self, and by this man I can't get out of my head no matter how much I try.*

"Your eyes!" Niles exclaimed; he seemed transfixed, and one of his wrists struggled briefly under her grip; she released him, and he lifted it to trace his thumb across her cheek. Since Gwendoline had no mirror, he nudged the boundaries of her mind, seeking to show her how her violet tinted irises had briefly changed to a steely gray.

Breathless, her body tense like a taut wire, she forced each muscle to relax as she stared down at him. She had a suspicion that he had allowed her to knock him down, but any indignation at that faded away along with everything else as they considered each other.

"Niles..." she said at last, her words halting, "I think I'm ready for my memories."

Niles caught her as she stumbled over a rock, not the first on their hike. Gwendoline huffed, tempted to refuse his hand. *Damn him,* she grumbled to herself, looking up to frown at his amused smirk. *I've hiked this path more times than I can count, and today is the day I have to stumble over every rock and acorn.*

"Are you enjoying me catching you?" Niles laughed at her, pulling her upright again. "Because if you wanted me to carry you up the trail, all you had to do was ask."

"Shut up!" Gwendoline snapped at him, annoyed due to her embarrassment. "I could just as easily accuse you of hexing me to fall so you could catch me."

"You could," Niles agreed with another chuckle. The sun filtering through the steadily shedding trees reflected off his eyes, once again autumnal in hue. The light melted into his black hair, where it drew forth hidden red fire if she looked close enough, and the dark jeans, fitted leather jacket, and black t-shirt he wore only enhanced the curious darkness that hovered around him, near the edges of her vision.

More than that, the clothes fit the shape of his body distractingly well. Once when he heaved a fallen branch out of their path—larger than one person should have been able to lift on his own—his shirt and jacket lifted several inches to showcase a toned back and abs well defined by labor. Time in the book hadn't diminished the labors the man had accomplished in the past to maintain his physique, and it was the person she felt drawn to as well as the body.

Flustered, Gwendoline distracted herself by plucking a few leaf bits from the sleeves of her overlarge cerulean sweater; perhaps she was supposed to be afraid of the dark, or at least worried about what it might be doing to Niles, who didn't show any awareness of the shadowy aura that surrounded him. But to her, it seemed like a cool, gentle dark—the sort she might encounter in a quiet library or near dusk in the woods—and she tried not to dwell on what it might feel like to fall into that comforting black.

Focus on the fact that these memories might make you not you *anymore,* she reminded herself as she and Niles continued the steady climb. *No more getting drawn in by the mystery of it all...not to mention his lean arms and broad chest and that dreamy hair...*

Frowning, she pinched herself on the wrist as punishment.

"So, why are we climbing up all the way up here to get this done? Won't my memories return no matter where we are?" Gwendoline asked, flipping back her long braid as she walked. Niles didn't miss a beat as he replied.

"Aesthetic, Gwendoline."

"Oh come on," Gwendoline couldn't help but smile. "Books aren't supposed to have aesthetics, or be snarky."

"I believe you and I both know fairly well that I am a man now," he looked over at her sideways, flirting again.

She strained her mind to concentrate, looking around at the natural scenery to avoid staring at Niles's back as he climbed ahead of her. "Do you have any idea what's going to happen once you return the memories?"

"I have a few theories about what might happen once I reunite the fragments, but it's not like this has been attempted before. I'm not sure which will prove true," he explained, holding up a low hanging branch so it wouldn't snap back and knock her in the face.

"That's reassuring," Gwendoline sighed, humming a short cast to keep her socks from falling down in her brown leather boots. The spell made her feel more like herself, as magic usually did, and she hung onto that feeling like a castaway sailor clutching a life-saving piece of driftwood.

"So? Your theories?" she pressed.

"I believe the soul will simply latch onto yours once I release its tether to me, and you'll remember everything you're supposed to when it links," Niles answered. "I'm not sure which memories will arrive first, but I'm hoping it's a gentler process than what I fear. Glenna's last moments were...unpleasant, and I'm not sure how vividly she preserved them."

"Unpleasant how?" Gwendoline asked, suspicion knotting her brow. Niles slowed briefly ahead of her, and a dull ache of pain that wasn't hers thrummed through her skull.

"Sorry," he said, glancing sheepishly over his shoulder at her. "I guess you could say I'm nervous, too."

"You shouldn't be nervous," Gwendoline forgave him for the slip up in spite of the headache she knew she'd have later; she had begun to sweat a bit from the climb, so with a silent breath she cast a minor cleansing spell. "You already remember what happened, so what have you got to be afraid of?" Niles held his silence and increased his pace. She had no choice but to jog along behind him, sensing that they neared whatever destination he had in mind.

After a minute or two, Niles diverged from the worn pathway, beckoning for her to follow. Curious, Gwendoline did so. This trail was familiar to her, no matter if summer flowers bedecked the trees or winter's first frost made the fallen acorns slick, but she'd never taken the time to explore the dense, pathless woods that surrounded the hiking trail. He led her on for several minutes, courteously clearing the way by culling branches and tree limbs ahead of her. In return, Gwendoline performed a quick cast that would ward off any mosquitoes or ticks.

Niles finally guided her through the last line of evergreen trees, which had been so visually impenetrable she couldn't glimpse the view beyond. When she saw what secret the woods had held, Gwendoline's lips parted with an involuntary intake of air.

They stood on a huge, pristinely flat gray slab of rock expanding out over the surrounding lower mountains. Their location afforded them such a magnificent view of the contiguous mountain swells that she marveled at the beauty, captivated. The sky couldn't look bluer, nor could the air feel more clear: autumn in these parts was crisp, and each stroke of nature's skilled brush rendered every object in sight lovely with sharp detail.

Yet, in spite of never venturing to this place before, Gwendoline felt that surge of recognition bewildering her senses again. She whirled to face Niles, who stood behind her, watching.

"Why did you bring me up here?" she questioned him again. He sighed, shoving his hands into the pockets of his jeans as he advanced to stand beside her.

"The Kinsley manor is the location of the Northwood family's original seat of power in Oloetha. Knowing what I do now, Averill probably had a hand in making sure any other eligible bloodline faded into the past so he could arrange his own rise to power. He's not actually part of the Kinsley bloodline, of course, but when his spirit began to rebuild he most likely arranged to gain some of that family's blood for proof to make his leadership claim legitimate.

"Anyway, back then much of the surrounding land belonged to the royal family, including this area. Glenna was more inclined to explore than the rest of us, even Leland," he explained, gazing out over the mid-morning horizon. "She used to come here during her spare time to practice some of her more complex spells...or when life at the castle would become unbearable."

"Unbearable how?" Gwendoline inquired. Niles frowned, hesitating, so she sighed and plopped down to sit on the smooth, marble-like surface. "You brought me all the way up here, so you might as well come out with it."

After a pause, he exhaled and complied, sitting down beside her. "She wasn't always unhappy. Glenna could be sharp-tongued, wickedly funny, and eerily introspective. She didn't make friends easily, but those she made loved her with ferocious loyalty," he said, leaning back on his hands as he stretched his legs out before him.

"Friends who loved her like you?" she asked; he gave her a side-eyed glance, making her regret her careless question.

"You could say that," he answered. Gwendoline shivered, suddenly cold, and Niles shrugged off his leather jacket and wrapped it around her shoulders without comment before continuing the subject they'd been discussing. "Up until the last couple of years before Averill broke the peace, she seemed fairly happy."

"What happened the last couple of years?" She was almost afraid to ask, but she needed answers, and now was the time. Plus, it was somehow not as easy to be concerned in the perfect sunny morning light, accompanied by a beautiful view and her crush's jacket hugging her shoulders.

"Glenna and Leland had always been close, since they grew up together. I myself didn't come to the castle for magical training until the previous head mage's heir died in an accident at sea...and my own tie to Fate revealed itself. Jael spent most of her time learning to be a princess and eventually a queen, so she didn't step into the picture until later. Even so, Glenna was hopelessly in love with Leland, and it showed to anyone who knew how and when to look." Floored,

Gwendoline felt her mouth drop open as the weight of what Niles said began to sink in.

"Glenna...loved Leland?"

And Niles loved Glenna, her thoughts echoed the unspoken after thought. In a way, some things made more sense. Niles's curious antagonism towards Colt, the bitterness that would seep through to darken a look or his speech: it all made sense now.

"She was devoted to him...until the end. The very end," Niles explained in a softer voice, purposefully not looking at her as he spoke. "Jael never knew, and I don't think Leland did either. The other knight of our trio, Abelard, never guessed. I was the only one who knew, and she would have preferred I never discovered the truth either."

"That I understand," Gwendoline admitted, tracing a floral design onto the slate surface below them; it glowed gently, glittery traces of magic lingering behind.

"We had our differences regarding the matter," Niles shook his head as if to clear away the spider webs of troubling thoughts, and a curl fell down over his brow. "I just thought I should tell you before you see it all for yourself." Gwendoline nodded, barely listening.

Picturing her and Colt together, and feeling no compulsion to be with him or to do anything other than laugh with him about the idea of them being in love, she squinted at Niles thoughtfully. Crushes had come and gone, and she'd been on nearly as many good dates as she'd been on disastrous ones. Part of the reason she went hiking so often was related to this: she frequently felt the compulsion to get away, to get out of the city away from her sad love life and the loneliness of doing without a proper family. In her bleakest moments, she'd contemplated packing up what she could and just driving away.

But this boy, this man, was simply different. She was drawn to him, entranced and utterly charmed, and she had been from the moment she'd freed him from her casting book. Could Glenna really have had no feelings for Niles? She couldn't believe it. Even now, when bits and pieces of Glenna had been seeping into her for some time, she didn't doubt that her own feelings for Niles were influenced by a strange sense of longing from her past self.

Misinterpreting her squinting, Niles huffed and ran his hands through his hair, pushing it back. "Gwendoline, I know you might have doubts about me still. But you know what? Glenna trusts me: you may not have her soul fragments yet, but like calls out for like. It's amazing, because the two of you are so different in your own ways, but you're similar where it counts. You already know I loved her, once upon a time. But you..."

"I don't," she interrupted as she reached out a shaky hand to place on his knee, her voice barely rising above a whisper. "Have doubts about you, I mean."

"No?" He smiled, teeth gleaming in the sunlight, though that didn't totally conceal his own anxiety.

"No," she assured him, louder this time; feeling bold, she lifted her other hand to his face, tracing his jaw with her fingertips. "I don't doubt you at all. I...I can't imagine feeling this way about anyone else. Glenna might have loved Leland, like you've said, but he didn't love her, and maybe she was just confused. Regardless...I'm me, and that's got to count for something, right?"

"You have feelings for me?" Niles leaned into her hand, rubbing against it slightly like a cat would have. Unable to contain a smile, she nodded.

"As far as feelings go, I'd say mine might run deeper than time would ordinarily allow. Hell, we've only known each other a few weeks...But have we? I feel like I should ask 'Is that all?' Well. I won't let who I was—who we were—in the past ruin our present." A faint breeze, of magical rather than natural means, filtered through her hair like a caress. It lingered much too long, as if tender, invisible hands lifted a few of the tendrils and caressed them. Wishing to reciprocate, she hummed, calling forth a special, rare kind of light that would reflect off of all the drops of moisture hovering in the air, making them sparkle like gems.

Mutually deciding they'd waited long enough, Gwendoline and Niles leaned into each other, coming together for a kiss as deep as the one they'd shared when she'd first met him.

It was as simple as him releasing whatever dam had been holding those memories back. They were kissing, and suddenly it wasn't just them anymore: she was Gwendoline, holding tight to Niles, savoring the sensation of his hands in her hair, then she was more, and this more brought her such agony that she stopped breathing. Through the pain, she got the sense that Niles hadn't meant to return her memories just now, that he'd tripped whatever mechanism held them back sooner than he'd intended.

Memories and knowledge filled her mind in a trail of unspooling pictures, blossoming with color and darkness and flashes of light. The actual process of Glenna's fractured soul merging with her own hurt immensely, so much so that she thought she'd die right there on the mountaintop.

Worse were the sensations she remembered—that Glenna remembered—right before she'd died.

Died?

Everything had been lost. The grief swirled up, threatening to choke her, and she cried out, falling back from Niles, whom she dimly noticed, catch her before her head slammed against the ground. Her darting eyes looked up at him, blurry from the pain and confusion, but Niles's eyes weren't right, they were all wrong. These were Leland's eyes, flat and lifeless as she'd last seen them, and now she understood. The reason she'd felt so bonded to Leland was because Fate had willed it herself, tying them together by their spirits, an eternal bond that couldn't be ignored, much less fought off or denied.

But had something gone wrong? For her, for Jael...and Leland...and Niles...

Blissfully, her mind couldn't handle her bewilderment and anguish any longer, and she fell into the last of the memories as consciousness slipped out of her grasp.

14

Before

After Glenna had fled the room where she had assisted Leland in preparing for his confrontation with Averill, she realized with an unpleasant surge of numbness that she had nowhere to be, and nothing to do. Jael and Leland were together, exchanging tearful kisses and encouragement, perhaps making plans for the future should the worst happen and calamities befall the queendom. No, she frowned as she considered, they were optimists. They would avoid discussing such a dark future at all costs. Leland would win, and take Averill's place, and that would be the end. Happily ever after was sure to follow. Right?

For their sakes, she hoped they were right. And she would do the best she could to ensure both their happiness and Oloetha's safety.

Glenna pressed the palms of her hands tight against her eyes as she endeavored to concentrate. She was sure she looked a fright, standing alone in the hallway trying to compose herself with her long hair hanging about her white face and her clothes plainer than usual, but thankfully no servants hovered about to witness her lapse in decorum. In fact, she realized as she lifted her face from her hands, strangely no one was around at all.

"I sent them away," someone spoke behind her. "There's no point in risking our people becoming collateral damage should the fighting exceed the bounds of the arena." Turning, Glenna saw Niles had come down the hall to meet her, perhaps knowing she'd already said her goodbyes to Leland.

Goodbye? Fate's blood, she hoped not.

She hadn't been alone to speak with Niles since two days before, after Leland had officially challenged Averill. It was still a blur: Jael had been the only person she'd consented to see, as she spent that time in her room—a different one from her previous bedroom where her maid had turned on her—searching frantically through her book for anything else that would help her adopted family. Of course, her search had proved fruitless, but straining her eyes and mind with too much reading and pointless spell practice had felt more profitable than sitting around pondering Leland's possible death, Jael's enslavement, and Niles's soul being stripped from his body and broken by someone as sadistic as Averill.

"Wise decision," Glenna spoke at last, too late to be relevant to the conversation and with a too husky voice. Clearing her throat, she tried again. "How long until—"

"He comes at any moment, I expect. The sun has set, and nightfall is upon us." True enough, the window in the hall revealed the rising of the ivory moon into a sky that grew ever darker as the seconds ticked by.

"I wish there were another way," Niles admitted softly, facing her as she stared resolutely at the moon. "I would hate to see Leland harmed. Did you perhaps find anything else in your book that could help?"

Glenna shook her head. "Only more about the fragmented soul concept. The only thing my book seems to be good for is sending me casting notes written in pure gibberish accompanied by dire threats of annihilation if I fail to use the spell at the right time." Out of her peripheral, she saw a ghost of a smile upturn his lips.

"I take it that's not how it's supposed to work?"

"No," Glenna blinked slowly, still staring out of the window. "I wish I knew why this spell keeps appearing before me. I can't see how it would help us in this situation if—"

"If Leland fails," Niles finished for her. Had he known she wouldn't be able to say the words?

"I suppose we'll need to prepare for that possibility," she admitted. It took effort, but she managed to distance herself from the idea, speaking about death like the whole matter was vastly inconsequential. "We're responsible for many, many lives should the fight turn foul."

"True. How shall we proceed?" Niles asked.

"Jael has appointed herself his second, so I believe if Leland...doesn't succeed, she'll have to take his place, or at least hold Averill off until..." she trailed off.

Until what? She'd never known so little about an enemy before.

"We need to find something to give her so she can dispose of him before he can get to her, or something we ourselves can use if he tries to harm her," Niles mused aloud. "But we've run out of time to come up with anything useful." His hard expression held his features tightly under control: the dark eyes, sleepless and fatigued, blazed with the alertness that came upon men right before battle. This once, with his slightly crooked nose and his strong, refined lips, he looked more potential king than Leland.

"There is one thing," Glenna dared venture, though she placed only doubt in this final piece of information she'd wrested from her studying. "A banishing cast. It's not relevant to our current situation, but—"

"Banishment," Niles repeated the word, a tone of finality in his voice just like the word. "I know of it."

"How do *you* know about it? I could barely find any information about it aside from a few phrases that my book gave me," Glenna marveled, recalling a bleary, candlelit evening of page turning and frustration that nearly had her howling with madness.

"Some information is too dangerous to record traditionally. My old master spoke to me of this hex only in whispers, calling it a true curse," Niles, frowned, his anxious expression further agitated.

"A true curse?"

"Whoever casts this spell bears the aftereffects of such darkness for the rest of his days," Niles intoned. "Evidently it was more common in the early days of mankind for magical folk to delve into the darker energy of our world."

"What made them stop?" Gwendoline asked, curious in spite of herself; she knew of what forces he spoke, though she had never needed to research them further, even in the midst of the drawn out, desperate scramble to place Jael on Oloetha's throne.

"I asked, but my teacher would only grumble. '*This power corrupts the minds of men, boy: the more gifted the scholar, the more absolute the corruption. Many who breach the depths of this earth find that they cannot draw back unscathed, and that those they care for suffer the weight of their actions for the rest of their short lives.'"* Niles cleared his throat after imitating his former master's distinct growl of a voice.

Gwendoline's hope at the mention of this spell soured with doubt. "How dismal. That sounds more like superstition than fact, if there's no history to back up such a threat."

"I did find lore regarding ancient kings who encountered the void, whether they were looking for greater strength or seeking to help their people, and on each occasion their story falls off at its darkest turn, clipping off into oblivion," Niles seemed reluctant to impart this information, almost like he had something else to tell her that he didn't want to.

"And?" Gwendoline pressed.

"I found the spell. I don't know how I found it, but it was like it came to me from nowhere," he admitted, not meeting her gaze. "I didn't even read it anywhere...it came to me in snatches of shadows from the candlelight, or in a whispered voice at the darkest point of night."

"Like cryptic passages in a book," Gwendoline breathed, a chill breathing down her neck. She knew Fate had chosen her for some purpose, but had Niles been chosen as well? The prospect of not being alone in this took filled her with a gratitude that took her breath away, and she felt a strange closeness to him.

She heard the betrothed couple approaching them from down the hall, rendering their hushed conversation impossible. She and Niles turned to face them.

Leland had removed his helm and held it under his arm; Jael had taken his other arm, and she leaned her head against his shoulder like a child seeking comfort from a nightmare. Some of her hair, uncoiffed for once, fell over her face, making her appear all the more haggard with apprehension. Still, they looked perfect together, and Gwendoline couldn't stand the idea of death separating them forever.

The four stood in a closed circle, silent and with serious expressions. Glenna tried to ignore the tear tracks lining Jael's drawn face, since she was too busy holding her own expression captive to impassivity to provide any solace to her friend.

"Whatever happens, you are my family," Leland addressed their little huddle with clear determination. He looked like he wanted to say more, but didn't know the right words. Silent, he looked around each member of the circle, lingering on Glenna while her heart skipped a few beats. She imagined what it would be like if just she and Leland rode off into the night, leaving Oloetha and its problems—leaving Jael and her problems—behind for good. Transfixed by the strength of his gray eyes, she briefly indulged in this other life, picturing the two of them raising horses in a distant village somewhere no one knew either of them.

"It's time," Niles interrupted the silence of the moment, stepping back as the first to leave their circle. Gwendoline's imaginings disappeared with a taut mental snap, reminding her of the precarious present.

Nodding to him in acknowledgement, Leland shrugged off Jael's embrace, taking her hand in his gauntlet-clad one as he led the way to the castle exit where only peril awaited him. Glenna and Niles fell in step behind, their presence a show of silent solidarity Jael appreciated with a watery smile. Beautiful even under strain, she too had run out of words adequate for their situation.

When they came to the place where the fight was to be held, Gwendoline saw Abelard waiting for them, tapping his sword around different points in the huge circle that would be the arena, no doubt casting protection spells so the damage would not trespass further than allowed. Averill could probably break these bonds, but they were betting on his desire to have a stake in the queendom and the castle to keep him from razing their home to the ground.

Abelard noticed Leland approaching, and all the concern and admiration a younger brother might feel for the elder voyaging off into the unknown filled his expression. Many outsiders were intimidated by the young night, seeing only his great bulk and his thick armor, but any who knew this knight knew he would only hurt someone under the greatest duress.

Glenna had so much more she wanted to say. She had to tell Niles that it would be safe to use the banishing spell, if Fate had sent it to him, and Jael that she would always be there for her, and Leland...well, she couldn't tell him she loved him. But surely something better than their last private conversation could be said? Couldn't she leave him on a better note?

Stop this, she told herself at last, *he will win this. He must, and he will.*

She glanced at his rugged face once more before it disappeared under the forbidding helm he fitted over his head and face. Melancholy, she wished him the strength of the creature it resembled.

A cloud passed over the moon, casting shadow almost completely over the makeshift arena, and when it passed Averill stood in the center of the clearing. He'd exchanged his formal wear for simple leather fighting gear, though he wore no armor and carried no weapons. His long snowy hair had been pulled back, lending youthful lines to his severe features, and his lips curled as he looked down his aquiline nose at his challengers.

Jael didn't betray any fear, though Glenna fancied she could see the pulse racing in her throat. Averill had never looked more savage, nor so close to unleashing the torrent of power a being like him had doubtless stored up for millennia. Her unease swirled up like smoke in her lungs, and weighed her down like an iron ingot in her stomach. No one had moved, but she was suddenly realizing how deeply they had underestimated their opponent. *This is all wrong...*

"Who challenges the Lord of this land?" Averill called. Indeed, his voice carried more of a growl than a human voice. Resolution setting his brow into a firm line, Leland stepped into the circle so only the two warriors, human and immortal, stood in the clearing.

"Princess Jael challenges you, and I take up the challenge in her stead," he spoke in a ringing voice, drawing his sword in one smooth movement.

"You fight wholly, as a champion with heart, spirit, and soul? No other is fit to come before me," Averill spoke the formal words of the challenge, the phrases heavy with eldritch foreboding.

"All are present and none will interfere with our battle," Leland confirmed, sliding into a ready stance as he lifted his sword in preparation. Perhaps he wouldn't notice through the eye slits of his helm, but Glenna wondered with a sick feeling at the premature smile of victory crinkling the corners of their enemy's mouth.

This is wrong... she thought again, panicking, but the answer to the question she felt she had neglected to ask stubbornly refused to show itself. A sense of failure radiated outward from her gut, knotting her brow and clenching her fists.

With the formalities dispensed with and no further warnings necessary, Averill attacked, shifting with an explosion of motion into his white wolf form. Leland barely had time to lift his sword, holding hilt and blade with both gauntleted hands as he blocked the beast from tearing out his throat. He held his stance and managed to throw off the wolf. It landed on all four paws, black lips lifted in a silent snarl.

"Already cheating?" Leland taunted, sliding into a crouch as he clenched the hand not holding his sword into a tight fist. Golden flames burst from both hands, sparking and too bright to look at directly. His sword blossomed with these flames, and the shape of his empty hand wavered as four blades of fire as long as a man's arm formed a daunting claw to rival the giant wolf. Glenna, watching, marveled at the savage beauty of this scene: the great beast of the woods, pure white against the night, facing off against the golden knight, the best swordsman and fighter in Oloetha and beyond.

Leland dove forward this time, his momentum carrying him forward enough for him to flank the wolf, though not fast enough for him to successfully flay the furred side with the fiery claws. Averill turned, whirling completely around as he stepped aside to avoid the grievous blow, transforming liquidly back into a man. This time, he wielded a sword of his own: a pale, wicked blade wrapped all around with black brambles of some accursed form of metal. On the offensive, he charged into the place he'd just been standing, swinging his blade to slice off his opponent's head.

Leland blocked, and metal screeched as the two swords clashed, edge against edge. Grunting, he swung his enchanted claws up from the side, aiming to puncture the ribs. Averill blocked with this hilt of his sword, the sleeves of his leather tunic flowing forward to form a fireproof barrier. Noting this, Leland stepped back to reassess his opponent.

Glenna, learned in battle knowledge and combat maneuvers though she was, would have been hard pressed to distinguish between the two swordsmen, so swiftly did they dance across the battlefield.

Leland's golden armor and flashing flames distinguished him against the night, and the swing of Averill's white hair or the gleam of his thorny blade flashed behind her eyelids whenever she dared blink. She had worried about Leland being outmatched, but he held his own with great skill. She itched to help him, every instinct screaming for her to intervene as she had always done: he would engage their enemies, and she would have his back with her blinding ice magic and her own warrior skills, taking a few lives with her own sword.

For Averill, she wished she could curse his heart into solid stone, and then carve it out with his own sword.

But she dared not step into the circle, not even when Averill shifted back into the giant wolf and knocked Leland onto the ground. The carpeting of grass ignited, fire spreading across each emerald shaft until it reached the protected edge of the arena. Beside her, Glenna heard Abelard's gasp, Niles's angry huff, and Jael's groan of despair. Leland's helm had fallen off, and the sweat beading on his forehead dripped to the ground with a tiny hiss where each droplet turned to steam from the heat of the flames.

Briefly, he looked over at the small group of people forced to watch him fight. His eyes met Glenna's, showcasing the clearest, brightest, most intense gray she'd ever seen. Knowledge, a knowing of the future without consciously accepting the reality yet, made her lips part as her own eyes widened in terror; she saw the same perception dawn upon Leland, his expression a mirror of hers.

How could it be?

Averill, seeing his advantage, leapt forward and clamped his jaws down on Leland's enchanted arm, ignoring the fiery gauntlet as he sank his wolf's teeth into the flesh and ripped the limb clean from the body.

Leland screamed as the beast shook the arm side to side before casting it away. Shifting back into a man, Averill stood tall before the fallen knight, his mouth burned and covered with blood not his own. Sword still in hand, he stalked Leland, blue eyes shining with a hunter's focus.

"Get up!" Niles shouted, his words calloused but necessary. *"Get up!"* Glenna felt true fear again, knowing as she did that Niles would not have let such an outburst escape him unless the end was truly near. She spared a glance for him, seeing that he stood at the arena's edge, desperate to enter.

Leland cut his scream off, unable to quell the low groan that rattled in his brawny chest. Gritting his teeth, he gripped his sword tight in his remaining hand, expending too much effort to bring it up to block Averill as the immortal mage attacked him.

"There's no need for that," the Lord said, almost conversational as he knocked the blazing sword aside and pinned Leland to the ground by shoving his own blade through the golden armor down to just below the thundering heart.

This time, when he screamed, Glenna knew he was dying. As Averill cruelly twisted the sword back and forth, driving the blade and the brambles deeper into one of the kindest people she'd ever known, Glenna unwittingly joined Niles at the edge of the circle. She would have broken through, but her fists beat against an invisible barrier, no doubt put up by Averill to keep them all at bay as he toyed with his fallen prey.

Showcasing impossible strength, Averill lifted Leland's skewered body into the air, the sword driving into him up to the hilt. Then, as if the hefty knight weighed no more than one of Jael's old dolls, he cast him aside, sword and all.

Dead before he hit the ground, Leland's body collapsed to the singed earth with an undignified thump. As he fell, the blanched sword diminished into nothing but fog, transparent enough that Glenna couldn't see it after a second or two. Expressionless, Averill bent to take up Leland's extinguished sword, turning the blade around and around as he studied the blue toned steel.

They'd lost? All the ties had been present...even Abelard stood nearby, ill and totally silent as he looked in the face of his hero's ugly demise. Jael was screaming, terrible, shrieking cries of agony and fury: Glenna saw him holding her upright so she wouldn't fall, and back, so she wouldn't run to Leland. Niles had trespassed into the warrior's arena, breaking through the magical barrier as he dashed through the flames that still smoldered as he knelt by the corpse of his friend.

Ruler, heart, soul, and spirit. All present, and all had failed.

But then, the whispers from her book and from that other presence made perfect sense. As she saw Leland's body falling to the ground, knowing he was gone before he landed on the place where sweet summer grass had once grown, all the confusing words that had been forcing their way into her mind for weeks came together to form a viable spell. Gasping for air to stave off the shock if she looked at Leland's body for even a second longer, she lifted her hands and called for her casting book to come to her.

Averill stood over the body, grinning down at the gore with a visible, shining aura of triumph about him. Blood spattered his black leather, visible only under the shining light of the moon, and his wintry eyes gleamed even brighter.

You won't succeed so easily, Glenna thought viciously, wishing she was strong enough to destroy the villain before her with a snap of her fingers.

"Niles!" Glenna called as her book shimmered into existence in her hands. Looking up from his friend's body with eyes red with hatred, he rushed to stand beside her an instant.

We must banish him, Glenna knocked urgently at his mind with her message. After an exchanged glance filled with fury and pain, she knew they shared a purpose.

To split a soul and banish him fast, a lass requires a perfect cast. The nonsense ditty spun through Glenna's thoughts, oddly helping her focus as she made her eyes gaze only on the book in her hands. She couldn't look up to see Averill stepping over Leland's body, approaching Jael with the walk of someone who is sure in his reward. Still screaming, Jael flew at him, but Abelard held her back, his youthful face white with rage or pain. He'd drawn his own sword, though compared to Leland's enflamed weapon it looked a feeble thing.

Words flowed from Glenna's lips, words she'd been worried of misusing before. Instead, serenity not her own filled her to the brim as she wove the cast. From the corners of her eyes, she sensed rather than saw a specter of a red serpent coiling around her neck, resting like a choker and thrumming with power.

Break thy heart, bind thy spirit, and split thine soul. Whatever else happened, Fate was with her in this moment as she felt her magic, every bit of it from every cell in her body, pouring into the spell, working quickly as Niles stretched his arm forward, casting a distinctly different magic.

Averill laughed at Jael as she struggled to reach him, tracing the ground with Leland's sword as he knocked Abelard far to the side with a harsh spell: strong as he was, the boy collapsed, unmoving as his head slammed against the ground. The princess flew at the white haired mage, green electricity snapping from her fingers as she clawed at his face, but Averill caught her slender wrist in a painful grip as he forced her down in submission.

But then a new darkness spread over the clearing, blotting out the moonlight. Glenna could not stop her cast to glance aside, or even risk the distraction of noticing anything outside of herself, but even she knew that there was something wrong with the magic Niles had taken hold of. Maybe no one else could sense it, but she could. The wrongness she'd felt ever since she'd walked out of the castle towards the arena only intensified.

Break thy heart, bind thy spirit, and split thine soul.

Averill, seeing the black of the abyss circling Niles as it wove unknowable patterns around his form as the fiery eyes drained to obsidian, frowned and released Jael, who collapsed to the ground with a sob. The princess glared up at him, all consuming hatred burning in her emerald eyes as her mouth curled into a mask of ferocity.

But at the last second, she realized what he was doing as he approached Glenna, sword in hand, and her expression changed to horror as Averill knocked the spell book aside and clinically pierced Glenna through with Leland's longsword.

She had wielded a sword for most of her life, and she had even been wounded in the past, but Glenna had never realized how fragile her own flesh could be. He had stabbed her in the gut, deep enough so only Leland could have healed her had he lived. This wound would drain her of life slowly and painfully; as waves of pain began to spread out from her mortal injury, she pressed her hands over the seeping line in her abdomen, gasping for breaths that fought their way to freedom. Yet, strangely, the murmured spell directly from Fate continued, her mouth moving of its own accord.

"Halt your cast, boy. I am owed a soul, and you will not cheat me by damaging yours with that spell," Averill called to Niles, pointing Leland's sword at him as Glenna swayed on her feet, struggling to stay upright. Falling to her knees, she heard a wicked laugh come from the man who had said he'd loved her again and again.

"You will have neither my soul nor victory," Niles said, but even through the encroaching fog of her injury, Glenna heard the strange, perilous quality rendering his voice much altered from the one she knew. "You will have nothing, and will become nothing."

True to his word, nothing did appear: true nothing, the empty of the void splitting the air and atmosphere like a rip in a tapestry.

This phenomenon he'd called into their world wasn't so much a banishment as a summoning. This darkness that fed on the night like a parasite, composed of deepest ebony and a pressure so intense it seemed to shrink their arena into total flatness, was summoned for Averill, and it pulled the white haired Lord towards itself. Impossibly, Niles stood beside this entity, guiding it with the inaudible hum of his power as a strong wind only he could feel swirled about the dark cloud surrounding him.

The emptiness made Glenna feel barren, more consumed by the void than Leland's death had made her feel. It was this type of darkness, the bleak outlook upon a surface that had never altered and could expect eons upon eons of the same, that made her feel utterly useless and alone.

Could she do nothing right? Could she only do nothing at all?

But there was something she could do to make this awful day mean something. Reaching outside of herself with her mind, out of this dying vessel that had served her well over the years, she allowed her eyes to slip closed as she searched. There wasn't much left in

Glenna, or in him when she found the fading strands of Leland's consciousness, but she gripped them tight with all of her mental and magical strength. Her heart pumped out the remainder of its blood with each beat, so she used the pain to channel her spell with razor sharp focus.

She had to tie these bits of soul to something, so they wouldn't leave the world forever: souls had to have a vessel, at least on this plane of existence. Now, the invisible bindings floated absently in space, curling and uncurling like sea grass before her mind's perception. After a moment, an idea came to her, and she smiled faintly. Fitting.

Fate hadn't helped them prevail, but she wanted them to have a future. It was so clear to her now, but she was glad she hadn't realized the truth before: the cost of fragmenting her soul, and Leland's soul, was her life. Averill might not have realized it, but Fate had guided his hand as he struck blow that killed her.

Glenna glimpsed the new expression of fear on their enemy's face as the abyss called him forward, pulling the wolf turned man into its heart. Waves of power shook the clearing, and the stones of the castle, and the forest surrounding them for miles, but to no avail: Averill had been called, and the void would have what it came for. Seeing now the true nature of this dark, fear for Niles stopped her heart long enough to make her lose consciousness.

Perhaps mercifully, awareness returned only once Leland's fading soul had clung to her casting book. She had almost done it: her soul had to go next. It was fading already as the magic took its toll and her body bled out as surely as the dawn would arrive at the end of this night. The book rested nearby, though she couldn't reach it from where she'd fallen on the scorched grass. She'd succeeded with Leland: that much she knew, and she smiled weakly as her mind winked in and out of consciousness.

When she came to for the final time, she sensed Jael nearby, hovering over Leland's body beside a woozy but hearty Abelard as Glenna rested in Niles's arms. Rested? Could one rest while dying? Wounds like hers took time to kill, but she was so frail now that she knew she had only moments more.

She could see Niles, though, and feel his arms around her as he pulled her into his lap. Any trace of that other presence, the terrifying black and even the red dyeing her vision to signify Fate's specter attended her, had disappeared.

"Did...did it work? The banishing?" Stupid question, Glenna thought as she coughed. He wouldn't be here if we'd lost.

"He's gone," Niles confirmed; something cool brushed against her skin, and she realized it was his hand smoothing her hair from her face.

"Glenna, I'm so sorry...the spell had me completely in its thrall, I didn't even see when he—"

"Shhh," she sighed; liking the sound, she made it again. "Shhh. We did it. We'll carry on."

"What do you mean?" Niles asked; he was rocking her slowly back and forth, which was pleasant, though she doubted he'd realized it. "Of course you will, I've got you now. I can heal this."

"No..." Glenna protested, though her voice was feeble. She looked up, really looked into those amber eyes which reflected Niles's heart so clearly. "No, you can't...that was never your strong suit, healing. But that's fine. I need to go, I need to—"

"Be here with me. Just...Just do that, just be here with me," Niles's voice sounded like the best kind of music, the sort that made her remember how it felt to climb the tallest of the elm trees outside the castle for the first time, higher than anyone else, or how it felt when she got her first kiss from a soldier who's name she couldn't recall. But she didn't have time to enjoy it, which made her strangely sad.

Lifting her hand, sticky though it was with her blood, she caressed Niles's cheek. "I don't have the strength, but you can finish the cast, I know you can. I think...I think Leland is in there, but I don't know if I caught all of him in time. Jael...and Abelard...I can only preserve them if they're dying, and I don't think Fate wants them to. Just let—"

"What cast? What did you do?" Any other time he would have been furious, and she would have been angry at herself. She lacked knowledge of far too much: she knew the book would preserve the fragments of souls she gathered, or a whole soul in Niles's case, but what for? When would those strands be freed? And the banishment spell...for someone like Averill, that couldn't be a permanent fix. The trial had failed, and he would return.

Just let me go, she slipped into Niles's mind, knowing he'd be open for her. He was, and he allowed his whole self to wash over her in return, his love for her shining forth in its purest form. Their mental contact allowed her to tell him her secrets, her encounters with Fate that led to this moment where the only thing that mattered was the cast. Even now, she was almost forgetting to care, forgetting at the speed of the garnet blood flowing out of the wound in her gut.

Finish it, so we can get it right next time, she whispered to his mind, unexpected agony coloring her thoughts as she next asked the impossible. *Bind yourself with us, so we can fight him together.*

Glenna? Niles hadn't been afraid when he stood alone, banishing Averill into the abyss, but she heard the fear in his voice now. *Glenna, no...*

Kiss me, Niles, and then go. Maybe...Maybe we'll meet again, maybe this will have meant *something,* Glenna returned his thoughts as she slipped further into the dark.

"Promise," she asked of him, her last word. Opening her eyes fully, she seized hold of his shirt, grasping it tightly. Tilting his head downward, Niles held her cold body to him, bringing his mouth to hers in the gentlest kiss she'd ever received.

"I promise," he vowed, his voice cracking. Glenna knew if he agreed he'd have to find her book to do as she asked, which required laying her body down on the burnt-out ground, but that didn't stop her from dreading the loss of his presence. She felt no pain as he set her down, but the mortal chill tingling over her skin with the pinpricks of a deep fog disturbed her.

Turning her head, she looked over to where Leland lay, her raven and snow hair spilling out behind her head. Jael crouched over the body, weeping into the blood-soaked chest of her fallen prince. Beside her, Abelard knelt to the side, true sorrow in every line of his military posture as he paid homage to his deceased mentor. Glenna paid no attention to them; by another trick of Fate, Leland's head was turned her way, and she let her vision tunnel so all she saw were those misty gray eyes she'd loved so much.

The knowledge that had dawned on them at the same time, before Averill struck the killing blow on Oloetha's knight flickered again in her mind.

Fated...tied together as true mates of the soul at the dawn of the stars...oh Leland, how did we miss this?

But then she was falling, even the sight of Leland's lifeless eyes going black.

Rekindle the fire, she murmured before her own consciousness slipped away for good. *Future sister, do what we could not*

15

Accompanied by a dull, throbbing pain in her temples, she crawled back into awareness of her surroundings. There they were, reclining on the mountain ledge like something momentous had not taken place. Niles's anxious faced hovered above hers, familiar in new ways now that she remembered what he had been like before. She could see the differences, now: the darkness in his eyes went fathoms deep now, deeper than with any completely human eyes, and she could sense how strong he was after all that time absorbing magic through the book, through his surroundings, and even from his age.

They say those who are talented in magic get stronger with age...how powerful must he be now?

"I'm so sorry, I didn't mean for it to happen like that—" Niles was speaking like he'd been talking to her for a while, perhaps pleading for her to wake up. Still gazing up at him, she inhaled slowly, a shaking, rasping breath that echoed hollow in her chest. How strange it was to be alive again! Her hands flew to her torso, groping for the hole where Averill had thrust Leland's sword once he'd...

She might as well say it. Her bonded, the man Fate had written to be hers and then cruelly given to another, was gone. Leland was dead. Dead dead. Niles didn't have any of his memories to pass on to Colt. Part of her had come back, though at the present she wished it hadn't.

"N-Niles," she spoke as she exhaled. "It's...good to see you again." These didn't feel like Gwendoline's words, but was she Gwendoline any longer? Had Glenna taken over? Judging by the pain, escorted with its sometimes welcome companion of numbness, she felt more like Glenna.

Niles cocked his head, careful impassivity a mask over his features. "Glenna? Are you...are you Glenna, now?"

"I don't know," she snapped. "Who do you want it to be?" Aggravated with her weakness, unable to dismiss the hope lighting Niles's eyes, she forced her prone body into a sitting position and exhaled again, her hands still clutching her currently whole stomach. There were so many other problems to consider, but her disoriented brain kept returning like a boomerang to one thing: Leland.

"Are you all right? Do you need anything?" Niles asked her. Ignoring him, and noticing that he had failed to answer, she struggled into a standing position and swatted away his helping hands.

Closing her eyes, she engaged in a head to toe assessment: she was hale and hearty, and nothing much was wrong with her aside from her disorientation. She recognized her body, welcomed all the sensations like old friends who had abandoned her only to return when she least expected them, and noted the differences with inquisitive interest. Glenna had been slender to the point of bony severity, but Gwendoline had managed to find the balance between skinny and curvy with ease. Gwendoline also wore casual light-wash jeans that Glenna would have liked to don for riding and sparring. As for the hair, the only difference was that hers was black and wavy, and Glenna's had been white and pin straight as well: both of them had styled their hair in hasty braids more often than not.

"I need..." she said at last, realizing minutes had passed without her moving or uttering a word. "I need to see Colt."

Perhaps she did. No, she did want to see Colt, if only to see whatever part of Leland was left. But this wasn't all Glenna, though her need to set eyes on him for herself pressed urgently. Gwendoline's emotional distress wanted to act out to spite Niles for the hope he'd expressed when Glenna had spoken first.

"Colt?" He had not gone cold, not yet. But she had only begun to hurt him, to punish him for so obviously wanting Glenna.

"What did you expect, Niles? Glenna loved Leland, believed he was the only one for her...did you think death would change her mind? My...mind?" She was furious, fuming so much she felt her cheeks redden from her rage. But uncertainty won out in the end, unclenching her fists and making her sway with dizziness. Nothing was the same, yet she and Niles had to keep on fighting...and she could see something Glenna couldn't now. She knew part of Glenna had belonged to Niles, too, though she had never told him, or even been able to admit it to herself.

Fate's blood, would the torment never cease? Had she merely carried her suffering to another life?

"I think we should get you home, at least for a while until—"

"Until what? Until you decide whether or not you want Glenna or Gwendoline?" She snapped at him again, her magic spiraling further out of control: her breath steamed out of her like smoke, shimmering the palest of blues. "Because I think you've already chosen Glenna, and if that's the case I can make it home on my own."

"Why are you speaking for me?" Niles demanded, his temper slipping as he scowled. "Do you not remember our conversation before I returned your memories?" Perhaps he realized he'd made a mistake, or perhaps his face paled out of impatient frustration. All the fight went out of her in an anticlimactic sigh; had she ever felt more drained before?

"I remember a lot of things," she said at last. Chilled from the mountain breeze that swirled around them, she pulled the jacket Niles had given her closer about her shoulders. "I remember a lot I wish I didn't. But as long as I recall the important stuff it was worth it, right?"

Niles stared at her, apparently at a loss for words. "I'm sorry."

She felt a faint smile wobbling onto her freshly kissed lips. "What for? You can't help who you love."

"Gwendoline, that's not what I meant!" He stepped forward, and she could see his longing to hold her shining in his eyes. Why were the irises dark now? Maybe she'd lost the ability to read him when she'd lost her assurance of what it was to be only herself.

"I don't feel like Gwendoline anymore, but I know I'm not Glenna. If I can't tell the difference, you can't be expected to either, but...I don't know," she rambled, losing her train of thought along the way.

"I know the difference," he said earnestly, each word distinct. "After all this time, why would you think I can't tell the difference?"

Because you can't, she thought, that brief, savage rage returning to her long enough to sour her thoughts. *Like I don't know who you expected to see when I woke up.*

"I need you to go," she whispered, hardly able to hear her own words.

It took him a heartbeat, but he knew what she meant. Sensing his power as she could, she knew it would be no trouble for him to teleport to a different location so she could hike back down alone. She'd never seen it done, had not met anyone that powerful, but she knew without a doubt that Niles could teleport away if she made him. Maybe she could too, if she'd had the energy to try. Glenna's power had joined her own supply, a formidable addition she'd have to explore when she could calm herself.

"I can't leave you like this," Niles frowned, "You're barely lucid, and it's a long hike back." She felt him then, brushing against her mind. He'd gone the extra mile and let her sense his emotions without holding back. Maybe Just Gwendoline would have cared. But whoever she was now, she couldn't handle that, and most of all she didn't want to see the flame that still burned for Glenna within him.

"Please," she said, studying the intricate puzzle of lines within the stone below her feet so she wouldn't have to see his face. "*Please.*"

A whisper of wind blew through her, teasing the wispy hairs that had escaped from her braid. Only when she'd looked around to make sure he'd really gone did she allow her confusion to take over, making her shiver uncontrollably as she began the long walk home.

By the time the glass door slammed shut behind her as she pushed through the entryway of her house, her whole body ached as tears tinted blue from her residual magic slid down her cheeks. Her breath continued to catch in her throat, the sobs choking her as she stumbled over to her kitchen counter to lean on the cool surface. The one thing she could take comfort in was the fact that Niles would not see her completely lose control like this. He at least would not see her descent into madness if she failed to master herself and her memories.

Still disoriented enough to be clumsy, she knocked over her purse: it spilled keys, pens, receipts, and several almost empty packs of tropical flavored gum onto the stone tiled floor. This mindless accident made her cry harder, and she viciously seized her purse and hurled it against the wall, a wail tearing from her throat. Deep down, she realized she was grieving more than her fight with Niles, mourning more besides her belief that Niles was truly in love with Glenna, not her.

Leland. Leland, Colt, Leland, Colt, Leland, Colt, her heartbeats all echoed the name, one of which she mourned with an anguish so complete she felt almost bent over with the pain in her heart.

He died. Better than Glenna, who was no stranger to the pain of unrequited love, Gwendoline knew the truth her former self had not discovered until she'd come to death's door.

Meant to be. We were meant to be...weren't we? Until the end.

"Isn't that...isn't that the most ridiculous piece of shit you've ever heard?" She said aloud, seeking comfort that wouldn't come in the sound of her own familiar voice. She howled with misery again, her furious energy unspent. Gwendoline's firm control over all the other aspects of her life was no match for the fury of the emotions burning through her in this moment.

We died, he didn't love me, and now he never will. The energy needed to go somewhere, she had to get it out, she must, or it would consume her so that even capricious Fate could not bring her back to face this again.

If she was burning, it all had to burn.

Gwendoline slammed her hands onto the countertop, palms flat against the surface. Fire magic was dangerous, most powerful when fueled by the caster's own emotions, and therefore all the more volatile; she rarely indulged in it, but in this case she held nothing back as she simply let go of her control. White flames tinged with deepest red at their core fanned from where she'd struck the surface, consuming everything in their path with a slow burn.

Objectively she knew she was acting insane, she was *burning down her house* to escape the agony that felt like it would kill her, but she watched the flames and inhaled the smoke without halting the destruction anyway. Part of her felt relief that, if she stayed, it would all be over soon. Selfish or not, she couldn't breathe, not when...

"Gwendoline!" She knew who that voice belonged to before she turned to face it. Sure enough, Colt stood in the doorway, staring with open-mouthed horror at the flames burning through her kitchen and living room. He cast his hands out over the flames, barking out a reversal spell in the private language all casters had. The flames cooled and faded, evaporating into mist. As they dissipated, the only destruction that they left behind were the clouds of unnaturally bright smoke drifting through Gwendoline's house.

They stared at each other from across the room, panting and out of breath.

"What the *fuck*, Gwendoline?" Colt said at last, coughing. He looked like he wanted to be furious, like he was about to shake her and demand an explanation for what he'd just witnessed, but the silence that filled the room after his one exclamation remained unbroken.

"Colt...what are you doing here?" she questioned at last, taking a tentative step towards him. Leland would never return, but Colt was here. That fact, wild as it was, grounded her enough to allow her to take a deep, consoling breath.

"Gwendoline," he spoke, frozen in place like he was an ancient marble sculpture, magnificent in its detail and beauty. His blue eyes—they were blue, comforting blue, not Leland's cool silver—bored into hers, and then she caught the thread of knowledge that had evaded her.

"You remember?" She asked hoarsely, advancing another step. *How does he have memories? Niles said there wasn't a chance they were preserved. But I preserved him. I caught his soul by the wings and bound it to my book...*

"I...I do. I remember everything," he replied. He gazed down at her steadily enough, but the turmoil and doubt in his eyes made her ache for him.

Everything...then he knew what she did. That last trick Fate had sprung on them, giving them knowledge of the destiny they had missed out on.

"How? Niles said he didn't have your fragments," Gwendoline clenched her hands into fists again, wincing as she noticed for the first time the shallow cuts on her palms.

"I don't know. Maybe he just couldn't sense them," Colt guessed.

"Maybe," she conceded doubtfully, not knowing what else to say. If he had known about their destiny, would he have interfered as he had in this timeline?

The atmosphere had grown heavier, too thick for any more talk. He was here—with her, not with Jael or Everleigh—and the present felt charged with electricity that seared them both. Neither one had moved, but Gwendoline felt the current between them both snap taut with enough energy to pull them together. It felt like her wretchedness was splitting her open, tearing her in two just as she'd been made a whole soul again that afternoon. Even worse, she felt like the bits and pieces flying off her in shreds were becoming something else, splicing with Colt to form something new and so intense that she had never felt its like before.

As if it had always been intended, Gwendoline threw herself into Colt's burly arms, dragging her hands through his thick auburn hair as she smashed her lips against his. Part of her, perhaps the Glenna part, expected that he would resist, pulling away to ask her what the hell she was thinking.

Everleigh was not Jael, since Jael had died long ago trapped in a timeline with neither friends nor family, and Niles was in love with a shadow. Neither one of them knew why their destiny had been to love, sometimes unknowingly, if Fate had kept them apart in their previous life. But the here and now in this life was what mattered, and this eternal draw could not be denied.

Colt pulled her body tighter against his, bending her against him as he kissed her back. It was only a kiss, though it was the type of kiss that tended to encourage more, but the release she felt at finally being able to show her true heart made her moan. When he echoed her sound, both of his hands splayed against her back, she saw stars behind her closed eyes.

She was hungry for him, ravenous for more, and he shared her desire. His hands wandered, both of them sliding down to the small of her back then coming to rest at the curve of her hips. His mouth tasted fiery to her, like cinnamon and clove, and while she couldn't get enough, she simply needed to pull his head back so she could kiss his throat, perhaps bite it just hard enough to tease forth some goosebumps. She certainly had them, as any girl would if Colt's hands were all over her.

They had to get closer, be closer. She pushed him back against the counter, tugging at the bottom of his blue t-shirt until he let go of her long enough to allow her to remove the garment. Gwendoline had seen him shirtless before, when he'd been playing soccer in the park with his friends over years of summers, but this time when she knew she was going to be allowed to touch, the sight made her shiver with anticipation.

But something made her pause, turning the enjoyable quivers to a wave of queasiness

"What?" Colt asked, breathless. He glanced down to where she was staring, then did a double take as he saw the new scars. The atmosphere in the room, so deliciously warm seconds ago, grew as heavy as a thunderhead. Setting his jaw, he looked up at Gwendoline to witness her reaction.

"I didn't know..." she began, but words seemed inadequate. Reaching forward, she brushed her fingertips against the deep red scar marking where Averill had impaled Leland. *You can even see where he twisted the sword,* she thought, nauseated as the memory of Leland's dying screams returned to her. Gritting her teeth, she set her other hand on his shoulder, slowly inching her way down his arm until she felt the raised scar marking where Averill had torn Leland's arm clean from his body.

"I'm sorry," she said, unsure of anything else to say that would communicate the depth of her sorrow. "I...I'm so, so sorry, Leland." In place of answering, or acknowledging her use of his old name, he closed his eyes, inhaling and exhaling twice in a search for peace.

Gwendoline mirrored him, feeling the hot tears that lingered heavily on her eyelashes, but she gasped when she felt Leland's hand begin to pull her shirt up. At first, she thought he had another goal in mind, but his expression remained serious as he slowly lifted the shirt until he saw the scar she should have guessed she'd have.

Her mark was not as large as his, just as her mortal injury had been almost surgical. Averill had simply stabbed her in the gut, seeking to kill her in a way that would be slow and inexorable. The scarlet line, the exact width of Leland's sword, ran in a straight line the right side of her abdomen, proof that yes, she'd actually been Glenna, and Glenna had died. How disturbing to realize that the sword Colt casually carried around most of the time was the same one that had taken her life in the past.

Colt wouldn't look her in the eye, though she tried to meet his gaze. He suddenly knelt before her, taller than most even on his knees, and she marveled that she didn't melt into a puddle as he held her hips in his hands and brushed his lips against her new scar.

"I thought you were dead before that happened," she whispered.

"Yet I knew when he killed you, somehow. My heart, living or dead, *felt* when it happened." Their eyes met as he drew back, communicating a shared pain.

Colt rose to his feet and effortlessly picked her up, lifting her so she could sit on her kitchen island. He yanked her head back by her almost undone braid, pressing his hot mouth to the pulse in her neck. A shudder of desire coursed through Gwendoline and she moaned, sinking her fingertips into his broad, bare back.

It's real, Gwendoline felt her racing heart slow at the thought. *If we do this now, we can no longer say it was a fit of madness, a sin in the moment.*

No excuses.

The moment of introspection passed as quickly as it came, and Colt tore her shirt off, shortly followed by the bra he expertly unclipped, and buried his face between her breasts. Gwendoline leaned back on the countertop of the island, twining her legs around him so she could pull him closer. His mouth worked over her pale skin, drawing forth a sigh here, gifting her with a love mark there. Had she ever been this complete?

Something about their connection sparked the magic within Gwendoline, and the same flames that had threatened to consume her home minutes earlier began to devour them both. The flames, golden instead of pure white, danced over and under their skin, the heat almost unbearable, but they felt no pain. Only the two of them existed in this time, and the one thing that mattered was their connection, centuries in the making.

16

Surely this couldn't be the worst Monday in her life...well, in this life at least. Gwendoline lay back in her bed, the too-warm sheets tangled fast around one of her legs. The rest of her, pale skin exposed, felt chilled by the morning atmosphere. She would have pulled the lavender print quilt up to snuggle into, but Colt had slung his arm carelessly over her torso, and she didn't want to wake him.

Turning from her bland contemplation of her ceiling fan, she stared listlessly at his peaceful, slumbering face. I can spare him from waking to this nightmare just a little longer, she thought.

Gwendoline wasn't sure how it was possible, but their frenzied coupling during the night—Colt's stamina had almost exhausted her—had provided such a catharsis to everything that had been happening to her lately that her overflowing emotional well had converted to a barren oasis. She'd wanted to talk to him, after, to try to wade through this muddle of circumstances they'd stumbled into. But then again, she hadn't really wanted to talk, or think about anything at all.

More than pleasure, she had sought the blankness of not needing to think.

Absentminded, she reached out to push a few strands of red honey colored hair from his eyes. Whatever else happened, they'd always have this night. That torn feeling scrambling her thoughts had faded, along with her confusion over who she was. True, she sensed Glenna within her, and perhaps always would. But somehow, now that she was calm, she knew she was Gwendoline, and that was the important thing.

If Gwendoline could have climbed out from the pit of apathy she'd stumbled into, her main sensation would have to be...guilt. What had she done? What had she done with Colt, who happened to be in a loving, committed, forever kind of relationship with Everleigh, her best friend. How would she explain this? How could she? Even Glenna had never learned how to describe the level of connection she had felt with Leland. Whatever reasons Fate had had for linking the two of them together, she certainly hadn't bothered to make that part any easier.

And Niles...what would he say? He hadn't come home at all last night, or she fervently hoped he hadn't tried to. She had banished him on the mountain where they'd come to some kind of understanding and kissed, then in her anguish she'd returned home and promptly fucked Colt who, somehow, still retained a part of Leland. Gwendoline turned away from Colt, suddenly wishing to be free from the weight of his muscular arm. Instead, she faced the window, where misty light peered down at them through the sliver where her semi-sheer curtains parted.

Abruptly, the shrill timbre of her phone's ringtone demolished the morning silence, disrupting her contemplation. Beside her, Colt snapped upright, blearily fumbling for his sword, which Gwendoline knew he hadn't brought with him into her house. Annoyed with the interruption, she grabbed the device from her nightstand and glanced at the screen. Her heart dropped when she saw the name displayed.

"It's Everleigh," she spoke in a frantic whisper, though her volume wouldn't impact anyone until she picked up the phone. Colt nodded for a few beats, not comprehending what she said until his brain caught up to his body's wakefulness. Then he paled, his blue eyes growing rounder.

"Are-Are you going to answer?" he asked, also whispering. Gwendoline frowned at him then glanced back at her phone.

Just do it, she told herself, *rip the band-aid off.*

"Good morning?" she said after she tapped the green button on the screen. Her voice almost squeaked, but she cleared her throat and it returned to normal. "This is early."

"Morning." Maybe it was her imagination, or the guilt taking root, but Gwendoline's friend didn't sound as chipper as she normally did. "Is Colt there?"

"Why—yes, he's here," Gwendoline admitted, steeling herself for the inevitable follow-up queries. Seeing the apprehension on Colt's face, she pulled the gray knit sheets around herself and sat up as well. How did she know already?

"Oh good!" Everleigh exhaled with relief, shocking her. "He ran off last night after we had a fight over nothing. He didn't seem like himself at all, he kept snapping at me about stuff and then he ran off. I assumed of course that he went to your house, or one of his college buddies, but...oh, I've been so worried!"

So she doesn't know, Gwendoline realized, ashamed of how swiftly relief spread through her before anxiety tainted the moment again.

Should I tell her? Should...we?

Colt held his silence like a protective aura, offering no input; it was strange to Gwendoline that now, however long this lasted, she could think of them as "we."

"He was here, and he's fine," Gwendoline said at last, holding Colt's gaze as she lied. "I've just woken up, but my couch is empty, so I guess he's headed off to classes already."

"Oh. Oh good," Everleigh's relief stabbed her again. "Well, I'll call him in a bit, then. Do you want to have coffee later? We can go to that newer place downtown, we haven't been there in ages. You know, the one that always has flowers?"

"I-I'll get back to you on that, I think I might be busy later," Gwendoline spoke all in one breath.

"With Niles? Is he going to bug you about those memories again?" Everleigh asked playfully. All was right in her world now that she knew Colt was safe, and she didn't suspect a thing. Gwendoline winced as she mentioned Niles, pushing the tangled mass of her dark hair back from her face and knotting it with one hand and a bit of magic into a sloppy bun. She'd forgotten that she hadn't told Everleigh about her plan to take Glenna's fragments from Niles.

"Hey, I've got to get ready for school since I'm running so late," she recovered from her flash of pain as she tried to excuse herself from further dialogue. "I'll catch up with you later."

"I want to hear everything about your magical date with Niles!" Everleigh sang as Gwendoline hung up.

It wasn't a date, it was a nightmare that ended in insanity, she frowned; then, looking over at Colt, she flinched again. *But the insanity had felt so, so good...*

"Your phone?" Gwendoline quizzed him, tossing her own back

onto her nightstand; the device beeped sullenly, reminding her that she'd forgotten to charge it the night before.

"In my car," Colt answered, rubbing the residual lines of sleep away from his face with both calloused hands. "But I forget my phone there a lot, so she won't be alarmed if I don't answer for a while. I always call her back." He was right; Gwendoline remembered Everleigh complaining once how he always forgot to call her back, so from then on he'd made a point to get in touch with her if he'd missed a call.

He stood too hastily, almost slipping on her polished wood floor before he righted himself and disappeared from her bedroom. A few seconds later, he returned with his shirt in his hands as he stumbled into his jeans. Gwendoline didn't like it, but her eyes traveled down Colt's defined tan chest to the place where he zipped up the well-fitting jeans. Biting her bruised lips, she forced herself to look away.

"A good friend would have told her...a better friend wouldn't have done this at all," Gwendoline sighed; abruptly, she realized she was the only one still nude, so with a few hums she called forth a fresh pair of leggings and a simple red shirt from her closet. Belatedly, she realized she'd forgotten a bra and underwear, but she didn't want her intimates zooming around the room when he was standing right there, not when he knew all too well what she looked like without them. The shirt and leggings would have to be enough for now.

"The same can be said for a long-term boyfriend, but that doesn't change what happened," Colt retorted, sharply enough that she caught the annoyance. "And now, what? What...damn, I'm not the kind of person to pick up and leave after a night like that, after waking up next to someone. Someone who happens to be one of my best friends."

"I don't think either of us are the same person we were before yesterday," Gwendoline said, avoiding his gaze as she stood to dress. Even so, she felt Colt staring at her. Self-conscious—but flattered—she tugged her leggings over her legs and bottom and shrugged her shirt on.

Now clothed, she'd run out of ways to avoid looking at him. They faced off in Gwendoline's bedroom, stock still and more awkward with each other than they'd been their entire lives.

"You know, it makes sense how I had such a crush on you back in high school," he rushed the words, almost stuttering. She hated how this endeared him to her. How could she think of him this way, how could she be so selfish?

"What? You did?" Gwendoline asked, caught completely off guard. She pictured Colt as a teenager during the point in their lives he'd mentioned: awkward, though more poised than many boys his age, and built like a man instead of a gawky youth. Still just as sweet and respectable, though he shared her irreverent sense of humor, and he often got in trouble with the hosts of friends a person like him attracted. What had she been like back then? Emo, of course: she had her own inheritance and relative independence, but she had to share families alternately with Colt Redfield and Everleigh Northwood after her stepmother ran off, and that wasn't nearly enough.

"Mortifying as it is to tell you this way, I did. I could get away with walking you to class because we were just friends, but I wanted to tell you stupid stuff like how I loved your laugh, and how I couldn't get enough of our spell practicing sessions. I spent the first three years of high school dreaming about kissing you...you had this habit of putting up your hair and taking it down all the time during class, and I wanted to kiss your neck every time. I couldn't seem to find the right time or the perfect words, though, and you always had a date to school functions…"

Perhaps they both remembered at the same time: senior prom, where Gwendoline had taken her side-guy-turned-boyfriend to the event, and Colt…

"You started dating Everleigh in high school," she said quietly.

"Yeah. I did." Colt came forward, beginning to reach out, but she leaned back on her heels and defensively crossed her arms. "I don't even think you realized I wanted to be more than friends, and Everleigh so persistently asked me out that I thought I'd give her a chance." Locked into silence again, each of them wondered how different their lives might have been had Colt voiced his attraction to Gwendoline in the first place.

"So, what are we going to do? You're going to abandon Everleigh and I'm going to abandon Niles? Is there a solution that won't tank the trust and lives of everyone we care about?" If the choice was between feeling heartache or anger, Gwendoline chose anger in a burning flash.

"What does Niles have to do with it?" Colt asked, thrown; then, understanding dawned in his eyes. "You…you like him?" The edges of his eyes crinkled into a suspicious squint: would he be jealous if she told him the truth?

"I…think I do?" Realizing how idiotic this sounded, Gwendoline huffed in frustration, looking down and toying with a loose thread dangling from the hem of her shirt. "Well, Gwendoline does, irrational as that sounds…and Glenna, too, at least a little." She looked up at Colt, gauging his reaction, but his face had become a handsome mask. How imperious he looked to her then, a distant prince avoiding a messy, complicated interaction with one of his subjects.

"I don't think…whatever else happened last night, I do love

Everleigh, and I don't regret a single thing about our relationship," he said, trying to sound unaffected but failing; lost in thought, he continued under his breath. "Not a damn thing."

"And...Niles," Gwendoline felt the weight of it all pressing down on her again, intent on grinding her poor being into the antique floorboards of her home. "He may love Glenna, and always will, but I'm still...kind of crazy about him."

For no reason, she laughed, if only because doing anything else meant that she'd cry. Colt laughed with her, a gentle chuckle that turned into a full blown roar of laughter that had him bending over with his hands on his knees. Gwendoline echoed his hilarity, the obnoxious humor of the situation expelled in a relief of sound.

"Th-This is absurd," he choked between breaths. Unable to speak, she nodded, a few tears pinching their way free from the corners of her eyes. In a moment or two, the surge of comedy passed, and they faced each other again, puffing with breathlessness.

"I'm going to head out," Colt said at last, serious again. "I need to...figure some things out, I guess."

"Right," Gwendoline agreed. Suddenly awkward, Colt realized he hadn't put his shirt on, and moved to finish dressing.

"Wait," Gwendoline internally groaned, embarrassed for remembering to correct this detail so her lies would hold up. Before he could put his shirt on, she hummed a cast, erasing the love bites she'd bestowed on him last night. Understanding her purpose, Colt hummed a spell of his own, smoothing away the hickies he'd left on her throat; perhaps it was wise that he didn't dare venture below the V of her shirt to remove the other marks.

"You should go," she murmured, looking down at his abs instead of at his face. Her hand lingered where she'd placed it, splayed flat against his warm skin.

Before she knew it, his mouth was on hers again, warm and reassuring. It was a comforting kiss, unexpected but welcome; she melted into him. Then, recovering herself, she gently pushed him away.

"I think you should go," she repeated, though as she looked up at him she knew her eyes told a different story. Colt knew, of course; one side of his mouth lifted, and he cupped her face in one of his hands, tracing her lips with his thumb.

"We'll talk later. We'll...get it right," he said to her before he withdrew with obvious reluctance. For now she couldn't see any other alternative. Maybe another meeting would help them solve this problem—if they could manage to stay out of each other's pants, which she doubted—this complicated love quartet that would get them all killed if Averill decided to start a conflict when they were all so very divided.

Irrelevant to the moment, an idea occurred to her, a solution to the problem she'd been puzzling over since the moment Averill tore out Leland's throat. *So divided, without any ties to bind us together...how can a heart, a soul, a spirit work when there's nothing to connect them?*

But then the notion disappeared, and she was alone in her house as the birds outside her window began to chirp their morning greetings.

After Colt's car rumbled out of her driveway, Gwendoline stumbled to the bathroom and leaned heavily on the sink. Knowing already how hung over she was going to look, she lifted her gaze to the mirror and scowled. To her surprise, the monster of remorse feasting on her guts hadn't yet travelled to her exterior, and her pale skin had a lovely flush about the cheeks that made her blue-violet eyes—

Everleigh liked to call her Liz now and then, after Liz Taylor—pop. Even her hair, twisted into a messy knot on the top of her head, softened her appearance to a gentle early 1900's vibe. Aside from her glower, Gwendoline could've actually competed with Jael's beauty today.

Snarling, Gwendoline froze her mirror solid with a barked cast, then heated it slowly, watching as the cracks began to spread.

Maybe she should have punished herself by going to her classes after all. It would be painful enough to count as some of the punishment she doubtless deserved, since she would be rendered useless by her complete inability to pay attention to anything outside of her thoughts. Instead, Gwendoline didn't have it in her to buckle down and suffer. Was that the problem? She was weak, and when a crisis had arisen, she'd settled for intimacy with the wrong person.

Or was he the *right* person?

At any rate, instead of class she'd taken a couple of hours to drive to the farthest park in Starford, a place where few tourists or city favorites ventured. The drive ended with a stop at a tiny café near the heart of this quiet district, since she'd skipped her coffee this morning in favor of fleeing her house like it was the scene of a terrible crime. In its own way, she guessed it was a terrible crime.

True, she wasn't solving any of her problems by avoiding everyone she knew and huddling alone in an overlarge hoodie where strangers could stare at her, but it comforted her to sit in the very back of the café just to think. Gwendoline looked up the local newspaper on her phone, but aside from the catchy headline speculating on the possible election related political swarm coming soon—Starford's elders must have somehow kept Everleigh's name a secret for now, since she hadn't seen her mentioned—she hadn't read a word in hours. Early morning had passed into afternoon without her taking note of the progression of time, except when she finished her first totally black coffee and bought another sweetened brew.

With so many problems to consider, like her night with Colt, or the possibility of Averill taking over the world one region at a time with a captive Everleigh at his side, she almost missed the flash of movement right outside the window of the café. She did a double take, almost spilling her brown sugar accented breve onto the smooth tabletop beside her newspaper.

A dog wagging its tail stood just outside, staring at Gwendoline with its head cocked to the side. She had never had a pet, since her stepmother hadn't been fond of animals and Colt and Everleigh had kept too busy for pets until the latter found her less than cuddly snake familiar. However, she was fairly sure dogs didn't behave this way, coming up to random buildings and staring inside at a specific person so intently. This dog hardly seemed real. She could tell it was a Dalmatian, possibly less than a year old, but its fur flowed much longer and silkier than she'd expected.

It even has a heart shaped spot on its nose. Unsure what to do about the staring, Gwendoline slowly tilted her head to the side as well and blinked at the animal, staring into its eyes, which were a curious shade of blue not unlike her own. *Don't most dogs have brown eyes...?*

In response to catching her attention, the dog's tail beat side to side at an increased tempo. Then it pressed its damp black nose against the glass of the window and *huffed*. Without noticing she was doing it, Gwendoline laughed, leaning forward as the Dalmatian snuffled against the smooth surface. She didn't see a collar or anything that would identify the beast, which saddened her.

The dog snorted again, leaving a fog of moisture and schnoodle on the glass. It about faced, prancing away from the café. She half expected the animal to turn back around expectantly, but it gamboled down the street alone.

Glancing between the disappearing black-tipped tail of the dog and the rest of her coffee on the table, Gwendoline checked to make sure none of the bored baristas were looking her way before she grabbed the cup with both hands and dashed outside.

It took some careful jogging—she had to cast a protection spell over her beverage to keep it in the cup and not all over her clothes or the ground—but eventually she caught up to the Dalmatian enough to get its attention again. It paused, waiting for her and standing still barely long enough for her to reach out and pat its head before it took off again.

Gwendoline hoped it wouldn't lead her on a merry goose chase through the whole of the village before she caught up to it again. She realized she was acting foolish, that the dog would probably be fine and had a loving family who lived around the corner in one of the cookie cutter subdivisions, but she couldn't let it run off alone. So, she trudged along behind, sipping from her coffee when she could.

The dog led her to an actual park, the type of flat, green, stereotypical commons suburban families took their kids to. Because the weather had started to get colder, and school wasn't out for the day yet, only a few people meandered about the area: a huff-and-puffing middle-aged jogger, a circle of teenage stoners cutting class, and there, sitting on an antique park bench...

Niles.

Fate, he was here, and for all her wasted time thinking things through, she hadn't thought up a single tale to tell him. Would she be honest? Would she lie to him like she'd lied to Everleigh? It's not like they were an official couple. But would he make that distinction?

The Dalmatian trotted up to Niles, its tongue hanging halfway out of its mouth. He reached out to pet it, murmuring "good girl" under his breath, and the dog lapped up a treat from his fingers. Then, it turned back to Gwendoline, jumping up suddenly in a bid for attention; the activity kept her from staring stupidly at him with her mouth hanging open.

"Where did you go last night?" Gwendoline asked at last, holding up her beige porcelain mug so the beautiful animal wouldn't knock it out of her hands in its desperate plea for more petting.

"I *am* capable of finding lodging for the night," Niles said. "The rest came easily enough."

Do you have to look this good? Gwendoline wondered, frowning as she stared at him again. He'd changed from his hiking wear yesterday, and the wine colored button down partially concealed by the charcoal pea coat suited him all too well. And was he wearing cologne? He smelled wonderful, *bad* wonderful, and she couldn't tell if it was just his scent calling out to her, or a little manufactured help.

"How...how did you find me?" she asked once she calmed the dog with a few scratches under her chin.

"I had reason to believe you would choose to abandon your classes, so I've been travelling between different areas of Starford and the little towns keeping an eye out for you," Niles explained.

"That's a lot of ground to cover in a morning's time," Gwendoline sighed, flopping onto the space of bench beside him; the remaining sips of coffee did their best to escape the confines of the cup, but her spell held. "I assume you had your new friend help you out?"

"Sort of. I actually went to a shelter last night as I was walking around the city, and Dancer had just come in. For some reason I couldn't leave her there..." Geller correctly surmised that by "Dancer" he meant the Dalmatian, and her tight shoulders eased somewhat.

"The hotel let you bring in an untrained puppy?" she asked, holding out her hand for Dancer to sniff.

"What they don't know won't hurt them. Besides, I already had to hex the innkeeper to forget that I hadn't paid for the room, so what's a stray dog staying with me on top of that?" Niles shrugged; a moment later, when she tipped the cup to her lips to finish her drink, she realized that he'd refilled it by magic without saying anything.

"You hexed the 'innkeeper?'" she mocked the old fashioned name for hotel manager, licking a dash of foam off her top lip; funny, this coffee tasted better than the one she'd already finished. "But most people are magical in this area, so that would require you bypassing his protective wards without him noticing—"

"So?" A cocky smile played about his mouth, which was outlined by a handsome five o'clock shadow, but it disappeared as she stared blankly at him. Perhaps recalling their last meeting, they both sobered. To avoid looking at him—on the off chance that he would perceive the secrets she felt were written all over her face—she reached out her free hand to caress one of Dancer's sleek black ears.

"You know, you used to write when you were younger how much you'd rather have a dog than a book for a familiar," Niles began, studying her; a moment later, he too held a mug like hers in his hands, full of dark, rich smelling coffee. "I can't say that didn't hurt, since I was in said casting book at the time, but I think you drew a few sketches of a Dalmatian now and then."

Suspicious, Gwendoline gave Niles the side-eye. "Did you conjure me a dog to try to apologize?"

"Well, Glenna loathed dogs, but I knew you enjoyed—why, would that work?" Niles smiled, clearly trying to break the discomfiture creating a barrier between them, but she couldn't smile back.

Another comparison to her, the irrational rage she as Gwendoline had felt previously flickered.

He tried again. "I mean, I felt culpable for your current lack of a familiar, since my exiting the book basically ruined the binding power a familiar would have, so...yes, if you want her, I found Dancer for you."

"Niles—" she began, trying to choose patience over exasperation.

"Look, whatever else happens, I don't think you should be alone, and at the very least she'll be an excellent watchdog. She doesn't seem all that bothered by spells, and that will be useful in the coming days, maybe," he interrupted.

Gwendoline glanced down, pausing as Dancer's gaze locked onto hers. Before she realized what was happening, a strange bond began to weave itself between them with invisible magic cords as she gazed into those cornflower irises. If Niles hadn't found the dog first, Dancer would have come looking for Gwendoline, or vice versa. Against all odds, she'd truly gained a familiar, the type Everleigh would call a traditional familiar, one who would live as long as she did and forever keep her company.

Everleigh...

"Dancer is a good name for her," Gwendoline said at last, setting her coffee cup on the ground next to the park bench so she could cup the puppy's face in both of her cold hands; her hoodie sleeves flopped forward at first, but she pushed them back. "Thank you, Niles."

She couldn't see all of his face as he took another sip of his beverage, but she could've sworn he was smiling. This irked her, though somewhere deep in her gut she realized that her illogical irritation was a defense against the raging torrent of shame surging within.

"So, you found me. What do you want?" Gwendoline said tersely.

"I want to talk about what happened yesterday. I wanted to see if you're all right, and I want to clarify a few things now that you've...regained your composure," Niles said. "More than that, I want to apologize for how everything happened."

"So talk," she sighed, slouching down in her seat and resisting the urge to pull her hood over her messy hair. He looked so poised and polished, damn him. Normally she tried to do the same, but today she looked and felt like a slob, and would rather not have been spotted by anyone she knew. Thankfully, the asthmatic jogger and distant stoner kids remained oblivious to the man and woman sitting on a park bench with a dog.

"I'm not sure where to begin, but I'll start with the apology, I suppose," Niles embarked on his explanation of events. "I didn't mean to throw you into the memories like that, I was going to share them a few at a time, if I could, and ease you into it. We kissed, and I just...it's like Glenna *wanted* to be joined with you. And I had hope for our future, suddenly, when I hadn't experienced that feeling in so long...but that's not really an excuse."

"Go on," Gwendoline encouraged, when Niles paused. He gazed out over the park, a gust of wind teasing his hair, and leaned forward with his elbows on his knees as he cradled his plain white mug in his hands. How different he looked from Colt! He was about as tall, true, and no scrawny weakling. But he was elegant where Colt was a bruiser, a dazzling rapier compared to a sturdy broadsword, and his words and voice could flow quick and smooth like poetry or the music she loved to compose.

"When you awakened, I didn't know what...who to expect," Niles continued, staring down into his cup. "I assumed it would be you, but I knew there was a chance it would be Glenna, and I had no idea how I would react to that. Even now, you seem like Gwendoline—like you—but some of your mannerisms remind me of her, more so now that you reclaimed the residual parts of her. It reminds me of the past more than I like, more than I think I can explain...though I'll try."

Though she'd just been comparing him to Colt again, Gwendoline felt another burst of temper singe her thoughts. Still, she held her peace. He paused, waiting for her to speak, perhaps hoping she would, but her silence persuaded him to carry on.

"I was a younger son in a wealthy merchant's family, a family concerned mainly with business, who didn't fuss about 'that magical nonsense.' They sent me away to a local mage to keep me out of my brother's way and to train away my frustrated outbursts, and then a mage from the palace found and tested me when he visited an old friend. I came to the palace, where I met Leland, Jael, and...Glenna.

"It didn't take me long to get used to my life as the head mage's apprentice, but it took a while for me to make friends with Leland, because Glenna was so determined to keep him to herself. At the time, she was also jealous of anyone else Jael took time to make friends with, though that changed over time as well. Then, seasons passed, we surpassed our tutors in both skill and style, and the civil war between Jael and her parents' greedy councilors began." A small, reminiscing smile graced Niles's face, a light in the darkness, but Gwendoline resisted the softening of her own heart.

"I don't know when I loved her first, but it felt like being kicked in the gut by Leland's charger once I realized she'd stolen my heart while I'd been focused on staying alive and advancing my career. Loving her was complicated, to say the least. At first, it only hurt because I resisted it, not wanting to risk our friendship, and partly assuming she would always have some sort of lover on the side. Then, the lovers stopped, and she grew thinner, and quieter over time," Niles's story came slower now, his expression more ponderous. "I presumed it was the effect of the war on all of us, the things we had to sacrifice to bring Jael to her rightful throne. But after that, when I finally noticed how she watched Leland, how she would sometimes be short with Jael for no reason, how gaunt her face grew as she pined for him, I packed my bags and went on a so-called 'diplomatic journey' through every province and town in the land to avoid seeing her in that much pain. I could see how much she loved him...how could I compete with that, with *Leland*?"

This, Gwendoline understood from her knowledge of Glenna's memories. Who could compete with Leland, indeed, or how could she have competed with Jael, the jewel of Oloetha, perhaps of the world?

"I fully intended to settle down far from the palace and marry a daughter of the nobility, even a peasant if that would take my mind off of her," Niles absently leaned down, patting Dancer's head as she gazed adoringly up at him. "But that didn't work, of course. I had to go back for the betrothal ceremony, and I saw her dancing with Leland in the armory wearing all the finery that made her quiet beauty shine...and decided, to hell with it, she's worth a try." Gwendoline remembered the rest: the conversation in the garden, the rose petals raining down from the ceiling like impossible summer snow as he kissed his way down her body...

Niles, perhaps recalling the same moment, cleared his throat. "I made my shot, it fell flat, and I experienced bitterness and heartbreak I had never known before. I swore I wouldn't let her get to me again, that nothing was worth this...this brokenness she could bring out in me. Then...Averill almost made her kill herself in front of us, and I felt my heart stop. I intervened. She didn't love me, but I was willing to give up everything so she could be free, and perhaps find happiness some day. And then...while she was saving us, saving my soul from slavery and torture after Leland's defeat, Averill killed her."

Gwendoline had been studying her drink during his story, but when he didn't continue right away, she glanced his way. He'd closed his eyes, tilting his head back to absorb what little of the sun succeeded in breaking through the dreary gray clouds.

"Why are you telling me this?" she asked, nudging him back to the present.

"So perhaps you can understand why there was a small part of me that wanted to believe Glenna was alive. It wasn't rational, it contradicted my very real hope that you and I could have a chance once all of this is over, if we somehow make it through Averill's disruption alive," he murmured. "Think, Gwendoline. Glenna did not trap me in the book, as I've said. I *willingly* chose to end my life for her because she was dying to save the land from Averill, and I couldn't imagine my life without her in it, even if I couldn't have her. How can that kind of...of devotion, misshapen and toxic as it undoubtedly was, be erased? Wouldn't you think there would always be some scar, some trace, some ache in the deep of winter like a fracture line in a broken bone?"

"You were not good for each other," Gwendoline held fast, closing her eyes as the images of Colt's scars flashed through her mind. "She used you, down to your very last drop of blood, and then continued loving Leland anyway."

The guilt swarmed like a host of buzzing insects, obscuring the clarity of her thoughts so she couldn't mold them into spoken words. The shame originated from her tryst with Colt, true, every second of that night burned into her memory with startling vividness. But was it possible she was feeling *Glenna's* remorse as well? For using Niles until she cost him his life?

"Used or not, well-suited or not, I loved her still," Niles admitted simply. "And I don't regret my sacrifice, if it means I can help all of us put that bastard Averill in the dirt for good this time. If it means I got to meet you, Gwendoline."

"Me?" *If you knew, Niles, would you still be glad you met me?* Gwendoline ached to confess to him, ached to be forgiven.

"You," Niles reached out to her, cupping her face in his hands so he could look into her eyes. "I see you, Gwendoline. I've known you for a long time. I've been in love with you...oh, forever, it seems. I knew you were the one the instant the book appeared to you at that market, even if I wasn't wholly human at the time, and as I learned about you over the years, I felt...connected, somehow. Breaking free from the book to actually meet you in person was like crawling on my belly out of a dark cave into paradise. You are familiar to me, part of her, but also a whole new breath of fresh air that brought me into the sun and taught me hope. Glenna is my past, and there's no changing that. But you are my future, and I...I just wanted you to know that I'm focused on moving forward. With you, if you'll allow me."

"You and me?" Gwendoline felt the water works gearing up for a new bout of crying—maybe Glenna had been weepy and she'd inherited that tendency with her memories—as Niles's hands warmed her cold face.

"Yes, if you want. You'll finish university, I'll go job searching, we'll take Dancer hiking, it'll be fantastic," he chuckled, wiping away one of her tears with the pad of his thumb. The fire in his eyes danced with the shadows that never faded completely away, and she felt her own eyes close as he touched his lips to hers. A mild burst of wind gusted about them, warm in a way that reminded her of summer. Strands of her hair swirled up around her head like she was flying.

Gwendoline felt that tearing sensation again, ripping at her heart as Averill had once torn Leland's arm from his body. Niles could fill her now, and fill her completely like the steamed milk in her latte had perfected her coffee.

But Colt could do the same, and the memory of Colt tugged at her and slashed through the beautiful bubble of hope she had begun to enclose around herself. Choking back a groan, she turned away, forcing herself to stand and back away from Niles. Dancer, who had been lying over her boot-clad feet, rose with her and assessed the situation, tongue hanging out again.

"What's wrong?" Niles asked, rising to his feet as well and clinging to her hands. "Are you hurt?"

More than you know, Gwendoline thought wretchedly as she shook her head.

"It's not meant to be, Niles," she said at last. "She will always be a barrier between us, in spite of what you've said, and now that Colt has Leland's memories, it's all more complicated than you can imagine." If she had been an artist, a truly talented one who didn't just dabble with sketches now and again, she could have drawn this moment perfectly:

Niles, seated against a picturesque autumn backdrop, looking up at her with his brows arched quizzically.

"How do you know Colt received Leland's memories?" he asked her. Gwendoline reacted before she thought, realizing that her decision whether or not to tell the truth or lie had made itself.

"He called and told me," she lied, looking into the abyss of Niles's eyes and endeavoring not to stumble over her words. "Turns out the fragments of his soul that had his memories hung around long enough for Glenna to save them."

"Did they?" Niles met her stare, hiding any surprise he might have felt, his return to her challenge filling the atmosphere with a tension specific to them. "How surprising."

Gwendoline lifted her chin, trying to appear stronger than she felt, or at least impassive, but she felt the volume of her heart thundering against her ribs would give her away. She'd sworn she wouldn't be the first to look away, but as he stared at her unflinchingly and leaned back against the bench, she doubted she'd hold out.

Then, the black blossomed with its usual vibrant color, and Niles looked away. There was nothing Gwendoline could say that didn't have the potential to betray her. She hated the suspicion almost certainly spinning gears in his mind, and she didn't think she could bear his disgust if he ever knew for sure of her duplicity.

"I can't, Niles. I just...I can't," she murmured after a long pause, crossing her arms over her chest as she stared down at Dancer, who looked up at her with interest. "I hardly know who I am anymore, and I can't...get involved with anyone when I don't know what I'm capable of giving." This part wasn't a lie: if Colt left Everleigh that minute and came to Gwendoline asking for a future together, she believed she'd give him a similar answer.

Niles considered her for a few moments, watching in silence as Gwendoline's eyes burned.

"All right," he spoke at last, surprising her as he slowly rose to his feet. "I won't add to your cares with unwanted persistence." Picking up his coffee mug from beside him on the bench, he passed it to his other hand like he'd forgotten what to do with it, but a moment later it vanished.

"I wish it were different, Niles," Gwendoline said, fixing her eyes on his collar so she wouldn't have to look at his face. "I wish..."

"I know," he spoke softly, shoving his hands into the pockets of his gray coat. "We'll focus on ending Averill, and then I'll go for good. For now, I'm simply walking away." And he did, turning his back to her as he headed away from them down the sidewalk of the park.

Dancer whimpered, long and sorrowful, causing Gwendoline to kneel down to her level in alarm. The big blue eyes stared briefly up into hers before the dog took off, dancing up to Niles and lifting one elegant paw for him to hold as she whined pleadingly.

You and me both, kid, Gwendoline thought, arms hanging limp at her sides. Niles turned, his strong profile striking to her perception as he took Dancer's paw and rubbed her head. He seemed to be saying something to the dog, but the wind carried his words out of Gwendoline's reach. Then, without looking back, he released Dancer and continued away from them.

If you ever call on me, I will answer, a gentle whisper akin to the caress of a sea breeze against her skin brushed against Gwendoline's mind, and she released a long, shaky exhale as Dancer trudged back to her side.

17

Time passed without anything of much importance taking place in Gwendoline's life. Her world was still in danger, as Averill's threat hung over her like an executioner's blade.

Heart and spirit and soul...what was missing, before? Everyone necessary was present at the arena. What went wrong? Pore over her reticent casting book though she would, her muddled thoughts refused to assemble anything helpful. She sparred alone in her backyard for hours, conjuring phantoms to engage with her, but she felt this was a pointless exercise. Averill would be so much worse than any poor shadow she could dream up.

She felt like she'd tripped into a tunnel, the kind that a person could fall into and never hit the bottom, and scenes of her life passed at strange speeds. She could spend decades lifting a fork laden with tasteless food to her lips, but classes and tests and bill paying and avoiding nosy neighbors zipped by in a blink. She had come home from her day at the quaint café and the park with a dog who seemed to resent her for her terrible decisions, noticed the few things Niles had garnered since he'd broken free from her old book had been removed, and sat alone in her empty house long into the night.

Averill's deadline for Everleigh, on which all their lives—and the lives of Starford's citizens, and eventually all the magically lacking folk in the world—hung, drew closer, but their group was no more unified than it had been before. Less, this time around, which made Gwendoline's already uncomfortable hopelessness weigh tons more. Last time, Leland and Jael had been fused in love and purpose, and Glenna and Niles were unified in friendship with them.

This time, Colt kept secrets from Everleigh while Everleigh avoided everyone except Colt, Niles had disappeared, and Gwendoline...well, Gwendoline knew she was a total mess, and Dancer's constant sulking proved her agreement with that fact. Long, daily walks and attempts at affection did not deter her depression, so the two of them kept to themselves and meandered about the house, accomplishing little more than existence and the status quo of survival.

Near the middle of that foggy two weeks, Everleigh and Gwendoline had one meeting between classes, where formerly three days couldn't pass without them hanging out at least twice. Gwendoline's apathy kept a solid barrier between her and her cares, but she faked normalcy as much as she could for her friend. Or was it for herself, so Everleigh wouldn't suspect her of the horrible thing she'd done?

"The council has advised me to stay out of Starford politics," Everleigh sighed as she lounged with careless elegance on one of the ivory couches in the student lounge. "Of course, they've agreed to reimburse me for my lack of involvement, since I am an official, viable heir to the leadership of this town."

"That sounds like a lot of horseshit," Gwendoline noted, plucking raisins from her bland breakfast muffin and exploding them with tiny pops into puffs of smoke; one of her exes, probably from her joke of a freshman year at Starford U, stared moodily at her from far across the lounge, but she avoided looking his way.

"I know, what an insult! I understand that I'm young and 'untried,' but that doesn't mean I'd be bad at changing things for the better in this town," Everleigh snorted, and then sighed again. Smaug danced through her fingers, delighted to be held instead of confined to bracelet form so he wouldn't scare Everleigh's teachers and classmates. Five minutes of silence slogged by before she spoke again, her tone softer.

"Then again, Averill is my opponent, and I don't think he'd be thrilled if I opposed him on the political battlefield. He's probably the one who offed Madam Kinsley, after all. They said she bled out from a wound to the neck, remember? He probably went all Vampire McFangerson on her ass."

"Since when do you give a damn what Averill might do?" Gwendoline swelled with bravado she didn't feel. Everleigh paused, a perfect statue with a golden serpent wound through her pianist's hands.

"Since he threatened to kill all my friends and family if I didn't become his undying bride," she said, whispering so the other students hanging around the lounge wouldn't hear her.

Gwendoline studied her, unwilling to compare Everleigh against Jael despite her mind instantly doing so. They were the same, in many ways: gorgeous curls—though these were rich mahogany instead of finest gold—petite structure, delicate, fairy-like features apparent in the small, almost pointy nose and childlike eyes. But Everleigh was leaner with more athletic strength gained from years of volleyball and cheerleading. Her brows were fuller, darker, and the line of her jaw more square compared to Jael. Gwendoline wondered if these traits had been inherited from Abelard, perhaps. It was remarkable, really, the comparison: Everleigh was merely a distant descendant of the old queen, but she easily could have been her daughter. Furthermore, to the fragments of Glenna's mind, it made sense that Abelard and Jael would have wed back in the past. Oloetha had needed an heir from its ruler, regardless if the princess's chosen was no longer living.

"We won't let him take you," Gwendoline spoke at last after an uncomfortably long silence; she'd drifted off again, Glenna's memories taking over not for the first or last time that day.

"That's what you said last time. According to Niles, that didn't turn out so well," Everleigh feigned indifference, but her chin trembled, and Gwendoline saw that the dark shadows under her eyes proved that she herself wasn't the only one losing sleep.

"What does Colt have to say about it?"

"Colt? Not much of anything, as usual lately. He says he has a lot of school work, or his Dad wants him to help out with renovating their house, or anything at all to keep away from me," Everleigh sighed, pausing her grumbling. "Do you have any idea what's the matter with him? He won't talk to me, but I think it's something to do with either failing his midterm, or because I could eventually be the most powerful woman in the city in a few weeks." Gwendoline winced internally as Everleigh smiled companionably, her trusting gaze expecting answers.

"No idea," she lied again, the words ashen in her dry mouth. "He's been avoiding me too."

At least that wasn't a lie. She hadn't seen Colt since their frenzied tryst the night she'd come back from the mountain hike with Niles. She wasn't surprised by his avoidance, but her confused heart felt like the thorns of guilt and loneliness pierced her flesh deeper whenever she remembered him.

"And you? Are you all right?" Everleigh probed, not for the first time. "Is Niles still absent?"

"Yeah." Gwendoline's reply was short, far from soliciting further questions. How could she tell Everleigh why Niles had gone without sharing the darkest parts of her memories as well as her present situation?

Sorry friend, seems like I've always been the type of person to covet another woman's lover, and this time around, I took yours and killed my chances with the guy I liked first simultaneously. Also, I have a dog familiar now who consistently screws up my magic because I pushed Niles away from me.

"What are we going to do with our boys?" Everleigh sighed, sitting up from her reclining position so fast that her curls bounced around her shoulders. Smaug, well used to his mistress's erratic style of movement, coiled about her arm and held still, though his eyes glimmered to show he had not yet been enchanted to sleep.

"We'll figure it out," Gwendoline promised Everleigh and herself, not only speaking about the boys. Shortly after, she made the excuse of class to her friend and booked it out of the student lounge. Instead of heading to class, however, she drove home in a daze, the familiar miles of her regular path stretching into eternity.

Thanks to the town gossips, word got out that Everleigh was heir apparent to a previously extinct bloodline. Without doing anything, she gained a following of supporters who didn't like the possibility of someone who had been as absent as Averill had been during years he should have spent getting to know his future citizens taking over their massive district. Could those who attended Averill's speeches—attempts to woo over a people inclined to be charmed by power—see through the charisma and leader's strength to the beast underneath that façade? How little they knew, that Averill already owned the land of a much wider region than they guessed, and would eventually work his way to more.

Gwendoline kept her promise to Everleigh, dutifully wracking her mind for any solution that wouldn't end the same way their lives had in the past. A small and mean part of her wished Everleigh had access to memories as terrible as the ones Glenna had given her, the kind of images that had her screaming into wakefulness night after night, but perhaps it was better this way. Out of the four of them, perhaps she had the clearest outlook.

On the first of the last three nights before Averill's deadline, Gwendoline sat staring listlessly at her television with a half-empty mug of Irish coffee in her hands. Beside her, Dancer lounged in a curled up ball of black speckled fur on the corner of the sofa, bright eyes half-closed in restless sleep. Gwendoline wished she could pet her without disturbing her rest, but she didn't have the willpower to endure the reproachful sadness of her pet. Besides, she had more to think about than a dog that refused to be comforted. The reporter on the news, irritatingly chipper in spite of her somber navy jacket worn to combat the unseasonable cold front sweeping in to announce winter's approach, had her full attention.

"The current favored heir for Governor, Averill Kinsley, has publicly issued an invitation to all local council members and law enforcement officials to attend a formal gala he will be hosting this Sunday evening at the Kinsley estate," the news lady eased into her new story with all the finesse of a freight train crashing onto the scene. *"Many prominent citizens have been invited, the majority pledging to attend, and Mr. Kinsley himself admitted to inviting the mysteriously silent and deeply contested heir, Everleigh Northwood. Miss Northwood was unavailable for comment, but Kinsley told us he is 'more than willing to work with the alternate heir if she herself is ready to cooperate.' We'll keep you updated on the status of the possible election as we talk to gala attendees at the much anticipated event."*

"And you're just *thrilled* to be invited, aren't you?" Gwendoline groused at the grinning journalist, sarcastically toasting the woman on the TV with her lukewarm beverage. She wished she knew more than the smug reporter, but Everleigh still hadn't shared her official plan on whether or not to run for the office that belonged to her by right.

Politics and magic sure are a funny mix, Gwendoline mused, chugging the last of her drink before she thumped the stoneware mug onto her coffee table. *How do you run for office and pursue democracy in a town that has never held an election before, and who already knows that the region belongs to you by right?*

The dilemma struck her as funny, and a hoarse, dry laugh slipped free from her pale lips before it quickly died. *Hard to think of an election when, regardless of that choice, Averill will come for you in the end.*

A knocking at her door startled Gwendoline, exasperating her dull headache. Dancer barked in alarm, leaping from the couch to dash to the front door so she could greet or assault the intruder as soon as the door opened. Following, Gwendoline quieted her pet with a hesitant pat on her head, and cautiously opened the door. Once Dancer saw who stood waiting to enter, she sniffed disdainfully and trotted back to the living room.

"Colt," Gwendoline greeted him with a sigh; her hand not holding the door open unwittingly lifted to cover her heart. The sensations she'd futilely attempted to bury boiled to the surface again, lining her face with a tense frown.

"May I come in?" Colt asked, perhaps oblivious to her discomfort. But no, he couldn't be: Gwendoline sensed a similar pressure bearing down on him, stiffening his easy poise into an awkward graveness as he entered at her nod of approval.

"Does Everleigh know you're here?" Gwendoline found herself asking as she trailed behind him as he led the way to her living room. Uncomfortable suspicion flavored her tone; she wished she hadn't asked.

"Yes...and no," Colt told her, unfazed as he plopped down into one of her stepmother's old wingback chairs; it wasn't the most comfortable seat, but the well-worn cushions accepted all. "She's been after me to somehow help 'fix things' between you and Niles, so we could all plan what to do about Averill together. I've declined interfering thus far. Tonight I told her I was going out...I didn't specify where, but she looked smug, like she'd finally got through to me."

"Oh," Gwendoline didn't know what else to say. Standing as she was in the entryway of her living room, she observed Dancer stare Colt down before she huffed and began grooming the one forepaw that was wholly black like the spots covering the rest of her. Colt, in turn, eyed the animal with some confusion.

"Since when did you get a dog? I thought you wanted to wait to get a pet until you graduated," he asked; whistling softly, he reached out to Dancer to urge her to come to him, but she ignored his proffered hand.

"My book doesn't work like it did before, and Everleigh was always after me to get a proper familiar, so..." Gwendoline shuffled into the room, tugging back the long sleeves of her sweatshirt so they no longer concealed her hands as she gingerly sat down beside her dog. "She came to me, and that was that."

And now you're not telling him the whole truth either? Her thoughts intoned balefully, making her feel like a wooden ruler was about to be rapped across her knuckles at any moment.

"Niles brought her to me," she sighed after a pregnant pause. "Judging by the odd ways familiar finding works, it can't have been just him...but he saw her first and brought her to me." She was babbling, she knew it, and Colt wouldn't care about that. A frown creased his forehead.

"So you have seen Niles?" he asked, studying Dancer instead of looking at her. Gwendoline felt a shiver rattle her. Was that jealousy she heard?

"Yes," she chose to answer honestly again, "though it's been a while since he's come around." Because I broke his heart again. Because of unfinished business between you and me. Again.

"Oh," Colt remarked after an uncomfortable pause, the sort that made the hairs on Gwendoline's arms prickle as she felt the urge to break the tension with an offhand comment or observation. She took her chance to scrutinize him, looking for signs of the emotional drain written in his bearing like it was on hers. The sight of his pallid skin, exhaustion rendering the bronze glow of health into a subtle pallor, cheered her even as she loathed herself for garnering satisfaction from his grief. The circles under the eyes mirrored her own, just as their relatively more carefree personalities of this present age had disappeared under the weight of their previous selves and the knowledge they shared. Their souls were their own, and fragments from the past wouldn't change that, but the memories contained in said fragments had already altered events more than either of them could have estimated.

Colt broke her reverie as she looked him over, his hollow stare unnerving her enough to make her cast her glance aside.

"Would you like some coffee since you're here? Wine? Bourbon?" Gwendoline offered, jumping to her feet so she could fetch a glass and whatever beverage he preferred from her kitchen. She was off before he could answer, but her slipper clad feet stuttered to a stop before she reached the entryway. The last time she'd been in the kitchen with Colt in the house, she'd offered and in turn received so much more than a drink. Dumbly caught in memories, she stood frozen for a few seconds.

"I don't need anything," Colt spoke right behind her, and she jumped from the shock of him suddenly standing so close. She almost turned, but he placed his hands on her shoulders, taking as much care as if she were a fragile and precious sculpture. Barely making contact, he trailed his warm hands down her arms to encircle her waist; though he didn't pull her back to him, she knew he wanted to.

"I miss you," he said at last, the words sighing free. "I miss you how I shouldn't. I love Everleigh, I do, but I can't get you out of my head. I miss my friend, but I miss you more." Gwendoline exhaled, closing her eyes as the familiar ache of loneliness began to dissipate under his touch. The sting wouldn't go away entirely, but a part of her felt inexplicably whole with him.

"I miss you too," she murmured, knowing he'd hear her low tone in the quiet of the house. "I hate that I do, but there it is."

"Agreed," Colt said. Turning her to face him, he gazed down at her face as some inner conflict held him mute. He was her friend, and had been for so long that the paths in her mind he'd ambled along bore his footprints down to her heart. The pain of this realization, the idea that she might just be in love with him too, squeezed her lungs too tightly for her to breathe, and she trembled with the desire to kiss him.

Neither of them moved, however. Their longing held them on the cusp of connecting again like they had after Glenna' s memories had returned.

But the source of Gwendoline's pain wasn't just from realizing Colt was her bonded in the oldest sense of the word. Something fractured within her, deeper into her very self than she cared to look. This dark part, unconsumed by the fires Colt kindled within her, wailed in the abyss, crying out for someone who wasn't there.

"We will have to choose, eventually," Gwendoline whispered to Colt, hardly able to hear herself think; reckless, she reached out her hand to take his. "We can't stay this way forever."

"I know," Colt admitted, entwining his fingers with hers; he frowned, but she glimpsed the same wonder and shameful elation she felt reflected in the cobalt gaze. Even now, when they understood the bond that linked them together, the astonishment in the face of such a spiritual connection neither of them had suspected refused to wear off.

"But...we do have now," Gwendoline reasoned, lifting her slender fingers up to stroke his well carved jaw line. "Perhaps this is enough." She couldn't think of anything else to say; neither could Colt. They lingered where they stood without keeping track of time, until somehow they ended up on Gwendoline's couch. There were no more kisses, no more inappropriate caresses since this time around they both felt the magnitude of what they had done too much to indulge in pleasure again.

Gwendoline felt herself drowsing in Colt's thick arms in spite of her quiet turmoil. The room, warm as it was, drew in close about them like a cozy blanket on a winter's eve, and the empty, contented minutes ticked away until sleep genuinely claimed her.

Dreaming had always been realistic to Gwendoline, but something about opening her eyes into the shadowed room struck her as eerie. Her waking had not been gentle, spurred on as it was by the sudden thrill of horror racing through her veins. The warmth of lying beside Colt echoed against her skin, but did not comfort.

Worse, she recognized this chill.

Steeling herself, and wrapping the plaid blanket around her body like chainmail, she rose to her feet. The wood was cold enough to freeze her toes and make her miss her comfy slippers, but she acknowledged the shock of sensation as a tool to ground her to her own existence. Dreams could be eccentric, manipulating reality and blurring at the edges. Magical interference in this plane, though she had never experienced it herself, would amp up the elements of chaos.

Gwendoline turned around and around, scanning the dark room looking for the source of the dread that drew beads of sweat from her white skin. Colt lay fast asleep on the couch behind her, proving further that this was her dream.

Come out, she willed the intruder, *come out where I can see you.* The temptation to call her ice shard sword into her hands or cast a protection spell around her made her tremble with the effort to resist. More magic in this dream might cause more harm than good; she was not practiced enough in this plane to risk any more unknown elements.

"How fitting that I should come upon you so shortly after your coitus with Everleigh's 'beloved.'" Averill's mocking voice sounded like it came from all directions at once, and the quiet tones were as overwhelming as they were alluring. "He did not surprise me with his infidelity...but you did. I expected this version of you to be stronger."

Gwendoline still couldn't see her tormentor when she frantically scanned the room once more, her hair whipping her face as she turned. "Come out and play, then, if you took the trouble to trespass here."

"As you wish," Averill acquiesced, materializing from the shadows in front of her like he had been standing in place for a while. Had he? Gwendoline shuddered, revolted by the idea that he had observed her and Colt.

In this dream world where Gwendoline looked pale as the moon and her hair as shadowy as waving seaweed in the dark ocean, Averill appeared to thrive. He shared her paleness, but his aura, though she could barely glimpse it hovering around his form, burned a deep scarlet. Dark shadows deepened his eyes, while impossibly brightening the blue in the iris to an almost blinding white. She noticed with a shudder how pointed his canines appeared when he spoke.

Has he fashioned this appearance for himself, or am I seeing his true form? Gwendoline wondered, comforted by neither option. Worse, she found herself imagining how it might feel to have those sharp teeth pierce her throat, melodramatic as a vampire film, and another shiver racked her.

"Why are you here? Everleigh doesn't have to make her decision for a few days yet," Gwendoline asked, knowing the stupid question might buy her a brief amount of time to plan her attack or defense if she needed one.

"I was curious," he said, casually spinning an errant shadow with his fingertips. The way he never broke eye contact gave his words weight that Gwendoline couldn't shake off. "I thought that perhaps our friend would deign to grace us with her presence."

"What do you mean?" She forced herself to ask after he failed to elaborate. He stalked forward, scrutinizing her with bestial concentration. Gwendoline twitched, wishing to step back, but at the last second she managed to deny herself the minute show of frailty.

"Surely you have some inkling. When you lived as Glenna, that luminosity surrounded you and echoed like a harmony in your speech. You knew before, even if she has denied you the knowledge and her radiance now," he spoke, soft and assured.

Before she could protest, his cold, long-fingered hands gripped her face, turning her up to look at him. Fear sludged through her, thick as tar, but strangely she sensed no predatory lust about him. She knew, however, the suspicion nestled within her heart like a poisonous viper. *Knowledge that wasn't her own, red words on a blank page, and that spark at the end of Glenna's life, renewing even as it consumed...*

"W-Who is she?" The query pressed free of her, anxiety pushing her forward when she would rather have held her silence to plan a way to break free from his clutch and wake up from this dark dream.

"Fate, Destiny, whichever name you prefer. She has eluded me these long years, refusing to confront the past, but in due time she will return," Averill seemed far away, even as his eyes bored into Gwendoline's with a dreadful force; again, the image of his teeth sinking into her neck flashed across her mind's eye again, and she shuddered. "When Everleigh is completely mine, she will return just long enough for me to erase her hold for good."

"So you're using Everleigh to get back at someone else? How remarkably human of you," Gwendoline's cheeky jab barely drew her own notice.

"Why you, Gwendoline?" Averill's sibilant doubts curling up to nest within her as he hypnotized her with his gaze. "Haven't you wondered? Everyone else has a purpose. Colt holds both the spirit and the sword. Everleigh is the ruler who will inherit the land, and Niles bridged the gap through time and death. But you? What purpose have you served? Why bring you back at all?" She could not deny it: his words disturbed her, teasing forth questions she'd buried deep within her subconscious. She'd rather impale herself again on Leland's sword rather than admit her curiosity, but she shouldn't have bothered: he read the interest on her face with ease.

"Does it matter?" She said at last, the bleakness she'd been experiencing these days leaching the color from her tone. "I am here, and that's what seems to count. Your issues with Fate don't concern me." He withdrew his hand from her face at last, the ice of his touch lingering a few seconds after. Had she not known better, she would have called his expression wistful.

"On the contrary, it concerns you most of all. For someone chosen to be her vessel, you aren't really like her at all. Ordinarily she chooses a puppet most like herself...but then again, Glenna was the one who emanated her aspect, radiated her frost and steel, not you." Averill hummed under his breath, a tune that sounded like the second part to a harmony he had committed to memory long ago. She recognized the music as something Glenna had heard when Fate's presence had filled her. Unbidden, the answering melody came to Gwendoline with a sweet flicker of strange, blissful peace. Her lips parted, her throat ached to release the music, but with some effort she choked off the connection.

"Vessel?" She asked instead, parts of her story clicking into place. She clutched her blanket closer to her body as if that would chase away the approaching terror of the known. A vessel was but an empty pot, waiting to be filled by something vital. Was that all she was? Would she be erased, if Fate came to claim her human vessel?

Niles...how would she tell him? Somehow, this information seemed worse to share than her dalliance with Colt.

Averill shook his head, studying her with both disappointment and satisfaction as he crossed his arms in front of his chest. "She won't show even now, when I've broken the rules by telling you what I have. Evidently, little relic, you don't have much of her protection after all. I am done humoring you."

A savage grin split his features, exposing sharp canines, and he seized Gwendoline's arm with no measure of gentleness. If he could hurt her in this dream the bruises on her arm would ache down to the bone. She cried out, struggling against him in a futile attempt to survive.

Don't bite me, oh please gods—

"I believe to make the best decision, Everleigh should have all of the facts. It's been such a victory already, watching you pine for each other and bumble around barely trying to oppose me. You are divided.

You are leaderless. You are *weak*." Averill taunted her; unfazed by her thrashing, his razor sharp smile wounded her with its anticipation. "Everleigh knows this, and she will come to me willingly enough...but I am confident that I can hasten her decision by telling her the truth no one else will." Pinpricks of despair needled Gwendoline's skin, reminding her of her vulnerability.

He did not attack her, as she had partially expected. Instead, invisible ropes snapped taut around her body, dissolving through her clothes to rest on her skin. Worse, a hex that burned settled like acid on her tongue, making her retch as the magical gag cursed her into silence.

"Come along, pawn," Averill laughed, his grip an iron cuff on her arm as he dragged her through space. "We have a heart to steal."

18

Gwendoline knew Everleigh wouldn't see her or Averill unless he willed it. That didn't stop her from aching to warn her friend about the sinister presence trespassing in the sanctuary of her bedroom. If she could have, she would have shaken her awake and told her the awful truth herself. More than ever, she wished she hadn't lied about her night with Colt.

Averill and Gwendoline, two phantoms in another person's dream, stood over Everleigh's bed and watched her eyes dart back and forth under their lids. A coating of faint pink smudges from yesterday's makeup that the cleanser product had failed to wipe away dusted her brow line. A plea to leave hovered on the tip of Gwendoline's tongue, but the muting spell kept her from speaking even to her captor.

Averill faced Gwendoline with a conspiratorial glint in his eyes, then his form blurred with magic. In a moment, Colt's likeness stood before her; it was a good reproduction, she had to admit, but Gwendoline winced at the sight of the garnet aura barely concealed by the heroic visage. Upon closer inspection, she caught the differences in bearing and likeness that revealed that the disguise more resembled Leland than Colt. They were the same height, but Leland carried himself prouder than Colt, and his eyes reminded her of the resolute gray of a thundercloud, rather than the welcoming blue irises she knew best.

Leland's smile fit like a mask over Averill's true face, and she sensed the gentling acted upon the storm of powerful magic within him as he seated himself on the edge of Everleigh's bed.

"Wake," he commanded softly, directing his focus on Everleigh to coax her into awareness. Gwendoline felt trapped, like she was a captive audience at a theater of horrors right when the curtain swings up to reveal the stage.

Everleigh stirred, a tiny frown crinkling her brows as she sat up with her eyes still closed. Her mahogany hair, damp from a late shower, spilled down her back gracefully; this coupled with the pink in her cheeks and the dusky softness of the dark eyelashes against her skin made her look like an ingénue about to be ravished.

"I had a terrible dream," Everleigh intoned in a vulnerable voice. "I had a dream that you left me...that you had gone far away. I dreamed I was the sun, your sun, until you decided you preferred the stars."

"Perhaps so," Averill replied in Leland's voice, playing along with the delirious princess as he took one of Everleigh's limp hands in his own. "But what fool would trade your love for someone else?"

A thin smile fluttered over her perfectly plump lips, but then the discomfort returned. Everleigh would truly awaken into this nightmare at any second. Gwendoline railed against her bonds, reaching out to grasp her friend's shoulders, but her hands simply passed through without making contact. Averill spared her an amused glance.

"Colt?" Everleigh questioned, sounding unsure instead of dreamy. Her fingers fluttered in Averill's grasp, delicate as a butterfly's wings. Finally, her eyes opened, the sharp green consuming all in this shadow world She stared at her visitor, unwittingly sharing the disquietude felt by Gwendoline.

"Is that truly who you prefer? After what's been done to you?" Averill reached out, taking Everleigh's other hand in his; he sought to charm her with his gallantry, but the poison and insinuation in his words couldn't be misheard.

"What are you talking about?" Everleigh asked, unease urging her to tug herself free from his grip. "Averill is my only fear, and that will make itself right, in the end." She sounded as if she had told herself this before, turning the meaningless words into a mantra to comfort her pining doubt. Gwendoline's cheeks burned with shame, knowing as she did the villain behind the mask.

"Averill is your great fear, then? Perhaps it is only because he's the enemy you know, rather than the liars who lurk in the background," he continued to trouble her.

"I have no other enemies," Everleigh insisted; fully awake, or at least awoken from her previous dreams into this manufactured one, she stared down the disguised Averill suspiciously, squinting as if looking into a bright light. "Why are you talking like this, Colt? It's not like you to be suspicious of others, or secretive."

"Is it not?" Averill scoffed, laughing darkly, the sound contrasting what his mask would have actually sounded like. "Surely you've noticed how I've changed towards you in the past weeks? Your deadline with Averill approaches. You've needed friends and at the very least your lover to stand by your side. Yet, where have I been?"

Everleigh blinked, the memory of hurt feelings scrunching her shoulders like a buffer. "You've been busy. It's not like you abandoned me..."

"But do I have any right to leave you when you need me?" Gwendoline hated Averill the most for this, almost as much as she loathed him for destroying their lives in the past; he plucked at Everleigh's strings like a master, drawing out the hidden misgivings she'd probably been forcing back in her own mind. "I'm always gone. The few times I grace you with my presence, I'm surly, rude, and unaffectionate. Do you deserve someone who would treat you such a way in your time of need?"

"You're struggling too," Everleigh didn't falter in her defense, though her agitation showed. She fidgeted with the sheets, straightening the hem with subconscious meticulousness. A bracelet glinted at her wrist, a sleeping Smaug who rested untroubled by the hidden menace in the room. Was the snake's presence an affectation of the dream, or was the small creature actually present? Gwendoline wished she could draw the attention of Smaug, if he could only sense her presence.

"But you are the one at stake. How could I be so selfish as to betray you in your time of need? For that matter, how could Gwendoline?" He had played his trump card, the one that would pave the way for Everleigh to guess the truth herself.

"Gwendoline?" She asked sharply, straightening her spine. "What does she have to do with anything?" Too restless to sit in bed any longer, Everleigh swung her legs over the side and stood on her bare feet. Averill watched her stride over to the window with hunger burning in his eyes.

"I've been absent, I freely admit. But who else has been away from your side?"

"She...she has stuff going on with Niles. Though..." The gears in Everleigh's mind were turning, whirring to compute a different conclusion than the one her consciousness was swiftly approaching. "Niles has been away too, hasn't he? Why...why is everyone always gone?"

"Niles knew the truth long ago, and couldn't bear to face it again. Few men have the strength to stand and watch the one they love devote themselves to another man," Averill painted a sorrowful expression onto the face that was not his own. Gwendoline saw his mask cracking, his anticipation of Everleigh's disillusionment rendering his sympathy hollow.

"He loves Gwendoline, anyone can see that. But...who does *she* love, if not him? I thought..." Everleigh knew: the knowledge had hit her in the gut before it reached her mind, and the cry of anguish bobbed silently in her throat as she swallowed.

"Gwendoline and Colt were preordained to love by Fate, two freewheeling souls spinning in the cosmos tied together in the young days of the world. How could you contend with such a destiny?" Everleigh didn't catch Averill's slip of referring to himself as Everleigh's boyfriend in third person. Instead of addressing his question, she faced the window again, her face blank yet considering.

"When she went to get Glenna's memories back, Colt acted so strangely that day. He...he mentioned Glenna, babbling about how he hadn't known it was meant to be her..." Gwendoline's breath whooshed out of her in a stinging exhale. So Colt's awakening into Leland's memories had been as torturous as her own.

Averill held his silence, letting Everleigh's mind spin as she traced the outline of a heart onto the fog of the windowpane. Gwendoline saw Averill's imposing reflection in the glass, since he'd remained seated on the bed as she had moved away. His eyes blazed with an indefinable craving, and his tense posture mimicked that of a hunting creature about to move in for the kill.

Wait, she thought with a surge of alarm, *this is* Averill's *reflection, not Leland's!* Her magic wasn't useful here, since this was not her dream and she could harm Everleigh's subconscious if she released any spells, but she concentrated her will into one thought.

Look and see him! She shouted at Everleigh with her mind. The connection was fuzzy, but she could just sense the edges of it.

Everleigh glanced to the side, smearing away the smudgy heart, and saw Averill's clear reflection looking back at her. What little color was in her face drained to make her appear ghostly as well, and she whirled to face her bed. Leland's façade fell away, revealing the true visage of her guest.

Anticipating an attempt to flee, Averill rose, towering to his full height as he waited for his prey to bolt. To her credit, Everleigh didn't stumble back or scream. Gwendoline twisted her fingers together, willing strength into Everleigh as she saw the verdant eyes widen with fear.

"You and your lies are not welcome here, Averill," Everleigh spoke resolutely enough, but her arms hung limp at her sides, the hands tightly clutching the folds of the boy shirt style nightgown she wore.

"Do I lie, Everleigh?" Averill held still, his tone insidious as ever.

"Just because you may have not doesn't mean you aren't lying now," Everleigh said, stubbornly clinging to her faith in Colt. But Gwendoline saw the defeat creeping forth from the shadows. Everleigh could be silly and shallow, but she had always been shrewd and difficult to lie to: the slump in her shoulders showed that enough of her believed Averill to seal the outcome of this dream sequence.

"I have not lied to you, and I don't intend to. In spite of what your ancestor inflicted on me in the past, I bear you no ill will. Unlike Colt, unlike Leland, unlike anyone you've ever known, I can see *you,"* Averill said; Gwendoline marveled at the bizarre, unforeseen sincerity in his words. "Your soul, willing or not, is open to me, and what I see is...magnificent." He took a single step forward, and Everleigh didn't withdraw right away.

"The 'magnificence' you see is my bloodline of power, I expect. Jael was a queen in her own right, and I'm only a pale shadow of her, not even a proper replica like...Colt is of Leland. The only thing I have now is the possibility of sitting on the committee that rules over this stupid city," Everleigh's attempt to sound angry and defiant fell flat as she almost choked on her boyfriend's name, and avoided mentioning Gwendoline altogether. "And that's what you want, isn't it? The legitimacy to rule as humans do."

Averill stepped closer again, locking gazes with Everleigh with those spellbinding eyes; again, Everleigh held her ground. "It is time this land, and eventually this world, was in the trust of someone who knows how to lead. So I confess, yes, your human right to wear the crown—however figurative it is these days—is part of why I would like you to come to me willingly. I can also say I would like to spare your friends in the process, as a gift to my future bonded."

"Colt is my love," Everleigh answered automatically.

"That may be so," Averill conceded. "But you are not his."

Finally, the realization of the doom of the most significant relationship in her life settled upon Everleigh's psyche like a veil of smoke. Blinking rapidly, she shuddered once from head to toe. Even then, the last of her strength held out: tears that lingered near the edges of her lashes stilled, refusing to fall before an enemy. Gwendoline knew she did not retort because she could not trust her voice to hold steady.

Averill took a final step forward, bringing him close to Everleigh, enough so he could hold her to him, if she would allow it.

"I could give you all, Everleigh, more than you can comprehend as you are. You have the makings of a true queen: it's in your blood, your bearing, and your heart. Yes, you have what I need to bring this world to heel at my command, the right to ascend to the throne...but there is more to you than royal blood. I can see that better than anyone." The disturbing sincerity shook Gwendoline again, almost deceiving her into tolerance. Worse, she knew that if she and Colt had fought through the madness that had consumed them with the return of their memories and had managed to stay away from each other, no honeyed words from the tongue of this serpent would have shaken Everleigh's faith in her knight.

Grimacing, she forced herself to watch this scene through to the finish.

"So I would have to go with you to ensure your victory in this town, and then accompany you—"

"You would be my ally, reluctant at first though you may be now, and you would stay by my side as long as I required it," Averill interrupted with the sum of the matter.

"Does 'all' include you leaving my friends and family alone forever? I won't let you harm Gwendoline, Niles, or...or Colt." Gwendoline, anticipating Everleigh's brave decision, reached out to her friend with her thoughts again, seeking one more window of passage to break into her subconscious. She shouldn't have bothered;

whatever magic had helped her before had been a one-time deal.

"I will not seek them out again, you have my word on that," Averill vowed, victory brightening his features. He locked gazes with his almost beaten prey, anticipating her compliance at any moment.

Everleigh hesitated once more, her face an uncharacteristic mask. "Do not think that I failed to see how you manipulated me into this position, Averill. I will not forget."

"You will learn to trust me, in time," he assured her, holding out his hand for her to take. "I will not betray you as your so called friends have."

"I would prefer not to speak of them any longer," Everleigh sighed, barely hesitating as she lifted her chin and took her enemy's hand. "Let's depart to your lair, since I'm assuming that's what comes next."

"Correct. We must prepare you for the process of becoming immortal after the election," Averill spoke in the courteous tones of a royal. Gwendoline felt bile rising within her at the idea of what such a process might involve for a being who craved blood as well as power, but she had no more time to contemplate Everleigh's misfortune.

Time slowed to a stop, until Averill and Everleigh and even the moonlight streaming into the defiled haven of rest appeared locked into a picture of stillness. Then, a voice trespassed in her head again.

"Worry not," Averill assured her, his speaking lips the only moving thing in this hell of paused time. "I saved the best for last, in your case."

What...? Gwendoline wondered, disoriented as the dream began to fade, blurring and pulsing at the edges of her vision in a nauseating pattern.

"I've already paid Niles a visit."

With that, Averill forced her into wakefulness, banishing her mind from the dream they'd invaded and screaming back to a waking nightmare too painful to face. Everleigh's expression of defeat, her sagging shoulders, and her brave despair as she submitted to that monster...each of these things would haunt Gwendoline for as long as she lived. The guilt broke her fragile heart all over again.

How did everything go so wrong? Gwendoline wondered, stumbling back into her own consciousness like a drunk party girl wobbling home with one broken high heeled shoe at five in the morning. *How did we change from hopeful, talented people into such a broken circle? Could this get any worse?*

Her answer presented itself the moment she opened her eyes and sat up. Colt had gone, laying her prone body gently on the couch, unaware that she had not been safe in her dreams. Dancer even had disappeared, probably up to Gwendoline's bedroom to curl up in her lonely bed.

But she was far from alone. A figure sat in the darkness in the corner of the room, shadowed by the predawn darkness created by the night. Additional fear might have crippled Gwendoline, but she knew who had trespassed in her house.

From the darkness, amber eyes gazed upon her with all the condemnation of a judge.

19

Niles took his time to speak, choosing instead to study her from the shadows. Goosebumps pebbling her skin, Gwendoline found that she couldn't cease her trembling any more than she could look away from the man in the corner. Mixed feelings slithered through her mind: elation that he'd returned, sorrow over their exchange of words the last time they'd met, and anxiety over what he would think now he undoubtedly knew the truth about her and Colt.

Averill had not lied when he'd said he'd visited Niles's dreams. The knowledge had him taut with tightly controlled fury that couldn't be mistaken for anything else. She had to wonder what horrors Averill had inflicted on him in his dream. She had been forced to stand and watch as he destroyed Everleigh...what had Niles endured?

Unable to stand the scrutiny any longer, and sensing herself turning unjustifiably on the defensive, Gwendoline bent her pride and broke the silence.

"I'm doing well, since you asked," she snapped. She still clutched the blanket around herself, tight enough that her hands ached, so she let it fall to the floor.

"I'm aware," Niles clipped his words with the dedication of a gardener attempting to shape an ornery topiary. "Colt and Everleigh, however, are not. That is in part thanks to you, Gwendoline."

"Why are we standing here arguing? We have to go to Everleigh!" Gwendoline regretted the shamelessness of her deflection, but she didn't believe she was wrong: Averill had taken Everleigh in the dream, but perhaps if they could get there in time—

"I've already checked on her. She's gone," Niles's expression darkened forebodingly as he announced their defeat. "I don't know what sort of dream Colt experienced, if any, but I saw him drive away from her house. Everleigh wasn't in the car, and I couldn't tell where he was headed."

Ridiculously, Gwendoline felt offended by the fact that Colt had left sharing a couch with her to go see Everleigh. The heinous yet somehow complete portion of her that longed for Colt to stay with her forever warred against Niles's quiet yet steadfast presence within. Stifling a groan, Gwendoline leaned forward so her hair fell forward as she covered her face with her hands.

"Do you have anything to say?" Niles asked after the silence stretched on a few more beats than was comfortable. His expression had been ominous, but his voice was deceptively mild.

"Yeah," Gwendoline spoke from behind the mask of her hands, taking a shaky breath before she dared raise her head to glare at him with bleary, tired eyes. "Where the hell have you been?"

"What?" Niles's question snapped with the echo of his annoyance, but thankfully he answered her, though he responded with a glare of his own. "If you must know, I've been attempting to puzzle out the reason we lost to Averill last time. Old libraries, ancient magical grounds, historic locations...I've been anywhere that might hold a clue. The requirements were met, we had our champion and the three ties to Fate were in place, yet still we lost. I think it's crucial we know why. I think it has something to do with the absence of one of the components..."

The three ties... an odd, suspicious little kernel of knowing pushed against the forefront of Gwendoline's mind, pressuring her to heed its urgency. *Nothing was missing...right?*

"But that doesn't matter now that Everleigh has willingly surrendered herself and the ruling right to Averill thanks to her broken heart," Niles continued, interrupting her train of thought before it could progress into helpful territory. Gwendoline's expression had been thoughtful, but her glare renewed as he chastised her.

"Do you have anything constructive to say? Anything that would destroy Averill for good this time?" she asked. It did no good to try to rein in the sharpness of her words; every piece of her seemed jagged lately, made up of shards good only for hurting those around her.

"I know for fucking sure that we can't defeat him the way we are now," Niles's voice rose as he held perfectly still, perhaps aware that moving in any way would break the strict control he held over himself. "I know that the reason we are a broken circle comes down to you and Colt." Gwendoline couldn't deny this, though the unwelcome heat in his eyes made her wish she could. What right had she to defend herself over her betrayal and the resulting consequences?

None, she thought.

Wiping her expression of any anger, Gwendoline inhaled and exhaled unevenly, composing her tumultuous mind by meditative breathing. The part of her that had belonged to Glenna assisted, humming a calming spell that Gwendoline had never heard before. She opened her mouth to speak, hesitant and unsure if her words were the right ones, but Niles spoke before she could.

"I knew, deep down, that you had...been together. I wanted to be the bigger man this time, to behave now as I should have back then. Your heart isn't mine to own or control, and it is not my right to shame you for acting how you choose and...loving whoever you wish," he began; his body remained tensed in that unyielding posture, but he spared her briefly from his gaze by turning to look out her window. "I am not your boyfriend, and I should not act like one.

"I did not believe Averill. Not at first, anyway, maybe because I chose not to. But, like Everleigh, perhaps I knew deep down that enough had already transpired. Still...to learn the truth from *Averill?* To have him invade my dreams and gloat? *We* are not in a relationship, Gwendoline, but Colt and Everleigh are and have been for a long time. How could you do that to her? How could you allow him to hurt her this way? I saw Glenna and Jael, and I saw you and Everleigh. She's your *best friend,* and he is someone you should want the best for."

"And why is it always your assumption that I am not the best for him?" Gwendoline challenged, old wounds opening to drain fresh hurt; unwittingly, she stood, seeking a position of more strength. "Even back then, you had Glenna convinced that she was not good enough for Leland. Why? Why constantly reassure me that I will never be good enough for him?"

Niles directed his focus on her again and paused, anger darkening his eyes. "That's not it at all, and you know it."

"No? I understand before better than I do now: Leland loved Jael deeply back then, so Glenna ruined her chances when she waited too long to speak her heart. Jael entered the scene, and that was it. Tragic, but true. But now...Colt came to *me,* Niles. Is it my fault his tie to Everleigh is not as strong as Leland's tie to Jael was? Is it my fault he decided I'm an option now?" Gwendoline asked. She wondered if Glenna would be proud of her new self, brave enough to say the painful things she'd avoided in the past.

"Has he said that to you? Has he said he'll leave Everleigh for you, or does he think your liaisons are a product of your confusion as split souls? 'Honorable' as he is, he broke down for *you* and cheated on the love of his life. Does that prove you are good together, that you bring out the best in each other? Hell, you're barely alike...does he even know you?" Niles's frustration was catching, like a spark leaping from a campfire to consume a whole forest.

"Does that matter?" Gwendoline huffed, crossing her arms over her chest; realizing her stupid error, she rushed to elaborate. "Colt and I have been friends since we were kids. Of course he knows me."

"Does it...matter?" Niles asked incredulously, his voice rising as he stood from his chair to tower over her. "Does it matter if the person you want to be with for keeps knows you through and through? Why not fuck someone else then, instead of your best friend's lover?"

"I never said I knew for sure I wanted to be with him for keeps!y But..." Gwendoline wished she had more time related magic, enough to nip back in time to smack herself for her stupid retort: perhaps then she wouldn't have to explain why she had taken this risk with Colt. "I think I might be *meant* to be with him. I think...I think it's supposed to be us. When Glenna and Leland were dying, we saw something."

"What did you see?" Niles held perfectly still, and in this moment, Gwendoline felt awed by him. One sharp eyebrow had lifted slightly, conveying his curiosity and his irritation with the one gesture. Somehow everything about his noble mien made her feel like she was a doe laying herself down in submission to a savage but beautiful predator.

"I'm not sure what would have happened if we had died for good, if we would have even seen the mark at all," Gwendoline dropped her combative pose, letting her arms fall to her sides listlessly as she looked up at him. "The process to trap part of ourselves in my casting book must have drawn out the passage of our soul fragments just long enough to seize the necessary remains for preservation. But Glenna and Leland saw that he and I shared a mark on our souls. Not really a mark, but a tie, a slender, crimson cord that bound the two together. I wouldn't have believed it before, but red is Fate's color, and I think she meant for those souls—*our* souls—to be linked." Concerned, Gwendoline scanned her midnight companion's face, measuring every detail of his expression in anticipation of change.

"Meant to be?" Niles spoke at last; unexpectedly, he lifted a hand to cup Gwendoline's cheek for the briefest instant. "You're right, that does make sense."

"Really?" Gwendoline almost flinched when he touched her. His hands were colder than she'd ever known them to be, but the contact was gone before she could adjust to it.

"My being...my very *self* was torn and crumpled and shoved into that damn book, and I felt every second of it, but it didn't matter. All I wanted was you to look at me as you were dying, to see how I saw you so you'd know you were loved after all. But...you never looked. Even when all you could see was him, *I couldn't stop seeing you.* I was willing to die because you were gone. And here it turns out you thought, at the end, that Fate would find a way to bring you and Leland together after all. I guess I never stood a chance, did I?"

"There you go again, lumping me in with *her*. I'm not Glenna. Yes, she's part of me, but I'm Gwendoline, remember? I hate this, I absolutely abhor the pain I've caused you and Everleigh, but I will not let you blame me for Glenna's actions. I am not the solution, the replacement for a phantom you once loved!" Gwendoline paused her tirade, realizing that she'd run out of breath in the heat of the moment.

"Well, *Gwendoline,*" Niles scoffed, his gentle touch on her face fading to memory as his resentment returned. "You can't keep saying you're only Gwendoline when you are using Glenna's tie to Leland's soul as an excuse to make yourself feel better for destroying Everleigh."

"That's not what I'm trying to do!" She heard her voice rising to a shout; a bit dizzy, she composed herself before continuing. "I barely know who I am any more. Yes, it's the Glenna thing...but now I'm the type of person to break my best friend's heart by sleeping with the only guy she's ever cared about? Now I'm the type of person who lies to everyone and worries about my own damn self instead of helping take down the biggest enemy Starford has ever seen?" Whatever Niles was thinking, he didn't reply. If he agreed with her entirely, Gwendoline couldn't blame him for that.

"Niles, I don't blame you for your hurt and your anger. I didn't lead you on by telling you what I did about my feelings for you on the mountain. I...I think there's a significant part of me that cries out to be with you, not Colt. But then my memories came back, and everything has changed."

"The more things seem to change, the more they stay the same," Niles mused aloud, his voice soft. She could stand neither his kindness nor his pity, if that was the aftermath of his anger towards her. Gwendoline directed her gaze to his neck, to the turn of his coat collar, to anything else but his face.

"I don't expect you to replace someone I used to love. Whatever remains of her soul resides within yours, a permanent addition of memories and pain. I don't mean to continue comparisons, but you are so very different from her, in more ways than you know. Gutsy where she was rigid, and reckless whereas she thought several moves ahead of most people to avoid ever making a mistake. You share her flippant humor, but she only shared her light with those in her circle. Jael was her closest friend, since Glenna was too much in awe of Leland to let him into her heart, and even she understood a rare few of her secrets."

"How shallow you make me sound," Gwendoline complained, though a faint smile edged its way forward on her lips. Even Niles smiled, bittersweet. As fearless as he made her sound, Gwendoline shuffled forward, tentatively pulling herself into him for an embrace. She hadn't realized how cold she was, but now that they were close she felt her skin absorbing his warmth.

"I want to choose you," she admitted, the words floating forward as a whisper. "But Glenna fought loving Leland instead of fighting *for* Leland for so long, and her ending was miserable and lonely. You are right, the fragments of her soul are in here somewhere, and that might be why I don't really feel like *me* anymore. I'm Gwendoline, but I'm also just enough her that the thought of losing Colt makes me want to end it all. And I know this isn't fair, but the thought of losing you...I can't even say it. I don't know if my feelings for you are purely Glenna's residual emotions or my new ones, but the thought of losing you forever..."

"Don't," Niles interrupted; for a second, he had begun to hug her back, but she felt him put distance between their bodies by straightening his spine. Embarrassed, she reversed her humble steps forward and looked up at him. He'd turned away, the line of his profile sharp and visible, and in an instant she knew he was picturing her and Colt together.

"Don't what?" *Still playing stupid? How mature,* her thoughts mocked her again. Her shivering returned, and an exhale of blue tinted smoke escaped her before she could halt the mixing of her magic and her emotions. Thankfully, he didn't see.

"I made the choice to step back and leave you before, more than once, and I would rather never go through that again," Niles spoke slowly, his eyes willfully blank as he finally looked at her. "I only came back to urge you to do the right thing by Colt and Everleigh. I guess I shouldn't have, since Fate marked you two for each other. Maybe I'll let events play out as intended this time." Was he mocking her, or himself? Gwendoline couldn't tell.

"Niles—"

"If Colt is who you want in this life, Gwendoline, then I won't stand in your way. I will tell you that I don't see happiness or fulfillment in your path if you choose him. Would you want your new love to start in the ashes of his old one, where you betrayed someone you both love? I can't seem to protect you in any way that counts, but I will always tell you the truth," The intensity of his sincere advice burned her like spell fire, and she wanted to scream that she didn't want him to go, that she didn't *know* yet if Colt was who she wanted for sure. Instead, other words came out.

"I don't want you to go," she admitted. A memory, one of another farewell after a night of falling rose petals and blissful comfort for a dying heart, flashed across her mind. But this time, like before, Niles couldn't be persuaded to stay.

"I must. Everleigh is lost for tonight, I think, but Colt must have gone to find her, and I should help," he said, his tone businesslike as he clearly attempted to distance himself from the emotion of their talk. Stepping back again, that familiar darkness began to blur the edges of his body as he prepared to teleport away.

"I'll come too," Gwendoline volunteered, her response automatic. She didn't move to prepare, however, as she realized that her presence in this mission might only jeopardize Everleigh further. Not only was she one of the chief backstabbers, but Averill's words about her being a vessel slipped back to haunt her. With as little knowledge as she had, was their circle ready for a final confrontation with Averill? Was she willing to take the risk? She hadn't even told Niles she was a vessel for Fate, let alone anyone else.

Niles didn't bother to stop her once he saw the knowledge dawn in her eyes. "I'll make sure you're the first to know anything." He took a breath to continue, but hesitated.

"Yes?" Gwendoline encouraged him to speak.

"Just...one more thing. Perhaps *you* are the one who has confused yourself with Glenna? Part of her remains, but it is you, Gwendoline, who holds the power," he told her; blinking, she kept her silence. "*You* are the one that matters now. Wouldn't it make more sense for you to make your decisions for you, and not for her?" He looked earnest and strange with the curious darkness consuming his body, and his eyes glowed amber as he spoke.

But before she could observe him further, his travelling spell carried him away, and Gwendoline found herself alone yet again.

20

Gwendoline held a pair of jeans against herself and grimaced. In her mirror, her shower damp hair and wan face grimaced back. Was there anything she could wear that would make Everleigh forgive her for sleeping with Colt?

Probably fucking not.

After last night's dream escapades, she wished to appear presentable to everyone. Nothing could possibly undo the damage she had irrevocably done to her friends, but somehow she couldn't help but feel that if she said or did the right thing she could set everything right and make amends.

Gwendoline glanced between her reflection and the pants she was holding again.

"Silly," the admonishment slipped from her lips alongside a beleaguered sigh. She dressed and pulled back her hair without further consideration.

Dancer accompanied her out to her car, clinging close for once as Gwendoline tucked a blanket into the passenger seat so no puppy claws would damage the leather. The weather had sunk into a deep chill, and both girl and dog shivered against the cold her BMW valiantly combated with its heating system. Perhaps she should have learned to use teleportation, like Niles; she was certain she was strong enough, especially now that Glenna's power supplemented her own, but magical travel would take more energy than she cared to spend on at least a twice daily basis.

Taking a deep breath in and then exhaling out so her breath fogged on the air, Gwendoline glanced sideways at her somber companion—no puppy had a right to have eyes that sad—and revved up the cold engine, beginning her drive to where she knew Everleigh could be found.

She had never before been to the Kinsley estates, not even to trespass on the grounds as pre-teens liked to do to prove they were too big and bad to follow any rules. Nothing bad had happened there to anyone she knew, but she had heard stories of magic causing strange aftereffects on trespassers. She had been rebellious in other ways, and the manicured grounds of the antique estate had interested her less than her rambling hikes closer to the mountains.

Still, she and everyone else knew where the leadership hub of their area was. The residence of the Kinsley line existed almost completely on the opposite side of town from where her stepmother's house was, and the road led straight through central Starford. She had expected traffic, even at the early hour of six in the morning, but it took her a quarter of her drive to notice the near total absence of other cars on the road. The few people she and Dancer did notice walking their own way didn't linger by the shops like tourists or workplaces like locals; tugging their coats and jackets closer about their shoulders, they kept their heads down and trudged forward as if through piles of snow instead of a stiff breeze.

Gwendoline's hands tightened on the scuffed steering wheel, and her foot eased off the gas as she caught sight of a familiar figure stalking along the sidewalk. Colt didn't see her at first, and unconsciously she slowed her vehicle and pulled closer to the curb to either roll down her window and speak with him or let him inside.

It took him a moment, since he seemed too busy brooding and marching forward with his hands stuffed into the pockets of his navy blue coat, but when he saw her he stopped. Their eyes met, and Gwendoline's fingers hovered over the switch that would roll down her passenger window. Instead, a heartbeat passed with an uncomfortable thud in her chest, and Gwendoline fled the scene as quickly as she could peel away from the curb in a car as old as hers.

He blames me, she thought, cringing over and over at the condemnation in his eyes. She and Colt were both smart enough to know that it takes two consenting parties to commit the betrayal they had, and not even searing guilt could erase the pull they felt towards each other. Still...he blamed her.

Gwendoline shuddered again, her mouth tasting unpleasantly acidic. She remembered how they had kissed, what Colt tasted like in the dark, and retched, not from disgust at the memory, but from the fact that the thought of their tryst made her desire another union. Here she was, off to rescue Everleigh from Averill, and she fell deeper into the betrayal she'd wrought with each passing day.

"We're fine," Gwendoline told Dancer insistently, forcefully loosening her clammy hold on the steering wheel finger by finger so she could reach over to pet her familiar's black furred ears.

As she absentmindedly drove forward, an unwanted string of thoughts circled the drain of her conscious mind so often that she couldn't silence them.

Glenna or Gwendoline? Am I a vessel, or am I just me? Decide as Glenna would have, or decide as I *would have before I freed Niles?*

At this point, she wondered if the choice was still hers to make. Niles had backed off, refusing to suffer any more hurt caused by her, and Colt...could she abide a relationship based in hurt and blame?

A while later, when she was pulling off the still uncrowded highway before the Kinsley estate emerged from the trees lining either side, she wondered why Colt was not on his way to rescue Everleigh himself. Didn't he have more obligation, or at least more drive, to make things right? Niles had called Everleigh the love of Colt's life, but how could that be true, if she had seen Colt fleeing in the opposite direction from where Everleigh had gone?

The iron gates blocking the long driveway into the grounds mocked her. Each bar undoubtedly had innumerable protection and warding spells tangled within each decorative coil, and worse: a bewitching spell had been cast on the gate and the area around it, so that try as she might, her eyes couldn't catch any details of the land past the entryway.

All this way, and it hadn't occurred to Gwendoline that there would be obstacles in her quest. She hadn't expected Averill or Everleigh to welcome her with song and dance, but stupidly she had expected her way to stay clear. Frustration made her grit her teeth together, her hands a vice on the steering wheel again, but she knew her aggravation wouldn't force the gates open for her. Dancer, too, seemed impatient: her long, feathery tail beat once or twice against the back of her seat, and a low, anxious whine sounded right under the edge of human hearing.

"It's okay," Gwendoline told her, not believing it for a second.

How could she make things right if she couldn't even get her foot in the door to give Everleigh the opportunity to slam it in her face? Everleigh loved drama: she was a master at the theatrical entrance or exit, and snide comments fell from her lips like jewels.

Frowning, Gwendoline shrugged her ivory coat more securely around her shoulders and got out of her car. She almost forgot Dancer, but a petulant bark reminded her to open the passenger door with a flick of her fingers. Together, girl and dog strode forward to the forbidding gate, Gwendoline's ballet tied flats clicking a pattern against the cement driveway. Her eyes strained to see past the concealment spells, and without consciously noticing, she murmured under her breath, sending forth gentle feelers to seek out any weak points.

Surprisingly, as her magic touched the invisible fibers of warding keeping trespassers away, the gates swung open without a sound, almost as if they were made of paper and the wintry wind blew them wide open.

Dancer growled, voicing her concern. Gwendoline spared her a glance.

"We don't have a choice, do we?" she told her companion. "We have to try, at least."

So, together, they followed the pathway up to the house.

The manor rested much farther back than she had first thought, so their walk took a few minutes instead of a few seconds. Another time she would have been tempted to sightsee, since these grounds had been famous for their beauty at one point, but the leaves had abandoned the branches of the innumerable trees early this year, due to the unseasonable cold, and only staunch evergreens remained.

What a house it was! Gwendoline had to admire the stately stone architecture, the sheer grandeur of the place. But the *presence* surrounding the house, regardless of whether it was wards alone or Averill's distinct corruption, disturbed her deep within her soul. It took much of her strength to lift her fist to the door to knock. Not as surprising this time, the dizzyingly tall double doors swung inward, beckoning her in as they somehow discouraged entrance at the same time. Shuddering, Gwendoline cautiously stepped inside, motioning for Dancer to follow as she adjusted her eyes to the dim light of the foyer.

Madam Kinsley had been old, reclusive, and, by all accounts, quite willing to leave the city to its own devices so long as she could sit up in her house and not be bothered. She had made headlines when she'd dismissed the greater part of her estate staff, keeping only a few unquestionably loyal members of the help on to manage the basic tasks required of a manor this size. Hindsight being what it was, Gwendoline guessed that Averill had had a hand in hiding the woman away.

Knowing this, Gwendoline marveled at the pristine, if gloomy, picture the house made as she looked around and around, staring at the expensive yet unexpectedly tasteful decor. Not a thing looked unkempt or out of place: for that matter, nothing had appeared in disarray outside, either. If no one had been taking care of the house, it didn't show.

Conversely, the place looked completely abandoned. This was a grand estate for sure, but it had never been a home at all. The lack of people made perfect sense, as if this house was meant to be empty, not even haunted by memories of the past. Were any memories here at all? Gwendoline wondered this as she strode forward, her steps softening as the floor changed from polished stone to sumptuous, fashionable burgundy carpeting. This place didn't have the familiar feel she had begun to recognize from other places.

This can't have been the same place, the same land Jael would have ruled from, she thought, doubting.

She rather felt like she was Belle from the original Beauty and the Beast story, where Belle had entered the castle to be observed and waited on by invisible servants. A nudge from behind almost made her yelp. Thinking it had been Dancer, she looked behind to scold her familiar for scaring her, she saw the Dalmatian had lingered by the front doors, imperiously sniffing a gilded coat rack.

"He's not here," Everleigh's familiar voice shook her from her reverie, startling her again so the hairs on her forearms rose in alarm. "Averill has gone out to plan for the gala announcing our decision to govern together."

Gwendoline turned slowly, hardly daring to breathe or move or speak. Everleigh's hostility felt like the biggest thing in the room, the biggest thing in the world as they faced each other.

"He didn't worry you'd fly the coop when he turned his back?" Gwendoline asked, her tone too deadpan for the sarcasm to fly as she studied her angry friend. A soft peach and ivory lace dress complimented her figure with its fitted waist and flowing skirts, and her Victorian updo framed Everleigh's lovely face to perfection while maturing her features ten years. Somehow, a night's stay in this forbidding place had had a reverse effect on her appearance, making her look light and carefree. Even the gray light coming through the windows of the foyer seemed intent on transfiguring the new mistress of the house into a paragon of beauty.

If she squinted and tilted her head to the side, she could imagine Jael stood before her instead of Everleigh.

"So did Averill have an orientation session set up to prepare you to become his vampire bride?"

"Don't do that," Everleigh warned. "You're not my friend, and I don't have any time or love to spare for someone who has hurt me like you have."

"Then why did the gates open for me? Why let me in at all?" Gwendoline challenged; she was not afraid of Everleigh, even this new nothing-to-lose persona of hers, and she wouldn't be chased off so soon.

That's why it hurt, really, when Everleigh smiled sweetly and cast a hex on her.

Gwendoline, caught off guard, summoned her wards to the forefront at the last possible second, though not quickly enough to block some of the damage. Her skin burned, not like fire but like someone had rubbed an itchy plant that she was allergic to all over her body. Worse, "all over her body" included her more sensitive areas, which took some delicacy in healing.

Fitting, she allowed the thought, though her temper was rising as she shrugged off the itch. Gwendoline had a lot of practice with unraveling hexes, and this one she dispelled with relative ease as she fought to rein in her temper. Dancer was less easily soothed: growling, she stalked towards Everleigh with her ears back until a sharp whistle called her back.

"I asked you to leave, and I really do mean it," Everleigh addressed her again, speaking again in a haughty, painfully regal voice that sounded like it didn't belong to her entirely. "I'm not interested in anything you have to say."

"I get that, but I'm not going anywhere. Not until you hear me out," Gwendoline insisted.

The jagged edge of another messy hex snapped against her face in a slap, punishing her for her insolence or her original betrayal. Narrowing her eyes, Everleigh glared at her with all of her anger on full display. Gwendoline couldn't tell what she saw, but like lava cooling over time, the rage faded into something more manageable.

"The election gala approaches, which is when I will take my new place," Everleigh all at once gave up her aggression. "You of all people know I wouldn't leave."

Gwendoline knew she was expected to take the bait for her apology, but the equally expected rebuff she dreaded couldn't be far behind. "Everleigh—"

"There's no need to apologize. We both know you don't mean it," Everleigh's voice rang cold, as if she were a teacher dismissing a needy student demanding a higher grade. "If you'd actually felt bad enough, you would have confessed right away. But who am I to interfere with destiny?" Her green eyes burned with carefully bridled emotion.

Gwendoline winced; sensing her distress, Dancer returned to her, bumping her long nose against her hand. "I did feel terrible. Awful. After it...well, I couldn't believe it had happened, and I didn't know what to do, so—"

"You don't have a single excuse that would be worth listening to. Gwendoline we were *best friends.*" The unspoken "how could you do this?" echoed in the room like the words had actually been said, but the question would have revealed her vulnerability, which would be anathema to Everleigh now.

Sighing, Gwendoline risked further comment, though she couldn't bear to meet her friend's gaze. "You're absolutely right, I shouldn't make excuses. I did an awful thing. But is my mistake worth condemning yourself to an endless life with Averill? Is it worth punishing yourself and everyone else for the mistakes of two stupid people?"

Everleigh pretended she hadn't heard. Her elegantly arched brows furrowed slightly. "I think, in a way, it's always been meant to come to this. Jael was weak, not strong enough to shoulder the burden that would have saved her queendom, her friends, and her...her love from ruin."

"It wasn't so much weakness as confidence. Jael had faith in her friends and...and she couldn't have known how unlucky her fate would have turned out to be," Gwendoline braved, studying the pattern of the marble stairs behind Everleigh to avoid the emptiness in her friend's eyes.

"She might not have, but I do. I will make the right decision for my people," Everleigh said. So she *had* taken up the ruling right after all, Gwendoline mused; only a princess spoke in such terms. Or she would have, if Averill hadn't conned her out of it. "People are weak, and I the weakest of all, but at least I won't repeat the mistakes of the past."

"This isn't you," Gwendoline whispered, her throat too dry to add volume to her words. This all felt wrong: Everleigh's bitter martyrdom, the darkness mixed with dim morning light in the foyer, the white knuckled exchange that made Gwendoline want to sink into the floor.

"No?" A wan smile sent pink into Everleigh's cheeks, and she chuckled quietly. "Niles said as much. Honestly, he's been here all of ten minutes, and he thinks he knows me enough to demand I return home? This is *my* decision. This is how a *leader* acts."

"There are other ways to keep us safe! I know it doesn't seem like it right now, but—" Gwendoline finally closed the distance between her and Everleigh. Reaching out, she attempted to take the shorter girl's hands in hers, cold as her own fingers might be. But Everleigh hissed, backing off as she glared.

"*Don't* touch me!" She ordered, her pert nose wrinkled in disgust as if Gwendoline had offered her a pile of toads. Dancer growled at Everleigh's tone, but Gwendoline silenced her with a stern look.

Everleigh continued as if no interruption had taken place. "Averill informed me of the consequences of breaking my promise to him this morning; perhaps you'd know what he's talking about. Do you remember the Rotten?" For a moment, Gwendoline's mind flew out of the present, cast back into Glenna's memories of disease and decay and ripping an unbeating heart from the chest of an innocent ladies' maid.

"He can't," Gwendoline protested stupidly, knowing damn well that Averill would do anything to get what he wanted, and he had the power to follow through.

"Can't he? And who would be the first victims? My friends, my family, my classmates? It was so *selfish* of Jael to refuse to save her people, really. Marriages of convenience were very common back then: indeed, with Leland gone, Jael married Abelard to continue her line, even though she didn't love him. Besides, even without Averill it's doubtful her little fairytale with Leland would've worked out, if you and he were 'meant to be' and all of that."

"I'm sorry, because I've hurt you, and I deserve every last bit of rage and scorn you have to throw my way," Gwendoline found herself saying, "but you can't talk about Jael like that. You weren't there, you didn't know her, and even then she made the right choice." More than ever, it showed that Everleigh would never possess the depth Gwendoline, Niles, and Colt did. She was enduring her own personal hell now, true, but the recollections of death and shining blood under the moonlight would never trouble *her* nightmares.

"How? How was allowing everyone she loved to die terrible deaths the right choice?" Everleigh's careful façade of blankness cracked again, her wide, childlike eyes beseeching Gwendoline for an answer.

Glenna's last moments flashed through her head again, bloody and chaotic. This time, she remembered Jael, screaming from the depths of her soul as she realized Leland was dead. The princess had lived, this she knew...but what had become of her life after that? Everyone she cared about *had* died horrible deaths. Niles had been the one to tell Gwendoline that Jael had married Abelard, though how he knew that he hadn't divulged, but who knew if Jael had found real happiness again? She had done her duty, at least.

"It's never the right choice to let evil take the reins, Everleigh," Gwendoline spoke after a long, introspective silence; seeking strength from herself and her magic, she cupped her hands together in front of her, holding them still as she breathed. "And Averill is evil, make no mistake about that. A power-hungry man who wants to rule the world as a tyrant isn't fit to rule anything, let alone a land like ours, or the rest of the world beside. What will happen to all the lesser magical people? I think you already know that."

"What choice do I have, Gwendoline?" Everleigh clipped off the end of each word, resisting the urge to shout. "He's won. You all thought you won before, though victory cost your lives, and he returned with the rest of you. Averill told me he's been back for many years longer than this...this version of you and the others. He's been waiting, strategizing for years and years, and that's what you want to fight? That's what you think you can win against?"

"I—" Gwendoline began to protest.

"Besides...thanks to *you*, I've already lost the main thing I cared about," Everleigh's tirade finished with a whimper instead of a bang; a stray curl slipped free from its styling atop her head as Everleigh turned. The light through a window shadowed her profile, making her resemble a cameo brooch, and Gwendoline found she couldn't look at her friend.

"I shouldn't blame you alone. Colt admitted he initiated your affair, but I'll never know if he was telling the truth. I'm sure you spoke with him since he came here last night. He might have even driven back to your house after leaving me, but I don't suppose I'll ever learn if that was true either," Everleigh rambled, almost in a whisper, like she was talking to herself.

"He didn't," Gwendoline felt obligated to say, but a glare discouraged any more comment; she felt more foolish than she had in a long time, and she clasped her hands together in almost prayerful protectiveness.

"I always thought *we* were soul mates, Colt and me. Childhood sweethearts, best friends, the whole package. Everyone we met agreed with us, too, and I was...I was so complacent about my perfectly planned future that I never dreamed anything like this would happen, especially because of *you*," Everleigh continued; mentally absent from the present, perhaps even the room, she lifted a slender hand to hover over her throat, where Smaug lay in the shape of an elegant necklace. "Averill was here when Colt visited, but he let me see him. I didn't care either way. I already had the answers I needed, so what if anyone else hears? I told him I never wanted to see him again, did you know? That if you were truly *fated* to be together, he should go back to you and stay there. I assume that's where he is now, waiting for you to get back?"

"He's not," Gwendoline confessed, gritting her teeth together. No, Colt would not be waiting for her.

"I told him to make a choice," Everleigh continued as if she hadn't spoken. "He said he couldn't. How does that make you feel? That he can't choose between you and me?"

More dreadful than you know, Gwendoline thought, her memory fixating on that one moment where she realized the depth of Colt's blame for their situation. She could hardly decide between Colt and Niles, yet she felt a stab of anger pierce her now that she knew Colt hadn't chosen her or Everleigh. Secretly, she hoped he'd choose her. What she'd do if he decided that, she didn't have a clue, but her wish lingered all the same.

"He will choose you," she said.

"That's so kind of you to say," Everleigh snorted, the irreverent noise making her sound more like herself, if only for a moment. "That's exactly what I need, more of your *kindness.*"

"What you need is to come home and leave this place," Gwendoline ignored the barb, instead directing all of her focus to the mission she came to this austere place for. "We'll figure the rest out. Our circle doesn't have to be broken."

"It doesn't? Oh, that solves everything, doesn't it? Gwendoline says it can't be broken, so of course nothing is wrong!" Everleigh unleashed her venom with relish, finally losing grip on the control that kept her buried rage and pain at bay. "Do you still not get it? It's already broken. We're divided beyond repair, and there's no bringing us back together. Colt and I are done, Niles is on his own, and you? You may have Colt, but you won't take the one thing I can make right away from me. I won't let your guilt get all of us killed." The last words hissed from her in a breath, fear and resolution lending a tinge of pain to her dialogue.

"I don't have Colt. I didn't have Leland. After all this, I certainly won't have Niles either," Gwendoline told her, trying and failing to be the voice of reason as her volume rose. "I understand I fucked up, I really do, and believe me I'll be punished for that. I am now that disgusting person everyone will learn to avoid, and justly so. But I can save you, Everleigh. We can make this part right without letting Averill destroy everything one power play at a time."

Everleigh crossed her arms, gracefully furious. For a moment, silence reigned. Gwendoline dared hope that she'd finally pushed through the armor Everleigh had set in place against her for the first time in their lives.

"I know we can't be friends again, not after what I've done," she continued, hesitating before she reached for Everleigh's hands again. "But you shouldn't pay for my mistakes. Not now, not ever." This time, Everleigh let her approach, and Gwendoline risked the lightest of hugs.

Then a great shudder ran through Everleigh, and she deliberately stepped back, leaving Gwendoline standing alone.

"Go," she ordered, once again the ice queen. "Go, and don't come back." Since Gwendoline had truly thought she'd made a breakthrough, this dismissal widened her eyes in surprise as Everleigh turned her back.

Worse, the house had apparently been programmed to respect its mistress's desires. Dancer growled, then whimpered in confusion as Gwendoline felt a pushing presence that nudged them back towards the front doors. Not wanting to get thrown out literally on her ass, she hightailed it back the way she came, exiting as swiftly as she could.

With crushing finality, the massive doors closed behind her, trapping Everleigh inside. She and Dancer gathered themselves before starting the walk back to the car. The scent of snow hung heavy in the air, but couldn't match the stench of defeat filling Gwendoline's perception. Everleigh's despairing expression as she unceremoniously dismissed them replayed over and over in her mind, and she felt unwanted tears threatening again. Since she was alone, she gave in, though her throat tightened near to choking her with sobs she held back for fear of losing control completely.

She had focused only on her walk back, looking down at the ground and watching her feet take one step at a time instead of observing the same dreary surroundings she'd observed earlier, so it took her a moment to realize that a figure waited by her vehicle, shoulders bowed slightly against the stiff breeze. Once she realized who it was, her throat clenched again and it took way too much effort to resist falling into the person's arms.

"How are you everywhere?" Gwendoline asked, attempting and failing to hide an undignified sniffle. The gates swept shut behind her without a sound, and there Niles stood, gloved hands stuffed in his pockets as he observed her with a clear-eyed gaze.

Perhaps Niles could tell that she was barely holding herself together, because he didn't toy with her. "I came up to try talking sense into Everleigh again. I'm so close to connecting the pieces of this puzzle...but she wouldn't come home."

"No, she won't," Gwendoline said curtly, looking up at the gray sky, watching for a few seconds as the outline of a bird dipped into a glide and then rose on the winds. Dancer nudged her hand, asking for a pat for her own reassurance or because she thought it might soothe her partner. But even puppy love couldn't quell the sting. Besides, she'd hurt Dancer too: the poor dog loved Niles to distraction, but out of newfound loyalty she kept her distance according to Gwendoline's reactions.

"We need to make her realize that if she doesn't come home now, she'll never come back at all," Niles said, and she brought herself back to earth and looked at him.

"Don't you think I know that? Why did you think I was here?" She snapped, regretting her outburst the instant it ended.

"I meant—" Niles began to defend himself, but then he stopped, shaking his head to deny himself the indulgence of pettiness. "We're all doing our best, so let's focus on what's important instead of lashing out at each other."

"You're right, I'm sorry," Gwendoline apologized, avoiding his gaze as she looked down at her shoes again. He looked good, too good. His face was clean-shaven today, sharpening his jaw line, and the cold transformed his embered eyes to crisp brightness. The wind had blown a few locks of his thick dark hair over his forehead, and she longed to touch him. But she refused to give in to that impulse.

The silence had stretched on too long; Niles broke it first. "Are you all right?"

"Me? I'm fine." The automatic reply made him arch one eyebrow in unspoken skepticism as he stared pointedly at the tear tracks lining her face. She met his gaze resolutely, daring him to comment on her appearance.

Liar, the thought barely brushed against the edge of her mind, a faint, teasing tone softening the accusation. She snorted, drawing a small smile forth from Niles. They looked at each other, really looked. It was just for a second, her blue-violet eyes meeting his, but a connection occurred that warmed the air surrounding them. She found she could breathe again, long enough to fill her lungs with a deep inhale she hadn't been able to enjoy in who knows how long.

"I know what to do," Gwendoline said abruptly, realizing as the words unexpectedly left her mouth that she really did have a solution. "We're pulling Colt out of the mud, we're going to that gala, and this time we'll get it right."

"We haven't figured out what went wrong last time," Niles protested, though he looked more intrigued than disturbed; studying her, he seemed to be encouraging her to better her plan, rather than discouraging her from acting rashly. His unspoken faith in her even after everything sent sparks of inspiration spiraling through Gwendoline. When he looked at her, especially like that, with his eyes fiery and interested and *kind,* she felt the knots in her stomach begin to unwind as frivolous butterflies took their place.

How could she allow herself to enjoy this when she'd hurt the people closest to her multiple times? Was she that self-centered? She tried to crush the butterflies with her guilt, but they proved too resilient for her.

"We need more *time,* Niles. All of us. We didn't have enough to figure it out last time, but this time...the gala is a few days away. I need a dress, you need a tux, and we need to come up with a plan," Gwendoline felt on fire, now that she had a mission, but strangely she felt misty as well. "It may be naïve, but I think there's got to be a way for all of us to be happy. I'll accept any punishment I might have earned with all of my terrible decisions, but it'll be worth it if I know I didn't destroy anything permanently."

Niles sighed, looking up into the sky as the clouds huddled together in preparation for a winter storm. "I wouldn't say you need any more punishment, Gwendoline."

As impassive as he tried to make himself sound, his tenderness touched her deeply. Words crowded her mind, battling to see which could reach her lips first, but none succeeded. Niles smiled down at her, fondly, almost as if he were her best friend. Neither of them could hide how they really felt from one another, but she wanted him to be able to free himself from her, if he was able, so she held her silence after all.

"Come on," she said, walking past him to hop into the driver's seat of her car. "We're going home."

21

The days preceding the gala kept Gwendoline busy with scheming out a solution. The local news was as fixed on the new political "power couple" as if Everleigh and Averill—she gagged at the idea—were a charming romantic notion cooked up by Cupid himself. Was no one at all shocked that right before Starford's first possible election an heir to the Kinsley line appeared as if from nowhere? Was no one suspicious that within a very short time he and the contested heir happened to form a relationship? She wondered how no one bothered to ask these questions.

Arranged marriages happened all the time. Everleigh's words from their haunting conversation occasionally traversed back to Gwendoline's thoughts, accompanied by a familiar sinking feeling. To an outsider, it wouldn't seem like the worst thing in the world for the two heirs to get along so well. Their region hadn't endured real conflict in hundreds of years, and wars could be fought over the line of succession regardless of modern democracy or not. Averill had stuck to vague descriptions about the changes he wanted to make, since he was wise enough to move slowly in the public eye if he wanted approval, and he had relied on his animal charisma to carry him through his quest. Everleigh was popular locally, since her parents were active in the community and well known. Her name would've been enough to rival Averill's contrived charm, so together perhaps they did seem like a formidable couple.

How little they know, Gwendoline thought to herself whenever she went out that week, which was a rare occurrence. Averill would rule with an iron fist, quash magical and even technological development, and any of those who barely possessed any magic at all would be in danger. Everleigh, whatever she believed, could not mellow that side of him. She wouldn't be able to save everyone.

Gwendoline had many reasons to stay housebound. Averill had promised Everleigh he wouldn't come after anyone she loved as long as she went with him, and so far Gwendoline hadn't seen him since the nightmare dream invasion he'd subjected her to. But she wouldn't depend on that vow if angels flew down from the sky to tell her the same thing. Niles encouraged her to stay home as well.

One of the main reasons involved the rest of Starford. Averill had not unleashed the curse of the Rotten, but a bizarre aura hung in the atmosphere everywhere Gwendoline went. People stayed indoors, which would have been normal in the early winter, but those few who did leave their homes developed a glazed, hungry look within a few minutes. She hated this so much that she quit attending her university classes as well.

Gwendoline shook moisture droplets from her hair and coat as she entered her house after an exploratory errand run through the nearest town. Two garment bags hung over her shoulder, also covered in water, and she shook them out without caring whether the moisture would warp her wood floors. Maybe it was stupid to risk an outing for party clothes, but she didn't have anything that would work, and they would need to blend in to get into the party. Averill would probably sense their presence, but there wasn't anything he could do about it right away if he wanted to keep his guests enthralled.

Dancer rushed through the house to greet her, her big paws thumping the floor as she pranced. With Niles back at the house, her sullen pouting sessions had become a thing of the past, and for the most part her Dalmatian acted like a regular puppy. Gwendoline greeted her with enthusiasm, tossing the garment bags onto the stair banister as Dancer jumped to try to lick her face.

Behind them, a resolute knock thumped against the door. Gwendoline jumped, causing Dancer to drop to all fours. She hadn't thought she'd been followed home, but she recognized the familiar knock and some of her tension ebbed away.

Indulging in a long pause, she turned back to her door and turned the knob to allow Colt to enter.

"I'm sorry I've been absent," he began, almost as if he'd rehearsed this speech on the way here. "I know you must be so mad at me for avoiding you, but staying away from you has been—" he halted mid-sentence, and without turning Gwendoline knew what had stopped his words.

Niles had approached from down the hallway, stalking casually forward in the navy sweats and a white t-shirt he'd been wearing to work out. His moving process hadn't involved much more than transporting the few articles of clothing and male toiletries over in a plain suitcase, but she hadn't seen this outfit yet and the simplicity of the clothes flattered their wearer.

Colt's expression hardened, his lips curling like an alpha male whose territory had been trespassed on. Inexplicably offended by both his antagonism and his attractive dishevelment, Gwendoline turned back to Niles to see his reaction. A disbelieving smile hovered about his mouth, but it wasn't a happy reaction. He shook his head, perhaps in disgust, perhaps in disappointment.

"We've been trying to call you. We should do this together. Get Everleigh back, I mean," she stammered, intervening to diffuse the tension. Realizing she was looking between the two men like a bobble head, she fixed her gaze on a safer spot, like the twisted zipper of the top garment bag flung onto the banister.

"That *is* why you're here, isn't it?" Niles questioned, his tone frosty even if he'd schooled his expression into something barely friendlier than disdain. A fleeting memory of Glenna's trespassed on Gwendoline's mind, a memory in which Leland and Niles had sat drinking after a sparring session, laughing at who knows what. Sadness not her own engulfed her, but thankfully it passed.

"Could you give us a minute, Niles?" Gwendoline asked, casting him an apologetic look. Niles didn't look surprised at her request, but she couldn't read anything else off him. Nodding curtly, he turned his back on the both of them. Dancer followed him with a displeased huff.

Colt watched Niles go, his eyes narrowed before he snapped back to the present as Gwendoline crossed her arms. She tried not to notice how his shoulders sagged from their vigilant posture into a more comfortable pose once they were alone. Well, she hoped they were alone.

"Look, it's not right for you to ignore my calls—" she began.

"You're living with Niles now?" They both spoke at the same time, their words tripping over each other in unpleasant dissonance. Raising her eyebrows, Gwendoline fell silent, giving Colt a chance to rephrase. He ducked his head, abashed, but didn't change his question.

"So...you and Niles?"

Gwendoline's frown deepened, and she snapped at him. "He's staying here because he has nowhere else to go, and we would all work better from a home base where we can watch our backs and springboard ideas on how to fix this Averill mess."

Also, it's not really your business what I do, she mentally added, lacking the guts to say it out loud.

Further shamed, Colt's wind-chapped cheeks reddened; she half expected him to scuff his shoe against the floor like a teenager who'd been caught shoplifting. "That's not a bad idea."

"Thanks," Gwendoline replied, failing to tune the sarcasm out of her voice. "If you hadn't ignored my calls, you would've known we wanted you to move in as well until all of this gets sorted out."

"The three of us? Living together?" Colt questioned skeptically. Clearly his antagonism against Niles would be more of an issue than she'd thought.

"*Grow up,* Colt! It's just for a few days, and we could all be dead within the week! *Dead* dead, not reincarnated to do this shit all over again. Pack a freaking bag, make your excuses to your dad, grab your stupid sword, and come stay here!" Gwendoline scolded herself for losing her patience, but the resentment boiling up within her couldn't be denied. He had looked at her with such blame the other day, when she'd been on her way to rescue *his* girlfriend, and here he stood daring to complain. She glared at him, tempted to shove him right back out her front door into the storm outside.

She saw herself in Colt's eyes, standing defiant with upturned chin and swirling frosty eyes as he looked down at her. Her stance conveyed more bravery and defiance than she felt in reality and magic seeped from her in a smoky, blue-tinted breath.

"I'm sorry. You're right, I just—"

"I know," Gwendoline interrupted with a sigh as she glanced down, tugging at the hem of her sweater to extract an imagined pulled thread. "We're all on the wire. But we need to knock it off, because Everleigh is in trouble, and we can sort out the rest later. We need to be whole, all of us. For her."

A new feeling—well, new to Gwendoline—filled her, sustaining her like a swallow of rum sipped in front of a blazing bonfire: loyalty. Not just loyalty to a friend, but to the person who should be ruling Starford, the descendant of the queen who had ruled Oloetha. Jael had earned her crown during the civil war in ancient days: by sacrificing herself to the beast that was Averill, Everleigh had earned the right to governance in this time.

"You're so..." Colt's hand twitched towards her, perhaps to brush an errant strand of hair from her face, but he kept his distance after all. "I'll get my stuff and bring it here."

"Good," Gwendoline replied, more harshly than she meant. She felt herself softening towards him against her will. She knew she'd been ill-treated. They all had stuff going on: terrible, identity questioning stuff, and yet in spite of her mistakes she felt like she was the only one of their duo trying to make changes for the better. They were both hurting, and somehow he was the one who'd hurt her the most.

"Gwendoline," Colt spoke her name like it was the forbidden fruit, dangling from a branch in a ray of sun. "Will you choose him?" He'd said it, which surprised her. She didn't think they were allowed to voice such risky, tumultuous thoughts.

Worse, she didn't have an answer, since she was too busy trying to stitch her heart together to make a whole person before she decided to sew it together with another heart.

"Will you choose her?" she challenged instead, beginning to turn away to trace Niles's path back down the front hallway. She didn't expect an answer, didn't expect him to do anything to stop her, but his big swordsman's hand caught her wrist to pause her departure. She faced him, questioning, but the look in his eyes stopped her from speaking.

Colt was no longer the easygoing yet thoughtful boy she'd known all of her life as Gwendoline, but he did not yet have the self-possession and assurance of the man Leland had been. His eyes were so blue: endlessly deep azure that she could dive into and never resurface from, which until recently had only endeared him as a friend when she'd only seen the shades as the calm surface of a familiar lake. But she saw something that terrified her this time, a hint of his decision that made her pulse skyrocket and then slow into near oblivion.

He had come here to choose her, she realized. *Colt had chosen her.*

"No," she sputtered, inexplicably angry and temporarily taken over by indignation for poor Everleigh, her once-friend and hopefully future sovereign. "You can't. Colt, we *can't*—"

He interrupted her, pulling her into him for an embrace so tight it stopped her trembling, and a kiss that made her shiver down to her heels. He tasted of new promises, promises made just for her, a flavor that reminded her of sweet iced tea on a warm summer holiday at Starford beach. He held her close, their lips moving in discovery and unexpected tenderness that mellowed their passion into what could only be called worship. The pretend stitches she'd firmly sewn her heart together with split down the middle, threatening to burst. The painful beauty of their kiss filled her utterly.

She had to do something, she had to stop this, because even though he'd decided, *she hadn't*. What about Everleigh? Gwendoline meant to say this, and her friend's name blossomed in her throat, working hard to separate the two of them from their kiss. But a different word broke free instead.

"Niles!" she choked, pushing Colt away, and failing due to his bulk. Panic seized her in its grip, though he'd already started to back off the moment she protested, but she didn't have any time to process as she felt air whoosh by as Colt's weight was lifted off her.

Blinking, Gwendoline steadied herself by leaning against the banister of her stairs. Once she refocused, she saw that Niles had answered her unintentional call by pinning Colt against the wall with his forearm, holding him back with apparent ease. Still, she noticed the muscles in his arms and chest straining under his t-shirt.

"Are you kidding me?" Colt protested, irritated at the violence. He gripped Niles's arm, intending to throw him off, but to everyone's surprise, for the first time in his life Colt failed to knock someone down. Niles stood fast, hardly breaking a sweat as he pushed Colt into the wall. Gwendoline heard a few cracks as the drywall supporting this feat groaned and splintered.

A memory of Glenna's intruded, or at least a sense of a memory. Leland and Colt shared the same brutish strength that could win most fights, and though Niles was strong and scrappy, he wouldn't have won a physical fight against either of them. Yet, here they were, and Niles had enough power to easily restrain Colt. Gwendoline saw the faintest hints of shadow swirling under Niles's pale skin, so subtle he might not have noticed them himself.

When you gaze into the abyss... These words were not hers, and they stung her thoughts with dread.

"Gwendoline?" One of them spoke her name, breaking her out of her trance, and she realized Niles looked to her for guidance. "Are you hurt?"

"No, she's not hurt! What do you think I'd do to her?" Colt shouted, still pushing against the barrier of Niles's arm. His face had flushed with the redness of exertion.

"Besides toy with her emotions?" Niles growled, fixing his glaring, charcoal black eyes on Colt. "You may be Leland reborn, but from where I'm standing, this version of him has been nothing but a disappointment." It wasn't like Niles to lash out like this, and Colt blinked in surprise. Unexpectedly, pain flashed in his eyes, eyes that for the briefest instant faded to a soft gray that echoed a former life. Gwendoline hesitated before stepping in.

"This isn't necessary, and I'm not hurt," she said; she felt like she should step between them, break the tension that threatened to escalate to violence...but she couldn't move. "Let him go, Niles."

"Are you sure? You're the one who called for me," Niles questioned her, his eyes slowly softening back to amber. She saw it in him, the calculation, as he shifted his gaze briefly back to Colt. He may not have been eavesdropping in a traditional sense, but he knew. He knew something had happened between her and Colt, something romantic and physical, and she saw his satisfaction, however meager, that she'd called for *him* in the midst of it. He didn't know she'd meant to say Everleigh's name to remind Colt of his duty, of how he'd been in love with a different woman not long ago.

Then again, no matter her intentions, she *had* called for Niles.

"Of course I'm sure, now *let him go,*" she ordered. Her

commanding tone didn't dispel her uncomfortable embarrassment, almost as if she'd called out the wrong name during the height of a sexual tryst.

"If you insist," Niles complied, lowering his arm as Colt stepped forward, his stance as threatening as if he wanted a rematch. This time Gwendoline did move between them, personally disgusted that she was the reason these two fools were at each other's throats.

Jealousy's a bitch, she thought.

"This isn't helpful. Nothing about this will help us save Everleigh, let alone the rest of the city. So let's...let's just stop," she tried to reason with them, her words hobbling forwards like teenagers forced to perform in front of family members as she pushed the two men apart.

Instead of agreeing or even answering, Niles nodded at her, sparing a last glare for Colt before he exited the narrow foyer at a leisurely pace. The latter tried to catch her gaze, but she turned her back to him, following Niles down the hallway to her living room. After a few seconds, she heard his heavy tread behind her as he followed her lead.

She should have felt furious, or resentful, or anything other than emptied out like a crumpled carton of forgotten ice cream. Inhaling deeply, she paused before she sat down in her favorite sand colored arm chair, the one that had been reupholstered at least twice. It took work, and a few more calming breaths, but she was able to dispel the uneasiness she felt with Niles sitting across from her on the same sofa she'd reclined on when she'd freed him from her casting book, and Colt leaning against the doorframe, not committing to entering the room.

Focus, she told herself. As an old habit, she called her casting book to her. With its arrival in her lap, so came the next idea.

"We need to reinstate the challenge, start the do-over," Gwendoline declared, stating the idea she'd been mulling over since she'd left Everleigh at the Kinsley manor.

Colt's answer was predictable. "We don't know what fucked us up last time. How can we go into this knowing we won't make the same mistake?"

"Would you rather we do nothing?" Niles needled him.

"Of course not!"

"Judging by the reason you came here, it doesn't seem like Everleigh matters much to you at this point," Niles prodded further, goading Colt back into fury.

"How is that your business? Besides, that's not true," Colt tried to keep his cool, but it was only a matter of time before he snapped.

Gwendoline listened to the boys argue, her unbound but hopefully still useful casting book open on her lap. The pages haunted her with their emptiness, but she flipped through them anyway, looking for a sign. Something niggled at the back of her mind, a familiar cord leading to a part of her mind that she somehow knew was not purely her own. For the first time, she recognized what this meant, and excitement dashed through the middle of her fear like a secret ingredient in a delicious recipe.

"Guys," she tried to get their attention as her vision pulsed, foggy as well as scarlet tinged. "Guys, I'm feeling a...a something?"

The boys ignored her for a moment, arguing amongst themselves. She had to call out to them again as a headache washed over her brain, making her wince. Niles was at her side in an instant once her casting book slipped from her hands and fell to the floor with an audible thump.

Fate, will you help us this time? She asked the presence in her mind, heedless of anyone else in the room. She expected no answer, or at least not enough of one to make sense of, but words as clear as if she had written them down in her own hand scrolled before her eyes like captions on a movie.

The circle is whole: heart, spirit, soul. The binding tie is present and in place. Time is Time to link the whole. This riddling talk reminded Gwendoline of past messages sent to Glenna, and even as she memorized the words disappointment with the lack of clarity sank in her stomach.

But then a presence that was both there and not there circled around her neck, the rasping scales of a snake brushing against the sensitive skin as more words followed.

You are ready this time, child. You have everything you need to defeat this Lord who has gone astray from the path. I will be with you, Gwendoline, as I was before.

For the first time, Gwendoline felt more whole than broken when Fate's presence left her. The spirit snake coiled about her neck felt comforting rather than constricting, and the ending of a euphoric smile she hadn't known she was wearing faded from her face. But the elation dissipated once she realized that, though they'd spoken almost directly, Fate hadn't really given any concrete answers. She still had to figure everything out on her own, and misery awaited them all if she got the answers wrong.

"Gwendoline? Gwendoline, answer me," Niles was commanding her again, his arms firm on her shoulders so that his fingers dug into her muscles as he shook her. She frowned, more from discomfort and befuddlement than pain. Then her vision cleared, and she blinked at the boys.

"Did you all hear that or do I have to repeat what I heard?"

"We heard you," Colt supplied an answer. "You were talking in your trance." They both knelt in front of her where she sat, close enough so she would barely need to reach out to touch them. But still, their figures appeared dim, as if through a veil of red her eyes couldn't clear. Gwendoline blinked several times, the same red goop in her eyelashes.

"Don't do that," Niles urged her. "Don't get any more in your eyes, it'll sting." With a sinking feeling, Gwendoline guessed what the substance hindering her vision could be. Shoving the boys aside, she staggered back down the hall to the mirror hanging on the wall there, steeling herself for confirmation of her suspicion.

Blood coursed down her face from her eyes, eyes that were impossibly full of the same so neither iris nor pupil was visible from the taint. She had been taken over by Fate before: normally pain came with the experience, and Glenna had experiences with blood during a possession before.

Could it be called possession? Gwendoline had still felt like herself.

"Are you all right?" Colt asked anxiously. The boys had followed her, but they kept their distance when she turned her crimson gaze on them and frowned. Colt looked ready to spring forward to catch her if she fell, and Niles ignored her warning and advanced to stand behind her.

Gwendoline returned her focus to the mirror, studying the blood. After a few heartbeats, she spoke.

"I am Fate's vessel, did you know? I'm not sure what makes me suitable for the role, and part of me wishes she'd chosen someone else. Given everything that's happened I'm not even sure I trust her. But she told us we're ready, and for Everleigh's sake, and Starford's sake, I have to believe that." Lifting her hands to her face and choosing to disregard the trembling of her fingers, she traced the lines of blood on her face to coat her fingertips.

She didn't have time to coddle anyone else, and she couldn't reassure Niles or Colt that she knew what would happen since Fate had concealed the future from her. The only thing she could control was her fear and her response to it, and that idea felt as oddly comforting as the finality of packing the last box in preparation for moving houses.

Thankfully, they didn't question her. Gwendoline expected Niles to flinch when she reached out to mark his face with the blood on her fingers, anointing his sharp cheekbones with scarlet in two sharp vertical lines, but he kept his composure and merely studied her, curiosity and dread warring in his eyes along with a growing battle fervor. Anticipating her approach, Colt too allowed her to stain his skin with the blood.

"We're going to crash that gala, bring Everleigh home, and unite against that bastard to kill him once and for all," she announced as she smudged the blood onto his face. "This time, we work together. This time, we win."

Gwendoline smiled, heedless of the blood that dripped down to stain her teeth.

22

Gwendoline couldn't believe the crucial night had arrived at last. Outside, the chill of the evening had settled in for the night, promising with bitter gusts that the worst was yet to come. This she knew already: they had a half-assed plan to save Everleigh from Averill—and herself—but so many things could go wrong that the Glenna fragments within her could scarcely bear the suspense.

Thanks to her encounter with Fate she felt powerful. Colt was late picking up his tux. Niles had ventured to scout out around the Kinsley estates to see if he could glean more information. He had yet to return, and Gwendoline resisted the urge to gnaw on her nails while she waited. Watching the snow fall with gentle pats outside her window reminded her of easier days spent relaxing with her friends, drinking cocoa and eating cranberry orange bread with their textbooks spread out all over her living room floor.

Glenna's even earlier days of hunting with her modified crossbow in the snow with Leland and Niles also starred in the playback tab of her mind, but tonight of all nights she didn't want to lose herself in her memories.

Lurking at her side as she sat on the padded bench next to her front door, Dancer channeled her restlessness into pacing. The Dalmatian knew she would be left behind and resented the exclusion. Gwendoline had explained that there was too much danger, that she didn't want Averill to use her familiar for an easy target, but she doubted she'd broken through her pet's stubbornness. The lack of her familiar's presence did have the possibility of tampering with her magic, but Glenna's fragments had been used to working without a familiar. Gwendoline was counting on this distinction to maintain her power.

A sound from outside made Gwendoline jump, her cultivated curls bouncing, but a second later she recognized the sound as Niles stomping his feet on her doorstep, shaking off the light coating of snow so he wouldn't track it inside. The door opened and he entered, several fat flakes of powdery snow clinging to his hair and coat. A gust of wind trailed indoors, cold enough to render the heat in her house briefly useless, and she hummed a swift spell that warmed both of them up enough to keep the shivers at bay.

"Are we ready?" Gwendoline questioned Niles as he shrugged free from his coat and shook the snow from his thick hair.

"As we'll ever be. Averill isn't a fool, so I believe he knows we'll try something, but I don't think he'll expect us to be addled enough to challenge him a second time." Niles's frown transferred to her own mouth, and she felt her brows crease with concern. "Regardless, his wards have been taken down, so he won't know we're at his celebration until we confront him."

And Everleigh, Gwendoline thought. She dreaded seeing her friend. Maybe it would be useful after all to concentrate on the past, to remember how she and Everleigh were friends before all of this changed their lives.

Concerns aside, a standard awkward silence took over the atmosphere. Gwendoline's teeth caught on her lip, searching for an errant piece of skin to tug, but she remembered the dark stain of her lipstick and clenched her manicured hands at her side instead. Niles's eyes were on her, glinting to belie his impassive expression and stance. He observed her from head to heel with the ponderous attention of a reluctant but admiring artist.

Straightening her posture, Gwendoline lifted her chin in a dare for him to comment on her attire. She should've picked something simple to wear, like matte black or a red deep enough to conceal any blood should they make it out of this crisis alive. Instead, she'd chosen a smoky silk and chiffon dream that swept from a reasonably low neckline to a sharply defined waist, and then down to the airy folds that swished about her ankles. Thin embellishments that could have been frost webs or vines decorated the satin bodice and the diaphanous sleeves that flowed loosely up to her wrists. Against her skin, the gray brightened her attractive pallor, accentuated the dark sweep of her hair, and enhanced the deep colors of her eyes and burgundy stained lips. The whole ensemble was a modern dress with an old fashioned twist, enhanced by the glamorous curled updo she'd bullied her hair into, and she wondered without wanting to wonder what he thought of her tonight.

Niles held his tongue, motionless black eyes unfathomable as he lingered on her face. A gentle whisper that she could barely name pressed against the walls of her mind before it faded almost immediately.

Raising an eyebrow, Gwendoline held his gaze as she lifted her hands to her throat, humming a note of costume magic that would turn the simple white gold chain she'd chosen into something else. Niles glanced down as she finished her cast, before turning away from her as if the moment hadn't taken place. She reminded herself that this rebuff was her own fault as she glanced down at the star sapphire pendant she'd wrought with her magic. Star sapphire...he'd compared her eyes to such in their fleeting contact, and she pondered the contrast her cool star sapphire would make to the flickering carnelian his eyes most often matched.

Niles had occupied himself with adjusting his tie in her hall mirror, and Colt found him thus when he finally burst into Gwendoline's house, already wearing his tux. She almost chuckled, since the formal ensemble fit him so terribly: broader than most men in Starford and perhaps most places, she couldn't guess how he'd managed to cram his athletic body into the suit. Scowling, Colt took Niles's place in front of her mirror as he growled a clumsy alteration spell. Sleeves and pant legs lengthened, his coat trimmed at the waist and broadened at the shoulders, and finally he looked the part of the contemporary prince Gwendoline expected him to be.

She had to change one aspect of his attire, however.

"Do you think Averill is blind?" Gwendoline chided as Colt picked up the sword he'd carried in with him to sling it over his back. He paused, glancing down at his favored weapon before he turned a glare her way.

"I'll need this if I'm supposed to challenge him again," he told her, obstinately fitting the sheathed sword onto its familiar place on his back. Gwendoline frowned. *It's not like the sword helped you finish this before, seeing as he used it to kill you.*

Maybe he was surly because of the fear and anticipation, but she would've sworn Colt had the same thought she had. His hard look failed to gentle into his usual stoic demeanor, but he didn't protest again. She heard the quiet notes of his casting, and the strap around his chest and the sword disappeared under a cloak of deceptive magic. Then his focus was on her, and a breathless sensation tightened her lungs when he looked at her with naked admiration and longing in his eyes.

Niles broke his silence, both from necessity and from an obvious desire to end the tension. "We'll arrive together, but I'll be leaving you to sneak in a different entrance. For the most part, you'll have to look after yourselves and find Everleigh while I search for Averill."

"Should we disguise ourselves too?" Gwendoline asked, already fixing a picture in her mind of what her disguise would look like.

"I've considered that, but no. Everleigh needs to be able to recognize you both," Niles halted her conjuring of a mask with his explanation. "I'll acquire one of the help's clothes as a disguise. Once I've blended in I'll keep you both as unnoticeable as possible. With the amount of people scheduled to attend even Averill shouldn't notice you for some time."

"Let's go then!" Colt's impatience made her turn to stare at him, her eyebrows lifted. He was too on edge, wound like a tourniquet fit to cut off a limb. If it came to a fight, he would lose: Gwendoline remembered Leland's purposeful clearing of his own head before any fights, and despaired. But then Leland had died in spite of his preparation. Maybe they needed Colt's fire, his drive to save them all. If they could kill Averill, would Colt be such a bad choice to take his place as Lord of the land?

The idea sickened her, eating her up with some unknown knowledge of the disaster that replacement could be. Still, who else had the right? Leland had been Jael's champion, as Colt was Everleigh's in spite of what he and Gwendoline had done.

Gwendoline had braced herself for more arguments, at least for more of the macho pomposity Niles and Colt had been showcasing lately, but the two men obviously felt like they had nothing worth saying to each other. If the showboating had been for her benefit alone, she might have felt a chagrined sense of flattery, but these two had issues that ran deeper than competition for one woman could allow.

Besides, Niles had renounced his claim: maybe he couldn't help but take the opportunity for however many snide barbs he thought of, but he'd kept his distance. Unlike Colt, who led her out of her own door with his hand splayed against her back. His skin felt warm enough to burn her, even on this cold evening and even through her coat.

Gwendoline insisted on driving, since they were taking her car instead of Colt's. She half expected a scuffle over who would ride shotgun, but Niles slipped into the backseat without comment. Colt filled the seat on the passenger side, folding his large body into the cramped space of her car. Silence ensued as she revved the engine, heating it as they began their journey to Kinsley manor.

Barely ten minutes passed before she couldn't stand the strain between the three of them: she had to speak.

"We find them, we convince Everleigh to leave with us, and then we fight Averill off. Worst comes to worst we banish him again, but I'd rather make sure he can't come back."

"Are you reviewing the plan?" Colt asked, fiddling with the air conditioning knobs as he tugged at the collar of his tux. Gwendoline smiled wistfully as she glanced to the side, recalling how little Leland had cared for formal wear as well.

"I'm just trying to make sure everything is in order. We thought it was last time, and we thought all the pieces were in place, but..." Gwendoline trailed off, knowing he understood.

"We're at the same level of preparation now, which isn't exactly favorable for the outcome of this night," Niles warned ominously. "Fate gave us one last message through you, Gwendoline, but have we really worked out its meaning?"

"She said we have everything we need, and she's here for us," she repeated the gist of the otherworldly message she'd received, grimacing as she remembered how tricky it had been to clean the blood from her eyes. She wished she still felt as brave as she had in that moment right after the trance. Any extra courage would be welcome company tonight.

"She's here for us?" Niles snorted. "That'll be a first."

"On that we agree," Colt interjected sharply, his expression darkening further. Sharing a glance, he and Gwendoline resumed the uncompromising quiet that had filled the car moments ago. They two above anyone had the most cause to question Fate's wisdom. Why bind two souls together in the beginning only to let them die suffering and failing to defeat one of *her* defiant Lords?

Sure, the magic in the land is at stake, and more lives than ours count on the scale, Gwendoline deliberated. *But does that mean our short lives have to be miserable? If destiny is so important and our souls share a connection, why allow Jael and then Everleigh to come between us? Why bring Niles into my life?*

She had no answers, and the long drive passed as wordlessly as if she were alone until Niles gestured for her pull over once they approached Kinsley's grounds.

"I'll let you know where I am once I slink inside," he promised. A second later he'd blended into the night, leaving no trace of his passage on the sheet of snow layered upon the ground. Freezing though it was, Gwendoline and Colt decided to park off the beaten track rather than risk the valet recognizing them and possibly reporting to his master.

Her teeth chattered as she walked in spite of the white faux mink coat she'd inherited from her stepmother, but the walk before them didn't take much time. Colt had eschewed his sensible jacket, choosing to warm himself with the heat magic that came to him easily. Reaching out, he gallantly offered to do the same for her even though she was capable herself, but she shook her head in a negative. Gwendoline wanted to save all her energy for Averill.

She had expected there to be some sort of bouncer, some poor creature Averill had enthralled to keep uninvited guests from entering his domain. Had this been a few weeks ago she might have made some calls to college societies throughout Starford U to arrange a riotous party crashing disaster complete with beer kegs and destructive athletes. But tonight too much was at stake. She glanced wistfully at the chandelier, imagining some of her wilder acquaintances taking pot shots at the opulent crystal ornaments with whatever magic suited them best.

But could it really be so easy to sneak into the gala? Socially, most people considered it the height of vulgarity if someone left their wards up during a party or social gathering, but it confused her as to why Averill felt the need to obey this custom. More than ever, she felt the surety of this all being a trap threaten to make her turn back, dragging Colt with her. But what else could they do? Leaving Everleigh to her unrewarding sacrifice—and leaving Starford and the rest of the world to be conquered by an unscrupulous, mightily powerful Lord—was out of the question.

Leading the way with Colt close at her heels, Gwendoline brushed past the large front doors she'd hope never to see again after her meeting with Everleigh. She'd meant to scan the gathered faces for their friend or their target, but someone seized her arm and yanked her backwards barely in time to avoid another less alert guest on the move from crashing into her.

"Careful," Niles cautioned, his tone soft yet alert in her ear; he'd been the one to yank her back. She nodded, and his tight grip on her arm relaxed. Without turning, she guessed his trick before he melted back into facelessness among the crowd. Niles knew well the power of even a simple disguise, and the mysterious hooded robes the servants wore provided the perfect cover. Sometimes magical concealment could be more obvious than a simple costume.

Averill, regal as he was, clearly owned the talent of a born showman. Gwendoline had expected noise, color, the elaborate and gilded entertainment of the wealthy, and she wasn't entirely off: the great room of the manor and sweeping stairs had the look of celebration, but it was unlike anything she had ever seen before.

Tapestries draped the walls, depicting medieval battle scenes in dull colors more muted than they should have been. The attendants slipping through the hushed yet talkative crowd with their trays of expensive delicacies wore moss green robes, hooded to conceal their features. One slipped her coat free from her shoulders right at the moment she began to feel too warm in the press of people, carrying it away almost without her noticing. Golden light from harmless floating torches and the great chandelier suspended by nothing lit the room, but this light was just as muted as every color but green and gold.

Strange, tinkling music fluttered like feathers in the wind against the ear, buzzing or ringing oddly at any given time.

Gwendoline, sensing the air of archaic ritual or sacrifice, felt nauseated. Which was the true sacrifice: Starford to Averill's power lust, or Everleigh to satisfy a different kind of want?

Colt, head and shoulders above the crowd, scanned the whole of the room with his lips pressed tight together. The fire blazing in his eyes could not be more obvious, and Gwendoline sighed as she tugged on the sleeve of his tux.

"I know subtlety isn't your usual game, but you're going to have to try harder than that," she hissed at him, drawing his gaze to hers with the urgency of her speech. "Act natural. If he doesn't already know we're here I'd like to keep it that way. Understood?" With an air of great reluctance, Colt nodded. Then, slouching slightly and rounding his shoulders, he allowed her to lead him forward.

Though there were guests aplenty visible in the main hall and surrounding social rooms, Everleigh and the master of the house had yet to make themselves known. The sweeping stairs leading to the upper levels beckoned to Gwendoline as they returned defeated to the entrance hall. Averill had to be waiting in the wings to make an entrance, and the ferocious part of her awakened by her last vision from Fate longed to seek him out and kill him herself. If only she could...but attempting to kill him outright would upset the balance of the magic in the land, and they couldn't risk that either.

Exploration was too risky, so they'd have to wait for Averill to show himself. Gwendoline envied Niles his disguise and secrecy: she and Colt had been noticed by one or two guests, though none had approached them, and the unwanted eyes glancing their way with curiosity made her ill.

"Come on," Colt suddenly said to her, beckoning with a large hand. "I heard there's dancing in the other room. That's subtle enough, right? We'll blend right in."

Gwendoline had to agree, so she took the offered hand and let him lead her through the assembly, down different rooms and halls to an exquisite—though just as eerie—ballroom. The source of the strange music originated here, and she had to admit she'd never danced like this before. Well, she as Gwendoline hadn't: Glenna might have been more familiar with the traditional waltzes and more complicated styles of dancing in her day. The music, played by an unseen orchestra, had notes of enchantment woven throughout the piece.

Clever, Gwendoline unwillingly admired the ingenuity. These notes, though vaguely jarring, guided the participants through the steps so they moved as gracefully as if they'd been practicing these steps since childhood.

She scanned the circular room while Colt led her as unobtrusively as possible through the dancers towards the center. Gwendoline saw signs neither of their quarry nor his hostage, but she did glimpse Niles circling the outskirts of the crowd, scanning the dancers for any signs of danger. His eyes met hers briefly, long enough to let her see them glimmer once he saw her dancing with Colt. He was becoming far too good at concealing what he felt from her, and annoyance intruded on her preoccupation with their mission.

"I imagine we look good together," Colt spoke, drawing Gwendoline's attention back to himself. He held her gingerly as they stepped around and back to each other with linked hands.

"What makes you say that?"

Colt rolled his eyes, nodding in Niles's general direction. "Might explain why he looks so sour."

"I suppose?" Gwendoline tried to guess at his direction, but another thought occurred to her. "Maybe we shouldn't dance together, then. Everleigh might be less willing to come home if she sees us together." A muscle in Colt's jaw twitched as he gritted his teeth and then unclenched them.

"You're probably right," he spoke at last. Gwendoline nodded, stepping back and away from him as she surveyed the ballroom again. But Colt held her fast before she could walk away, both of their hands linked as the dancing drew them back together. Gwendoline opened her mouth to speak...then closed it. She could think of nothing to say to improve the situation. She hadn't made her choice yet. Besides, when all was said and done, they might not be around to choose anything. What was the point of dithering?

The minutes passed in a complete daze for a time. Gwendoline felt like she could barely catch her breath, the atmosphere was so thick with tension, and her cheeks flushed from the heat in the room and the warmth of her dance partner. Tiny things like the swish of her airy gown about her legs and the soft brush of her hair against her nape felt like the most significant sensations in the world. Music thrummed against her ears, tinny and oddly pleasant as it guided her steps and locked her into a faceless stupor that reminded her of being drunk. Or drugged...

Gwendoline gasped once she realized the truth.

What is it? Niles was knocking at her mind's door as her distress slammed her back into true awareness.

The music. It's more than a track for dancing, she sent him her knowledge with her eyes half closed as she concentrated. Colt, who had still been dancing, slowed to a stop as he blinked rapidly in succession. Gwendoline planted her feet firmly on the floor, her heels clicking against the smooth yet tractable stone surface as she whispered an antihex to herself. Averill had done his work well, if it was he who had bothered to engineer this hex rather than one of his minions. Even in her confusion, Gwendoline felt disgust rankle her composure. Clearly, the Lord of the land was taking no chances when it would come time for Starford to decide who ruled.

Colt shuddered as he banished the befuddling sorcery from his own mind. "I hate these games. Why can't people settle things with a good old fashioned brawl?"

Gwendoline laughed weakly, stepping to the side of a still bewitched couple—prominent voters on the building committee, she recognized—and then leading the way to the sidelines. "Really? You sound like someone who's never touched magic. Could you really live without it?"

"I think I could learn to, but I suppose I'd rather keep it. There are other things I couldn't do without."

"Like?" Gwendoline asked stupidly. Colt glanced down at her with his eyebrows lifted high. She flushed, exasperated that she'd missed her cue and secretly irritated that he kept pushing her into something she couldn't be ready for yet. But deep inside, the part of her soul that was tied to him jumped for joy.

Niles, still in his medieval waiter's garb, joined them briefly once they'd left the dance floor. He'd even bothered to steal a tray of fizzing champagne that sparkled in gold tinted flutes.

"I haven't found Everleigh, but I've sensed Averill nearby. Don't drink that," he interrupted himself as Colt reached for a glass. "If the music is hexed, we don't know what else might be tainted."

Gwendoline, who had almost reached for a glass herself, sighed as she mourned the dryness of her throat. "I can take care of the music, and you can make the rounds to antihex the party fare. He won't win so cheaply, at least."

"No," Niles shook his head, his features darkened by the hood he wore. "We shouldn't interfere until we know where Everleigh is."

"So we just leave them to suffer whatever plan Averill hatched for them?" Gwendoline protested, tempted to knock the tray of sparkling flutes onto the ground. "No way!"

"Lower your voice," Colt intoned, glancing nervously around the circular room. Gwendoline felt it too, the approaching sparks of a higher power. Instead of allowing the distraction, she slipped away from Niles and Colt, melting into the crowd as she tried to track the unsettling music to its source. Though both men mentally shouted discouragement for her new quest, she recognized too many faces she knew and would regret not seeing again as she passed through the throng like a silken gray shadow.

There: a corner of one of the grimmer tapestries—a unicorn sacrificing itself to a dragon to save the maiden cowering behind it—fluttered in a breeze that couldn't exist, and she gingerly tugged aside the swatch of artwork to see what she'd find. Only bare wall presented itself with gleeful blankness. But Gwendoline refused to be deceived. Hesitating long enough for the boys to catch up to her, she set her palm flat against the cool stone.

Nothing happened, and she exhaled her relief as she began unwinding the hex and binding it into something harmless. She sensed her friends behind her observing apprehensively, waiting for a curse to crash down on her like a concrete slab.

Sure enough, after the strands of the hex felt her touch, they lashed out, burning her palm with unseen acid. Biting back a scream,

Gwendoline choked back her outrage and finished the reweaving as her hand burned.

Niles roughly seized her wrist, yanking it back almost before she'd finished her work. Not bothering to hide her relief like she'd tried to hide her pain, she squinted her eyes shut. She would have cradled her injured fingers to her chest, but Niles hadn't let go of her wrist. He turned her hand over and over again, staring at the flesh so burned it had started to turn black. Gwendoline bit her lip hard enough to bleed as she silenced herself, but she needn't have bothered: Niles healed her with a soft cast of his magic, surprising all of them. It took a few minutes for him to undo the complex curse, a curse that had intended to mark the person who dared interfere with the musical hex for later retribution, but his will won in the end.

"That was stupid," he murmured, looking up at her. Yet Gwendoline could see his admiration, and a tremulous smile crossed her lips. He curled her fingers closed and released her, her hand whole and unpuckered by burn scars,

"It appears to have worked," Colt remarked, gesturing to the surrounding people. He took no issue with Niles healing her hand, even though that was area of expertise, and was too distracted to feel any surprise. Gwendoline congratulated herself on her cleverness to keep the part of the hex that helped people dance, so there wouldn't be a sudden cessation of dancing to draw attention to them. But, more importantly than her little triumph...

"Why would he bewitch them, though?" she wondered aloud, staring around and around at her fellow citizens in distress. "He's won over half the city and districts to his cause, and that half is mostly who's here tonight."

"True, but he wants it to be unanimous, I think," Niles

rationalized thoughtfully. "He's not above using his considerable power to manipulate the outcome of the election, meaning that he wants to inherit by might and erase Everleigh's Northwood bloodline claim altogether, but he wants everyone to be open to whatever ghastly idea he comes up with."

"He wants to be loved," Gwendoline whispered, the truth dawning on her at last. All those encounters when he would study her as if waiting for something to happen, or for someone else to arrive suddenly made sense. When she had been Glenna, when he had threatened her life by her own hand with the knife to her throat, he'd been hoping to goad Fate into coming to her aid. Then again, in the dream he'd hijacked, he'd threatened her then too, telling her enough of the truth to see if Fate would descend to punish him.

But then he'd killed Glenna, and Fate had done nothing to stop that.

Appalled, Gwendoline shared her revelation with her companions. "He's got a thing for Fate, and he's been using Jael and then Everleigh to replace her all this time. I'm her vessel, but he doesn't want more of the same: he wants to punish Fate. He might want Everleigh's heart as well, but Fate is who he's after." Colt, thunderous in his anger, nonetheless looked nauseated by what she'd told him.

"That's sick," he growled under his breath. "He's crazy as well as power hungry."

"More importantly," Niles intoned, sounding no less angry. "Fate has been using us to spurn her jilted lover instead of taking care of her own problems. We've all died for her while she's abandoned us, and for what? Here we are again, centuries later, about to make the same mistakes." Gwendoline had never seen him so angry, so mutinous.

Shadows clung to him, sucking light from the room as the hovering torches dimmed. Their eyes met and she could see what he was picturing in her own mind's eye: Leland's ravaged body with his arm flung to the side like garbage, Jael standing over the carnage screaming out her grief, and Glenna's own lifeless face as blood trickled out of her mouth.

I will be with you, Gwendoline, as I was before.

But you weren't with us! Gwendoline screamed to no one in her thoughts, unsure if her attempt to make contact with the being who would use her as a vessel would even work. *We died. All of us. You bound me and Colt together in two lifetimes, and we aren't free in either one. What was the fucking* point?

Hesitating for a second, Gwendoline reached out and rested her hand, the one he'd repaired after Averill's spiteful curse, on Niles's arm. She couldn't justify one bit of the horrors they'd experienced at the hands of one sadistic blood Lord and a debatably worse being of the stars. But they were here, they lived yet, and if she could only offer him a little solace then that would have to be enough.

The torches had dimmed to mere embers by the time Niles let himself look at her, and she concealed a shudder as the flat blackness of his eyes roved over her like a beast's. Yet the attention thrilled her simultaneously, locking her gaze with his in unspoken challenge. Slowly, as the shadows coalesced into a visible aura, Niles lifted his semi scarred hand from under his cloak and placed it over hers.

But Colt...she'd forgotten Colt, she'd been so lost in the moment. Thankfully, he hadn't noticed her connection with Niles, but Gwendoline couldn't be too grateful. She followed his line of sight to the top of the elegant stairs, when an angelic figure had appeared in glittering finery to address the assembled guests.

23

"May I have your attention?" Everleigh, for all her willing captivity, looked stunning. No sign of distress marred a face enhanced in comeliness by the wide green eyes outlined with brown and gold. Indeed, she glowed where she stood at the height of the stairs. More form-fitting than the dress Jael had worn at her own interrupted betrothal ceremony, the golden fabric flowed over the graceful lines of her body, accentuating each one with skill.

More importantly, a golden circlet embellished by a single yellow teardrop diamond ornamented Everleigh's brow, declaring her royalty in an outrageous display of opulence any town member ordinarily would have balked at. Even for a gala, crowns were considered over the top. Twin bracelets around her slight wrists matched the unofficial crown, making the set a simple yet elegant declaration of what a true leader of Starford would look like from now on.

She looked over at Colt, assessing his reaction. Fury and concern kindled in his eyes, warring with his struggle of keeping control over himself. He looked up at Everleigh like a dying man keen to pass into the light just so he could speak to this creature of serene beauty, but something held him back. Jealousy wanted to prevent Gwendoline from admitting that she noticed the desire there as well, but practicality won out: who could not desire this golden goddess?

A whisper of magic to her left distracted her: Niles had disappeared, even his presence untraceable. His absence left a vacuum that couldn't be filled by Colt's heat. She marveled how Everleigh's eyes failed to seek out the source of this fatal blaze of attention in the hall of her new home. Not too long ago, the magnetism between the couple would have drawn their attention to each other instantly. Gwendoline grieved how out of tune her friends were.

Everleigh's profile, more demure than Gwendoline had ever seen it as she modestly cast her eyes to the ground, was something an artist would have wept at the desire to capture. The layers of brunette curls, some strands gilded with highlights of the same gold that ringed her eyes and the bracelets around her wrists, fell over her bare shoulders as she turned. Averill himself approached from the other end of the hall, subtly yet vividly royal in a navy tuxedo that portrayed his features and figure with sharper lines.

"May *we* have your attention," he corrected Everleigh, making the moment seem like a private one even though he spoke loud enough to set the guests to chuckling fondly.

The music, harmless now, faded upon his arrival. Demurring again, Everleigh ducked her head, affecting a wan smile as she rested her hands on the smooth stair banister. In this dim light, the golden bracelets could pass for handcuffs. Smaug was not even in his usual place around her wrists: Gwendoline searched for the telltale curl of serpent, and was relieved when she spotted the flick of a tail around Everleigh's throat. She wanted to wave to get Everleigh's attention, foolish though that action would be if their enemy saw her, but she doubted her friend would notice since she seemed totally occupied with studying the whorls in the wood of the banister.

"We'd like to thank you all for attending our gala on this election eve, since we have much to disclose regarding Starford's line of succession," Averill began, stepping forward out of the shadows to join Everleigh in the figurative spotlight; he shrewdly scanned the crowd, but Gwendoline had anticipated that move and dragged Colt down into a crouch before he spotted them.

As much as she hated seeing her bubbly friend so cowed, Colt had to be feeling even worse. It took a good amount of her strength to subdue him enough into ducking his head, blending in with the crowd so his fury wouldn't draw attention to themselves before they were ready to act. She half expected him to reach for his spell concealed sword, but even angry he couldn't be that reckless.

"Where's Niles?" Colt asked her sotto voice while Averill waxed eloquent about Starford's prestigious history. Gwendoline shook her head to indicate her lack of knowledge. Her eyes skimmed over the crowd, searching for the telltale flip of a cloak, but she saw nothing and instead refocused her attention on Everleigh.

"Everleigh and I are in complete agreement that Starford doesn't need an election any more than it needs the conflict of an heir of Madam Kinsley arguing with an heir of the Northwood line until the end of days," Averill was saying, approaching the zenith of his speech. "My great aunt wanted me to spend my youth travelling, which is why I haven't been as much a part of Starford as I would have hoped. Her death, lamentable as it was, has gifted me with the opportunity to make this land what it should be."

Gwendoline snorted. However else she could denigrate his

actions, she had to admit that they were clever: he certainly had the power to fool the magical tests used by the council to determine the legitimacy of an heir, and in his world power was what mattered.

Everleigh had guessed as much before, but she didn't protest the lies any more than she rejected the pretender to her ruling claim when he rested a hand on her back in a public show of ownership. Instead, when she spoke, she sounded as serene as she looked.

"This is an opportunity I feel shouldn't be squandered. Starford has grown with each passing year, so why not dedicate the time and passion of two rulers to our city?" Whatever else Averill had made her do, he had convinced or compelled her to sound genuine; looking over at him, Everleigh appeared the picture of satisfaction, as any regular girl with a new boyfriend and the world on a string might.

"Well said, Everleigh," Averill praised. He was too much the royal to stoop to grating smugness in the face of victory, but even he couldn't hide the triumph in his eyes. "Therefore, to best serve Starford and its people, we have decided to combine our efforts and our hearts to give this town a ruling couple utterly focused on restoring our home to its former glory and beyond."

Polite if hesitant applause filled the hall, as if an orchestra had finished playing a masterpiece too obscure for anyone to recognize. Gwendoline glanced around at her neighbors and the wealthier citizens of Starford, all gathered here to witness this spectacle before they threw their rights away for Averill. Most of them were talented with magic, each in their own way: Mrs. Llewellyn had what you could call the gift of a green thumb, so she oversaw the beautification of the city and its districts. Councilman Roster didn't have as much of a gift for gardening, but he was a talented negotiator, and often kept the peace in small disputes in the higher circles of city management. She scanned the faces of others that she recognizing, hating that she was mentally making a list of who had the least magical ability. Those would be the people Averill would target first.

Colt was shaking his head, almost vibrating with rage. No longer caring if he was seen, he stood to his full height.

Everleigh flinched, a nearly imperceptible twitch near her lips that froze her celebrity smile into a mask that could crack at any second. Averill had taken her hand in his own, gazing at her dotingly as he brought it to his lips for a kiss. Knowing what she did, Gwendoline searched for a sign that this display was merely for show or genuine. She couldn't tell either way.

"Don't do this, Everleigh," Colt broke the silence, stepping forward; Gwendoline started to reach for him to hold him back before lowering her hand back to her side. He needed to do this, and the die was already cast regardless. Praying for perhaps the first time in her life, she cast up an entreaty towards the heavens.

Be with us, my lady. Let past mistakes remain where they are. Save our future.

People made a path for the warrior among them, parting like the seas so Colt could walk to the bottom of the left stairway. Golden drop earrings dripping with bright canary diamonds swayed as Everleigh's head snapped to the side to look at him. She stared at Colt, the man she had considered her soulmate before all of their lives had changed, and her lips parted in surprise. Perhaps without noticing, she withdrew her hand from Averill's while her green eyes burned feverishly from hope, then despair, then anger.

"You shouldn't be here, Colt. I don't want you here," she spoke, glancing to the side where Averill stood in silence. Gwendoline, reluctant to witness the moment she'd helped arrange, averted her gaze to study their enemy. He didn't seem worried: indeed, his lack of concern eased his features into a secretive smile. Had he been waiting for this to happen?

"I don't care. I know you're furious with me, and you have a right to be. I was a huge ass when we last talked, and..." Colt trailed off, pausing his ascent up the stairs. "I messed up. I have my reasons...but I hurt you, and almost threw away the biggest thing I care about. I can't believe I was that cruel."

"Me neither," Everleigh whispered, her true personality seeping through her cultivated mask as she began to shed the layers of faux contentment Averill had encouraged her to show. "But it doesn't matter now. I've made my choice."

"So you've said." Taking another step up, Colt painfully reminded Gwendoline of a fairytale prince climbing a tower to reach his beloved. "But it's the wrong one. I may have lost the right to tell you that, but that doesn't stop me from caring. I have no pedestal to stand on, and my pride has no place here, but I'm asking you not to sacrifice yourself this way. Please, 'Leigh."

Walking as if she were trapped in a dream, Everleigh left Averill's side. For several heartbeats, there was no sound in the hall aside from the click of her shoes on the marble floor; the assembly had been whispering amongst themselves before, commenting and judging, but now they held their silence with bated breath. Once again, Gwendoline felt like an unseen shadow as the two golden beings approached each other with their undeniable magnetism pulling them together.

But how could that be, when she and Colt had Fate's invisible cord linking their souls together? How could there be both?

"You left me, Colt Redfield. I needed you, and you left me for *her,*" Everleigh accused; though her manner came across as composed, her cheeks flushed with emotion. "No one has ever treated me with such...such lack of care, such disrespect. But this is about more than myself. More than us."

"I know. I know that," Colt admitted. Closing the distance between them, he spoke so quietly Gwendoline would not have heard him if not for the silence in the room. "But I would rather we fight outright, for you and for Starford, than give you over to that beast. He may have promised to hold back for your sake, but we know that won't last. He's tried something tonight, and I can't let you sacrifice yourself for a lie...or to save me."

This was it. Gwendoline tried to prepare herself without knowing the outcome, summoning magic to her fingertips in uneasy silence; it lingered there, unformed crackling energy she could configure into something else at a second's notice. She looked up again at Averill, but aside from raised eyebrows saw no concern in his demeanor. Niles still refrained from revealing himself.

"Jael could not—or would not—save Leland. Why shouldn't I save you?" Everleigh said, her voice dropping to a near whisper.

"I don't need saving. But right now, you might. Let me do this for Starford. For you, 'Leigh." Colt dared lift his hand to her face, tracing the line of her cheekbone with his thumb. From where Gwendoline stood, nearer to the staircase than she'd like, she saw the indecision on Everleigh's face come to a conclusion that made her smile more truly than anything she'd seen tonight. Tender enough to reveal the depth of her own feelings, the modern princess lifted her hands to Leland's, holding his hand to her as her eyes welled.

"Good," Averill's voice rang from above, and he stepped back into the light with his teeth bared in a feral grin. "I was waiting for an excuse."

Then, with barely a lift of his finger, a screaming fireball burning with white hot flames flew down the stairs towards Colt. The energy seared the hall, drawing screams from the ladies and gentleman still gathered in their finery. So swiftly did the fireball descend that Gwendoline didn't have time to bring up a magical shield to halt it.

Before the flames could utterly consume whatever was in their path, Niles materialized in front of Colt and Everleigh. He'd discarded his hooded cloak, and on his arm he bore a huge shield of solid darkness taller than himself and wide enough to fill the stairway. Moving so fluidly she could barely hold his form in her vision, he slammed the shield into the ground in front of the fireball's path and held his stance. Gwendoline thought he'd stagger back as the fireball crashed into the magical shield, but the black front absorbed the heat and fire into itself as a gust of wind extinguished all of the torches in the hall.

Feeling the rush of bodies pressing against her in the sudden darkness as the terrified guests madly dashed towards the exit, Gwendoline relit the hovering torches into blazing brightness with a wave of her hand. The return of visibility wouldn't halt the stampede, but at least no one would get trampled.

Her eyes free to see once more, she looked up towards the stairs as she dodged people to reach her friends as quickly as she could. Summoning magic again, she didn't pay attention to what weapon or defense she called until she glanced down to see the sword made of silver blue light clutched in her right hand. The single star sapphire set into the base of the weapon winked at her, a greeting from the past.

Aside from casting the deadly fireball Averill hadn't deigned to descend the stairs. Colt had drawn his sword, holding it up and at the ready; he'd tried to push Everleigh behind him, but she'd refused to budge. Instead, she'd unclasped Smaug from his binding around her neck. The golden snake grew, lengthening and thickening into a serpent headed golden staff whose red eyes burned with its mistress's fury. Still in front of both of them, Niles panted behind his obsidian shield; after a moment, it disappeared into black mist. Beneath where the shield had been, Gwendoline saw the split and cracked marble stair that Niles had crushed when he'd slammed the barrier into place.

You have everything you need. The thought came to her as she saw all of her loved ones, her family, ready to fight and die again. More importantly the thought was accompanied by the missing link that had ruined their battle with Averill in the past.

Time is time to link the whole.

The whole...it wasn't enough for Leland to fight. He was the sword and spirit, but the heart needed to guide him and the soul was his shield! Gwendoline almost laughed, laughed with relief that she had the answer at last and had solved this fatal puzzle. Ready to fight, she hefted her shimmering sword and balanced on her toes as she flowed into a fighting stance. Standing behind her friends, she would be the rear guard.

"You." Averill remarked on Niles's sudden arrival as if he were discussing the highlights of a particularly boring weather report; still, his feral eyes gleamed with intrigue. "I sensed the others, and indeed, I expected them to try to intervene tonight. But you...how did you conceal yourself from me?"

"Pure dumb luck," Niles quipped, his face deadpan. His eyes glittering with menace, deep seated rage flowed from his pure black eyes to materialize in his hands as two large circular glaives that sparked with heat and flickered in and out of reality at a dangerous frequency.

Averill's lips twitched as if he were hiding an indulgent laugh. "You still owe me your soul, boy. I look forward to flaying it layer by layer to see how you have come by this dark power. But for now...I have another old enemy to destroy."

Something was still amiss. Gwendoline and her friends looked around—except for Niles, who saved his baleful glare for their enemy alone—and noticed all the Starford citizens who lingered in the room. She wondered why in hell they were stupid enough to stay until she saw how the great doors had slammed closed to lock them all in.

No...

Before it happened, she almost guessed what would take place. Someone seized her from behind, tugging her back so she fell down the stairs. Her head smacked against the round end of the banister, making stars dance before her eyes but thankfully failing to knock her unconscious. Gwendoline struggled, kicking and shouting as she stabbed her rapier under her arm to attack whatever had grabbed her. A putrid scent filled her nostrils, gagging her. She would have been able to free herself were it not for another individual grabbing her sword arm and twisting it so her deadly blade flickered out of reality.

Whipping her head to the side to see her attackers, she already knew what she'd discover: the waiters and servants of Kinsley manor had transformed into Rotten.

The music must have kept them and everyone else docile, and the effect lasted even after I removed the hex...the cloaks hid the decay...Averill had promised to leave us alone, but he expected an attack and prepared to murder us again. All except for Everleigh.

Niles materialized by her side in seconds, slicing one of the creatures—who the person had been before was unrecognizable—clean in half near the heart. Gwendoline gathered her concentration and to free herself from the other Rotten: she heated her body with magic until it was too hot to hold, and materialized Glenna's now familiar rapier in time to stab her captor in the heart and twist the blade to make sure it stayed dead this time. Nearly black blood stained her lovely smoke colored dress, but she couldn't care about that now.

"Are you hurt?" Niles asked her, gripping her arm as he searched her face; gore spattered his, but in that moment he looked so beautiful, his concern mingling with his rage, that she couldn't speak. She shook her head, then looked around the room as she noticed the screaming for the first time.

There were more ordinary people present than Rotten, but enough of the wait staff had been turned by Averill's curse to trigger a wholesale slaughter of the gala attendees.

Those who could fought back. Bolts of electricity and spurts of fire crackled through the room from the magically talented and properly trained guests, but too many lay on the ground already, savaged by the Rotten who hovered over them like hungry beasts. Worse, even the people with magic hadn't the first clue about how to properly dispose of this menace: destroy the heart, destroy the creature.

But Colt...and Everleigh! Exchanging a glance with Niles, Gwendoline rushed to attend them as Niles took off through the press of people, cutting down and burning Rotten in his path as he tried to save whoever he could. The creatures were but a distraction, which was why Colt and Everleigh hadn't moved to fight them. Averill still refrained from entering the fray, but a cold wind swirled around him, showing his readiness to fight. Tears of helpless rage filled Everleigh's eyes as she gazed at her fallen people.

Colt ascended the stairs, hefting his sword in preparation for a powerful blow as golden flames sprang up around the blade and cross guard. Under such a furious gaze, with pure hate consuming those fearsome blue eyes, surely anyone would crumple.

Gwendoline felt panic incapacitate her again as memories from another time and Glenna's voice filled her with internal screaming. *Not again...*

Colt! Gwendoline mentally shouted his name, intentionally broadcasting her thoughts to him, Everleigh, and Niles. Bounding up the stairs, she grabbed Everleigh's arm to bolster the connection. *You are the ruler's champion, but you can't fight alone. The three ties of Fate must fight with you and through you. We didn't do that last time. I'm so sorry, I misunderstood...*

In a moment that felt like it held eternity in its depths, she felt the eyes of her friends pierce her, a heartbeat ticking by as their thoughts joined in an unspoken goodbye in case this went wrong, in case the past repeated itself.

"Do you see now what revolution will cost you, Everleigh?" Averill was gloating as if he'd already won. "I promised you I would seek neither your lover nor your friends, knowing that they would seek me out anyway to 'save' you. Tonight I will crush any hope you have of escaping me, as I would have with Jael had not this upstart meddled with the power of the abyss."

"My meddling served me well. You disappeared for quite a few years, didn't you?" Niles taunted; he had joined the group to make their circle whole once he'd unwound the hex on the doors holding them barred. As he spoke, the few guests that remained fled the scene, leaving only the four and their enemy behind.

"Do you have any knowledge of what horrors you entangled in your desperation to banish me?" Averill taunted. "Even so...the same trick will not work for you this time, let me assure you." Lifting his hands, he called forth the sword of thorns Gwendoline recognized with a shock of dismay. Within her, Glenna's soul recoiled from the instrument.

"No?" Colt challenged. "Maybe this will."

Working in tandem, he and Everleigh stretched forth their weapons, staff and sword linked in magic as they cast a bolt of golden light at the blood Lord. Expecting neither impact nor pain, Averill barely bothered to step aside. Yet as the magical blast struck him, passing through his left arm with the sound of meat sizzling, his bestial eyes widened in surprise.

Gwendoline took wicked satisfaction from his shock. *We can do this. It won't be easy, but we can kill him and end this.*

Then Averill laughed, his focus turning to Gwendoline as the flesh wound piercing his bicep began to heal.

"So," he jeered. "You puzzled out Fate's riddle, and now you think you have the keys to the castle. I must admit, you *do* have a chance to defeat me now." Opening her mouth to retort, Gwendoline had an irreverent remark ready.

But he disappeared, rematerializing behind her in half a second. His voice invaded her mind, bypassing her wards with little effort.

But did you know that I conquered Fate in combat? It would take more than your small army to defeat me, pawn, make no mistake.

Gwendoline whirled around right on time to deflect his sword from piercing her back, her rapier whistling through the air as the blue-white of her sword clashed with his thorn-wrapped weapon. As blade met bramble, the torches flickered into blackness again. Averill laughed again, an evil sound that let her know that the fire would not rekindle by any hand but his own.

Another invading thought broadcasted to each of their minds, though he goaded Niles specifically. *You spent time in the abyss while that book held your soul for me, Niles Graeme. Let us fight in your element, then. This darkness should feel familiar to you, should it not?*

Through their link, Gwendoline felt Niles shudder as *something* within the recesses of his mind and soul rose as if from a long slumber and shook itself like a sleek animal tousling its own fur and yawning lazily. If she dared reach out to this thing, or to Niles, she had no idea what she'd find in this creature.

This, perhaps, could be Averill's first lethal mistake.

All around her in the darkness Averill hand plunged them into, Gwendoline saw her friends' weapons light up the pitch black room next to the thin, wavering shine of her enchanted rapier. In the dark, she could pretend the golden longsword and yellow-flamed claws belonged to Leland instead of Colt. Everleigh's staff glowed right next to him, the red eyes hypnotizing. Niles's weapons absorbed light instead of bestowing it, but white sparks occasionally crackled in the darkness.

This is it. We finish this tonight.

Then the wolf attacked.

24

First the wolf fell upon Colt, vivid white fur and teeth flashing in the darkness as the fire of sword and claw revealed its shape in the blackness. Colt, anticipating the assault, heaved the beast off of him, swiping at it with his blade as its weight lifted off him. A stream of bright green insects, buzzing and burning with an awful sizzling sound, erupted from the head of Everleigh's serpentine staff. The bugs, shimmering with enchantment and hex mingled together, clung to the wolf's fur as they targeted its nose and eyes with their stingers. Snarling in rage, Averill leapt back, swiping at the pests with his paws.

Gwendoline took the advantage, diving forward and thrusting her sword towards the beast's unprotected side. Before her rapier could pierce its hide, the wolf disappeared, replaced by the white-haired man who parried her attack with his own sword. Deflecting, he swung at her head, aiming to decapitate. Perhaps he had forgotten that Gwendoline possessed Glenna's memories as well, and she had been a gifted warrior. She blocked the advance, and danced backwards to choose a better opening for attack. The darkness obscured her vision, but the glowing weaponry helped her see well enough. She lunged forward as an impossibly darker shadow raced past her, roaring in the hoarse, shrieking way of a creature she couldn't yet name.

Averill, taken aback, barely had time to transfigure back into the wolf as a huge panther-like creature with blanched claws dove at him with its mouth wide. Aghast, Gwendoline staggered back before she glimpsed the amber eyes of the panther.

How did he do that? Where did he get enough power to take that form? She marveled, staring at Niles in his new shape.

Wolf and hunting cat battled, crashing through the stair banisters and cracking the marble floor as their awesome weight landed on the ground. They rolled about with great battle cries escaping their throats, first the howl of the wolf, then the shriek of a wildcat eager for slaughter. Gwendoline searched for an opening, but couldn't stab into the whirlwind for fear of wounding Niles instead of her target.

Colt had no such inhibitions. Bolstering the fire on his sword with Everleigh's willing flow of power, he rushed into the fray, swinging his sword down in a powerful arc as Niles pinned down the wolf's muzzle with two fierce claws that drew blood onto the pale fur.

But the beast that was Averill roared a protest, the atmosphere around its body vibrating with silencing magic. Gasping for breath, Niles shifted back into human form as the flames of Colt's weapon briefly extinguished. By the time their personal lights reactivated, beast and man had disappeared.

"Admitting defeat already?" Colt taunted, furious that he'd missed a chance to end this for good. "I didn't peg you as a coward, *my Lord.*" His mockery elicited no verbal response, but Everleigh cringed in the light of her staff. Then, her eyes widening, she opened her mouth in a silent scream as her hair lifted to float eerily around her head like a halo.

"He's cursed her!" Gwendoline shouted as Everleigh gasped for breath. Her own breath whooshed in and out of her body with effort as the temperature in the room dropped to a subarctic level. "She can't breathe!"

"Unwind the hex!" Niles shouted, his voice burned raw by the yowling panther he'd become; his duo of glaives spun in his hands. "Colt and I will cover you."

Gwendoline dashed to Everleigh's side as Colt and Niles took positions on either side of them, staring out into the dark with light blinded eyes. Seizing in pain, the besieged ruler collapsed, her staff tumbling from her hands and clattering noisily against the floor as its owner trembled with the beginnings of a fit.

No you don't, Gwendoline thought, allowing herself to feel only her wrath instead of the terror that would incapacitate someone weaker than herself. As she laid hands on Everleigh, something from the shadows yanked Colt into the darkness, the yellow fire flickering into mere embers as its master disappeared. Casting a last desperate look at the two women, Niles followed the trail, seeking Averill as the white bramble sword flashed in the darkness, the flame engulfed longsword rising barely in time to clash against it.

Gwendoline cast a feeble protective field around Everleigh and herself, muttering every antihex she knew as she lifted the brunette into her arms. They were both shivering as the crackle of forming frost echoed throughout the mostly empty room, and despair pierced her through as Everleigh's clear skin tinged blue from cold and suffocation. Frustrated and reckless, Gwendoline's muttering changed to shouting as she slammed her hand onto Everleigh's chest, bruising her body if not breaking any ribs. *Please work...*

At the same time, Averill reappeared with a heinous grin on his human lips, engaging Colt and Niles in battle with twin swords made sharper and more deadly by their thorns. Snapshots of images cast in light and then in shadow pressed imprints into Gwendoline's mind: Averill's mockery and his rage, Colt's fury and determination, Niles's unexpected savagery as the edges of his form blurred and refocused as if he was struggling to stay himself.

Everleigh's eyes fluttered close, but she coughed, tainted blood spewing from her mouth onto Gwendoline's face as the curse wavered. Suddenly blinded, Gwendoline noticed curl of a snake around Everleigh's throat right before her vision was compromised by the poisonous blood.

Did Smaug break the curse? But no, the snake had been red scaled, not golden. *Fate...*

Gwendoline screamed, screamed louder than she had in either of her lifetimes as teeth sank into her throat. She had been blinded, but she saw herself in her mind's eye, frozen by the cold as Averill materialized right next to her and sank his fangs into her neck.

How is this happening? She wondered fearfully as her thoughts began to scatter. *How are we losing again? We're all here, and we're all fighting this time! What more is there?*

Something coalesced her wandering mind into a functioning unit before she passed into unconsciousness, but the mental hand gripping her in its vice could not be anyone who wished her well. She had not expected the teeth to feel so cold, like twin knives of ice coated with venom worse than the poison compromising her vision.

I have allowed this disrespect to carry on too long, and I will not engage with your game pieces a moment longer, Averill's voice slammed into her mind like a truck breaking through a flimsy handrail on the freeway. *I know you are here. Show yourself, or I'll drain every drop of life's blood from your last remaining vessel.*

He wasn't addressing her, Gwendoline realized. Her throat was raw from her screaming, her voice a whimper in the darkness, but only seconds had passed since he'd bitten her.

I'm not dead yet, her mind chanted, deriding her attacker as his teeth tore the skin on her neck to shreds. Summoning her rapier again to her fingertips, she brought the blade down in a sneaky arc that would've wounded him deeply if he failed to dodge the blow.

Relying more on her hearing thanks to her sightlessness, Gwendoline heard the wolf howl as his terrible weight was lifted off her. The panther, who'd tackled Averill away from her, screeched as brutal claws raked its face, drawing blood that glowed in the dark.

Cool hands covered Gwendoline's eyes and then her neck, making her shiver more from their touch than from the cold spreading a layer of ice throughout the room. A second later she could see, not just free from the poison, but as if her eyes were made to pierce the darkness with her sight. Breathless, Everleigh hovered in front of her, panic easing in her eyes as Gwendoline stared up at her. *I expected this from Colt...but maybe I underestimated my friend.*

The wolf had Niles pinned, but Colt lunched forward, his sword shifting and twisting with bright sparks of metal into the most impressive battle axe Gwendoline had ever seen. With a start, she realized that the hunting cat shifting in and out of reality as the beasts had circled the room, hunting each other, had been the distraction so Colt could make his play. Niles even grinned, his huge fangs gleaming with saliva as he reached up both paws to hold the canine in place for its execution. Even Everleigh had played her part: magical chains green as grass wove themselves around each massive white paw, binding the wolf to the ground more surely than real chains might have. Even if Averill had shifted, the chains would not release him.

Besieged on two fronts, Averill seemed to be in the ideal position for defeat. Gwendoline felt her heart soar: victory could not be closer. Heart, spirit, soul were all joined together to defeat the worst enemy their home had ever seen, past or present.

Yet would the red snake have chosen her throat to encircle next if that was the case? It tightened like a python as new fear joined the adrenaline racing through her as if blood still pumped from the wound on her neck.

Time is time to link the whole.

The wolf, howling with demonic laughter, shook off the chains and shifted back into the man. It disappeared as Colt's transformed weapon slammed down. Grunting with effort, Colt barely halted the descent of his axe in time to keep from killing the panther. Rolling out of the way, Niles matched Averill's human form and disappeared, leaping to his feet and searching for their enemy. He was losing it, even preoccupied Gwendoline noticed: the shadows, the marks of the void surrounding Niles that she hadn't been able to define, suddenly made sense.

The banishing spell linked him to the abyss, and casting himself into my spell book only bound him to it more. Who exactly is in control?

She couldn't think, she couldn't assemble any more coherent thoughts as the serpent no one else could see tightened around her throat. It wasn't suffocating her, but the multi-patterned scales stung her skin on every edge. *They're here, all of them, and they will die before you again if you don't* think.

True enough, Averill's voice rang throughout the room, tainted by the growl of the beast. "I *know* you're here, you conniving bitch! I feel your presence. Show yourself now, or I take their souls as well as their lives! Maybe if you surrender to me I'll spare your pets."

Suddenly exhausted, Gwendoline raised her sword, looking around to see the pale, haunted faces of Colt and Everleigh after Averill's shout faded into silence. She heard rather than saw Niles, the huge cat only slightly darker than everything else in the room prowling the perimeter in search of their quarry. *We're united and more powerful for it...but we're still fighting individually.*

It came to her then, the idea a tickle of fresh air coursing down from the heavens to bless this pit of hell.

Time is time to link the whole.

Niles had spoken of this long ago afternoon in the gazebo when Averill hadn't even been a shadow cast over their minds: *"You're sort of the bonus piece, a chosen nearly exact reincarnation of Glenna. I think she was sort of the binding, the glue that holds all of the pieces together. As you are in this time."*

Averill, choosing his human form as he descended from the ceiling in a fantastic burst of light with white wings of flame holding him in the air, bore down upon Colt with both of his swords poised to murder his rival. Gwendoline had little to no time to act upon her new discovery.

Hoping her friends would forgive the invasion if they miraculously survived this fight, she shoved her way past their mental wards and seized at the powers within them, holding them tight together with her mind as she lifted her sword with both hands towards the sky. She hadn't known she could do that, she hadn't known she could hold the essence of someone else's power in her mind and bend it to her will, but as the tie that bound all of them together she knew this was possible.

As Fate's vessel, as the instrument acting out the will of the unseen hands who had guided rulers and Lords into place since the dawn of humanity's time on this planet, only Gwendoline could bind the three ties together to smite Averill through the chosen champion. Biting her lip in concentration, she savored the iron in the blood that filled her mouth as she gripped the threads of her allies' magic and forcibly linked them together with the magic of her own soul.

Averill's descent from the height of the vast ceiling seemed almost paused, time had slowed so much in this moment. Gwendoline had seconds to witness the change of his expression as he refocused on her instead of Colt. Dismay changed his features from haughty to alarmed, but Gwendoline was in control now, and he could do nothing except watch her defeat him.

Colt, Everleigh, and Niles all shouted in her mind, agonized and in pain as she ripped power from them like a shark taking huge bites from a whale. Holding control over this vast well of magic wasn't easy: her arm wavered with the sudden heaviness of her sword, the weapon of her willpower and light weighed down by the others' magic. But this was something that, as a vessel, only she could do, and she'd be damned if they lost everything to the same enemy twice.

Sweet triumph filled her soul like a cup running over with wine.

If she didn't have to concentrate so hard on keeping a protective shell around her mind in this howling gale of power, she would have smiled as she sent a bolt of magic—searing with Colt's fire, crackling with Everleigh's electricity, and enshrouded about the edges with Niles's amber sparked shadows—screaming from the tip of her sword towards their enemy.

In the wake of such power, and under the strain of holding it together within her vessel primed body, Gwendoline's consciousness wavered and she collapsed without a sound as all the lights flickered out.

The last thing she heard was Colt's agonized, heart-rending scream.

25

Stars, more than Gwendoline had ever thought existed, wheeled above her head as she lay on a carpet of warm summer grass, her long hair waving out behind her like a fan in a breeze so gentle it felt like a lover's caress against her cool skin. Colors on this alternate plane bloomed more vivid than she'd ever seen: the empty field with waving grass and calming lavender blushed with greens and pinks and purples that took her breath away, and the white stars and dusky moon created perfect accents against the indigo sky.

Am I dreaming? Is this the afterlife? Gwendoline wondered, not particularly perturbed by either outcome.

Sitting up and stretching as leisurely as if she'd woken from her own bed at the start of an ideal weekend of relaxation and fun, she grinned as she shook her head from side to side, enjoying the antigravity making her hair flow like she was underwater.

The clashing noise of battle caught her attention like an irritating fly buzzing around her ears. She wanted to ignore it, but part of her knew this was a memory: her brain was trying to catch up, to make sense of the trauma that had happened to her. The blinding light of the magic she had bound together into a deadly weapon flashed through her brain, making her gasp as it all came back to her.

Scrambling to her bare feet, Gwendoline felt the silk of her unsullied dress tickle her skin as she spun around and around in this endless field, looking for something, anything to make sense of why she was here and not back with her companions. Was she dead? Were they all dead?

It didn't work, she despaired, her heart breaking as she scrubbed her hands over her face.

"It did work, child. Do not trouble yourself on that count." Gwendoline's spine stiffened as the voice, familiar and yet not, echoed down from the sky. A presence, ripe with power and yet gentle as the mother she'd never known, descended behind her from the sky. When she turned, she saw the mistress of the world standing before her.

Fate didn't look how Gwendoline had expected. Maybe that was due to the fact that her only encounters involved Fate interacting with her more as an ethereal presence rather than an individual. But even if she'd known better what to expect, this woman wouldn't have been her first idea.

"You." Gwendoline acknowledged her, at a loss for words as warring emotions overwhelmed her. The beauty of this strange dream world ceased to charm her.

"Me," Fate nodded, smiling fondly at her. Averill's regality stood no chance against the authority and nobility that this womanly figure possessed. Hair the color of brightest steel flowed like water down Fate's back, the eyebrows sharing the color as they arched over eyes as yellow as Colt's flames. White skin, blemished neither by mark nor by time, complimented the long, aquiline nose and commanding mouth.

Willowy, her figure flowed tall and unbowed, slender fingers and pointed ears reminding Gwendoline of a faerie queen. She wore a simple ivory shift dress, but had she been clad in nothing or in rags she still would have looked like an empress.

"I know there is nothing adequate I could say to ease the pain of your past or the new scars of this present day, but you have my thanks and my congratulations for defeating my wayward Lord," Fate began; she stepped forward to embrace Gwendoline's wooden form. "He is as human as they come now, and without magic thanks to you. All that remains is to decide who shall take his place in the fabric of this world."

"Who...who takes his place?" Gwendoline sputtered. Of her tangled feelings, rage was rising as the victor, flushing her dreamy skin with red as she panted for breath. If she'd had her sword, if she had been gathered enough to remember her magic, she would've engaged this arrogant creature without a second thought.

"I must confess, I rather thought Colt would have insisted on striking the final blow himself. Niles was born—in a figurative sense of course—to succeed my dear Averill, and he will play that role better than any of us have dreamed. Indeed, I fully expected Jael or at least Everleigh to choose him as champion. But still...Colt might surprise me again, and I am rarely amazed by mortal doings." Fate said, studying her broodingly. Holding Gwendoline at arm's length, she smiled faintly as she patted down the night dark hair floating like a crown around her head.

"My...my dear Averill?" Gwendoline, mired as she was in this swamp of fury that continued to boil up dangerously within her, spat the words as she staggered away from Fate. "Your 'dear Averill' destroyed us before, and almost did again. And...and here you show up after the fact, after we've already won, acting like you did nothing wrong?" *More like you did nothing at all, and now you want the credit*, Gwendoline didn't say that thought aloud, since she'd exhausted her oxygen and didn't seem to be able to capture more, but this dove haired angel appeared to have heard her anyway.

"The conditions of my bargain with my Lords involved me not interfering directly," Fate explained, her tone gentle even if her yellow gold eyes glinted with the hardness of steel. "When Averill convinced the Lords to let him challenge my rules for their conduct, the wager we set had very specific rules. Aside from sending coded messages to my vessel that held only a little truth, I could not interfere. If I had, you all would have died more surely than if I killed you myself, and Averill would have ruled the lands and taken me prisoner to his will. Sweet Gwendoline, I am sorry for that." Nothing about Fate but her voice conveyed apology: she looked down her long nose at Gwendoline, her pale lips set in a straight line.

"You couldn't interfere, but you could bring us back for another round that almost killed us?" If she could have, Gwendoline would have swung her fists at the youthful yet motherly figure of Fate, her violence a shout into the void. "You could mess with our love lives, tampering with the hearts of truly good people, all the while hovering in the background next to useless?"

"Truly good people excluding yourself?" The shrewd query threw Gwendoline; she took another breath with effort, glaring at the deity.

"Get out of my head. You've *no business* snooping around my mind."

"No? Hm," Fate mused as if Gwendoline hadn't spoken. "Are we not of the same kind? You, my vessel, have taken as much from me as I have from you, and I tell you that the person I have such a bond with cannot be wicked."

"No?" *Would a wicked person destroy the people they love in the ways I have? Loyal Everleigh, broken enough to sacrifice herself...Niles, wounded to the core by my selfishness...and Colt, dragged down into the dark right next to me. We've won, but I've still lost everything.*

Sweeping forward with the intricately woven locks of bright-steel hair flowing behind her, Fate studied her at close range, looking into Gwendoline's face curiously. "To be sure, there is a darkness in you, a touch of the inky black that cradles this little blue planet in its womb. But then, I could not use you without that touch. Niles especially carries this shadow within him, by himself and by the doing of that which he summoned to carry Averill into its fathomless heart."

The banishment spell, Gwendoline thought, her heart sinking. Maybe Niles had been the one to truly lose everything after all.

"Had you thought as much? No, this isn't something you could have predicted. See, here? He has a dark soul." Gwendoline watched as Fate casually materialized a magical orb into her hands. The dark lit, silver outlined orb rotated in her talon like fingers; she smiled, too, her hair falling forward over her face as her golden eyes gleamed. "Few have souls such as this, and fewer still fight for the good. Niles is as rare as he is beautiful, I'm sure you'd agree, and his soul more so."

That's his soul? Gwendoline shied away, at once inexplicably attracted and horrified that Fate could access his soul this way. Yet, taken aback as she was, the spinning orb that could only be a soul drew her towards itself, willing her to touch it. Whether this was some power of Fate's, some trick of a soul, or Niles's actual being calling out for her, she couldn't tell.

"Then why, Lady," Gwendoline finally dared speak, "Would you pair me with Colt's soul and not with Niles?" Fate looked up, studying her like she'd forgotten she wasn't alone as she turned Niles's soul over and over in her hands like a special toy.

"Where Niles is dark, dark from his past and dark from the powers that have brushed against him over his centuries in your casting book, Leland was and Colt is the sun, in a way. The sun does not compete against the beauty of the moon, but it has its merits... And a light sent into the dark shines all the brighter, perhaps."

"You speak in riddles." Normally in her dreams, she could only sense her emotions clumsily, like she had to wade through a tub of molasses to access them. Maybe this wasn't a regular dream, then, since Gwendoline felt her very thin patience ebbing away with the tide of her anger.

"Do I? Perhaps you do not listen. Perhaps, human as you remain, I must show instead of tell you." Without ceremony, Fate zipped to her side with a predator's speed. Reaching into Gwendoline's chest, somewhat below her heart, she gripped SOMETHING that made all the stars around them cease their spinning.

With a strange, wet, sucking sound that echoed in her skull, Fate pulled out Gwendoline's soul from her body.

It hovered, tethered to its host by a transparent, ultra violet cord made up of what looked like hundreds of tiny, ornately intertwined steel braids. The mere fact of her soul being outside of her body, held by such a capricious being as Fate had turned out to be, made her shiver to the depths of the orb held in someone else's hands.

"Do you see, sweet Gwendoline? Your soul is dark as his, dark with fewer points of light," Fate explained, rotating the white haloed sphere atop her fingertips; unlike the only other soul she'd ever seen, this one swelled slightly larger on one side, its aura iron gray instead of pure black. "You also bear the mark which makes you a vessel. I cannot engineer that brand: I merely wait for it to appear. You are the first to bear a dark soul and have my blight, as it were, for normally my soul is attracted to light...to those like Leland, or even like Everleigh."

"You have a soul?" Gwendoline marveled, distracted from ardently wishing Fate would return her soul to her body. Amused, eyes that were yellow in both pupil and iris laughed at her.

"Yes, we all do. A higher power than I designed such things as souls. I merely tinker with them. But how marvelous the mystery of what would come to pass if a light soul matched with a dark one. It has not yet happened, at least among us beings with power. Averill bears a darkness I cannot touch, dark as pitch like his spirit. I sought that, once, near the beginning of my recollection...but see what misfortune that has accomplished."

Gwendoline began to untangle the direction of her rambling explanations. "If I am dark and Colt is light...did you force us together only to serve your curiosity?"

"Curiosity? No!" Fate said, taken aback as she cradled the tethered soul in her grasp like it was her newborn child. "I can be kind, Gwendoline, especially so to those chosen by Above to be my vessels. Leland would have fulfilled you, and you him. It is a good match, and would have remained so...in its time. Now I am not so sure." She remained lost in her inscrutable thoughts, the soul in her hands spinning faster and faster until Gwendoline thought she'd scream from the tension.

Finally, Fate slowed and ceased the rotation and ever so gently pushed the soul back into Gwendoline's body. "Here, child. Your soul is again yours...As are your choices. I do so wonder who you will choose."

With a flick of her wrist and her thoughts, Fate materialized before Gwendoline's eyes the scene she'd been most anxious to see. As if through the glass of a two way mirror, she saw the darkness of Kinsley manor's main hall lit up by Fate's light and the stars behind them. She was an outsider looking in, but she felt more present than ever as she noticed her body standing in the unblocked doorway with an empty expression. In the destruction that had occurred, scorching walls and floors and destroying tapestries, she noted with awe how Averill's descent upon wings of flame had utterly destroyed the ceiling, leaving the remains of the walls reaching up towards the sky like cracked, broken fingers of stone.

None of her friends had noticed she was absent from her body: they surrounded Averill's fallen and pinned form, glaring down into his feral eyes as he howled with insane laughter. Everleigh's hollow eyes and Niles's scarred and bleeding face drew her attention first, but her eyes paused at the sight of Colt's ravaged face. So that was why he had screamed before Gwendoline had blacked out: Averill's conjured fire had sought him out in one last vindictive burst of power, scarring the unblemished skin on one half of his face and ruining the rugged beauty she'd come to love.

*Oh, Colt...*Gwendoline, trapped in the dream-like sequence of Fate's design, fell to her knees as sobs racked her body. Struggling to come to terms with Colt's new injuries, with the burns and disfigurement even he wouldn't be able to heal, she dug her fingers into the soft earth, anchoring herself as she tried to remember to breathe.

In the mirror, snow fell in swirling patterns as placid as any other winter's evening. She might have been looking at a painting, and not a window into the real world.

Colt held his sword loosely at his side, but he needn't be the one to take up the mantle of Lord. Everleigh was ruler by right, so she couldn't take anyone's place, and as a vessel Gwendoline herself could not be chosen. It had to be one of the men.

"It's your choice," Fate reminded her gently, kneeling beside her and rubbing her back. "But make it soon."

"Me?" Gwendoline protested, recoiling from that gentle touch as she clambered back to her feet. "Why the hell should I be the one to choose? Isn't it your job to decide the destinies of other people?"

"Don't be petty," Fate chided, a tinkling chuckle bestowing warmth upon her imperious face. "It doesn't suit you."

The destiny of rulers and Lords had to be decided here, and here the mystical hand guiding the powers of the world stood cracking jokes and tossing the responsibility to Gwendoline like it was the keys to an expensive new car ready for a joy ride.

Worse, the choice Gwendoline considered disgusted her with its self occupation.

"Who is my fit match? You have always chosen for me in the past. Leland was Glenna's soulmate, as I suppose Colt is mine," Gwendoline felt her spirit twitter, but her soul, newly revealed as dark as pitch, rebelled within her. Fate's lips pulled back to reveal teeth sharp as Averill's.

"So? Averill is mine, but he and I shall never join again. It is the choice that matters, Gwendoline, a choice made with your full being and not your heart or spirit alone. I know what Glenna chose."

"Yes, Glenna chose Leland. But you gave him to Jael." There, she'd addressed the elephant in the room. Many actions of Fate, explained away by forfeiting her rights in the wager, had wounded her, but none more than Glenna's pain at seeing Leland choose Jael. "Why?"

"Ah, I wondered when you'd ask me that," Fate sighed; lines appeared in her face, aging the youthful beauty twenty odd years, but they disappeared as quickly as they came. "In the new days of the world, Jael's ancestor saved the bloodline of my vessels at great peril to herself and her love. Her bonded died in the conflict. Overflowing with gratitude and generosity, since I was much occupied at the time with exploring my new home planet, I swore to her that her descendants would never suffer what she had. And they didn't: I always made sure to grant them the love they desired. Yet the first time I bound one of my vessel's soul to a mate, that tie conflicted with the vow I'd sworn."

"Shouldn't you have unbound us, then? Or caused Jael to love another?" The accusation in Gwendoline's words revealed her anger, but unwelcome tears threatened to overwhelm her at any moment. She couldn't speak, she couldn't breathe: inundated with grief, she clung with both hands to the edges of the mirror into the real world, staring down the frozen scene and willing herself into composure.

"I wished I could, my dear. You don't know this, but ordinarily I avoid inflicting needless distress upon my vessels. I hated to cause you pain, but it is...not in my nature to break vows, nor could I unweave the binding on your souls. I made the difficult decision of letting events play out by themselves, and I hope Everleigh's ancestor understands my dilemma once you make your choice." Fate's hands came down on her shoulders, tenderly turning her body to face the silver haired fallen star. "I will say...but should I?"

"Yes?" Gwendoline felt breathlessness choke her voice as she locked eyes with her mistress. Indulgent, Fate brushed away the tears crowding her lashes.

"Like goes to like. It is no coincidence that Niles loves you, nor a pointless tragedy. I may have matched you with Leland based on your souls...but I am not in charge of such things entirely. Above matched your whole being to Niles, I think, and I merely made it possible for you to choose between two ideal persons."

Gwendoline opened her mouth to voice a forbidden request—*choose for me then, choose so I will hurt them the least*—but at the last second she closed her jaw with a snap. *Too easy.*

Instead, another unbidden query slipped past her defenses to reveal her desperation. "Do you know what Niles has chosen? Because—"

"Because you don't think he'll have you any longer? Because for a time you chose Leland over him, and then Colt? Because your rejection of him was so complete for so long that he may want to give up whether you choose him as Lord or not?" Fate stung Gwendoline with her icy tone, freezing the tears in her eyes.

Yes. Because I wrecked him again and again and I think our chance is lost forever, the thoughts burned her like hot oil.

"To tell you the answer to his choice would be...how would you put it...*cheating,*" Fate turned her vessel again, both of them facing the mirror to observe the scene within. "Besides...you who so value choice would not want me to invalidate his by giving you answers to questions he should address with you and you alone."

"Right," Gwendoline replied softly; she felt her shoulders would have slumped if they could. The idea of Niles giving up on her at last, just when she realized what actually mattered...how *he* might even matter the very most to her. Well, it made her give up her will to fight at the very least.

"You still have something precious in your possession, love," Fate said, smiling down at her from the side of her eyes. "*You* have choices as well. Your heart is your own, even if the ties that bind it tug it every which way, and you can decide what it needs the most. You could choose to spend your life with Colt in a mortal world where everything is wondrous and new. Or you may choose immortality with Niles. As my champion, he has done me a service, and I will not curse an eternal one with a mortal mate, leaving him to walk alone as the others must, where duty will be at your sides for eons to come. Neither choice will prove easy...but believe me my child when I say I have faith you will make the best one."

Had Fate given away her plan without intending to? From what she'd said, had she calculated that Gwendoline would choose Niles to replace Averill as Lord of the land?

But no...Gwendoline had already made that decision. She'd gazed into the mirror, she'd seen the hearts of both men, and within her dwelled the surety that Niles would be the best successor for power in the land. With this conviction she found the answer to her other choice: she did not wish this power upon anyone, least of all those she loved, and she knew now that Niles was the last person she wanted to sacrifice to the needs of this world.

Oh Niles...

Fate nodded, her sharp chin dipping briefly as she confirmed the guess. Ignoring her, Gwendoline stared at Niles's bleeding face in the mirror, wishing she could reach out and touch him.

"If you live a sixth of the time I have lived, you may be able to discern the patterns life settles into. Cycles, wheels, turnings of the moon...parallels. In journeying through these, we often wind up right back where we began. As Glenna, you pined for untouchable Leland, but as Gwendoline, you were unaware of Colt's love for you for years. Averill halted the betrothal ceremony in the past, and this night you and your friends have interrupted what would have been his betrothal to Everleigh.

"If it helps you, one constant in either timeline has been Niles.

Your soul and Colt's might be freewheeling stars in the cosmos, tied together only by my design in the early times of the world, but could not Niles be the magnetic center around which you orbit?" Her words, flowing as they did like poetry, were fit to dazzle Gwendoline further into confusion.

But she understood...how well she understood.

Fate elaborated. "Destiny can be...hm...poetic. I may have tied two souls together long ago, but how interesting that to draw another man's soul forth from a book, the key would be a kiss? I am familiar with earthly fairy stories, and how many humans desire to be part of one. Do not many such tales start or end this way, with a kiss? Such a small action can bear so much weight..."

"You must like the sound of your own voice," Gwendoline quipped, some of her old humor returning to her in a feeble effort for her brain to normalize this situation.

"I am more often one of the stars in the galaxy than I am in this form, and as my vessel, you are the only human able to perceive this shape," Fate returned. "So yes, it's nice to chat with someone every few millennia or so." Startled enough to laugh, Gwendoline bubbled with mirth.

Fate waited for her to collect herself. "I see you've decided. Niles will be Lord of the land, and you will pursue him. As for Colt and Everleigh...well, we'll have to see." Something about her tone made Gwendoline wonder. She understood now, as she hadn't before, that this choice couldn't be simply one man or the other: she'd chosen Niles, but part of her would always be bound to Colt. Maybe that scar would never heal. With a shock that made her eyes widen in surprise, Gwendoline realized that regardless of her quest for Niles, the best thing she could do would be leave Starford behind her forever.

Maybe then Everleigh and Colt can find the happiness they deserve, she thought, ignoring the twinge in her spirit that cried out at the notion of Colt loving anyone else but her.

"Goodbye for now, sweet Gwendoline," Fate whispered to her, placing something heavy in her hands. "Once again, I am sorry for the pain I've caused you, child."

Before Gwendoline could look down to study it, gentle hands nudged her *through* the mirror—no, it wasn't a two way mirror, it was an open window into the real world—and she fell through it, collapsing into herself endlessly as the gorgeous dream world faded into mere memory.

Averill's crazed laughter broke upon her eardrums with all the subtlety of a maniac playing the drums at a rock concert as Gwendoline awoke within her own body. Unlike her dream self this physical body *hurt*: she was sore from fighting and covered with small bruises and wounds she'd have to inspect when she had time. Shuddering, she nearly dropped the object in her hands, but her quick reflexes kept it from tumbling to the ground.

"Well, my love, has it not played out like I assured you it would?" Gwendoline's voice flowed from her like wonderful music, halting the laughter with its beauty as every head in the room turned in her direction. But no, it wasn't her voice. Fate had dismissed her from their personal audience in that alternate plane, but her presence filled Gwendoline to the brim and took over her voice. A *vessel's* voice.

"It has indeed, *dearest*," Averill answered after a pause, coughing as Colt's foot pressed down on his now human chest; no feral magic burned in those haunting eyes, but danger shone in his bared grin. "Tell me, what took you so long?"

"Gwendoline?" Everleigh, the first of the trio to question the new voice, approached her cautiously, exhaustion slowing her steps though wariness held her serpent staff at the ready.

"No, not yet," Fate assured her through Gwendoline. She would've comforted her further, but Niles had flashed through the space between them, his hand tight around her neck in less than a second.

"Leave her alone," he threatened, heat rising from his skin as he glared dangerously. "I know what you are, and I will burn you before I let you consume her." In the glow of eyes Gwendoline saw herself. Well, mostly herself: her own eyes had transformed into Fate's curious yellow, brighter than the dawn.

"Do not let the shadows running in your veins erase your own will," Fate warned through her, though she didn't deign to struggle in Niles's painfully strong grip. "I will return Gwendoline to you once my business is complete."

Are these the actions of a man who does not love you? Fate's real voice, the one from the dream world, teased in the depths of Gwendoline's mind. *If that is the case, I wonder what he would try to do to me if he* did *love you.*

Niles considered his options for a moment before reluctantly releasing her. Gwendoline would have rubbed her bruised throat gratefully, but Fate had other concerns. Besides, the object Fate wouldn't look down to let her see still rested in her hands.

"Do you think it was foolish pity that stayed my hand, even while you cheated at the wager? After what you did to my beloved Ys, my

Atlantis, did you think I would let you live a second longer than you had to?" Unexpectedly, pain that wasn't hers burned in Gwendoline's heart. *Averill was her bonded...*

"Not pity, never that from you. I require a mate, my love, as you know. Deprived of you...I would take one of only the highest humans in this world. Jael, for all her mortal flaws, would have served me well...and Everleigh even better." A harmless snake in the grass, a toothless wolf, Averill smiled menacingly at Everleigh as if he still had the full scope of his power. "The real deciding factor was that you have a soft spot for her bloodline and her ancestors. If subjugating her to my will would come even a little bit close to retribution for your abandonment of one who had fallen beside you that eternity ago, then it would've been worth it."

"A futile pursuit, as I told you and your brethren when you sought to rebel against my wishes," Fate sniffed, disdain hiding the ache in her breast. "I never encouraged you to make your mistakes, Averill, and unfortunately you know the bounds of my power as well as I do. You took advantage of the terms you set in the wager, and for a time you were victorious."

"Hardly. Your *boy* cast me into the void for far too many years while I reassembled my power and myself," Averill growled. But he knew, Gwendoline saw from the backburner Fate had set her on, that his end was near, and his fury failed to conceal his fear.

"Can we be done with the talking?" Colt interrupted, leaning harder on Averill's chest so the breath whooshed out of him. "I never want to set eyes on this snake again."

"In due time," Fate snapped at him, irritated with his impertinence. "Even one such as he has the right to last words."

"Words?" Averill snarled. "I have nothing else to say to you." For the briefest of seconds, eons of time passed through Gwendoline's mind, the images swirling quickly around the part of her that Fate commanded. *Averill and Fate, locked together in a celestial dance, in their human forms, then as stars, circling so fast and yet so cosmically slow that it drove her mad...*

"Pity," Fate spoke at last, approaching Averill's prone form to kneel by him. "I almost wish you had something to say to me, but I see that was too much to hope for."

"So come out of that useless shell and talk to me," Averill taunted, his teeth gleaming as he grinned. "Show me the true face I've missed."

"Even for you, that was a poor effort," Fate laughed as if partaking in a private joke. "Lords need no vessels to walk among humans, but I would destroy this continent if I shed this body. But that was your intention, was it not?" Averill turned his head to avoid her mockery, but she laid her hands on his face and guided him to face her. With one hand still on his cheek, she wordlessly lifted the object she'd brought from the dream world from Gwendoline's lap and set it over Averill's eyes.

It was a crown of sorts, though its strange position functioned in part as a blindfold as well. Even for a crown, it looked rather scrappy to her eyes. The silver was tarnished, and the ornate scrolling around the edges of the pointed diadem was chipped from age and neglect. There was a hole in the center where a gemstone once might have rested, but it was empty now.

Yet even as they all watched in silence, the depression in the silver for the gemstone began to fill, swirling with magic as it rested on Averill's head. As the process went on, his skin paled further and his face twitched with anguish. But a second later a fathomless garnet filled the empty spot, and Fate removed the crown from her former

Lord.

"Now," she began, guiding Gwendoline to stand as she gripped the warm crown in her hands. "I know who I have decided to replace Averill once one of you strikes the killing blow. But are you, Colt and Niles, in agreement?" When they all stared at her in dumb confusion, she sighed with exasperation and elaborated.

"This is the Lord's crown. It can only be accessed by me or by the Lord it was made for when a new Lord is crowned or when all of the Lords commune together. We are about to crown a new Lord, and I will place this relic on the brow of he who succeeds Averill."

If Gwendoline doubted who she loved the most before, she couldn't any longer. Niles drew her eyes as he glanced at Colt. Clearly he felt like he should speak, but he didn't want to take the choice from the person who had the right as Everleigh's chosen champion.

"Aren't you literally Fate? Shouldn't you decide?" Colt voiced the question Gwendoline had earlier asked on her own. He was panting, out of breath as he struggled against the pain of his seared face. His eyes had the bright look of someone who'd been drugged, and the burns had been partially healed thanks to his own curative magic. But the damage...with a drooping eye, part of his nose melted away, and much of his scalp burned...

That was the most he could do? Gwendoline mourned in her mental prison, part of her longing to reach out to touch the partially healed scars in a gesture of sympathy.

"I am a celestial being, knight, but I am not omniscient," Fate intoned, ignoring her wishes. "You may call me Fate, but I merely arrange souls and events in ways I know will work the best. I'm not always right, but..." she trailed off as Colt stepped forward, his transfigured sword hefted over his shoulder.

"I am the ruler's champion, so it's my responsibility," he said, though he had the look of someone walking to the gallows lingering in his eyes. "I'll do it."

Gwendoline found herself smiling at him as Fate's emotion showed on her face. Her feet carried her close to him, and she lifted the hand not holding the crown to the whole, unmarred portion of his cheek.

"See, you are not as dishonorable as you feel," she whispered, caressing him; in the background, she saw Everleigh shifted her weight to her other foot and cleared her throat. Fate, maybe remembering that she wore Gwendoline's face, changed tactics. "But this is not a burden you would learn to bear well, is it?"

"No," Colt's voice was barely audible. "No, it isn't, but I'll carry it if I must."

"I know you would," Fate assured him. "I know your heart. It isn't much, and I won't be able to undo what has been cast upon you, but I can fix some of the damage."

Colt's skin flowed like water, sickening and disturbing as underneath the surface his nose, eye, and twisted lips repaired themselves. The skin would remain charred on one half of his face, but his hair rapidly grew to conceal the scars that had crept up to his scalp, and after a minute or two he looked much improved.

Gwendoline heard Everleigh gasp at the transformation, and Colt himself sighed as much of his pain went away. He still looked injured, and always would...but he was whole underneath the damaged skin.

Fate at last approached Niles. Gwendoline's heart thudded with awkward starts and stops under her ribs as she looked up at him through Fate's misty influence.

"I meant for you to be champion, Niles Graeme. I didn't link your soul to anyone else's for that reason," Fate told him, lowering her tone so he would be the only one to hear her words. "Sometimes even I make mistakes, and for that I am truly sorry."

Niles held perfectly still as she held the crown before him, asking permission to set it over his eyes. When he didn't move or protest, she lifted it to his face and gently set it over his eyes. If Gwendoline had expected to see any change, she was surprised.

But then she remembered the body of their enemy lying on the ground, so unmoving she thought he was unconscious. He lived, but something about wearing the empty crown had taken something from him, so perhaps very little of his spirit actually remained in this world.

Accepting this change of plans, Colt passed Niles his weapon without comment. Though Gwendoline had expected Niles to be blinded by the crown, he glanced down at the axe and in a shimmer of sparks transformed it back into the sword Leland had carried. After so much struggle she had anticipated more fanfare for the final defeat of their enemy, but now that it was here this moment reminded her more of an execution.

Now you understand, Fate told her as sadness for the tragedy of this moment distracted her from Niles standing over Averill and lifting the sword with both hands. *This should never have been, least of all with Averill. Replacing a fallen Lord is one of the saddest moments on this planet, sweet girl.*

But it had to be done, Gwendoline, trying to comfort her, worried she'd misspoke or come across too harsh. Either way, Fate kept her own counsel as Niles glanced up at her through the blind eyes of the tarnished crown and plunged the sword with a clean stroke of finality into Averill's heart.

This time, the transfer of power wasn't just obvious, but

explosive. Niles screamed, in pain or something else, as eye stabbing white light filled the room. His crown was the only thing Gwendoline could see in the light as the silver changed to a metal blacker than anything she'd ever seen, and the red gemstone transformed into the same color as the brilliance filling Kinsley manor.

Interesting, Fate remarked, thinking of the darkness of Niles's crown. *How fitting that the symbol of his power reflect the hold the abyss has over him.*

But after a moment it was over, and the light sank into Niles skin as he froze statue still over Averill's body. Or rather, the place where Averill's body had been. Now the tip of Colt's sword rested against the cracked marble, a smear of dark blood marking the only indication that Averill had even existed. Niles looked down at the empty floor through his transformed crown, his lips a thin slash though his face showed no other viable expression.

"I have cast his body among the stars from which we came," Fate told him through Gwendoline as moved to stand beside him; she laid a hand on his shoulder. "You are a Lord now, Niles, and I trust you to hold the position well and with honor. You must seek your new brothers to make your position known to them, but for now this...this is enough, and I am grateful."

He didn't speak, but he did turn to look at her through his crown. Before Gwendoline's eyes, the royal ornament vanished, becoming wisps of dark smoke that filtered away through the cold air to reveal the changed eyes beneath. Certainly everything had changed, though only those who knew him would see how: the eyes that gleamed amber or onyx at any given moment had settled for now onto a fire color that echoed Averill's bestial glow, the flames within set to consume all in their path. He'd always been regal, even when joking around, but now he'd gained the bearing and nobility of a Lord.

Within Fate, Gwendoline had a strange urge to bow before him.

Then with little fanfare, Fate *was* gone, disappearing from her mind with only a sigh of farewell that let Gwendoline realize she didn't intend to leave her for good.

Whatever had changed in Niles, he held his silence as he studied Gwendoline a moment longer with his new, power filled eyes. She had no doubt that, as Averill could have before they defeated him, Niles could snuff out their lives as easily as a gale blowing out a single candle. Unwillingly, fear weakened her knees, but she stood her ground under his scrutiny and eventually he looked away without giving any indication of his thoughts. As an afterthought, she noticed that the slashes on his face had healed without a scar.

In silence, he walked over to Colt—his new strength carrying him there faster than he'd intended—and returned the sword without flourish. Nodding to him to show respect, Colt took his sword and cleansed it with a hushed spell before returning it to its scabbard across his back.

They faced each other, communicating something in the male language that Gwendoline couldn't understand. Then Colt's bluest eyes flashed in her direction, partially in apology, partially in sadness before he turned his back on her and faced Everleigh. If Gwendoline hadn't already chosen another man, this wordless goodbye would have hurt her worse than Leland ever could have.

Everleigh stood aloof, her expression a mask as she clenched the hand not holding her Smaug staff into a fist at her side. But her eyes gave her away, wider than normal and green beyond belief as she stared hungrily at Colt.

"I can't begin to undo what I've done, Everleigh, and I wouldn't want to, not entirely," he began, his voice shaking as he humbled himself before the woman he loved. "I think this was inevitable, that we all had to go through this. While that doesn't excuse my behavior, not even a little, I have never been more certain that you're the person I want to be with. I knew...I knew when I saw him next to you, treating you like property, that I had almost ruined everything when I hurt you. When I cheated on you.

"The truth is, I love you, and knowing now what it is to lose you, I never want to experience that again. I think...I think after everything, now that we've won, I think we could be happy. I am broken, I'm no longer completely...whole. But I am here for you, 'Leigh, and I don't intend to leave ever again." Hesitant, Colt gathered Everleigh's stiff but svelte form into his arms and pressed a kiss against her lips that would make any onlooker ache to see the tenderness.

Automatically, as if by habit, Everleigh kissed him back, her staff crashing to the ground as she slipped her hands behind his head to pull him even closer.

When their fairytale moment ended and they separated except for their joined hands, Gwendoline could see in his eyes the expectation that Everleigh would forgive him. His plea for redemption had been heartfelt, and Gwendoline's heart broke for the role she'd had to play in his betrayal. Worse was the guilt she felt, standing watch with Niles at her shoulder.

Everleigh's eyes, half-moons of sad, contemplative quietude studied Colt, her hands limp in his grasp. Even in this moment of tragedy, they set a pretty picture: a princess radiant in her ragged edged gown, and her knight, damaged but devoted in a tux half consumed by spellfire. Gwendoline wished nothing but their happiness.

"No," Everleigh spoke at last, shattering both the tense silence and the painted pose their stillness had created. "I can't. I'm sorry, even though I don't have to be."

"What?" Colt, genuinely surprised, let go of her hands; Gwendoline could no longer call her fragile, for she had seen the strength her petite friend possessed.

"You..."Everleigh paused, composing herself as her throat bobbed in an effort to squelch any tears. "You hurt me, Colt. You were the last person I thought would hurt me, especially this way. But you did this."

"I—"

"Yes, I know about the binding ties. Trust me, I've heard enough about them to linger in my mind forever." Gwendoline exchanged glances with Niles, who appeared equally nonplussed by this outcome. Everleigh didn't sound bitter, and had conveyed a resignation to heartbreak up until this moment.

"In the past, my ancestor Jael found happiness with another. She ruled her realm, and sat beside an honorable man. So I've been told," Everleigh smiled sadly, turning his face back to hers with a gentle touch. "I am trying not to find fault with you, Colt. I am a fresh person, without the weight of memories like yours. But, if I could not even compete with Gwendoline, how could I compete with the shadow of Leland's adoration for *Jael*?"

"Jael," Colt echoed the name, leaning into Everleigh's hand like he never wanted her to withdraw. But withdraw she did, straightening her spine to steel herself.

"I don't want to be with you like we were, not anymore. It's not fair to either one of us, and I...I think I have to learn to need only myself. Not only so no one can hurt me like that again, but because you and I were together so closely for so long that I think I forgot how to be just me. And as someone who needs to pull Starford together, I know I need to find out how to do that. Without you." Everleigh finished her speech with great aplomb, though her voice stumbled over the words. If Gwendoline didn't know better, she would've thought this was a cold way to dismiss someone from your life, especially for Everleigh. But her words made sense, loathe as she was to admit it, for Colt's sake.

Colt...if this had been Glenna with Leland, she would've been comforting him any way she knew how by now.

"Do you understand, Colt? I don't want to hurt you, I really don't, but—"

"I understand, Everleigh," he spoke at long last, her name heavy like it was the saddest word in the universe. "I...I wish things were different, but I want you to be happy, even if it isn't with me."

"My," Everleigh remarked, two tears breaking free from her eyes as she reached up to brush her fingertips along the line of his jaw. "Look at that, you've grown already."

"Is it enough?" Colt quipped. Gwendoline felt like an intruder in this scenario, she and Niles both, though they stood three feet apart looking on without speaking. But she couldn't just leave. Somehow, no one had planned what to do after they defeated Averill.

"No," Everleigh shook her head, lowering her hands back to her sides even though her whole expression begged with quiet desperation for him to hold her. "No. I need to be me, without you. I need to go tell the council that I'm their new ruler, since I earned the right through blood and tears, and I damn well better be sure I'm a whole enough person to lead."

"Go do it then," Colt encouraged her firmly, but not unkindly. "I believe you can." His eyes remained dry, but Gwendoline saw the pain in his face and it made her whole internal being squirm. If Everleigh noticed this, she didn't care enough to comfort him. But Gwendoline understood.

So, on her own, the new ruler of Starford left Colt behind, marching out into her new future. All of them watched her go, watched the light reflect off the tattered yet glittering golden fabric of her dress, and not a one of them knew what else could be said.

Together in this moment, the three remaining looked up, up through the empty ceiling through which the stars could be glimpsed in their great multitude.

26

Dawn had never bloomed so beautifully in the sky, at least not to Gwendoline's perspective. Her car hummed peacefully under her direction, and Dancer sat safe in the passenger seat with her head hanging out of the window as air almost as welcoming as a springtime zephyr sifted through the long fur on the dog's soft ears. With Averill's demise, the harsh deadening of an arctic winter had relinquished its grip on Starford: autumn remained, but the weather had warmed enough for casual jeans and cozy sweaters instead of layers upon layers of clothes.

The weather couldn't dispel her nerves completely, or even a little, but peace had wriggled its way into her healing heart.

Just in time for it to break again, Gwendoline mused pessimistically.

The darkest hours of the night had remained after the conflict had ended, and with it Colt's and Everleigh's relationship. After rekindling the torches, the three had searched throughout the house for any stragglers or wounded. No one that remained had lived through the battle—those the Rotten had savaged had died before the fight began—but when they'd made their way outside, they found a crowd of people lingering around the manor, awaiting news of the outcome. They'd heard the terrible noise, seen the flashing lights...obviously, no one had come to their aid, but Gwendoline hadn't been able to find fault with them for that.

An awkward moment had passed when Colt had seen Everleigh waylaid by a news crew in an especially picturesque spot right outside the intimidating gates. If the modern princess had felt any trepidation at either the attention lavished on her or the invasive personal questions, it didn't show on her face. Someone had mended her gown, cleaned the blood from her face and dress, and arranged for her to look presentable for the late night news. Her shrewd eyes had passed over them as she addressed the interviewer, announcing a repeat of what she had said to her friends about leading Starford, but she was loyal enough not to draw attention to them as they slipped out of sight and left Kinsley manor behind.

And then Colt, his jaw tight and his shoulders military straight to show no weakness or strain, said he was going to the hospital to see if any wounded had shown up and if his healing magic could help. Gwendoline had felt obligated to do the same, though fatigue pricked annoyingly behind her eyes and through her sore muscles. Niles had offered to accompany the two of them, though as a fresh immortal he couldn't know for sure how much power he now possessed. Suffice to say he bore no signs of injury or fatigue: of the four of them, he'd emerged from that awful place more whole than when he'd entered.

Once they reached the hospital after a long uncomfortable drive—if someone knew the secrets of negotiating a drive with one ex lover who'd just been jilted and a man who had essentially been gifted godly powers, Gwendoline would've liked to speak to them—the three of them had parted ways to work. Colt, marching off with the sternest of expressions, tended to any injury he could lay hands on, heedless of what the magic cost him. People stared, appalled at the burns on his face and taken aback by the poorly repaired tux, but once he began his healing incantations they forgot their dismay.

Gwendoline took it upon herself to help with administrative duties: the emergency room nurses and doctors knew their stuff when it came to day to day trauma, so she expected some posturing and resistance, but the truth was they were more than happy for any magical assistance in this sudden flood of cursed injuries.

The worst part had to be contacting the families of the injured or deceased. Some people she knew, some she didn't, but since Gwendoline's guilt didn't allow her to skip this task, she mentally shoved aside her own problems and devoted herself to each phone call. *If I had figured out the clues as Glenna, would these people be suffering now?*

Niles had found enough to occupy him for most of the night as well, in a way no one had expected. Many Starford civilians kept wandering in the hospital doors, complaining of a strange, lethargic sickness that had lingered for days with no change. These people had looked sick enough to keel over dead at any moment, and their skin stank with a familiar scent. Gwendoline had been appalled at this new realization of how many people Averill had corrupted and cursed, intending to build an army of Rotten from the lesser magical folk. The damage he would have inflicted upon Starford and the world would have been so much greater had she and her friends not defeated him.

As the new Lord of the land, Niles could lift the deadly hex with ease as each person came to him. But as the new Lord, he hadn't learned to contain his aura of power: the shadows that seemed to always accompany him now had a corporeal quality, and though his eyes hadn't changed from their amber color, they burned with that ferocious light Averill's had possessed. Though she had expected something of this nature, it grieved Gwendoline to see how obviously inhuman the man she loved had become. Worse, that the very people he had sacrificed so much for avoided him if they could, skirting around his imposing figure like he was a gargoyle standing guard over a haunted estate.

Still, those he helped thanked him and lost their fear of his aura. Gwendoline had felt that Niles would handle his newfound power well, but his kingly demeanor and benevolent words made her pause with pride swelling in her heart as she watched him. She couldn't help that, as she sat at the desk she'd claimed to arrange paperwork and call families, her eyes lingered on him, studying his progress with each patient and his conduct throughout.

If he noticed, he paid her no mind.

Colt watched too, studying them both. She caught him at it once or twice, and futilely wished she knew the right words to say to him to ease either his pain or his pride, but she had nothing. Worse, she knew it wasn't her place: the only person who could help him now was Everleigh, and she'd cast off that burden for good.

But that was all last night, the long hours dragging on until dawn arrived. Colt had remained at the hospital, Niles had disappeared as soon as the last of the accursed had been cleansed, and Gwendoline had stopped by her house to pick up Dancer, clean up, and pack a hiking bag.

In this new dawn, she found herself driving back to the trail where Glenna's memories had been returned to her, hoping against hope that Niles hadn't left her behind yet. She hadn't rested—she couldn't remember the last night she'd slept soundly—and her skinny jeans and black sweater were some of the plainest clothes she had. But Gwendoline had smoothed the shadows away from under her eyes and schooled her hair into soft waves, so maybe she looked attractive enough to remind Niles that he had desired her, once.

Foolish, the wiser portion of her mind reproached her. *That isn't why he loved you, and you'll have to do more than look nice to heal the breach you caused.*

Don't you think I know that? Panic, though not as terrible as the constant frayed nerves that had troubled her since Averill had trespassed in their lives, threatened to shatter Gwendoline's peace. But then Dancer whimpered at her for pets, and she remembered that whatever else happened, she wouldn't be alone.

Finally, she reached her destination. The packed dirt road, lined with gravel once though the stones had long since worn away, was just wide enough to allow her car to carry its passengers up far enough to save her some walking time. Out of habit, Gwendoline parked in the most secluded spot she could find before she shouldered her simple leather hiking bag and exited the car. The temptation to rest her head on the bar of her steering wheel and give in to her anxiety simmered under her skin, but she held out.

Please don't let me be too late, she thought in a steady mantra as she began her uphill walk. Dancer traipsed along happily, first lagging behind, and then bounding ahead with a puppy's indefatigable energy.

They kept a good pace, enhanced by the four shots of straight espresso Gwendoline had chugged. Worn thin though it was, she'd duplicated the sure footing spell she'd cast on her formal shoes the previous evening: unless an outside force physically threw her onto the ground, she wouldn't stumble or slow.

For one final time, she doubted her decision. Starford was her home, had always been her home, and the people she loved most lived here. Glenna had sacrificed herself for Oloetha, and Gwendoline had nearly done the same thing for Starford. Was the price always going to be death or exile from everything she knew? Her friends, her beloved university where she could learn and learn...could she give them up for untold years with Niles?

Yes. She could. But even if she couldn't, if he wouldn't have her, if he doubted her surety...there was Colt. And Everleigh. The romantic in her wanted to believe they stood a chance, that they could figure things out and fall back in love. But even if they could overcome Jael's powerful memory, and Leland's strong hold over Colt's soul, could he overcome his bond with Gwendoline? Could she, if Niles rejected her and she dared linger in Starford?

If she stayed, neither one of them could move on. And therein lay the crux of the issue.

The zenith of her hike approached more rapidly than she'd anticipated. Dancer blew past her in long, nimble strides, and part of her was tempted to follow at the same pace. But Gwendoline had a hard time catching her breath as it was, so she maintained her speed until the little path Niles had showed her weeks ago came under her feet.

Then, after hiking this small, winding trail for several minutes, she came upon her destination and the man she sought.

The sun, rising with lazy, effortless glory, burned deep orange and pink on the horizon, shot through with a gold that showcased the true wealth of nature. Niles waited for Gwendoline, though his back was to her. Her heart raced at the sight of him, and her hands trembled down to her fingertips. She glimpsed the wavering mist of her own breath hovering before her, tinged pale blue with her magic.

"I doubted I'd ever see this again," Niles spoke softly without turning around. "When I started to wake up when my soul was in the book, I wasn't sure if I'd ever get free. And I knew with Averill's return, there was a possibility none of us would make it through the struggle."

"It doesn't seem possible that we've won," Gwendoline stepped forward to stand beside him, her gaze focused on the tips of the evergreens swaying far beneath them, their outline darker under the sunlight. The last fragments of Glenna's soul, dormant though they were, swelled inside of her own being: they'd won. They really had.

After a pause she waited for him to fill, she spoke up. "Were you expecting me to follow you here?"

"No," Niles confessed; his profile sharpened as he almost turned to look at her. "I knew you'd know where to find me, if you chose to look, and I thought I was foolish enough to wait for you...but I predicted I'd leave Starford alone."

"You waited for me, and I'm here," she pressed. "So maybe you guessed wrong." Her boots crunched a stick onto the flat rock beneath her feet as she shifted her weight, but she ignored the sound. Obedient to the idea of her commands if not any she actually voiced, Dancer sat back at the tree line, watching the scene before her unfold with her tail thumping periodically against the ground.

"Did I?" At last he looked at her, leveling the full force of his eyes on her in a way that made her want to fall to her knees and weep. He'd always been taller than her, though she was taller than many women her age, but now she felt that she had to crane her neck back to look up into his face. Even if she did, his carnelian eyes that glowed brighter than this dawn would have blinded her, and the startling beauty in his stately nose, stubble decorated jaw, and wind teased hair made her breathless with longing.

Suddenly ashamed, she looked down. *How I've hurt you, Niles, and you never deserved it.*

"Do you have plans for the future?" Niles asked her when she failed to answer; he appeared confident enough, but she heard the uncertainty in his voice as he shoved his hands into the pockets of his coat.

"I'm leaving Starford for good, whatever else happens now," Gwendoline told him as she scuffed the tip of her boot against the stone below them. "Things are...different. I can't stay here."

"I can't either," Niles intimated, surprising her. "I thought I'd stay afterwards, when I thought Colt would be the next Lord. But now I've taken Averill's place and... I don't think I could stay here. It's not my home anymore. Besides..."

"Besides?" Cursing herself for her cowardice, Gwendoline willed enough boldness into herself to look up at him. She saw no judgment, no condemnation for the choices she'd made or planned to make: only something else, the one thing she'd prayed she'd find.

"If you're leaving, I'm coming with." Gwendoline, relieved she'd spoken even if the words were barely audible, dared herself to continue. "It wasn't in Glenna's nature to say sentimental things, but it is in mine. You're...you mean more to me than you know, Niles, and I—"

"You what?" Niles questioned her with a faint smile, one he was trying and failing to hide. But he wasn't really asking her: he knew, he *had* to know, what she was going to say.

"I love you. I...I really, *really* love you, and I can't call any place my home unless you're there. With me." Any time she'd pictured this moment in her head, Gwendoline had kissed him naturally, the connection a graceful and serene gift of her love. In reality, she felt out of breath, and her heart thumped ahead too quickly for her to manage, and imagined she'd never felt more vulnerable and embarrassed than she did now.

Even so, she cupped his face in her hands and stood on her tiptoes to brush her lips against his. He tortured her for a second, hesitating before he kissed her back with all the ardor she'd been missing. Gwendoline clung to him, relishing in the sensation as his mouth moved against hers and his arms wrapped around her so his hands could rest on her back and pull her closer to him. Warmth filled her tip to toe, and when she saw herself in his eyes when they separated, she saw a glow coming off her skin similar to the dawn's light gracing the land.

"I could've sworn you'd go after Colt," Niles told her; unwilling to release her entirely, he held her tapered waist in his hands, his thumbs chafing the soft fabric of her sweater. "When Everleigh rejected him, I imagined you going to him to offer comfort, if not yourself."

"I want *you,* Niles. I knew I wanted you when Fate asked me who I'd choose to take Averill's place, when my answer was to spare you because I didn't want you to endure one more moment of sacrifice or pain. I had to choose you after all, since you were the right person, but it broke my heart. I knew before that, I think, deep down...but it was easier to let the past take control, to let my tie to Colt take the lead. *I* want *you,*" Gwendoline said insistently. "I didn't go to him because I didn't choose him. I won't lie to you, there's a part of me that Fate designed to always want him, and I can't change that. But she gave me a choice. So I choose you."

Unexpectedly, Niles laughed at her, kissing her again with a faint but friendly growl of possession echoing from his throat. Unable to resist, Gwendoline laughed too, weaving her fingers through his mass of dark hair.

"Say more things like that," he murmured against her mouth as his arms tightened around her. She obliged.

"I choose you. I will always choose you. Given time, I think Glenna would have loved you after Leland and Jael's wedding," she said; this made him laugh again, this time against her neck as he kissed the tender skin there in a way that heated her body in the best places.

"I choose you too," Niles said, his quiet assurance making her heart soar to greet the sun. "You're mine from now on, as much as any one person can belong to another." Gwendoline let her head fall back as he dipped her back in a fairytale kiss on the mountaintop, her eyes sliding closed as she relaxed under his touch.

But then something burned her, searing her down to the bones in her wrist so she cried out from the pain. Niles caught her as her feet gave out under her, but the throbbing pain was already fading by the time she sat on the ground.

Calming her thumping heart, Gwendoline tugged back her left sleeve and stared at the new mark that had appeared. As she considered it, a familiar voice filled her mind with a soothing presence.

With Niles's choice, your destiny is thus far sealed, Gwendoline, Fate's tone bore the weight of proclamation, and thought she'd made her decision and didn't regret it, Gwendoline felt a surge of trepidation twist her guts. *I told you before that I would not curse Niles with a mortal mate. To maintain order I cannot gift you with immortality myself, but you will accompany Niles as he seeks the other Lords, and they will contribute what is needed to make you as immortal as he is.*

Furthermore, Fate continued in a darker tone, coloring Gwendoline's thoughts with disquiet she could not obscure from her vessel, *all is not as well as I had hoped after this conflict. I will protect you the best that I can, sweet child, but you may find more than you bargained for as you seek out Averill's brethren. In the meantime, I've given you a token both of appreciation and protection. Half of the benefits of becoming eternal kind will suffice for the present, I think...*

When she broke out of her trance, Gwendoline repeated what she'd been told back to Niles as they stared down at the new, faintly swollen serpent tattoo gilding her wrist. Red scaled and outlined in gold ink that actually shimmered, each line had been etched by magic with delicate detail down to the gleaming eyes. Whereas pain had radiated from the mark before, now power such as she'd never experienced bolstered her own store.

Unbeknownst to her, her new power had changed her in other physical ways. Blue-violet streaks the same color as her eyes had woven through her hair, hidden unless the light hit them. Any flaws in her skin, any faint lines showing her age, had been smoothed away by a new layer of ethereal luminosity that faded any blemishes into oblivion. Gwendoline had no idea if beauty came part and parcel with immortality, but if so this at least was a gift.

As changed as Niles had been when he took Averill's crown from her hands, she too had altered so the naked eye could see she wasn't entirely human.

"I love you," Niles said to her, offering the comfort of his arms as she inhaled the clean mountain air with senses newly heighted beyond the normal human range. Abruptly, Dancer broke from the trees, barking in a way that somehow remained dignified as she pounced on her mistress and licked her face.

Once she'd recovered from the effusions of joy, Gwendoline shakily rose to her feet as Niles helped her. With no more words necessary, she took his hand and they faced out towards the rest of the mountains.

To the future, Gwendoline mentally toasted, wondering what eternity might hold for her and Niles.

EPILOGUE

3 days later

Perhaps I should've bought more boxes, Gwendoline mused. Despairing of ever getting her house packed up, she gazed around at her home. Magic had helped her pack, organizing her furniture and belongings into impossibly small boxes where not even the most fragile of her crystal champagne flutes would crack, but she still had a lot to do. Worse, Dancer had been distracting her all day: newly filled with the exuberance of a puppy now that Niles had returned to live with them in their few remaining days in the city, she had spent much of the morning bringing Gwendoline toy after toy to encourage play time rather than business.

She scratched absently at the mark adorning her wrist. The tattoo Fate had burned on her skin tingled on occasion, but otherwise did not bother her. Still, the presence of the snake troubled her with its implications.

Half immortal until the Lords officially elect Niles...once he finds them, that is, Gwendoline pondered the information they'd been given that had decided the first direction for their eternal wandering. *How can I be* half *immortal?* But it was true: her shining hair with its brightly colored streaks never tangled, her skin glowed, her power had surged to new heights so that she never tired while using it, and any signs of her aging further than the peak of her youth had disappeared.

Dancer bounded onto the bed, dislodging most of the remaining clothes Gwendoline had transferred there from her closet. Her pet's high spirits would have distracted her if she wasn't already engaged in other ponderings not related to her moving out. Try as she might, she couldn't leave her home behind forever without closing a few loopholes, but she was debating on whether or not this would be self-serving or the right thing to do.

By the time twilight circled in the skies, Gwendoline had finished packing and come to a decision. She'd told Niles she would meet him just outside of Starford by moonrise, but she still had enough time left to do what she felt she had to. She wouldn't have been able to accomplish this when she was completely human, but now she possessed a deeper well of power.

With a sensation like diving into a perfectly still pool of deep water, she cast her mind out towards the person she sought.

Everleigh's house looked the same as always, except for the fact that a small moving truck was parked in its driveway. Gwendoline would've been surprised, except she'd already heard that the new ruler had "inherited" Kinsley manor and would be moving there Starford's magically gifted renovation group finished the repairs on the damaged estate.

For a moment, Gwendoline was tempted to make herself known. She didn't have the guts to go to Everleigh personally, but maybe a conversation between minds would be doable for her courage. Instead, she hungrily studied her friend, searching for signs of the familiar. Everleigh didn't have the benefit of an immortal blessing to heal her minor bruises and cuts: shadows smudged the skin under her eyes, her face looked thin and drawn, and under her fluffed hair her throat sported a fantastic pattern of purple bruises. When she waved at a passing neighbor Gwendoline was too preoccupied to identify, her sleeves slipped down her arm to reveal a series of tiny, self-inflicted abrasions. Had she clawed off the bracelets Averill had foisted on her?

Gwendoline pitied her, but she had to admit that her exhaustion and overall poor appearance had an air of something triumphant about it. Her midsummer green eyes flashed brighter than ever, feisty and inspired by the promises set for her future.

Starford won't know what hit it, Gwendoline mused. She watched Everleigh finish packing her truck with help from the occasional family member, but mostly by herself. Before, Gwendoline would have been right there with them helping her friend transition into the next phase of her life. Now, she had questions. Would Everleigh take a break from Starford U to learn politics and leadership? Would she change everything in an explosion of activity, or would she be the type of ruler to work with her people first and gain their approval? Jael had tried things both ways and it had worked for her. But this was not Jael, and Everleigh didn't want to live under that shadow.

Gwendoline followed in her ghostly guise as Everleigh reentered her house and wandered around searching for items she'd forgotten. Colt's absence from the Northwood house became glaring and obvious as she noted the empty spots on the walls where picture frames had resided, especially once Everleigh reached her room. True, everything she owned and wanted to take with her had been sent to the truck, so there wasn't much to point at, but her girlish bed and simple nightstand stood barren of all but her journal, a cold cup of tea, and one picture from Colt's and Everleigh's beach vacation from the previous summer.

Gwendoline's shadow studied the picture with Everleigh, wondering if her friend was also thinking about how happy the two of them looked. She also wondered if the picture brought forth any thoughts of her, since she'd been the one to snap the picture: the tip of one of her fingers had even blurred a corner of the photograph. After seeing this image for the hundredth time, Gwendoline noticed something that made her breath catch. Everleigh, tan and bubbly and glowing with happiness, stared directly into the camera as if inviting the object to share in her joy. But Colt, unscarred and smiling though he was, had been looking past the camera at Gwendoline with a look she had learned to recognize in recent weeks.

In the end, she had ignored the bond linking their souls and chosen to follow Niles. Colt had made a point of choosing Everleigh, or so Gwendoline had thought. However, this familiar photograph gave her second thoughts about what had really happened. Colt had said he'd loved her for years, before Everleigh, but his affection for the petite brunette had been genuine. Still...maybe Colt had more in common with pining, heart sore Glenna than he realized.

Maybe that connection wouldn't fade with time, as Gwendoline had convinced herself to hope.

Someone knocked on the bedroom door, startling Everleigh into dropping the picture frame. It thumped gently against the carpet, and she shoved it under the bed with her foot like it was a guilty secret.

"Sorry," Niles said, since he'd been the one to enter the room. "I didn't mean to intrude, especially when you're so busy with moving, but I thought I should—"

"I know you're leaving, yes," Everleigh stood, smoothing her dusty palms against her embroidered jeans. "I assumed you would be, after everything."

"Well, you're right," Niles agreed. Gwendoline wondered why he'd decided to visit Everleigh without telling her. More than ever, she sought to conceal her wraithlike apparition from their awareness.

"And you've come to say goodbye? That's sweet, but I'm not sure why you'd come to me. We're not that close," Everleigh, shrewd as ever, toyed with the arm band form of Smaug, plucking nervously at his scales.

"I'm here for Gwendoline's sake as well as my own," Niles intimated quietly. "May I come in?" He hadn't entered the room yet, courtesy leaving him to hover awkwardly in the doorway. Her frizzed curls bobbing, she nodded.

"Gwendoline and I will be leaving Starford tonight, probably for good. I think she feels unwelcome here, so I doubt she'll come to tell you herself," Niles told her.

Accurate, Gwendoline sighed internally. She couldn't face the Northwood parents any more than she could face Everleigh herself.

"Gwendoline's leaving?" The brunette slowly lowered herself back onto the bed. Several emotions passed over her face, furrowing the defined brows from their intensity: shock, regret, and finally acceptance.

"I imagine that's for the best. She...well, as much as she could with her soul yoked to Colt's, I assume she feels some love for you." From anyone else the bitterness in these words would have soured the communication completely. "I have to say, I thought she would have chosen Colt over you. I'm shocked she's not staying here with him...though I can't say I'm upset she's leaving."

Niles didn't waste his breath defending Gwendoline. "I see things differently, but I can't blame you. I just thought you should know, and...I wanted to apologize."

"Apologize?" Everleigh questioned.

Apologize? Gwendoline echoed her mentally, bemused. It had hurt to hear that Everleigh was so eager for her to leave, but she couldn't say she didn't deserve the dismissal.

"Again, this isn't really my place, but I...I feel responsible for the turn your life has taken," Niles hesitated, his aura filling the room uncomfortably full as he drifted near one of the widows; the Northwoods had always been blessed by wealth, so Everleigh's room functioned more like its own wing rather than just a room. "I don't expect I will ever see you again, since Gwendoline feels like it would be better to leave any bad memories from all of this behind...she wouldn't tell me for sure, but I know she was thinking of you as well when she decided this with me. You have the right to a fresh start without any of us, since that's what you want.

"Regardless, your life was upended completely by my return, and no one ever...I just felt that someone at least should make amends for destroying everything you knew and loved." Gwendoline's pride in Niles couldn't grow any bigger than what she felt as she heard him speak. Sunset progressed with dusky hues outside of the curtainless window, the colors muted as the cold of evening returned. The last amber rays settled in the fire of Niles's eyes and the highlights in Everleigh's hair as Gwendoline watched her stand and approach the widow to stand beside him.

"Don't you think on it another minute," Everleigh spoke softly. "It's not even a little bit your fault, and what you brought me with your arrival was, in its own way, so much more than what I lost. Averill didn't break us, and..."

"And?" Niles and Gwendoline both waited for the continuation she seemed hesitant to voice.

"We're too good for them, Niles. You and I both. I don't wish them any harm, I honestly don't, but I don't understand how Gwendoline ended up with everything she ever wanted after all the mistakes she's made. I know it's a double standard that I've slipped into: I can forgive Colt for his betrayal, but not Gwendoline? But...I don't have it in me anymore to let things go, and I wouldn't want to still be that way."

She wouldn't have spoken this way, least of all to someone she knew as little as she actually knew Niles, but the conviction in her voice wounded Gwendoline more than she would've ever voiced. Jealousy raised its blunt head with her, sniffing disdainfully as Everleigh turned the force of her summer eyes on him. Gwendoline couldn't bring herself to believe it was totally on purpose, but neither could she ignore the invitation the fresh ruler offered to Niles. She couldn't entirely blame her, but shock rooted her to the floor all the same. Once again she debated revealing herself, but she thought better of it.

Smiling so as to not hurt Everleigh's pride, Niles shook his head. "I think we can agree to disagree here. You don't have any memories from before, but I think you might understand better if you did."

"That's what it keeps coming down to, right?" Laughing bitterly—though not at him—Everleigh switched off her affected allure in the blink of an eye. "All three of you are so important with your past lives and your complicated memories. I could've done without the drama and the angst of two matched souls thwarted by the princess I'm descended from, but I really *really* wish I had somebody else's thoughts rattling around my cranium. Maybe it would help me understand. Maybe it will help me lead. I don't know." Frustrated with her lack of control, she raked her hands through her thick hair and exhaled loudly.

"You know, I think I can help with that, actually," Niles interjected on her moment, his smile returning. Without elaborating further, he strode over to the simple antique nightstand, picking up the yellow journal and flipping it open to the center.

"Hey!" Everleigh protested, diving to rip it out of his hands, but he silenced her with a look and closed his eyes so he looked like a priest pondering his prayer book. A whisper of magic darted through the room, stirring the pages into movement as Niles hummed an intelligible spell. Once the pages stopped fluttering, he closed the journal and passed it to its owner.

"I was trapped in a book, once. But as long as she lived, Jael never stopped writing to me, or to Glenna. Most of her notes she directed towards Leland, but she did charge me with passing on her messages when the time was right. It never felt right to share her writings before...I didn't want to overcomplicate things while we were hovering on the brink of annihilation. But now..." Everleigh didn't seem like she was listening, but she held the enchanted diary in her hands like it was the most precious book she'd ever known.

"I'm not sure I want to read this," she admitted in a whisper, tears trickling from her eyes. Gwendoline wished she could comfort her, but it wasn't her place any more. Worse, an increasingly loud part of her wanted desperately to see what Jael had wrote to her—to Glenna. But in the end she supposed it wasn't her place anymore.

"Give it time, Everleigh. You have your whole future to figure everything out. Perhaps you will come to a place where you can pass

Jael's messages on to Colt without pain. I...I wish you the absolute best, my lady." This time Gwendoline saw him disappear, though a distracted Everleigh didn't notice until he was already gone.

It was time Gwendoline left as well. Taking one last long look at the girl who had been her best friend, she let her ethereal form return home.

She had one more person to see, and this time she intended to show herself. This time, she was relieved her physical body wouldn't be a burden here. Sure though she was in her decision, she didn't want to measure the trust she had in herself while risking that the magnetism between her and Colt would draw them together. It would have to be enough, that her essence and her image would be present for him.

Eventually, she found him treading the familiar walkways of Starford University. They had often come to this spot for studying or magical practice. Gentle willows swayed along the ancient brick walkway, so imbued with magic absorbed from over the years that their leaves shimmered without any light reflecting from them. Since it was nearly night time, the rest of the student populace had found other places to be, so he walked alone with his hands in the pockets of his leather coat.

Inhaling and exhaling purposefully, she jogged to walk beside him and revealed herself.

"I knew you were here," Colt began before she could even expect to have startled him. "I sensed you."

"Is...Is that all right?" Gwendoline hated the hesitancy of her voice, loathed this rift between them, but she couldn't think how to bridge the gap.

Colt gave her the side eye; without meaning to, she'd chosen to walk on his good side, and his familiar face looked whole from this angle. "I expected to see you before this. We have a lot to say to each other," he said.

Gwendoline looped her fingers through the empty belt loops of her pants as she moseyed along with him. This form felt human enough, and she felt very present with him.

"We do," she agreed, "but I can't remember what those things are now." Gwendoline did remember, though. She wanted to ask him how he'd known Everleigh was the one he wanted, if that was really what he'd chosen, and she wanted him to know that she was leaving and she would miss him with that devoted part of her that could only belong to him. Arranged by Fate or not, they had been connected, and she knew they would both feel that bond for all of time.

"It's about choice, isn't it? That's why we're here," Colt interrupted her musings, pausing his walk so he could face her fully. His blue eyes glinted as if he'd read her thoughts, drawing more of her attention than his scars, and then she realized he had: she'd projected them onto him without noticing.

"We fought Averill so he couldn't decide everyone's future. Fate gave us back our options...well, in a way. Whatever else happens, I'm grateful that I still have that," he declared.

"That's...that's a very positive way of looking at it."

"What other choice do I have?" The acrimony Gwendoline had expected to find, especially given Everleigh's state of mind, finally showed its face. "A short time ago, I could've called myself happy and content. I had a woman I loved, a future I could predict, and a healthy dose of self-respect. Now..."

"Everything has changed," Gwendoline reached out, laying a ghostly hand on his shoulder. He let her touch him briefly before he stalked ahead, seemingly unable to contain himself to stillness. She tottered after him, caught off guard by his speed until he slowed to walk with her again.

"I don't regret my time with you. I never will. But betraying Everleigh is one of the worst things I've ever done, and it's changed both of us forever," he murmured, exhaling as he looked up into the darkening sky. "Together, we defeated Averill. That is an honorable deed, an act of someone worthy of love. But I am no longer honorable, no longer worthy, and I don't know what my future holds."

"Colt...ah, Colt. We really messed things up, didn't we?" Gwendoline said. Because she understood: she understood perfectly how he felt. Everleigh was right, it didn't seem fair that Gwendoline, who had thrown away her integrity the second she'd kissed Colt, was walking away from the aftermath with her heart's desire at her side. Destiny worked in the most befuddling ways, she couldn't deny it. Why should she get what she want while he ended up alone?

Colt laughed, the sound as harsh as a old dog's bark. "That's an understatement." They continued down the winding walkway in companionable silence, enjoying perhaps the last few moments they would ever spend together.

"I knew...I knew I'd chosen Niles when Fate summoned me into the dream world and asked me who I thought would replace Averill the best. I didn't want to lose him, and I didn't want to place that burden on him...not that I wanted to burden you with it either, but that's when I knew."

"You loved him more," Colt's voice cracked, his expression hollow under the sidewalk lights that flickered on as the light began to disappear. "I'm not as sure when I chose Everleigh. I didn't know I'd chosen her until I had. Truthfully, until that moment, I thought I'd chosen you."

Pain, expected this time, stung Gwendoline's eyes with tears. Though she understood Fate's intentions better now, she spent a few seconds hating her for putting them in this impossible situation. They each loved their chosen partner more, regardless of the outcome of their choice, but that didn't erase their feelings for each other or their inescapable connection.

"I'm sorry, Colt. If it's any comfort at all, you did the best you could. I wish you had a better outcome than what you have now. Part of me wishes I could stay here, if only to be your friend, if only to help you heal...but I can't. I can't, and I'm so sorry," Gwendoline risked pulling him in for a hug, though this form barely had any substance at all. Even so, she felt his arms close around her as they embraced for one final time.

"I love you, Gwendoline. I hope you find everything you want," Colt kissed her transparent cheek as they separated. Tempted to turn her head so their lips met, she instead pulled back and laid a cold hand on his defined cheek.

With nothing else to say, she smiled at him, desiring his last picture of her to remind him of happier times.

By the time she returned to herself, back in her nearly empty house with Dancer nosing her fingertips, night had truly fallen and there was nothing left to keep her in Starford. Her face felt wet, damp from the tears she'd shed, and she felt worn out even though her magic had been barely affected by her spirit travelling all across town. She'd contacted her friends one last time for closure, but the only thing that felt different was the wider margins around the emptiness wailing in her.

In time, it would close over: the wound of loss wouldn't ever disappear completely, but she would feel it less with each passing year.

But she planned to enjoy many more years than humans were normally allotted: how much time would it take, then, to forget this pain?

She had run out of time to dwell on it, for now. Niles's mind brushed against hers in the most intimate of caresses. For him, this was the beginning of an adventure in which he gained everything he'd ever dreamed and more. Gwendoline smiled, wrapping her arms around herself as if for warmth as he sent her an image of them together under the stars; a surge of power accompanied the mental image, zapping her nerves with delicious electricity.

Waving her hand so all of the boxes shrunk to fit into a sizeable suitcase, Gwendoline hefted the bag onto her shoulder with a grunt and called Dancer to her side. Once she'd locked the door, she took one last look at her childhood home before she traipsed down the front steps and got in her car.

By morning, Starford wouldn't even be a blip in her rearview mirror.

ACKNOWLEDGEMENTS

What an adventure this book has been!

It all started in 2009 with a few pages in a notebook hastily filled with scribbles during school. I've been writing for over half my life, so I quite literally have old story ideas and concepts stuffed around every corner of my house like inky ghosts. Skip ahead a few years: it's NaNoWriMo (national novel writing month) 2016, and I decide to go through my older files searching for inspiration to descend upon me like a gift from the heavens.

Thus, Long Grows the Dark was born.

Throughout the next year or so of writing (obviously I didn't finish this novel in the allotted month) I experienced a few life changes. My husband and I found our Scottish Terrier, Fannie Mae, who's greatest delight lies in acting as bratty as she possibly can. Shortly after that we spontaneously chose our second dog, a Whoodle we named Heidi Rose. By October, we had a bobtail black cat I named Phoebe Moon...and after three wild pets who had little interest in being trained, I put my writing on hold for a little while. But now this book is finally complete, and I have some people to thank.

Thanks to my editor, Paige Bagby, for contributing her wit and expertise to help make a messy first draft a readable book. I appreciated every single comment. (Thanks also to my reader friend Caroline, who also helped a lot with her comments.)

Blessings to my best friend Kerrie, who was with me on this journey almost from the beginning. Our work days involved a lot of talking and coffee/tea drinking somewhat more than actual writing or painting sometimes, but they were instrumental in helping me talk through a lot of the plot points and small details of this novel. Kerrie was going through some personal stuff, too, so that makes it even more amazing that she was so there for me during this time period. Here's to many more work days ahead of us!

It's standard to thank the cover artist, I think, but honestly I'm so grateful for the beautiful work she provided me with so Gwendoline's story has a unique image to accompany it. I'd been following Salome's art on social media for a while, and I never dreamed I'd get to have some of her work on any books of mine, but here we are and I'm still in love with this book cover. So thanks, lady!

My family, though some are readers, has never really understood the whole writing thing. I'm still that weird little oddball who keeps to herself and spends a lot of time at the computer typing loudly and occasionally blasting music. Still, they've always been supportive, and I love my parents very much. Thanks for, you know, life and all. ☺

Finally, to my husband. It's also traditional to thank the spouse, I suppose, but I mean this part too. Daniel, you're not a reader, and you'd rather play some Overwatch or go hiking than read most of the time. But not only have you listened to me talk endlessly about this book, about each detail and new idea I've had, you've supported me and never once doubted my ability to get this done and out into the world. Plus, you've helped me get a decent author photo I'm not embarrassed about, which is far from easy. I love you, and I'm apologizing in advance for how I'm going to talk your ear off about my next books.

To you, reader, thanks for giving me a chance and picking up this book. I hope you enjoyed it, and of course I couldn't do this without your support.

Endless love,

Catherine Labadie

Catherine Labadie

lives in the mountains of the scenic Carolinas with her husband and her three pets. *Long Grows the Dark* is her second novel, and she plans to write many more.

Follow Catherine on:

http://authorcatlabadie.wixsite.com/catherinelabadie

Don't miss Catherine's first novel!

Vixen

In a post-war world, Sierra Maurell and her three fox attribute brothers must use their cunning to endure the cold rejection of the pure-DNA human race. When a new series of desegregation laws force Sierra to spend her last year of high school at a former human-only institution, social antagonism compels her to lead her fellow half-breeds towards equality.

But one human refuses to treat half-breeds as less than human, and their meeting creates a new line of fate which might change Sierra's world forever.